Paths of Promise

DONNA J. GRISANTI

ISBN: 0970886012
ISBN-13: 9780970886019

For Clinton.
You wanted it, so this one is for you.

"Therefore, since we are surrounded by such a great cloud of witnesses, let us throw off everything that hinders and the sin that so easily entangles, and let us run with perseverance the race marked out for us."

- Hebrews 12:1, *New International Version*

PROLOGUE

EMERGENCY ROOM AT 10:30 A.M.
CHICAGO – 1967

"I don't want to talk about it anymore. Please, just start writing!" Ruth
Yuell ordered in an uncharacteristic brusque tone. "I know I've got a bump on
my head…and I'm just 'dusting close to my thirties,' as my grandmother would
say, but I don't want to *talk* about writing my story *anymore*, I want to get it *done*!"
Ruth frowned at Norma, her dear friend since their college days. "There's nothing
else to do while we're here." In an otherwise peaceful demonstration for fair housing rights, overzealous police officers had rushed to quell some enthusiastic dancing and clapping. Getting pushed overt a police barricade as the crowd changed
direction had sent Ruth to the hospital.

Ruth looked around the drab, khaki cubicle, pulling her thoughts together.
"I want to begin with the time they thought I was a murderess." Ruth put her
hand to her aching forehead, trying to concentrate. "Not the first time when I
was in high school, mind you, but the second time, when I was in the university
with you!" Ruth looked at Norma, who started writing. "As you know, the first
time they accused me of killing my cousin and her child, the authorities were trying to cause trouble, divide the Negro community, and tarnish the Yuell name."
Norma looked at her friend with worry furrowing her brow. "So we'll start with
the second time—the *real* killing. Think that's what I want to do."

"Are you sure?" Norma asked, looking at the shiny gauges of all the medical
equipment on the wall. Ruth's story was riveting but Norma never thought she'd
be asked to write it. "Well, you've said your sister, Thelma, says no one but a
Yuell should tell the story." Norma gulped sheepishly. "I am a…a white woman

and…and you and your family are black." Norma wondered if her use of what some Negroes eschewed as a needless new term to define Ruth's race might further upset her dear friend.

Ruth gave Norma a penetrating look, which could mean trouble. "I've been called a Negro, colored, black, African-American, and other names, back and forth till my head spins from more than this concussion. To think after all those dangerous months of canvassing and protesting down in Alabama, and this peaceful Chicago Open Housing protest got me injured!" A fleeting, wry smile came to Ruth's face. "At least I'm in a hospital and not a jail, like before. But don't you think for one minute I don't want you to get your pad and pen moving right now. We've known and trusted each other since college! Talked about every subject on God's green earth, looked out for each other…and I want you to write it. Whether white, black, or Martian, I've chosen you and that's that." Ruth sniffed and patted her upper lip with a tissue. "Write it, edit it, and get it published in a newspaper, book, or something-or-the-other! I want to tell everyone what you can go through and get through…and still stay true to yourself and what you believe in."

How many times had Norma seen Ruth's determination shooting from her dear friend's crystal brown eyes?

Norma always relished unexpected assignments—and this one took the prize! As a journalist, she'd been in war zones with bullets flying….and felt more calm in those places than with this assignment for Ruth. Norma decided to do as Ruth wanted and deal with the consequences later.

"We've always said, 'We're in this together!'" Ruth cleared her throat. "Promise to get it in book form or some other which way or you'll add to my headache!"

"OK. OK. I promise." Norma knew her steel-willed friend needed rest or the doctor might incorrectly diagnose Ruth's agitation as something other than their disagreement. "I'm only saying Thelma is so proprietary about family things. You know that…and then there's Sylvie. What about Leroy or Lady Dee?"

Ruth huffed, not seeming mollified. "All I know is that I'm one fifth of the remaining Yuells on this earth and if I don't get something started, the story might *never* get told." Ruth tried to straighten her sheets. "Thelma's always acting like she's the boss, but being born ten minutes before Leroy doesn't give her the power…and she doesn't know *all* my part of things which need telling." Ruth's stone-eyed glare made Norma flinch. "After all these years and everything we've been through, if I can't trust you, *then who can I trust?*"

This latest picketing incident of broken glass and twisted metal compelled Ruth to begin her storytelling, no matter what the setting. At the very least she'd ask Norma for a pad and pen, start a list of stories, and keep things rolling after her discharge from the hospital. "So write things down…or give me a pad and pencil. I'm ready to go!" Ruth frowned again. "If you're going to write it, I'll check things over if that will ease your mind."

Norma felt with her uncertain heart that they had other things to deal with before they began. "I know those were pivotal points in your life, Ruth, but I think we should start at the beginning." Norma kept talking, praying Ruth would understand the rationale and stay calm.

"People, especially white people who've never stopped to consider anything beyond their own backyard, need to hear things from the beginning, so they can understand how *really different* things were—context for the more sensational stuff." Norma twirled her pen in the air. "They'll want to know things about St. Louis, about your family, how you were raised, and your family's rise above all the roadblocks of segregation and inequality." There were other things to consider. "Your story is a microcosm of having to live a life with two faces: one in the safety of your own neighborhood and another in the white community." Norma bit her lip. "You also want to tell them the great things the Negro community did on all fronts, even with the threats of violence and death." She rested the pen on the pad and gently put her fingers on Ruth's wrist. "We want people to learn…and remember."

Ruth looked unsure of Norma's suggestions. Mutinous amber depths threatened to spark in her eyes. "I've been a victim of sensationalism enough in my life. You know some people are more than willing to lap up gossip like fresh cream to a hungry cat. Don't want to start this the wrong way."

"I tell people stories all the time, Ruth," Norma reasoned. "Readers like sensation…and celebrity…but they are *moved* by the lives and circumstances of *real* people even more."

"Fine. I'll go along for the time being," Ruth replied, letting the steam of her anger dissipate while trying to recall and arrange the details of her life. "So you want to ease into my story?" Norma nodded. "But your way better hold people's attention to my satisfaction…or we'll do it my way." Ruth sat back against the gurney pillows. "If I can't start with the murders, I'll start with talking about my parents and the down-to-the-bone difficulty of living under segregation."

Both women took a deep breath and thought, "We're in this together!"

CHAPTER ONE

ST. LOUIS – 1939

The newly minted Doctor of Medicine and impending father for the third time, Edgar William Yuell, sat listlessly at his parents' kitchen table. Work far exceeded sleep these last few weeks. Mother Yuell saw him yawn and languidly stretch his tired back. She fussed around him in her loving way, having him sit down with a cold glass of water for his thirst and a thick china cup of freshly brewed chicory coffee to ease his fatigue. "Another birth for you and Lady Dee right around the corner."

"Yes. Only a couple of days now till the baby's born," the young doctor noted, taking his recent thoughts to happier places.

Mother Yuell only nodded, wanting Edgar to tell her what was *really* on his mind. He'd been brooding since Mrs. Hawkins died three days ago.

"Can't afford to send my own wife to the hospital," he began with deep sadness. "I'm a doctor and I can't afford to send her to the hospital like she did when the twins were born."

Mother Yuell squeezed her son's shoulder blade in silence. *What could she say?* There wasn't any money this time. Last semester of school needed to be paid and the roof of her son's home needed immediate fixing after the last storm. She and her husband had a few dollars in savings but the funds weren't enough, and when they offered, neither Edgar nor his wife, Lady Dee, would take it.

Mother Yuell's son looked around the room. He *wanted* to think some happier thoughts. *Where was his lovely wife, Lady Dee?* Lady Dee was probably doing two things, he thought with a slight, crooked smile: making sure everything was ready when the new baby came and lovingly attending to their almost-past-toddler son, Leroy, and his twin sister, Thelma.

Edgar thought of what his wife, Lady Dee, had said. "I don't want Leroy or Thelma's feelings to be hurt by all the attention sure to be lavished on the new baby." Lady Dee needn't have fretted because every time he'd looked for their son or daughter, both were either being talked to, held, smiled at, or hugged in such extravagant fashion their feet hardly ever touched the ground. *Having a new baby in the family was a happy thing, wasn't it?*

"It's going to be different for you, baby," he said as the glass's wavering crystal-cut rainbow splashed the wall and enlivened the empty room. He looked down and rubbed the tender knuckle on his left hand. Several days ago, he'd bumped it on the rough-hewn wood during Mrs. Hawkins's deathbed visit.

Sophie, Mrs. Hawkins's daughter, had her son, Elias, come and get him. Mrs. Hawkins warned them, "It was time to go to the Lord." No one doubted her word.

As the car engine grudged to a coughing start, he'd ordered Elias, "Get into the passenger seat!"

In her clapboard three-room shotgun house, Sophie kneeled at the bedside. Just like Mrs. Hawkins had been when her beloved husband died three years earlier. The same bed Mr. Hawkins had built for himself and his bride fifty-five years ago.

Edgar sadly replaced his stethoscope into his doctor's bag when he listened to her chest. Indeed, it was Mrs. Hawkins's time to follow.

"It's so nice of you to come, Dr. Yuell. Reverend Fredericks will be along soon, too. Come sit by me," Mrs. Hawkins wheezed in a panting whisper as if she'd run a long distance. Her thin, bony hand lifted from the bedcovers in welcome. "Come sit a spell and help sing me to heaven," she politely invited without opening her eyes. "Come, sit here at my side before my piece of time is gone." He'd skinned his knuckle on the bed.

"She'd like us to sing, Doctor. She's been planning her going for awhile." Sophie wrapped the wound as a lone tear escaped her red, puffy eyes.

Edgar started to sing in his baritone voice. He hoped his efforts were worthy of the celestial choirs welcoming Mrs. Hawkins home to heaven. Knowing by heart all the songs her family sang endless times with the congregation at church, Mrs. Hawkins smiled occasionally and lifted the edges of her blue-tinged lips as meaningful lines and passages from their makeshift chorus seemed to please her. The young Reverend Fredericks slipped in and added his warm tenor voice to the hymns.

"You know I'm going back to freedom, Reverend." The words jolted Edgar. They always did. Her words graphically reminded him of the hateful racial divide forcefully separating his black community and the white community. Sadly, the chasm of racism had only narrowed slightly in his lifetime thus far—if at all. Mrs. Hawkins was one of only a handful of black citizens left who remembered the "days of freedom" that followed the Civil War. Mrs. Hawkins's grandparents and parents, former slaves, pooled the money they saved for twenty years or more to buy the land where her three-room home now stood. But the laws had changed, legalizing the segregation of rights and races once more.

Shortly after the war, the Southern states enacted Jim Crow laws bent on squashing the Fourteenth and Fifteenth Amendments to the Constitution, firmly reinstating the racial segregation and vise-like Medusa of legal bureaucracy with which his people now lived. There were slightly more freedoms in St. Louis than the rest of the state, but Edgar knew if he got on the wrong side of a white citizen or the law, he was in trouble as serious as his Southern relatives in Alabama and Mississippi.

The former slaves' freedom and short-lived civil liberties lasted barely a generation. Negro-owned land was legally snatched away like a brutal theft in the night. Both state and federal officials, especially in the South, turned blind eyes to protests from the black community as voting registrars asked black citizens to recite entire chapters of the state code in order to get proper voting cards. Any protests on land and voting issues from the Negro community were turned aside with vicious cross-burnings, tar-and-feather incidents, and many deaths. "Slavery to legal statutes has replaced human bondage," Reverend Fredericks agreed as he patted Mrs. Hawkins's hand. Bitterness filled Edgar's throat.

The Hawkins situation was just one of many other sad cases. Taxes, drought, and illnesses in both their livestock and family members forced them to sell all their hard-won holdings, except for the house and a small yard in the front and in back. Times had been hard but Mrs. Hawkins vowed, "I'll hold onto this land. This land shows all the world, or whoever inquires, that Negroes are capable of the responsibilities and banking requirements of land ownership." The Hawkins place stood as an earthen testament to that earlier time when all Negroes had been free. Fortunately, Mrs. Hawkins would not have to face the soon-coming reality. Sophie would have to sell the rest of the Hawkins' land for back taxes. Sophie and Elias would be able to get along in rented rooms but the land and this humble house would be gone. The earth would remain but the monument would become a memory.

The yellowed, faded deed to the property hung nailed to the wall in a simple frame—the Hawkins family remembrance of land ownership and freedom. Mrs. Hawkins, her late husband, their parents, and grandparents before them, kept the stories and the history of both their slave and free days fresh in their children's minds. They'd taught everyone well. Sophie, Elias, and the entire church congregation could recite these true tales of bravery and freedom to keep them alive. All their fellow church parishioners wanted to extol the accomplishments of their race and savor the days of past freedom. Besides the Bible and His Lord, this was the truest thing Reverend Fredericks preached every Sunday.

"You heard about the airplanes? Those fliers?" Mrs. Hawkins asked in a tiny, breathy wheeze.

"Yes. Yes," Reverend Fredericks whispered, gently patting the elderly woman's hand. "It must be a glorious thing to fly like those brave men down in Tuskegee."

Edgar took a moment to look at the quiet pride flickering beneath Mrs. Hawkins's pallid face. Arnold Pratt's nephew had been telling about the airmen down at the barbershop. The news traveled to Mrs. Hawkins's bedside. It was wonderful to reflect on this first opportunity allowing black pilot training near Tuskegee Institute; a true example of all men being created equal down to their souls, so help them God. So Negroes would have to keep praying, working, planning, and enjoying the stories of accomplishment against formidable odds. And cherish their work and dreams of freedom.

Mrs. Hawkins roused everyone from their private thoughts. "I'm going to fly, like the Reverend says. On wings made of spirit and mother-of-pearl feathers. I'm going to fly...back to freedom," Mrs. Hawkins whispered, from her thin, smiling lips with her last breath.

Amen. The doctor's mind returned to his kitchen as he massaged his healing knuckle. The untouched chicory coffee was cold and his ignored water glass sweated droplets onto the oilcloth table cover.

In the four days since Mrs. Hawkins's death, the same dark thoughts endlessly carouseled around Edgar's mind. The echoing question repeated in Mrs. Hawkins's deathbed hymn lyrics, "How long, Lord? How long, Lord Jesus?"

Edgar knew he needed to talk to someone to get his head straight. With their new baby coming, Lady Dee didn't need any more burdens now. So besides praying to his heavenly Father, Edgar decided to forego his healing chats with Lady Dee and talk to his mentor and business partner, Dr. Thurgood Elison Means. Dr. Means provided work and encouragement for all the long years it took to become a doctor. Now they were going to work together in their community, side-by-side in their medical practice.

Edgar drove to the white clapboard house with the yellow trim, unable to outrun the sick helplessness still hanging on him and nagging on everything good, including his peace of mind. Perhaps his friend would have some answers.

Dr. Means quickly opened the door and let his young partner in, ushering him to a comfortable, worn, stuffed leather chair that had been in the family for as long as the younger man could remember. Mrs. Means wore an apron but was still dressed in her favorite dark blue frock she'd worn that afternoon for the Hawkins's funeral. Work papers and medical journals covered the dining table.

Mrs. Means didn't like the cloudy amber in the younger man's brown eyes and she hastily tugged at her apron as she started for the door, "Mother Aires is feeling poorly and resting in her room. I'm about to change my clothes."

Edgar waited politely for her to leave, then spoke without preamble. "Thurgood, it's just so hard. No money for a hospital for Lady Dee and the baby. Doubts nagging at me. Can I say to myself that things are getting *better*? Can I stand up and say, 'Go on. Go on'? Can I continue to teach my children what it's like to be colored when they're in the white community?" Edgar's hand slashed the air. "Teach them the restrictions, the rules, and the limitations of not being white-skinned?"

Dr. Means knew not to interrupt. Young Edgar still needed to let off steam. Mrs. Hawkins's funeral had affected them all. His young partner's tone was rising with each angry word.

"It's truly a glimpse of hell, hearing about the victims of lynchings done for no reason! Watching daily humiliations of our brothers and sisters at the hands of ignorant whites and having no legal recourse! The fact of one drop of colored blood determining our identities by the white community! Miscegenation they call it. Ha! We are not, nor have we ever been, inferior before God or man!

"In *Crisis* magazine, the tally of lynchings hasn't gone down. Thurgood, you've read about them, too. Seen the sickening, degrading pictures in a newspaper. Several lifeless men with their lives snuffed out. The whites were laughing, smiling, and posing underneath their dangling, dead bodies like it was a holiday! Some brave Negro mothers' sons were dangling and the whites had a picnic under the shade of the trees and their bodies!"

Edgar shook, inside and out, at the injustice. He saw Dr. Means's silent razor-cheeked face and grieving brown-black eyes. Realization flooded Edgar, slapping his passion with cold, stinging awareness like a flame gutting in a pool of drowning wax. *Ranting in front of such a respected man—and his business partner to boot? The older man had fought for justice all his life.* Edgar's cheeks burned with mortification!

Dr. Means felt relieved when the light of reason finally returned to the younger man's eyes. *Give Edgar a chance to find his way back to reason.* Thurgood reached for his Bible on the side table to hold the words of peace, hope, and justice on which he built his life. "Anger helps relieve the pressure but it doesn't get anything done. Does it, Edgar?"

Edgar ran his hand over the back of his neck and tried to relax his tightened jaw. "The rage delighted…and surprised me." Edgar sat there shame-faced. "For a moment, it felt wonderful. It billowed, surged, and shook me. I lost control of the evil weight just at the same time I realized control was what I needed most. The exact antithesis of the Hippocratic oath I've worked and waited so long to take." He stopped a second and stammered, "I repent to you and to the Lord. I'm so glad that these four walls and you were the only witnesses to it."

"I'm no plaster saint myself, son," Dr. Means replied with in a sad sigh. "The good Lord knows...I've done my share of hollering with witnesses and without many, many times. With a few more years, you'll come to fully understand that you, your time, and damnable temper belong to the Lord. Also, remember every soul is forgiven when the Lord is asked for pardon." The older doctor shook his head as he took off his gold-rimmed glasses. "Don't know why things are the way they are, this side of heaven. I only know we'll be free and so do you, deep down. So do you. We're doing our best to move toward freedom but it's still an unjust and sometimes loathsome world." Dr. Means looked down at his folded hands and then back into his partner's eyes to make sure Edgar was listening. "It's Mrs. Hawkins and your children stirring this up, isn't it?"

The younger man delivered a curt nod. "I just felt so sad. She'd lost her freedom in this life. Will my children ever gain theirs? I just don't know..." his voice drifted off.

Simple words could never describe the unjust impact of the Founding Fathers sidestepping the issue of slavery during the forming of his beloved country. Sitting there, in the twenty-fourth state within the United States of America, as college-educated, tax-paying Negro doctor, in the fourth decade of the twentieth century, Dr. Means and all black people of the nation still felt the damning repercussions of that misstep. About freedom too long denied. Dr. Means's frown deepened.

"Let me assure you, I—and any other Negro doctor worth his salt—have had his own violent tussles with this issue. We all have doubts sometimes." Thurgood let out a small humorless grunt. "We've come from a history of pain, loss, and broken promises...but we're still here, Edgar. At times like this, it bears repeat-ing." A deep breath rumbled his shirt front. "God put us all on this earth for a reason. Even though the white folk don't want to admit it, or sometimes we ourselves question the progress, we are *truly* going forward." Dr. Means paused to collect his thoughts. "We're heading for freedom with all the dignity and integ-rity we can muster. It's for the respect of those gone before and with God's help."

Dr. Means put the Bible in his other hand. "We are here to recount the tales of those who have gone on before...to honor them with our blood's own dignity and integrity. Need I say more?"

Edgar shook his head, thinking of at least twenty stories from gone-before members of the congregation relating to their lives as slaves.

Dr. Means continued wanting to recall the chronology Mrs. Hawkins talked about before her death. "The Revolutionary War soldiers and 'freemen,' the free time after the Civil War when many more Negro people succeeded as self-suf-ficient individuals capable of full citizenship. The Jim Crow laws reinstating segregation slowed things, like a knotted pipe, but with the church and more and more professional Negroes coming along, we'll change the laws back!" He nodded with satisfaction. "Maybe we should have been lawyers," Dr. Means said with a slight smile.

"So *I think* we live to save lives, to keep stories *alive* like those of our ancestors and the Hawkins' family *and* encourage today's success stories as we work *hard* toward our rightful freedoms as citizens." Dr. Means got up from his chair, walked behind his partner's chair, and touched his shoulder. "If it's not to come for ourselves then it *will come* for our children. Understand?"

Edgar met the gesture by pinning the weathered hand with his own and squeezing it gently. "Guess I just needed to hear someone say it all again, Thurgood....and to see the futility of my raging." Edgar looked wistful. "Such energy could have fueled a powerful and futile vengeance; a vengeance unworthy of my calling as a doctor. I just have to remember the good, fine things in our history and the good, brave people." He tapped his palm on the tabletop. "We just keep working for freedom on this side of heaven, too."

The older doctor squeezed Edgar's shoulder again. "That's some words to live by. Stirs up some righteous hunger. Want some early dinner?"

The younger man walked after his partner's receding form into the kitchen. "Thanks, but I gotta get home."

So the young Dr. Yuell returned home and sat at his own dinner table. The memories of the afternoon lingered as he and Lady Dee prayed before their evening meal. The familiar shadows outside were disappearing in the twilight. He took a deep breath; thankful he had hashed it all through. Once again, Edgar repeated with greater conviction, "Too late on this earth for Mrs. Hawkins, but it's going to be different for you, baby mine...and for us all."

❧❦

The very next day, the Yuell's new baby pains started. As Pastor Fredericks said, some people were born as the fall winds snatched the paint-glorious leaves from their branches and danced them to the ground. Other babies came when the skeletal tree branches were robed in ice and snow. There were some who showed up at the same time the crocus, tulips, and leaves reappeared. Ruth Scott Yuell showed up a bit later. In the year of our Lord, 1939, on the first warm very early spring morning, her mother, Doris Alwilda Yuell, known in the neighborhood as Lady Dee, felt birth pains. "Oh my! Two weeks too early!"

"Leroy and Thelma," she called. Her frightened yell jarred the sturdy twin toddlers playing on the picnic quilt spread on the patchy, still winter-brown grass near the door. "Come on now, honeys," she coached, gritting her teeth against the pain. "It's time to call Mother Jones, the midwife. Our new baby's coming."

At the borning time, Ruth didn't know it but she had an older brother and sister waiting for her. Her brother, Betchem Leroy Yuell, tried and failed to lord over his twin sister, Thelma Elinor Yuell—the oldest by mere minutes. Ruth became the third, and last, in sibling command behind Leroy and Thelma.

Lady Dee wiped beads of sweat from her forehead and upper lip while she turned off the gas stove. "Now I said, come here!" Her newborn's healthy arrival was still in doubt and hours away, so everything else could wait.

Lady Dee's call to her toddlers alerted Mrs. Higgins from across the street. Mrs. Higgins knew Lady Dee never called her first-born children in anything other than a kind voice unless she was angry or something was wrong. "You ready, Lady Dee?"

Lady Dee nodded confirmation against the strong knifing pain. Heading down the backstairs, Mrs. Higgins knew to set her steps toward the house of the midwife. What a time for Lady Dee's husband to be way across town caring for Farmer Burton's gout! The old skinflint didn't have a phone even though he could have afforded one. "Don't worry. Know Dr. Means and he missus are visiting in Detroit. I'll go get Mother Jones."

Mother Jones wasn't easy to find. On the midwife's worn screen door was a paper scrap pinned to a dish towel on the doorknob with instructions to find her at the Duggins' place. Mrs. Higgins pursed her lips in exasperation as she saw the Phillips' oldest girl heading for the market. "You there, Esther. Can you stop and leave a message at the office of young Dr. Yuell on your way while I take my steps to find Mother Jones? Tell the office nurse, Lady Dee's laboring! Please tell Mrs. Phelps in Dr. Means's office. You understand?" Esther, grateful to have some excitement added to the market list, started running toward the doctors' offices.

Mother Jones showed displeasure at Mrs. Higgins arrival at the Duggins' back door. She'd been busy. Too busy these past two weeks with the no-money times still hanging on tighter here than in other places. The evidence was all around.

Mother Jones's porter nephew, who worked on the New Orleans-Chicago railroad route, talked about the hard economy. "It's better now up in Chicago but still a bit hard here, I see." No one had to tell Mother Jones. Little sleep and aching bones going from birth to birth told her the predicament. No Depression in having babies here, just no money for the hospitals and such. So they came back to her midwifery services, Mother Jones thought tiredly, as she put the Yuell home as her next stop and tried to figure out how she'd get two babies born when there was only one of her.

The Duggins boy was not anxious to be born after several days of off-again, on-again visits and the Yuell's baby wanted to enter this world early. Mother Jones would bet good money, if she had any, that their new arrival was going to be a girl. These labors had been preceded by the Minors' twins, both boys, and the Slocums' tricky breech birth, now a healthy baby girl they named Alice. "No rest for the good or the weary," Mother Jones said to the air after a deep sigh as she folded her hands in prayer. "Know it's not good to complain, dear Lord, but couldn't the almost-Dr. Yuell deliver his own baby?"

Mother Jones called out to Mrs. Higgins, "This is her second pregnancy, right? With twins the first time?" Mrs. Higgins walked over the door threshold and nodded.

"That's good. Tell Lady Dee I'll be there as soon as I can. She knows what to expect. You stay with her and send for her kinfolk. Have hot water, newspapers, and towels ready for her…and strong milk-coffee and a meal ready for me." Mother Jones opened the screen door, listened to her stomach growl, and watched Mrs. Higgins disappear down the sidewalk. "Make sure there's some pound cake if you please," she shouted as an afterthought. "I'm mighty partial to Lady Dee's recipe."

❧❧

Lady Dee didn't have much time to think as the pain worsened. It seemed like a long time since Mrs. Higgins had left. She put away the clothes destined for the washboard and steel tub, shoved the beginnings of dinner back in the icebox, and dried her hands. Fixing the family car for Edgar's future duties and the roof leak required all their savings toward a hospital birth and a wringer washer. Perhaps she should have sent Mrs. Higgins to her mother-in-law and grandmother first before sending for Mother Jones. The party line phone failed to reach anyone. Lady Dee didn't remember how many people were assigned to her number, but even the busybodies who listened in on every conversation trying to find out everyone else's business weren't home.

No one was at home on this first warm day hinting of spring with the breeze and bright sun begging to be enjoyed. *Would Edgar be able to get home? Could she get out of bed and get over to the Blasedale's to get help? It had been a long time.*

Lady Dee straightened her spine and regained focus. *This was just a problem, not an emergency, so a field holler across the yards to alert her neighbors would be undignified.* With Mrs. Higgins gone and no telephone here at the house, she'd have to walk to the Blasedale's house for help.

After a quick scribbled note, Lady Dee scooped up Leroy in one arm and Thelma in the other as another birth pain wrenched her insides. More pain-sweat formed on her upper lip and brow. "This isn't going to be too easy, children. Can Mama's big boy walk?" Lady Dee asked as she put her son's sturdy legs on the dirt alley and grabbed his hand. "We might have to stop a few times while we walk," she said. "You look at the trees and the birds when we do." The walk took more time and energy than Lady Dee expected but Mother Blasedale and

Grandmother Cameron were home. Mother Blasedale took the twins to her house and Grandmother Cameron left to find Edgar. In the distance, Lady Dee saw Mrs. Higgins. She closed her eyes in silent thanks and headed for her own back door. Once inside her house, Lady Dee stripped off her sweat-soaked dress, ran a cool cloth over her face and neck, and put on her nightdress. She thought about the rest of her family. "When will they get here?" Lady Dee whispered in a tired sigh. "I'll just have to wait till they do."

Mrs. Higgins helped Mrs. Blasedale watch the toddlers until Mother Jones and her overflowing black carpet bag arrived two hours later. Seemed like two days to Lady Dee. Lady Dee's energy was spent and she was about to say so but Mother Jones cut her off as she checked her list of impending deliveries. "I've been working hard but there's a lot more to come. The Bates' baby has yet to signal birth pain and the Clemons' twins are still safe and warm for several more days, at least. No word from the Addleys yet. You're a mite early, according to my calendar. Not due for calling for a week or after, but that's the way of it. "The pear falls from the tree when it is ripe and ready. So you have me now."

Mother Jones bustled around nodding in silent thanks to Mrs. Higgins's preparation of clean sheets and rag towels, alcohol, newspaper, and a pot of water on the stove to boil. "Look at this," Mother Jones exclaimed. "A remnant from a tablecloth Miss Bee and I made for Mother Blasedale. Been thirty years or more." She spread it out on the bottom sheet where Ruth would be born. "Your people are coming," she continued, indicating Mother Yuell and Grandmother Addison were within sight of the kitchen window. "You washed up? Time for bed and birthing."

Mother Yuell and Grandmother Addison entered the house and quickly removed the hat pins from their netted felt hats and hung their coats in the closet. "I'm usually right about these things...didn't think Lady Dee would have her baby early, so we went to the prayer meeting," Mother Yuell said in an out-of-breath gust as she poked her head into the bedroom and scooped Lady Dee up for a hug. "We're here now."

The twins were safely cared for, the remaining chores would be done, and she could get on with birthing her third baby. Lady Dee relaxed against the mattress.

The clarion call went out to the neighborhood, "The Yuell baby is coming. Early!" People walked, ran, and sauntered down the sidewalk, over dirt paths, around fences or initiated back-door conversations heralding the birthing event and starting plans to take care of the Yuells.

"Mrs. Anderson, did you hear Mother Jones is with Mrs. Yuell?" and, "Hello, Mrs. Bates, did you know that Mother Jones been called to the Yuells?" or, "Yuell's baby on the way, early by at least a week!" Just as Ruth's mother had done so many times for others in birth, death, or need, now the women in the Negro community went about their afternoons with one more casserole, cake, pie, batch of fried chicken, or fresh crock of buttermilk put aside in praise of the "new" doctor in their community and his growing family.

☙❧

Daylight passed, evening was gone, and now it was several hours into the early morning of a new day. Lady Dee was beyond tired, edging on exhaustion. The labor pains weren't coming regularly or close anymore. Leroy was asleep in a blanket bed in Mother Yuell's arms while Mother Addison and Thelma slept propped on the other doily-covered arm. Edgar sat weary-eyed at the kitchen table occasionally laying his head on the oilcloth cover to rest or pray.

"Your labor's just not getting along. Pain's lasting too long to allow sleep but it's too short to birth a baby," Mother Jones noted, stifling a yawn. "Even though he's a doctor, I told your husband to get some rest at the kitchen table. He looks as worn out as you." Mother Jones frowned a bit. "This baby is coming between the stars and the bluebird sky, which is a good sign, so you'd best get to doing it."

Even though things were going slowly, Lady Dee liked laboring at home so much better. Smells of fresh air, instead of the hospital ether and ammonia, comforted her. Mother Jones being so patient when the people at the hospital would have given her chloroform by now and pulled her baby out. Memories of the so-called delivery room flooded her mind, making her grimace even when there was no pain. In the Colored ward, dust moats the size of baby fists floated below the hospital cot over a sea of forgotten gray dirt. The formerly white porcelain on the metal beds and bed tables were so scarred and old that the finishes were more black than white on most surfaces. Edgar and Dr. Means tried to find some community moneys to make things better but resources were stretched thin.

"Can't get done this way." Mother Jones placed her hands on her knees and rose heavily from the worn, overstuffed bedroom chair. The structure beneath the faded flower-patterned upholstery creaked against her weight as she headed for the kitchen. "Seen it happen sometimes. Having some blackstrap molasses and condensed sugar milk in some strong tea is the next trick to consider. Perhaps a whispered story or two. Guaranteed to speed things along."

"Are you sure?" Lady Dee asked, too spent to voice skepticism. "Perhaps we should ask Edgar?" She hadn't seen her husband but for a brief kiss and hello before Mother Jones shooed him from the bedroom. Birthing and babies were for the women, an occasional doctor not related to the laboring woman in question, and that was all, Mother Jones reiterated in her mind, lest the mother was dying and that wasn't happening here. The midwife looked through the kitchen cupboards. *Lady Dee was not dying.* Mother Jones stood her ground, barred the door, and made the tea.

"That's my idea for it," Mother Jones stated emphatically. "Doing this will make the labor go faster." She handed Lady Dee the steaming mug. "Now let's consider the night sky out there." Mother Higgins bit her lip and thought how to describe it. "It's like Mrs. Elrod's night-blue velvet holiday dress." She turned her tired gaze to the ceiling and pointed upward like they were both outside and could see the sky. "The stars are like white fists of cold fire. Like you could touch them and not get burned." A slow smile came to the older women's face. "It's going to be a cloudless, clear-as-crystal, bluebird-sky day tomorrow."

To Lady Dee's great surprise, as she drank the tea and listened to Mrs. Higgins's thoughts about the night sky, the contractions quickly got stronger with a speedy progression to a healthy daughter's birth, none the wiser of the slight delay into this world. At 5:33 a.m., as the sun of a new day rose, life's clock began ticking for the Yuell's new baby girl.

Lady Dee just laid there and smiled. "A boy and a girl together, and now another girl. How perfect!" Everyone was pleased. They named their daughter Ruth Scott Yuell after the Old Testament heroine and her dearly departed Grandmother Scott.

Mother Jones walked slowly out the door after prayers, cleaning up, and hugs with an extra wax paper bundle of pound cake slices. "Child, that's how it is sometimes. The old starry sky helped things along. Babies that come early, sometimes arrive late."

CHAPTER TWO

EMERGENCY ROOM AT 10:45 A.M.
CHICAGO - 1967

"So Thelma and Leroy were born in the hospital and you were delivered by Mother Jones?" Norma asked as she checked her notes. "We might have to check to see how long the trend lasted."

"Probably as long as people didn't have the money to pay for hospital births," Ruth answered pragmatically. "Race was an obstacle. Disease was another hazard. There were no wonder drugs yet. Our medicines were mustard, hot water teas, camphor, a review of the almanac remedies if you couldn't afford a doctor, like my father or Dr. Means, and prayer. Many lives were crippled and lost to measles, polio, and diphtheria epidemics. A common cold could turn deadly in a few days in the young, old, or weak. In the protective custom of women retreating from the outside world after childbirth, Lady Dee was ensconced in her bed and I slept in a wooden cradle squeezed between the bed and the wall so no one could get to us."

"Lady Dee told me she wasn't allowed to leave the bedroom except 'for a few minutes a day for air and sunshine,' as Grandmother Addison insisted, but she slipped out to have evening meals with Daddy. The twins were with Grandmother Yuell and Great-Grandmother Addison, who acted as sentries in the kitchen and living room, taking the covered dishes and desserts from friends, neighbors, and father and Dr. Means's grateful patients. Both shooed away anyone 'without enough sense God gave them' when people tried to peek at me. Even my toddler siblings were firmly bottom-patted away from the cradle...."

ST. LOUIS – 1939

Ruth's dedication day's sky was bright blue. In both directions along the street and hard-packed dirt alleys and paths, well-wishers, friends, and family in their Sunday clothes waited to greet the Yuell's new baby girl. After the formal church service, everyone gathered on the lawn to wait for Dr. and Mrs. Yuell to present the days-old guest of honor.

"What'd they name her again?" Mrs. Phelps asked in a loud voice as she tapped Mrs. Smith's shoulder.

"Her name is Ruth," Reverend Fredericks whispered close to the woman's ear. He intervened knowing Mrs. Phelps was rather deaf and could probably neither hear nor understand the answer without further shouting.

Dr. Yuell proudly escorted Lady Dee with Ruth in her arms down the church steps. Everyone gathered in a lazy circle like a bureau-laid black pearl necklace for this celebration of life and community.

"We," Edgar said as he reached for his wife's hand, "offer our welcome and introduce you to our new daughter, Ruth Scott Yuell."

In this traditional family parade, Lady Dee, with her husband's hand gently at the small of her back, walked slowly around the courtyard revealing the baby's cherubic face from the confines of the soft pink baby blanket.

Thelma and Leroy stood at Grandmother Yuell's side, quite proud of themselves; they had been the first besides their daddy, Lady Dee, and their grandparents to see baby Ruth—even before the church elders and all the rest. Having grandmother's special-made apple fritters waiting for the toddlers if they were behaved didn't hurt either.

While Leroy and Thelma thought of their fritters, other people speculated about the looks and features of the Yuell's new baby. Emma Clavors emphatically stated that the baby, without question, looked like Lady Dee. "It's quite plain for anyone to see, Mrs. James. Ruth has her mother's eyes and oval face."

"Now, don't be too hasty. I think she looks more like her father, the doctor. What do you think, Mother Addison?" inquired Mrs. Clavors.

"Don't put me on the spot! All three of my grandbabies are special to me," Mother Addison stated, trying to avoid taking sides in the discussion. "Did you bring your coconut cookies, Minna?" she asked and turned to Mrs. James. "Ethel, are those vanilla cake slices?" The women stopped arguing. Mother Addison led them to the refreshment area where the plates and platters of food were being set out. Several men had come over early to help Reverend Fredericks put wooden tables under the hundred-year-old oak tree.

Reverend Fredericks took up his post at the head of the line. "Dear ladies and gentlemen, thank you so much for coming to see little Ruth. Please, please, follow after the Yuells to the tables for the refreshments our Women's Guild has so kindly arranged from the dishes you've shared from your kitchens. Dear Lord, thank you for such a special time, this glorious food…and memories made here this afternoon. Amen." After these few sacred words, the noise level exploded like a vintage champagne cork as children and adults followed the Yuells to the food line. Lady Dee made sure Edgar had charge of their plates and sidestepped the crowd to where the family's baby buggy stood. Mother Addison quickly said her goodbyes with instructions to watch over her great-granddaughter as both she and the infant sat in the veiled quiet, each enjoying the sights and sounds of that happy day.

ᐒᐧᐸ

"Today has not gone well since I opened my eyes this morning," Lady Dee pushed damp strands of her hair back into the unusually haphazard chignon at the base of her neck, which irritated Lady Dee because she always prided herself on having a tidy appearance, especially on Sunday. "I haven't even been able to go to church. Leroy has a molar coming in and he's been feverish and fretful all night and this morning. The sassafras tea hasn't helped quickly enough but at least he seems content for a moment. Ruth's been crying loud and long too, echoing her brother, in this hot, humid weather. Colic, I guess." Lady Dee frowned. "The celebration air of Ruth's dedication ceremony has faded a bit more quickly than I wanted," she confided to Mother Addison a few days later.

"No fever, spots, or throwing up, thank the good Lord, so this doesn't mean anything more serious," Mother Addison pronounced as she finished inspecting her great-granddaughter's sleeping body, placing her on her back. "All Ruth is doing is being cranky, twisting around, and kicking the air?" Lady Dee nodded but she wasn't as sure as Mother Addison when she intoned, "It'll pass."

There had been so much rain this spring, Lady Dee thought glumly, alternately watching the leaden gray skies out the window and Ruth, sleeping an exhausted slumber. Her husband's melancholy thoughts echoed and intensified her sorrow, heavy as the sodden skies. *I know exactly how he's feeling.*

Feeling down had started to affect Lady Dee even before Ruth's birth. At least now their baby girl was here, but she couldn't shake the sadness.

Birthing blues, Mother Yuell had thought, seeing Lady's Dee's behavior, hoping they would pass and not wanting to say anything to her son or dear daughter-in-law.

Mother Addison noticed, too. "What's the matter, Baby?" the older woman asked as Lady Dee heard the thump step of Grandmother's worn-out hipbones and saw the sketchy outline of her age-stiffened fingers on the door panel.

"I'm not the baby anymore," Lady Dee replied softly with laughter showing in the edges of her near-whisper. "Ruth is."

"So how does a woman saying she's so happy let out such a forlorn sigh?" Mother Addison questioned, now whispering herself. "You're worried about your husband." Before Lady Dee could issue a confirmation or denial, Mother Addison waved her hand to keep her granddaughter-by-marriage silent. "I saw the sad look in his eyes, too. I've seen that look a time or two in other men's eyes. Life isn't easy."

"Mind you, I'm not complaining, but I think Edgar's sad I wasn't able to go to the hospital to have Ruth," Lady Dee said, trying to explain. "It must hurt him deeply, being a doctor and not having the money to send me for a hospital birth."

"I'm a young woman in an old woman's body, I think," Mother Addison started as she sat heavily in the maple rocker. "I like this dim light. Easier on me when my tired eyes hit evening."

If Grandmother Addison wanted to say something, Lady Dee would listen to her wise counsel.

"I've been alive long enough to remember better, freer days. As a child, I can remember a few times when I sat with the white folk. No trouble or nothing. They might not have liked it but there was nothing they could do about it. Not then. I remember my grandfather going to vote for something or another—wish I could recall what it was. No matter, *it was so*. But now times are different for men and for women with colored skin. Money's got a little to do with it. It's a sour thing, for sure. You can't let a sour thing fester. Gotta' clean it out or it'll kill. Told your father-in-law the same thing, years ago. He knew it already. But sometimes, a body gets tired of carrying the load. We all do. Landmark times can be the worst of it, as with the birth of Ruth here. So let's get all the gripes out into God's sweet air. You hear me, Baby?"

Feeling emboldened, Lady Dee started speaking in an exasperated whisper. "It's so much better when we're visiting up in Chicago." Near tears, she swiped at her cheeks as she looked at Mother Addison. "It's so unseemly, having to stop to use bushes and the woods to go to the bathroom when there are restrooms aplenty for the white folk. But I must say, with the rundown bathrooms we have to choose from, I'll take the bushes!" Other injustices flooded Lady Dee's mind just waiting for her tongue to speak. "I'm tired of sitting in the colored section of the movie house when we go south. That old balcony is so small. It gives me claustrophobia when they pack us in there so tight. The screen seems so far away I feel like I'm looking at the movie through a pop bottle!" Her grandmother-in-law began rocking in slow, even motions. "Then there's the signs saying, 'No Negroes or dogs on the grass!' I'm tired of going on family outings with so much stuff," Lady Dee tapped each addition on her fingers as the right index finger met the left ring finger. "We need mason jars with water for cleaning and several old, clean towels to use for drying or spills. There's the towel remnant for wrapping the soap. Then there's all the food!" Lady Dee's thoughts came faster and faster. "Let's see, there's the water jug for drinking and the lemonade. Bologna and bread for sandwiches and meat snacks. If we'll be away for dinner or Sunday supper, I'll have cooked fried chicken. I have to save boxes from the grocery store or ice those old galvanized tubs we use for traveling. Even though the white grocery stores sell to us, sometimes the people are so rude and uppity; I prefer not to use them when we're traveling, especially south.

"When we go south, you know there are no restaurants where we can sit in the main dining areas. Why must we be treated that way?" Lady Dee cried with exasperation. "No using the benches, beaches and, sometimes, no getting gasoline for our cars. Just because we're colored. Just because of our skin. Our food has to be paid for in advance. We eat in the cramped places and get served from the kitchen windows or back doors of the white establishments. Just a few feet away, white patrons sit inside the restaurant, eat from a menu with more selections,, greater portions, and far friendlier service. I'm so tired of keeping a mental road map in my head to remember the safe places to sleep, bathe, eat, and get water and drinks. We shouldn't have to be afraid," Lady Dee's voice rose to a painful shout-whisper tearing at her throat. "You *know* we're always on the edge of danger. If we forget the rules for Negroes or are in the wrong place at the wrong time, we could be hurt or even killed. For nothing. *For nothing.*"

"Feeling better, child?" Mother Addison intoned.

Tears were streaming down Lady Dee's face. Mother Addison rocked forward, stilling Lady Dee's quivering hands as she finally uttered, "I know, I know. I've been there many-a-time myself. Fussing and fuming. Being proud of who I am and putting my mood down so low at the same time. It's the strain of the truth on one layer and the baby's blues plopped on the top of it, I think. You're looking up from that 'low place' and heading for the light, again. Just letting the sourness out. That's all. Sometimes it'll be tears and shouting and other times it'll be tears and whispers, like right now."

"Same kinda' fading spell came upon me every time I gave birth and lots of times in-between. Guess it was all about bringing a new life into the world and sifting over the good things and the bad things that might be ahead...for us all and for this beautiful, sleeping little girl." The older woman leaned over and stroked the tiny, golden chubby cheek of her great-granddaughter with her gnarled hand, then tickled the baby skin with her knuckles. "That could make anyone, a woman or a man, think or say something they didn't really mean. Did I tell you the time that my dear husband and I..." Mother Addison began but Lady Dee was only partially listening. The tears had stopped and she cherished the words that this sage woman, her God-gifted grandmother-in-law, had spoken.

When Mother Addison stopped speaking, Lady Dee queried, "So it's just a passing feeling for me...and Edgar? Him too?"

A twinkling brown light shone in Mother Addison's eyes.

"'For the Lord will provide me with wise counselors...' like you, Mother Addison." Lady Dee stood up, wound her arms around Mother Addison's neck and this time when she unwound them, instead of a sigh, she breathed out laughter.

Lady Dee took Mother Addison's advice to talk to her husband about the comment she overheard him make about things 'going to be different' for Ruth after Mrs. Hawkins' funeral and the dedication. Edgar talked to her about it, too, at the encouragement of Dr. Means. They cleared the air about the question of the hospital birth and Mrs. Hawkins's death. They both felt so much better.

ᏇᎧ

EMERGENCY ROOM AT 11:05 A.M.
CHICAGO – 1967

"What's the matter, Ruth?" Norma asked. "Do I need to get the nurse? Are you feeling OK?"

"I'm fine. I'm fine," Ruth said dismissively, not wanting to start talking about her own sad times...just yet. She closed her eyes against the pain, dizziness, and the blood-red thoughts by squeezing her eyelids together tightly. "There's plenty of time to talk about the sadness. I need to tell a happy story now, please."

"What would you like to talk about?"

"You want to talk about *my* memories, Norma?" Ruth lifted her head, gave one pillow a sideswipe to erase the wrinkles and eased back again.

Ruth thought she might as well start with the moving day and her brother, Leroy. "I sat in a cardboard fort of packed and unpacked boxes listening to Granddaddy explain why we had moved so many blocks away to the larger brown brick home."

ᏇᎧ

ST. LOUIS – 1945

The five Yuells were moving from Archer Street. Ruth, at about age five, got lost in all the large rooms on the first floor.

"Changes are hard to make, my dear Ruth, even at age five." Grandfather Addison unpacked the table lamp he and Mother Addison had given them as a house-warming present. "Now that you have moved, you can have a bedroom of your own. This Depression's been long and hard, followed by this war. So finding you a house has had to wait a bit. Do you understand? Granddaddy wants you to understand what is going on."

Ruth was close to her first year at school. Ruth knew she wasn't happy and they'd moved away from their small frame home. She wished they lived closer to her granddaddy again and told him so.

"It's not too far. Just go from the alley to where the pavement starts, travel a mile, turn left at the chestnut tree, and the street leads to our house." Grandfather Addison smiled reassuringly.

Besides, Ruth's whittled animal playthings, chocolate cloth rag dolls, and tea set had been misplaced in the move and Lady Dee was too busy to watch her daughter play outside. So Ruth was stuck sitting and playing by the boxes. Neither her brother, Leroy, or her sister, Thelma, were there to alternately play and annoy her in their normal daytime cycle. Her siblings caught a summer cold and their coughing and sniffling postponed their coming with the family. Mother Addison was trying to douse them with camphor salve, cod liver oil, and hot-honey tea. Besides listening to the rattling of packing paper, some workmen, and birdsong outside, there was nothing for Ruth to do but sit and watch the constant flow of people in and out of the door, who all seemed to want to do everything but play with her.

"You want to see your room?" her father finally asked, coming through the dinning room arch. "Thought it would be the first thing you'd want to see when you set foot here. Come on." He proudly ushered Ruth up the stairs, like a magician extending his hand after an especially difficult illusion, opening the door to a large room that seemed to swallow her old bed. There was a bureau and dresser in it she'd never seen before. "A gift from the previous owner," he said, as her eyes lit up in wonder. "They're moving to a smaller place. They didn't need them and now they're yours." With open-mouthed surprise, Ruth walked over to caress the pieces like they were giant wooden babies set at her threshold. They were the most beautiful things she'd ever seen outside of the wooden pews in Reverend Frederick's church, with carved wood rosettes in the middle of each drawer and a squatty, curved carved leg on either side of the front panel.

"They're so fine. You and Lady Dee didn't want them in your room?" Ruth asked incredulously.

"No. No, Ruth. We're just fine. We thought you might like them here." Her father smiled with love and satisfaction.

What were Leroy and Thelma doing? Were they going to have new bedroom pieces like hers? She hoped her siblings would be there soon and not miss out on any of the new discoveries. *Did they have to pick this time of all times to be sick? Together?*

Ruth missed their attention, good or bad. Ruth knew that when Mother Addison's grandchildren were sick or wanted to act like the grown-ups, Mother Addison would put some coffee grounds into sugar-sweetened milk and put the mixture through her sieve, so they could pretend they were drinking grown-up coffee. Not only that! Ruth bet the house smelled of freshly baked rolls, bread, or biscuits because of tomorrow's Ladies' Spring church luncheon. Leroy and Thelma were having Mother Addison fix them some milk-coffee, eating fresh biscuits, and then, Grandmother Addison was probably going to let Thelma win in a game of dominoes!

Even if she could have, Ruth didn't want to go outside alone. Outside the front door there was a porch with several cement steps with brick and cement-capped railings, sitting like sentries on either side. The number of driveways between the old and new house seemed like the distance from the earth to the moon.

She might know a few of the people and children in the houses but it wasn't with the same knowledge and comfort as the people she'd grown to love on South Archer. As Ruth stood on the first high step, she felt she was perched on a small mountain. She didn't need to be hoisted in her father's or Lady Dee's arms anymore to see the long swath of cement sidewalk or the wider patched asphalt street. Ruth scampered back into the house because her heart was beating fast.

There was a knock on the screen molding. The light was blocked by a tall, thickly-built woman in a severely plain dove-gray suit. At the knock, her father stood up from unpacking the last bookshelf box while trying to fold down his upturned cuffs, button them, and open the door, simultaneously. "Mrs. Wilcox, I didn't realize it was two o'clock already." *Hadn't Lady Dee said something about the Wilcox family?*

"I understand. Understand, quite well." Mrs. Wilcox jovially gained a position among the boxes. "You're finally getting a bit more space than the other house."

Ruth noticed other changes, too. Colorful ration tickets and Granddaddy's stories changing to tell more about Negro men fighting in World War I and now this war, World War II. Several of the families in their church had sons or grandsons in the Army. Prayers had changed at church to not only praying for the country but including prayers for places like Europe, the Philippines, and China.

Dr. Yuell looked into Mrs. Wilcox's face. "Just seemed like we were getting out of the Depression finally, and now this terrible war. So many lives lost already."

"Yes. Yes. Terrible thing, but a valiant cause. Virgil Collins is leaving next week. He told me so when he was helping with your move just now," the woman replied.

"We'll have to continue to organize our plans and prayers for the families with servicemen. How are you getting along over there?" Dr. Yuell inquired. Lady Dee had said something about taking care of Mrs. Wilcox's cousins.

"Don't worry about us," Mrs. Wilcox assured the doctor with a wide, tooth-radiant smile. "We're doing just fine," Mrs. Wilcox changed the position of her head and spoke again. "Miss Ruth. That you sitting over there?"

"Come here to Mrs. Wilcox." Dr. Yuell pushed Ruth forward toward Mrs. Wilcox's strong, beefy arms. "We're going to get to know each other quite well. Your mother will help to care for my cousin and a younger niece about three, maybe four years older than you, I think."

"Mrs. Wilcox's cousin and niece need some day- and after-school care while she's working at a munitions plant," Ruth's father replied. "You'll be meeting them in a few days when we're settled." Nothing would happen for a few days. "She and her family go to Reverend Monroe's church."

So that was the answer. The Wilcox family didn't go to their church or travel down to South Archer Street, so they had never met as far as Ruth could remember.

◔◡◔

Soon Leroy and Thelma were well. So well that Ruth found Leroy sitting on the back porch steps with a soap bar in his month and a towel on his lap—a sure sign of punishment. "Now don't you go bothering Leroy while he's considering the error of his ways," Lady Dee recommended. "Your older brother has decided those slang words he hears in impolite conversation should become a part of *his* vocabulary. Your father, the soap, and I will convince him to reconsider." Lady Dee picked up the laundry basket. "Only correct English will be spoken in this house. Your parents, grandparents, and great-grandparents represent a proud heritage of proper elocution and grammar…which will continue or there will be soap wasted until things change."

So Ruth waited for the punishment to end to tell her brother and Thelma about feeling strange for not knowing the Wilcox family or Mrs. Wilcox, in turn, not knowing much about South Archer Street.

"Now that I'm out of the dog house with Lady Dee, I can take you around the property. We've got lots more land here," Leroy offered as they sprinted together into a wooded area of grass-green trees. They scrambled over the small, surprisingly sandy rise to see broken-down fences of what had been animal pens. "These all belong to the Wilcox family," Leroy informed in a businesslike manner as he started to point. "Was a working farm once but the houses and city have choked it out. Had this land for ages and ages, I guess. Heard someone say they're land-rich and money-poor, so both Mr. and Mrs. Wilcox work to hold onto things." Leroy must have read the look on his sister's face because he calmed his voice.

This was the first time Ruth had been out exploring since moving into her new home. *What other surprises were in store?*

Leroy made everything sound so much bigger and more important. "And over there used to be a hog pen. Nevin Anders fell in there once and Bluebell, the last sow they kept, stomped him. He'd taken a bet he could walk the entire pen rail but Nevin said he hadn't counted on the sow's yellow-hot, beady sow eyes looking at him the whole time. And his challenger didn't tell him Bluebell just had a litter two days before and she was one angry, protective mother."

Leroy laughed at his own retelling of the story. "All the mud, pig anger, and Nevin's legs flaying all over the place as Bluebell punished him for breaking her and her piggies' peace. Bluebell pinned him over there where the trough used to be!" Leroy's arm fell to his side. "Mrs. Wilcox said that would be the last pig for awhile, or perhaps forever, now that her cousin and niece were coming to stay."

"Then there's the garden behind the grass and brick border. We'll plant, tend, and grow everything right here. Tender plants grow near the shade tree over there. Plan to plant a new tree each year on Arbor Day," he stated, pointing to the treetops behind the property they'd just left. The plot was about an acre. Uncle Benjamin's truck farm was about five acres.

"Does the clay taste sweet here?" Ruth asked. Leroy frowned and looked surprised. She stammered as she said, "Uncle Benjamin says sweet clay near planting ground shows the soil is good." Ruth was happy to be able to contribute something to the tour and conversation.

"I don't know much about sweet clay but with a good rainy season, the soil'll give us enough to eat for the year, if we're careful. We'll be canning and raising steam clouds in the kitchen every morning till frost comes except Sundays and the Fourth of July. You wait and see. There's enough glass jars to go from here to downtown!" Quite a picture for Ruth to see in her mind!

Leroy sensed her unease. "Let's go see the school. It's two blocks down the street from our new house." He stuck his hand out. Ruth slowly lifted her hand, grabbed it and the two siblings walked slowly to the three-story red brick school building. They went from the sidewalk and bright sunlight to filtered yellow haze. A puff of dust motes rose as they walked through tall metal doors. "We'll stay here a minute. Let your eyes get set for the dark."

Ruth nodded her head, tightening her grip on Leroy's hand. "There's school for Thelma and me for a few more weeks, after chores and breakfast. Then lunch, more classes, home for chores, and more studying in the afternoon according to the schedule father's set out.

"Better get started looking at your new school here!" Leroy loved adventures and talking and telling. "In September, you'll be in first grade...and you'll need to know your way around. You're tall for your age but a bit scrawny. Have to be smart and sharp all the time to keep out of trouble." *How was she supposed to remember all this information and be adventurous at the same time?*

Leroy was still talking and explaining while Ruth was feeling lost and sore inside like she'd fallen good and hard on her ribs. It felt like that old sow had stomped her instead of Nevin Anders.

"We're at the auditorium. There's the long piece of cement between the school building and here…and the big doors we just went through," he said as we rounded the corner and came to a halt. "Here's the music room. My most favorite thing is when they play the instruments," he informed. "Follow me."

In the dim light, Ruth could see a large opening and hear Leroy's shoes step-slide over the polished wooden floor.

"Isn't it beautiful?" Leroy said as the black hole became lighted.

Ruth looked at the cavernous empty room with an elevated stage clothed in curtains so red they were almost black.

"The curtains sure are pretty," Ruth said softly.

"Real burgundy velveteen. The cord to pull it is right over there to the left, anchored with a big silver bolt," Leroy recounted proudly. "There are five steps up to the stage with some closets and scenery in the back. Mr. Ambrose, the music teacher, teaches drama classes at the high school and says no one can go there without permission. Chairs are back there, too. All put away for waxing the floor in the summer. Sliding slick. Did it once with rags tied to my feet. Felt like I was flying once or twice."

Leroy whirled around with his eyes closed. "They have dress-up dances here and the couples twirl and twirl around to the slow music. It's like a Cinderella ball." From his description Ruth could almost see the couples dancing in their fine clothes. "Then there's the kitchen for serving lunches mostly down the hall and those are classrooms there. All the students are getting ready for graduation and summer vacation now. Then it will be more like everybody's dead and gone, it'll be so quiet here." Leroy pointed in the opposite direction. "Here's the cafeteria dining room and back there's the kitchen. Bigger than the city restaurant where we ate for Dr. Means's birthday."

Most of those places only allowed white folk. But Ruth stood in a large restaurant place now. Not quite as fancy, Ruth admitted to herself. Long tin-clad tables, but lots of them, and the chairs were lined soldier-straight along the walls. "Mopped the floors last Friday. Put the chairs along the wall. Put the tables back after it's dry. See the counter here?" he pointed. "The food gets organized from the cook pots and platters. You stand in line to get your plate."

Leroy was in the kitchen now. "Come see the stoves, ice box, and sinks," he called. "The sinks are really deep. I think they got them from an old hotel. You could almost take a bath in them. Time to go up to the second floor. Not much to see there except rows and rows of classrooms."

After they wandered through the entire school, they headed back home to do their chores. Leroy pointed to the Wilcox property. "Did I tell you the Wilcox place still has a chicken coop? I gotta' go feed 'em. You can hear 'em scratching and fussing all day long. Better go now and take care of them before dinnertime."

Ruth walked with Leroy to the Wilcox chicken coop. *What was he going to show her now? And would she remember it all?*

"The rooster, Brutus, crows so much you'd think his throat would hurt," Leroy began. "The neighbors don't seem to mind since the eggs are good. Mrs. Wilcox sells the eggs and meat real reasonable when the hens get old. Eggs been kinda scarce with the war and all." Ruth spied a huge brown-feathered rooster. "He's nasty as Bluebell was in his own way. Chases all the chickens around till they do what he says. Time to feed 'em."

"Where's the feed?" Ruth asked. Leroy pointed to the galvanized bucket on a tenpenny nail in the coop. Leroy opened the wood-framed, chicken wire-clad door and closed it tightly to ward off any chance of escaping poultry. Brutus swooped down from his three-foot perch. "Stop it, rooster, er...Brutus," Ruth shouted. "Uncle Benjamin's got a nasty rooster just like you. Next time you get the business end of a broom if you try that again," she announced, in her best Uncle Benjamin impression. "And if you peck me, maybe we'll have rooster for Sunday supper instead of hen. Now get." For the rest of the visit, Brutus sat on his perch while Ruth threw the feed with an even-handed throwing motion, secured the bucket on the nail, and closed the door.

"Fine job. Fine Job," Leroy complimented. "I know it isn't right but I hate that old rooster," he whispered. "Likes to scare people and the only good chicken is a fried chicken as far as I'm concerned."

Finally, she had impressed her brother. *But in all the things they'd done that morning, did it have to be concerning chickens?*

❧

A few days later, after saying prayers over the evening meal, Dr. Yuell cleared his throat. "I've been over to the Wilcox house next door and there's an older girl and a young girl, from the extended Wilcox families, who have come for a stay." Dr. Yuell stopped for a moment. "The younger girl has set herself right at home because she already calls Mrs. Wilcox and her husband Grandma and Grandpa." Lady Dee and Dr. Yuell decided not to share the fact that so many children during those Depression and war years were left with extended family and friends so couples and single parents could find work farther north and then send for their family members later—even a sadder case for these two girls. Their relations came to the Wilcox home with the girls in tow and then left several days later with no future plans in place. The doctor continued, "Mr. and Mrs. Wilcox have jobs in the war plants, so they'll need someone to watch their cousins Sylvie and Nettie, and Lady Dee has agreed to supervise the situation so she can stay home and care for us, too."

Edgar and Lady Dee looked at the wages Lady Dee earned in her position as a part-time domestic and the intermittent salary from her work at her husband's and Dr. Means's practice. This money was just as good and she'd only have to travel between their new home and the Wilcox place through a path behind their property. Ruth looked at her parents and nodded, getting back to the field peas and mashed potatoes on her plate. "Good then. There'll be some time to get to know them before school starts."

CHAPTER THREE

The next day, Dr. Yuell, Leroy, Thelma, and Ruth walked down the pea-gravel path leading away from their home. Ruth could see several people in the side yard on the edge of the Wilcox property. Patches of late spring wildflowers waved in the breeze as they watched three people busily washing sheets and hanging laundry.

As they slowly walked the last few yards, Mrs. Wilcox wiped her hands on her apron and called out, "Almost done here. Woulda had you over earlier. Washing clothes isn't any way to have you meet Nettie and Sylvie and Emil's started scything down the weeds."

Ruth looked at the man sweeping his arms in a rhythmic motion nearer the trees but was startled by the sound of someone rushing towards them.

"That's Sylvie," Mrs. Wilcox informed as Ruth watched the pumping run of large-booted feet before a thick-bodied young woman in her late teens burst from behind the other side of the laundry-brimming clothesline.

"Nee-Nee," Sylvie called as she stopped and pointed at Ruth.

"Sylvie, it's just Dr. Yuell, the twins Leroy and Thelma, and little Ruth," Mrs. Wilcox replied.

Sylvie continued to nod her head quickly. "Nee-Nee." Her bright-eyed, friendly face and stance were those of a tomboy but her size and the muscles under the slim-sleeve shirtwaist were like the workmen across the street or the farmers visiting her father's practice. Her head was large and a bit misshapen in the back as she turned her head to look at Mrs. Wilcox. "Nee-Nee," she said a third time.

"Sylvie, don't go scaring her," a small voice came from behind a muslin sheet flapping in the breeze. Ruth hadn't notice the small, thin, barefoot girl looking all arms and elbows in a billowing, faded yellow dress. The girl was about Ruth's own size but with the eyes of a much older woman. While Ruth's attention was fixed on Sylvie, she'd stood there twining a fat single braid around her index finger. "I'm Nettie. Wanna go exploring?"

Ruth nodded her head, grabbed her hand back from Leroy's grasp, and ran after her new acquaintance as the yellow-dressed girl released the braid to fly down her back. Both girls disappeared behind the sheets. Sylvie's heavier step was close behind.

Dr. Yuell waved. "I'll be back later," as Ruth saw her father and the twins turn to say goodbye to Mrs. Wilcox and head back toward home.

Things might be more fun in the new house now.

"Sylvie's sick sometimes," Nettie shouted back matter-a-factly. "Granny calls it 'being slow.'" Her breath began puffing. "She'll always be like a child even though she's over eighteen and something. But it doesn't bother us too much except Sylvie gets powerful sad or afraid sometimes. The medicine in the dark bottle helps her to rest and get going on the right track again. Granny will decide when to use it." Nettie gave information and changed subjects with lightening speed as Sylvie and Ruth chased her past the clothesline and out unto a tiny meadow. "I can play after chores. Jump rope, too. I'm going to find some work to do to make extra money. There's lots of work when the school year starts and enough during the summer, too, I hear." Nettie was brimming with information. "We came here from Kentucky. We're staying with Granny and Grandpa from now on. Sylvie's like a much older sister. How about you?"

Sylvie looked at Ruth as if she had all kinds of precious secrets to tell. Ruth made what she thought was a pitiful declaration about moving from one house to another.

Nettie seemed satisfied to Ruth's relief. Sylvie seemed very pleased as her eyes shone brightly and she smiled. "Nee-Nee," she said yet again.

"She's named you, sure as I'm standing here. I'll call you Nee-Nee, too. You mind?" Nettie started again in her rapid-fire style. Ruth didn't have a chance to react. "Settled then," Nettie said and started off running again. "Sylvie's got a favorite book. *The Three Pigs*. Have to read it to her at least six times a day but I don't mind. You want to try reading to her? Grandma Wilcox says they had pigs here but gave them up."

Ruth nodded her head. When they went back to the house, as soon as Sylvie saw the well-worn book, she came and sat next to Ruth so tightly that Ruth thought she might fall over. Sylvie's eyes shone brightly and she frequently repeated some of the words Ruth read, bouncing gleefully and clapping her hands.

"If Sylvie lets you read her book, then she's friends forever!" Nettie declared with a smile.

Just as Nettie had predicted, Sylvie called Ruth "Nee-Nee" from that very first pleased-to-meet-you day. Never knew why she called Ruth that. Sylvie couldn't explain. Ruth and Nettie grew into best friends and Ruth traveled the sidewalks of the new neighborhood answering to two names: Ruth and Nee-Nee.

❧

The next morning, Nettie was at the screen door just as Lady Dee got the breakfast dishes on the table. "Can I play with Ruth, Mrs. Yuell?" Nettie said as Ruth picked up her milk glass. "I want to teach her how I jump rope. They say I'm a real expert. 'Mary Mack all dressed in black' is my favorite!"

Ruth's milk glass hung in the air almost forgotten because it startled Ruth to hear her mother called "Mrs. Yuell" and feared Nettie, the only person her age who had befriended her in this new home, had made some mistake in her mother's eyes by doing so.

To Ruth's relief and pleasure, Lady Dee laughed and said, "Mrs. Yuell is my husband's mother. We don't want you to get mixed up, so please call me Lady Dee." Most all of the wives in Ruth's memory got called "Miss" or "Lady" or something else besides "Mrs." until their mother-in-laws died. Like royalty.

"Let Ruth finish her breakfast. I'm in charge of making sure you have your breakfast, too. Now and when school starts. Sit down to breakfast now, Nettie. Please come over at the same time as Sylvie and be ready to eat in the future." Lady Dee finished looking at the colander where the beans for the evening meal were soaking. "I'll have Sylvie sit on the porch for a few more minutes while you eat."

"Thank you kindly...Lady Dee." Nettie's muffled reply came from her mouth filled with a piece of bacon snatched from Ruth's plate. Ruth gulped again. They were always told to watch their manners at the table. Nettie's style scared Ruth. She wasn't in the door a minute and Ruth's heart had already jumped and nearly stopped twice already. Either Lady Dee didn't see it or Nettie had the best luck of anyone Ruth knew because Lady Dee handed Nettie a full breakfast plate without a word of reproach. It was truly miraculous.

After eating at a pace faster and louder than Lady Dee's code of manners allowed, they sprinted for the hallway. "Now, Ruth. Mind your manners and be back in time for your chores. We'll have to discuss what needs to be done now that we're settled."

Things would be different, Ruth thought, but at least she'd met Nettie and Sylvie. Nettie seemed to know everything and be able to do most everything she wanted here.

"Let's go upstairs. Where's your bed?" Nettie ran toward the stairs.

"I used to sleep in a bedroom I shared with my sister and brother. Now we've moved into this house and we have our own bedrooms." Ruth followed Nettie into the first bedroom next to the stairs.

"Well, you've got all the room in the world, it seems." Nettie darted from the room. Ruth thought they were going to play upstairs. She found Nettie hanging over the banister of the white-walled and pine-spindled staircase. "Come on, Ruth. Let's see what else!"

Ruth raced in her bare feet, feeling the slick, cool stairs on her feet and toes. "You've got plenty of room here," Nettie hollered as she ran into a long rectangular room built above the living room on one side and sitting over the kitchen on the other. "You can ask your daddy if it's allowed for you to have me come here to sleep over. Your brother..."

"His name is Leroy," Ruth informed.

"Leroy's got his own room and Thelma does, too? That's fine. Whenever your daddy or Lady Dee pleases about me staying over, I'll be here," Nettie stated.

"If they please," Ruth amended.

"I could sleep over here with you if you were scared to sleep alone," Nettie offered.

"I'll ask." Having a sleeping party with Nettie might be fun.

☙❧

During that first summer, Ruth quickly identified that Nettie liked to embroider and embellish almost every story. Nettie was *not* overstating when she said there would be a marked change when they started school. Two Sundays before Labor Day, Thelma pointed out some of the children who were going to go to school with them. So far, Ruth knew Hugo, Jacob, and Alice. "I'll point out several more when the church service is over." They craned their necks, tucking their legs under themselves to be higher in the pews so they could see the other children. "You'll be going to the welcome meeting on the weekend."

On their last free Saturday afternoon, the PTA had set up tables in the cafeteria so students and parents could have refreshments while getting their books and finishing their paperwork. The echoing halls of the summer-deserted school crackled with activity. "Sure hope Lady Dee's got a better pickle relish recipe than the principal's wife. According to Grandma Wilcox, there's too much vinegar and liquid in the jars for Grandpa Wilcox's taste. Had to throw it out."

Vinegar was the least of Ruth's concerns. Ruth liked Lady Dee's relish but who could tell if Lady Dee's recipe would please any of her new school friends?

Nettie nodded her head. "Jars blow up in the pantry with too much vinegar. That's what they all say."

As they walked by the registration line, Ruth noticed each student was dressed in their Sunday clothes. The older girls walked excitedly with light sweaters covering their blouses and boys strode in knife-pleated, cuffed, or straight-hem pants. Excited trills and baritone laughter filled the once empty spaces.

"Don't try to remember all the names," Nettie teased. "It'll be like you've known them all your life...soon." Nettie floated through the crowds like she'd been there all her life, like a beautiful red kite with a multicolored tail, bobbing and weaving through all the people, listening for all the talk and categorizing all the information and gossip like a trained librarian.

◔◔

School life started in earnest. Experienced students helped the new ones. Routines were set up on the chore list. Mrs. Gant was Nettie and Ruth's teacher on the second floor of the grade school part of the building. Nettie was several years older than the rest of the girls in their class. Nettie blithefully explained she'd missed more formal schooling because she'd traveled to many exotic places, which was a *fine* education in itself.

Ruth became familiar with people and could even recognize them if she was sent off to find somebody. If Ruth couldn't find someone, Nettie always had helpful ideas on where they could be found. Barney Field, an eighth grader, nicknamed Ruth and Nettie "the shadows" because they were so efficient and so inseparable.

Nettie wasn't too particular about attending school every day, to Lady Dee's dismay. "When my wife can't get off from the munitions plant, we need Nettie over at the house. Lots of work to get done with Sylvie and all. Teacher says her grades are fine, she's smart as a whip and the money's too good. So, sometimes, we'll keep Nettie home."

When Ruth asked her mother about it, Lady Dee would reply, "Your father and I are adamant that our son and daughters attend school on every scheduled day."

Nettie amazed Ruth. Nettie seemed to have a gift of being able to do her schoolwork, chores, and still know everybody's business within fifty miles. "Got my schoolwork done for tomorrow. Got some lemonade when I walked down to the school cafeteria. Mrs. Leeds had her baby and Mr. Hill's spring seeds came in the mail today."

As Mrs. Monroe, the school secretary, laughingly said, "There'll never be an ounce of fat on that girl because she goes so fast and knows so much but she better stop rolling her waistband. Every girl in our school needs to be prim and proper."

◔◔

Life at the Yuell household began at 6 a.m. Nettie could always be seen every morning with a biscuit in her hand telling Ruth the latest news. The standard weekday fare was biscuits, home-style gravy, hot cereal, and grits. On weekends, Lady Dee fixed eggs if the Wilcox chickens were laying plentifully. Home-cured ham and bacon were added, when money allowed. "Like Mrs. Jasper says, your family's still paying off your daddy's education bills, I bet," Nettie whispered.

Lady Dee stretched the family food budget by accepting farmers' invitations to glean the fields in repayment for her husband's medical services or as a gesture of friendship. She, her children, and sometimes Nettie, carried their burlap picking sacks and lunches to gather the produce, grains, or fruit, picking the too-large or too-small, overlooked, bruised, or misshapen fruits and vegetables left in the fields behind the harvesting crews. Just like their ancestors, each chose an old slavery hymn or popular song to sing, in turn, trying to creatively pass the time of the monotonous, sweaty work. "But these times are different. These farmers own or rent this land. Tastes the same as store-bought vegetables." So they'd take everything back home for meals, canning, or to give to the needy at church.

During the winter, Lady Dee and some of the church members looked over seed catalogs to select the right varieties of vegetables for the upcoming year's garden. "The beans weren't good this year," Lady Dee would tell Elly Mae Mason. "Spindly-looking and didn't hold up well in the canning. We need a heartier variety for this wet soil. What does the Tuskegee information say about wet soil?"

"Let's see here. Beans...beans. Some of these newer varieties can go in the ground a few weeks after the trees are budded and others must wait till the earth is warmer, I think it says," Mrs. Mason replied as she scanned and fingered the various pamphlets, catalogs, and farming reports.

"Don't care what the pamphlets say," insisted Mrs. Babcock. "The peas are not ready to plant until I get back from visiting my cousin in Memphis."

By the end of spring, the bickering would be over. All the garden plots were finally planted with the last of the seed when the school year ended. With extra hands available, the garden-tending schedule for the Yuell family began in earnest. The ground always needed hoeing, weeding, and watering. If the weather was dry, all the water came bucket-by-bucket from the yard spicket by the garage. Nettie and Ruth always prayed for rain to relieve the back-breaking chore, tending the garden in the cooler morning times so the bugs wouldn't be thick and the sun wouldn't dry out the leaves yet if the plants were thirsty.

"You finished watering?" Lady Dee would call from the kitchen. "I need help with picking and the jars need washing. Can you help?"

"Just got to feed the chickens 'cause Leroy's at school helping the janitor this morning," Ruth called back. "Then I'll be there."

"I'll be there just as soon as I check on Sylvie," Nettie said, trying to string out her last leisure moments between chores. "Grandma Wilcox has the day off for canning, too, and Grandpa Wilcox went to see if there was any work at the railroad yard this morning." Nettie swallowed and yelled. "Sylvie may need some water. Sometimes she forgets."

Canning was another job done best in the morning before the daytime heat. Everyone put straw hats and old kerchiefs on their heads to protect their hair and gathered the sweat as they worked. Ruth arrived in the kitchen to find either her father or Lady Dee starting the large water-filled kettles on the kitchen stove. "Gonna get a newer model gas stove next year."

Superheated steam clouds rose from boiling the Mason jars ready for the washed and cleaned produce. Large containers of sugar, salt, and vinegar provided the proper preservative mixture as well as paraffin if the filled jars required a protective coating.

"Lotta work today," Thelma said as she hoisted another load of cooled jars on a tray to take to the pantry. "I love the taste of our canned tomatoes, sugar peas, and beans."

"And don't forget I really like the pickle relish recipe that Lady Dee makes," Nettie said with a mock shiver. "Miss Buella's is terrible. Too much salt and vinegar!"

Lady Dee asked, "Have I ever told you the story of when I picked cotton?"

"You picked cotton, mama?" Ruth cried.

"You picked cotton?" Nettie echoed.

"Yes, I picked cotton," Lady Dee laughingly replied. "I picked cotton for several years, actually. Needed school money. I had a talent for it. My mother and I could pick four rows at a time," Lady Dee smiled as she remembered the accomplishments rather than the heat, sweat, and back-breaking work. "Tended lots of chickens, too."

There was never a holiday or season of rest from the chickens unlike the winter fallow garden. "Animals are just like people," Lady Dee said. "Both need daily love and care."

There were piles upon piles of fertilizer to muck out of the coops. "Foul-smelling stuff, but they'll be no eggs or chicken meat if it doesn't get done and they get sick," Thelma reminded them while mucking out on an especially hot summer day.

"The heat makes it smell so bad!" Ruth remarked. "Sometimes I want to put my scarf over my mouth instead of on my hair."

Thelma didn't have much sympathy. "They're God's dear creatures. I love them just like I love other animals. Father's chores included three cows and four fattening pens when he was young, which was much more to care for than chickens. You'll have it done if you don't take time for complaining. Gonna be waiting for you either way."

Getting the chicken meat to the table was hard work, too. Grandpa Wilcox handled the chore of "ringing" the chicken necks. To help the feathers come off easier, the carcasses would be plunged into an oil drum filled with boiling water set on a wood fire grate tended by Thelma or Leroy. Then Nettie and Ruth would sit there for what seemed like hours plucking the feathers. The feathers were saved in burlap feed sacks to sort and save for pillows, so none could fall in the mud or dust. "Even after washing with lye soap, I still smell like 'em all day after working here. I hate chickens." Nettie rolled her eyes as she grabbed handfuls of feathers. "When I grow up I'm going to be treated like a fine lady and have other people pluck my food."

❧❧

EMERGENCY ROOM AT 12:25 P.M. CHICAGO – 1967

Norma stopped and turned another page in her notebook.

"Thought good times with Nettie would last forever. Going to high school and college, getting married, and having our babies. Nothing turned out as I planned." Ruth stopped talking and sighed.

Ruth had to tell Norma about the day when Nettie's *true* history was betrayed. It was a hurtful, bungled affair and no one's business outside of Nettie's family. "But people love to gossip and muck sticks to anyone who lets a secret slip away." And nothing was ever the same.

❧❧

ST. LOUIS – 1951

Ruth skipped a grade that last year because she did well in her studies and she was now a grade ahead of Nettie, although Nettie always said she was "more sophisticated" than her childhood friend in an earnest breathy tone.

Nettie liked talking about her age now and mentioned it frequently in their conversations. "You know I'm almost fifteen and what I lack in book-learning I've got in natural smarts." Nettie nodded emphatically. "Can't help it…and don't see as I need to go to high school, where I should be now, if things hadn't got messed up when I was young. Feel adult already!"

With Nettie's newfound sophistication, Ruth felt surprised Nettie agreed to go fishing with her and Leroy at a river pier. Sylvie had a chest cold and was dozing in bed.

"Can we go down to the pier now, instead of later?" Nettie asked.

"Your other chores finished?" was all Lady Dee asked.

As Nettie and Ruth nodded their heads, Nettie responded, "Even got all Sylvie's cough medicine in her before she fell asleep."

Lady Dee seemed pleased with this. "Go ahead then."

"Lots of friends from school are going to be there," Leroy offered. "Ned and Kenny are usually through with the mucking out at the stables in the park by now."

Nettie stayed quiet on the walk to the pier and while they got the fishhooks baited but after they put the lines in the water, Nettie started grousing, "Why don't they get hungry and bite the hook? These flies are fierce today."

"If you don't stop squirming and yelling, we'll never catch anything," retorted Ned. He'd been the first one there on the pier. "Now sit or go." Nettie threw him a sour look and plopped on the cement landing.

To avoid any further confrontation, Ruth suggested, "Why don't you go downstream to the picnic spot and sit on the limb overlooking the shallow water?"

"Why, thank you, Nee Nee. I just might do that," Nettie replied sarcastically as she got up. So much negative energy came from Nettie's voice and pose, Ruth didn't think there was any left for the rest of Nettie's body.

"Gonna be a no-account just like her mother," Ned retorted angrily.

Ruth gasped and choked at his vitriol. She sprang to her feet, almost crying while looking to see that Nettie was still traveling toward the picnic spot and hadn't heard his nasty remark. "Ned Brown, wh...what a terrible thing to say! Nettie's my best friend!"

"Sorry...but it's true," Ned's tone changed as he continued sheepishly. "Her momma left her and Sylvie here several times after she was born. This time's just the latest. Went up to Detroit or something. The Wilcox family kept them 'cause they're supposedly kin and all. I'm not so sure." His doe eyes gained some heat again. "Never heard of since. Just hightailed it."

"Does that make it right to gossip about it?" Leroy seethed half-angrily at Ned for telling Ruth, and half at himself, for not being able to protect this sister from the truth any longer.

"Nettie acts so flighty and uppity sometimes," Ned offered, trying to explain.

"That's no reason, far as I can see. Think you...and everybody acts that way sometimes," Leroy emphasized with a wave of his arm accidentally causing the pole to slap the placid water.

"Gosh darn," yelled Amory Gillins, the boy nearest to them, "What ya doing!"

"My fault. My fault, Ame. Lost my balance and I let the pole fall to keep from hitting Ruth. Sorry!" Ned called. Ruth wanted to escape from them seeing her turbulent and embarrassed tears. She ran to the woods to swipe them from her face. *Did Nettie know people were talking about her?*

"Slow down, Ruth." Leroy grabbed at her thin shoulders. "Our father's not here now, so I have to do the telling and I'm telling you people can be cruel, even to their own!"

Ruth felt sick inside. She didn't know the answers but she did know one thing. Fishing would never be the same.

❦

Ruth was out of sorts all that afternoon and next day. She didn't see the looks passing between her father and Lady Dee. Lady Dee sat her down to feel Ruth's forehead before going to bed. "I noticed you didn't eat much last night and that you've been quiet today."

"Yeah," was her daughter's monosyllabic reply.

Lady Dee persisted as she was pinning the pattern for Ruth's new Sunday dress, "Anything wrong? You haven't seemed yourself since yesterday?"

Tears welled up in Ruth's eyes so quickly; Lady Dee was almost too startled to reach for the dainty white hankie in her apron pocket before she opened her arms to Ruth. "It's about Nettie," Ruth sniffled as she looked into her mother's eyes and saw her mother already knew all about Nettie. "I just found out about her mother leaving and all. They might not be related to Mr. and Mrs. Wilcox."

"We just have to live good lives and think the best of people," Lady Dee replied. She would always talk about the larger character and moral issues in any situation. "You understand why we need to think positively and be our best?"

"Yes." Lady Dee's question got her thinking about their many conversations of the other unhappy, unjust subjects of slavery and segregation.

The story was always the same. Many, many years ago, before she was born, people of her race were denied freedom on many levels. Her father and Lady Dee had nothing to do with it. They told Ruth she had nothing to do with it. Their community flourished under the leadership of fine black citizens and the church as best they could, despite the social and legal opposition to their race. Still, it was difficult to live and progress without the respect and cooperation of the white community. Things had even gotten a little worse with the no-money times caused by the Depression and war. It was a pity and an injustice that even though they worked in their businesses and homes, the white folk refused to recognize and appreciate their race's contributions to the community and culture. Without warning, the hate and the prejudices of the white community could flare and black citizens suffered, even died—innocent victims of power and anger-crazed people.

From her earliest memories, Ruth recalled white people choosing to talk and whisper about the more unfortunate members of her community, not giving any credit to the hardworking, upstanding citizens she knew. They'd talk about

Mr. Malley, a hard-drinking man prone to loud singing on his frequent weekend benders. He didn't sing on the streets of their community but they talked about him anyway. What they didn't know was Mr. Malley lost his child to diphtheria; his farm to several floods, a drought, and the Depression; and, shortly thereafter, his wife to scarlet fever. That's when he started to drink, her father said. But it didn't matter. The pretty poison of what people *thought* they knew mattered to them—not the truth. There were so many others who were taunted and mistreated—countless in number. "So Nettie's like that, too? Talked about…but it's not her fault?" Ruth asked. "So we should ignore it?"

Lady Dee nodded her head and Ruth laid her head back on her mother's shoulder and thought some more. "But it's our own people talking," Ruth said staunchly.

"We'll just have to set people straight in a kind way," Lady Dee replied. "We can't gossip, but we can stick up for our own." She turned her daughter's face to look deep in her eyes. Ruth knew what her mother was going to say next even before her lips started moving. "Tell the truth and be a friend."

Ruth thought about the white community. It seemed nobody from their side of town wanted to be friends with the Negro community. "Being laughed at by strangers is hard."

"Just ignore it and hold your head high," Lady Dee replied.

"I've managed to ignore most of the time," Ruth replied truthfully. Things were good within the confines of the black community most of the time, not withstanding this dust-up about Nettie.

"Just remember what I've told you when things get a bit ugly," Lady Dee said with a steely tone. "No one on this earth has ever been, or ever will be, a nigger! We are *all* created in the image of God! You can look it up in Holy Scripture." Lady Dee wiped her hand on her apron. "We only have one life given to us, so we must take care of ourselves and then go out and love others." Lady Dee cupped Ruth's chin in her hands and looked deeply into her eyes. "If Nettie has problems we'll help her, but she's got to tame some of her God-given curiosity tinged with the stubbornness she's got. You'll help her and we'll help her, if she wants." Lady Dee repeated, putting her hand under Ruth's chin. "Don't let fear own you, Ruth. History tells us that people can own your body but not your mind. You've got to keep your mind free. Just be careful of what you know could go wrong in life.

"There's danger. Yes. Death. Sometimes it comes before you're old. Look out for the loose boards in life but keep living. Run your own life. Can't help some circumstances but you're dead already if you let fear or your problems own you!"

Lady Dee jumped as the screen door slapped on its frame to announce her husband's arrival.

"What are you talking about?" Dr. Yuell asked as he walked up to the long table.

"I just hope Nettie, er, someone will do well," Ruth stated, trying to put everything in a few words. "Mother got me through it but I'll tell you about things if you have the time."

"May I speak to your mother, first?" her father asked. "It's about Mrs. Exner. She's finally passed." Lady Dee nodded her head and bit her lips in understanding. "None of her people are left here anymore. So her memorial service will be on Saturday." He broke his gaze from Lady Dee's, looked down at Ruth, and exhaled the gloom from his lungs as he tried to brighten his spirits.

"People are talking about Nettie and Sylvie. Gossiping and saying they were abandoned here and all," Ruth stated without preamble.

"Child, Nettie can make it through. If she stays strong, works hard, and pays attention to her schoolwork, it'll count. When people say bad things about her, it won't matter. There'll be so many other good things to say in her defense. Just deal with adversity and move toward what you want," her father retorted. "Right, Lady Dee?"

"Right, dear. Hard work and prayer," Lady Dee added.

Dr. Yuell walked toward the door. "Now, if you ladies will excuse me, I've got to pick up my messages in the office and make that call to the pastor."

"Bye." Ruth's head felt tired from all the worrying. She saw Nettie's familiar shadow in the twilight of their porch light.

"You'll never guess. Mrs. Exner died," Nettie said as Ruth walked out of the screen door. Before Ruth could tell Nettie, her father had already told her. Nettie added, "She's got a high-yellow daughter in Chicago passing for white." Nettie's voice accidentally rose so she looked around again before concluding, "Imagine that!"

"What!" Ruth declared in a strangled whisper as Nettie tugged at her arm so she wouldn't get too loud.

"Hush!" her friend replied in an angry tone. "If anyone hears us, I'll get a whippin' for sure! Just got no one else to tell, really."

"Well, maybe we shouldn't talk about it at all," Ruth felt unease after just listening to her parents talk about living good lives and moral character.

"But this is news, Nee-Nee," Nettie said as she tried to sidle even closer to Ruth's side and added conspiratorially, "...about nothing ever happens here that's this juicy."

So said the snake to the woman, Eve. Ruth remembered one of Pastor Fredericks's sermons.

"Heard it from Miss Ellen as she came by for some peas from Granny's garden. Her wanting to make a casserole for after Mrs. Exner's services," she informed. "You know how she loves to make comments about everybody's skin and all."

In the distance, they could hear Mrs. Wilcox calling Nettie. "Gotta' go. See you tomorrow."

Ruth had heard talk about such things many times before. Dr. Yuell and Lady Dee mentioned people wrongly focusing on skin color. People even chatted at times about Negro people trying to pass as white folk. "Don't understand it myself, Ruth," her father said. "Living a lie and all." Then he sighed and shook his head. "We were put on this earth by God to be what we are and do what God wants us to do. Cuts the community up. And I don't even want to think of what it would be like to keep away from your family and kin because of a lie. Can't imagine it," he'd say in sorrow and exasperation. "What could it be like to worry some part of every day your secret will come out?" *Would it be like always being stalked by a bear? Would it be like waiting for a bomb to explode like they talked about with the soldiers and all during the wartime?*

❦

The rest of the week's schedule included Mrs. Exner's services. Since she'd died late into the afternoon, the visitation was on Friday night and the funeral was scheduled for late Saturday morning, so people could pay their respects and do their work before coming to the funeral. "Won't need too much food for supper Saturday evening," Lady Dee said. "With all the food for the funeral, no one will be hungry."

Funeral services meant several trips to the funeral parlor plus the church and the cemetery on Saturday. "Church two days in a row," Nettie complained. "Only good thing about it is that people will be doing plenty of talking."

Traffic in and out of the mortuary door was brisk whether there was a funeral or not. The men of the community treated it like a men's club. A few armchairs, several wooden pews, and rows of wooden folding chairs seemed like a big living room if a person ignored the wooden coffin between the two tall electrical lamps throwing light on the ceiling from either side of the rectangular box. Guess the men just ignored the coffin and concentrated on the fact that there were over-stuffed chairs where they could converse in comfort. Nettie observed with her constant practicality, "Corpse dead and gone. Past caring and all." Ruth winced a bit at that, but she couldn't refute Nettie's cold logic.

Some concessions were made in the solemn setting. The gentlemen of the community didn't smoke their smelly cigars and cigarettes when a coffin was there. They didn't curse or play cards either, Nettie reported.

Mrs. Exner's walnut-tinged coffin perched on a fringed box of shirred purple velveteen like Ruth had seen on fancy banquet tables. There was a center aisle with the first two pews with cushioned benches made of the same purple velveteen as the coffin drape in front of four rows of wooden pews. "Heard they got the pews from the AME church when it got remodeled," Nettie said as she and Ruth scooted into the last aisle of folding chairs, placed soldier-straight behind the pews.

"Neeland said that's where they do the embalming," Nettie said, pointing to a locked oak door at the far side of the hall. "Kinda pickles the people up so they won't spoil before the funeral's over, I hear." Ruth hadn't even thought of that part, as her stomach got an empty feeling. Nettie didn't seem to notice her friend's distress as she continued, "If we're real quiet, people won't notice we're here. That's when they say the good stuff. Just pretend we're talking and keep your ears open. I can move my mouth soundlessly and still hear just fine. Wanna' try?"

Suddenly, Miss Ellen arrived. "She'll sit in the chair by the door. That's her favorite. Then she'll look around to see if it's safe. Then, she'll start talking. Now, come on Nee-Nee," Nettie ordered. "Concentrate and let's see what we can hear."

It didn't take Miss Ellen any time to warm to her subject. "Poor Mrs. Exner, in her coffin so dead and all. It's a real loss to the community. Never saw a husband and a wife so happily married in my entire life, I'll tell you! Looks so natural there in the casket. My, my, how they doted on their daughter...and her being their only child and all. Mrs. Exner being black as coal and all. Mr. Gladdins, the mortician is an artist, I say. Looks just like herself. Who'd have thought her only daughter would have such light, snowy skin and have all that straight brown-black hair. Who would believe it? Best that Mrs. Exner be in heaven, not to mention the pain in her body."

Miss Ellen's head brushed the fan palm next to Ruth's seat, making her jump. Nettie put her hand up to Ruth's mouth and glared disapprovingly. "Yes. Lord, yes. So disgraceful. More than one time poor Mrs. Exner's daughter's been rumored to be passing somewhere north," Miss Ellen gestured pointedly in the direction of the door. "Yep. Up north, I hear."

Mrs. James returned stoutly, "Mrs. Exner denied it and said she heard the rumors. Didn't believe in gossiping. *Not a bit.* Said her daughter was busy in Cincinnati with her secretarial school and then with her work after that. Got letters from her daughter all the time, telling her about her work and all. She'd believe none of the gossip."

"See," Nettie whispered. "Mrs. Exner's got a daughter passing as white."

"That's not what was said," Ruth retorted, trying to clarify. "Miss Ellen claimed it was so and Mrs. Exner, God rest her soul, isn't around to deny it. Besides, Miss Ellen isn't always right. Remember when she told everyone Eddy Paul was ill. Said it would start a big measles epidemic last spring. He only had a rash from eating too-early strawberries. You had to stay inside two days and drink castor oil until my father could convince your grandmother of the facts. Remember?"

Nettie didn't look so sure anymore. "Well, she was wrong. Just that one time, I admit. But she sure sounds convincing now."

ᏆᏇ

Sunday went as usual, except Mr. Climms's mule cart mired itself in an alley ditch. Several of the men, including Mr. Wilcox and Dr. Yuell, had to leave their Sunday dinners to help him get the wagon back to the street.

As Mrs. Wilcox's voice called Nettie home for the evening, Ruth looked up to see only the lamplight coming from the window in her father's office. Usually Dr. Yuell had the office light on because the lamplight was too dim for him to read. She heard her father's voice and another higher pitched voice—an unfamiliar woman's voice.

"Thank you for seeing me, Edgar. This is diff...difficult for me," the woman began. "I'd be talking to Pastor Fredericks but several of the old biddies at church will have his place staked out, ready to pounce like cats if I show up there."

"This isn't a happy occasion, Eva," her father said. "What are you doing to yourself? There has been talk." His tone was flat. When there was something wrong, he sounded like that, Ruth remembered. Fear cemented her in the shadows of the entryway.

"What kind of talk?" the woman whispered sharply. Her veiled head snapped up at the doctor's words.

"Can't you guess, Eva? Can't you guess," Dr. Yuell replied wearily. "About Cincinnati or Chicago or wherever you're hiding yourself. About you not coming back since you went there. About your skin. I don't like to traffic in gossip, Eva. Are you sure you want to hear it?"

"I've already scandalized everyone for not showing up to the funeral," the lady named Eva laughed mirthlessly. "The lady at the last boardinghouse I stayed at in Cincinnati didn't get the information to me in time. I haven't been there in three years." Dr. Yuell leaned back in his desk chair. "You know I went to Cincinnati to go to secretarial school. Better myself. I didn't want marriage, kids, and a farm. Not yet...not here."

The lady shifted in her chair again and pulled out a gold cigarette case, opened it, and then shut it. She fingered it for a moment and then tossed it back into the purse disgustedly. "I'm trying to give them up," she stated. "Helps when I'm nervous though." She looked at the door and Ruth thought she had been discovered. But Eva turned back to her father and said, "It was all so easy, really. Didn't know if I had the brains to do it. But I did it. One of my teachers here,

Miss Collins, told me at school that I had less brains then a peahen." They both chuckled gruffly at the long ago memory.

"I finished secretarial school. Did real well. Interviewed for that big Negro-owned insurance company in Chicago. I was so happy. Thought I'd go over to celebrate at this club there. Hadn't been there before, but the girls at school said there were plenty of people there and that it was fun. Thought some of them would be celebrating, too." She sighed and swallowed. "Got there. Looked around and didn't see anybody I knew. Was about to leave when this white fellow got real rowdy. Bouncer as big as that old horse, Julius, ran past me and picked the guy up like a feather. Mr. Climm still got horses?" Dr. Yuell nodded. "Anyway, the bouncer as big as Julius picks the guy up and throws him out. I get tapped on the shoulder and this dignified-looking white guy asks me if he can get me a cab. At first, I didn't put it together. You know my peahen brain and all. He thought I was with the drunk, rowdy guy. I finally caught on as he started asking questions. Bought me a drink. Told me he was sorry there were such cretins in the world. Didn't know what a cretin was till I looked it up in my secretarial school dictionary. Can you believe that?"

Doctor Yuell looked toward the floor and didn't answer. "He touched my hand and said, 'You were unnerved by all this. I'll take you home.' Before I even knew what I was doing, I nodded my head in mute agreement and I was off. We drove around for about five minutes before he asked where I lived. I closed my eyes and sealed my fate when I told him the address of a young ladies' boarding hotel. For whites only. I'd seen it in the local newspaper. Asked me to write my name on the back of his business card. I almost stopped breathing when I looked at it in the passing streetlights. He was a lawyer in one of the biggest firms in town. My mind raced. I told him that I didn't give my number to any man. That if he wanted to see me again, he could meet me in the lobby of the Parkland Hotel the next afternoon."

The lady lifted her veil, as if emboldened to continue now that she'd gotten this far in her story. "Told myself if he wasn't there, then that would be my answer. I'd be Eva Exner again. Well, not only was he there, but no one at the Parkland asked me to use the side door or called me dirty names or anything! I walked right in, sat down right in the lobby by the registration desk, and no one said a word. If it were my momma, they'd have hustled her out the front door or to the kitchen or maid's room, but not me. So with some light skin, my interview suit, and secretarial diction training, I was sitting in the Parkland Hotel with a white man who was glad to see me." Doctor Yuell exhaled disapprovingly. "Canceled my interview. Had my belongings shipped to the young ladies' boarding hotel. Called to take care of my so-called shipping error and forwarded them with no trouble. New person. New hotel. The man even taught me how to drive. Got my license here somewhere. Don't need it though. We have a driver. Married the man two and a half years ago. Have a daughter and a husband and a life far away from here and Mrs. Exner."

"Mrs. Exner! Mrs. Exner! That Mrs. Exner was your mother!" Doctor Yuell hissed. "You turned your world upside down, come back here and expect me to listen? And now you've brought an innocent child into it!"

"I had a right to a life, Edgar," the woman countered.

"You had a life. You manufactured another," Doctor Yuell replied. "You turned your back on your mother, your community, and yourself. You've lied, cheated, and denied your heritage? Why? Because it was inconvenient, Eva? Didn't provide enough benefits?"

"It wasn't like that. Not at first," the woman admitted shifting in the chair. "Don't know what I thought. Just knew it felt good to be important. I won't deny that."

"But you would deny everything else," Doctor Yuell continued. "What did you tell your husband about your childhood, your education, and your friends? Are there a lot of holes in your story? How many lies have you had to tell in order to keep your 'importance'?"

"So you won't help me?" the woman stated angrily. "I do have this situation of my mother's death to take care of."

"Eva," Doctor Yuell said tiredly. "This situation is your mother's passing and you being the only Exner kin left. Your great-great- grandfather worked the land and passed it down to your mother. It was to go on to your daughter and any other children you have."

"That's impossible now. Sell it and transfer the money to this account," the woman shoved a piece of paper across the desk.

"All right. All right," Dr. Yuell said wearily. "You know Eva. I attended your mother's funeral today, looked over the appointment book on days filled with sick people, and helped pull a mule from a ditch. Now I'm headed off to see my family. Best of all, I know who I am and don't have to look over my shoulder for any lies to pounce on me. For all your importance, can you say the same?" He escorted the woman to the office door past the shadows where Ruth was hiding. "Take care of yourself and your daughter, Eva. Take care of your husband, too. Don't think I'll be seeing you any time again soon but I hope before I die, that before God and the law, we can just *be* and forget all these pretenses and strategies. I'll be able to be your friend and you'll be able to be mine. Maybe even go to the Parkland Hotel, use the front door, and sit in the lobby together."

The woman looked into Dr. Yuell's face but didn't say anything more as she put her veil down. She turned wordlessly and headed for the big, black car parked in the Legion Hall parking lot. Dr. Yuell took the piece of paper she had left on his desk and looked at it for a long, long time. Finally, he banged his fist on the desk so hard it scared Ruth and made her eyes tear up. Then, Dr. Yuell rushed past his daughter hidden in the shadows into the night.

Ruth sat in the shadows for a long time. Her father would keep Miss Exner's secret and, so then, would she. No use turning lives upside down again. Thought of Old Humpty-Dumpty. Wouldn't help anybody and certainly wouldn't help Mrs. Exner. She was at peace now. Reverend Fredericks had given her a nice church and graveside service.

❦

Nettie asked Ruth the next day, "Elder Brimley said that there was a strange car in the neighborhood last night. 'Big, black one with a silver hood ornament and smoke-glass windows in the back,' he said. Elder Brimley asked your father about it and your father said that it was a person who had lost their way. The person wasn't about to take his directions, so your father just said goodnight and the car left. Can you believe that?"

"Sounds very sad. That person could still be lost," Ruth said.

"Bet not," Nettie replied, losing interest.

"Can I ask you something, Nettie?" Nettie nodded as Ruth continued, "What if you could be anything you wanted but you'd have to leave everything here. Leave everyone—Sylvie, Granny Wilcox and Grandpa Wilcox, and me. You'd have to leave us all."

"Have to leave you all behind? Couldn't talk to you or nothing? That would be a powerful hurt. Wouldn't want to do that. No letters. No phone calls. No nothing?" Nettie said as she considered Ruth's words. "That wouldn't be what I would want to do, then. Even if my skin was high yellow and I could pass. I couldn't leave you all here. If you're here, I'd want to stay."

A warm glow filled Ruth. That's what she wanted her friend to say. Ruth felt the same way.

❦

Ruth saw her father later that day. "Father," she said, "I was there when Miss... Miss Exner came by last night." She swallowed and looked into her father's bland expression, which turned to exasperation.

"I can see by your expression that you're sorry. Shame on you, Ruth. You've never eavesdropped before...that I can tell, at least," Doctor Yuell said. "You picking up any bad gossipy habits?"

"No. No, Father. I never have. Promise. Please forgive me," Ruth said pleading for his understanding. "I saw the lamplight...and by the time I saw you, Miss Exner was there, too. I didn't know what to do. I just froze."

"Just don't tell me you were sneaking around," he replied.

Before she could stop herself, Ruth retorted, "You raised me better than that."

"Of course, I hear the talk and the gossip. With all the talk about Miss Exner, high-yellow coloring and brown-black hair," he said as Ruth sat astounded by his knowledge. "I choose to ignore it. Information has the power to hurt people and people get hurt enough in this world and our community without our adding to it. Understand?"

"Yes, father," his daughter replied in a small voice.

"There's always going to be talk. So you remember to not gossip and always be proud of who you are." Doctor Yuell looked away for a moment as if lost in thought.

His daughter gently prompted him, "Anything else?"

"Oh, yes, Ruth. Sorry. Don't mind who anyone marries, but it can't be based on lies. And, Ruthie," her father raised his eyebrow and looked at his daughter intently. "The rest of this matter will be remembered but not shared with anyone else." He cleared his throat and walked down the polished hall. "Oh...and Ruthie. I think Lady Dee was baking molasses cookies in the kitchen. Think you might want to go have one?" Ruth ran to the kitchen for his peace offering. There were two more things to remember. Ruth wouldn't deny her family for anybody. No sir. And her daddy forgave her.

That evening was torn up as well. Ruth heard the commotion before Dr. Yuell came to her door. "Wake up, Ruthie," he said quickly. His touch was light but his voice was troubled. "Lady Dee's with Mrs. Wilcox. Sylvie's had another seizure spell. We're sending Nettie over here to get some rest for the remainder of the night, so you just stay quiet while I set up the cot."

CHAPTER FOUR

On the porch the next day both girls were subdued from the lack of sleep. Ruth thought about Nettie, Mrs. Exner, her daughter, and Sylvie, being ill and how hard making decisions seemed lately. "You've been looking and acting peaked the last few days, not just because of Sylvie's spell last night. Are you feeling sick, too?"

Ruth was just about to answer Nettie's question when their attention was distracted by the hissing sound of steam coming from under the hood of a red convertible roadster rolling to a stop on the street. Nettie and Ruth sat for a second and then headed for the car. There were three white people, two adults looking like a husband and wife and a boy about their own age, in the small back seat. The man opened the door revealing red and cream upholstery as he disgustedly stripped off his jacket and loosened his tie. "We'll be late for sure now, Mabel."

"Told you to take the turn back there, Bud," the lady with the red and white cotton sundress and wide brimmed straw hat whined. "Of all the luck—and in this neighborhood, too! Look out! Some of *them* are coming over." She said fearfully, "Buddy get in the front seat next to mama."

"Need some help, ma'am?" Ruth asked. Her husband stood concealed by the billows of white steam still hiding the front of the car.

"Bud. Bud. They're talking to us," the lady said as she fluttered her white-gloved hand toward the water-smoke.

"What you saying, Mabel?" the man shouted over the hissing noises.

The lady looked at Ruth and Nettie fearfully, clutched her purse and her son closer to her. "I said *they're* talking to us."

The man appeared quickly and swiped at the girls with his forearm. "Get away. What you doing, scaring her that way? You niggers bothering my wife?"

"No, sir. No, sir," Ruth stumbled back at the harsh words and the arm swipe. "I just asked if you needed help." Her heart was beginning to pound and her mind was racing off questions about her behavior. Soon, she'd be crying, if she didn't swallow hard.

"Can I assist you, sir?" Dr. Means enunciated tightly. He'd come out of the office unnoticed. "No need to bother the children with this. I'll call the garage on Main St. for you. Nettie! Ruth! You go back in the house now. Isn't it time to set the table for supper?" Ruth nodded her head, even though it was several hours until supper, relieved just to get away. She grabbed on to the excuse and Nettie's hand at the same time. Ruth didn't look back until she was safe behind the screen door. She was shaking.

"Did you hear her? That lady telling her husband we were bothering her?" Nettie huffed.

"I didn't hear you say anything," Ruth replied, "...and all I asked was if she needed any help."

"Sounded just like Mr. Johnson, that prune-faced white man down at the hardware store who hates anybody with black skin. Calls us all kinds of names and laughs. Slapped Allan Jones before he quit working there and moved up to Chicago. Allan said he'd never let another white man touch him again. That's a fact! Otherwise, they'd probably beat the snot out of him."

"Allan Jones?" Ruth asked.

"Allan Jones. Mr. Bernard Jones's third son," Nettie shuttered. "Left when you were visiting your grandparents, I guess. Took his cardboard suitcase one afternoon and hopped a freight going north. Had to. Mr. Johnson was talking crazy about the Klan, burning crosses...and using ropes."

Even at their young age, they knew of people who had suffered. Nettie mentioned Allan Jones. He was lucky. He'd gotten away. But there were others. Her father and Lady Dee didn't talk about such things in front of their children. Didn't let their children talk about such things either or they'd get a lashing with a hickory stick. Blatant racism in the public eye usually didn't come this far north to St. Louis. But there was, more often than they wanted to think about, a malignant ugliness represented by the people now standing by the broken-down car. The white woman clutched her purse and grabbed her son as if they had to be afraid of a doctor's daughter and her friend who only asked to help. The man swiped at them as if he had a right to hurt them because they had black skin. Ruth knew Nettie would say some kind of joke and they would laugh at it later, but now it hurt to be treated so badly.

"Miss Ruth, may I come in?" Dr. Means called as he walked to the door.

Ruth started for the door as she said, "Yes, Dr. Means. You need me?"

"Just wanted to talk to you and Nettie. Your father home?" he asked.

"No. He went to Mrs. Rollins."

"Is Lady Dee here?" he continued.

"Yes. Yes. She's in the office doing work."

"Good. Good. Nettie, you go get your grandmother and bring her here, please." Dr. Means and Ruth walked slowly to the office to the slow rhythm of their shoes hitting the polished hardwood floor.

Lady Dee looked up from her deskwork to see Dr. Means and her daughter. "Doctor Means? Ruth? Can I help you?" A telltale frown line came to Lady Dee's brow.

"There was a car breakdown out there. White folk from Fort Smith going to Springfield. Ruth kindly asked them if they needed help and they weren't kind in return. They got flustered, said some nasty things and used bad language. I've sent for Mrs. Wilcox and Edgar," Dr. Means recited.

Lady Dee handed Ruth some pencils and paper. "Do your sums until everyone gets here."

ༀ

Ruth's father came home from his afternoon house call and left his doctor's bag on the sideboard as Mrs. Wilcox entered the office. "Hello, Dr. Means. Lady Dee. You here, too, Ruth?" There was a frown line on his brow, too, Ruth noted.

"We just need to talk about a few things, Edgar," Dr. Means said in a clam, pleasant voice. "Please sit down, Mrs. Wilcox. Nettie, you sit with Ruth on the chair over there." Dr. Yuell pulled a wooden chair closer for Nettie and Ruth. "You said you wanted to talk to us, Thurgood?" When everyone was comfortable he faced Dr. Means and asked, "What's this all about?"

"There was a car breakdown," Dr. Means began.

"Saw them getting towed to the Main Street garage when I got back from downtown," Dr. Yuell replied.

"Ruth and Nettie acted like kind little ladies and asked the wife in the car if they needed any help. The woman said some hateful things," Dr. Means informed.

"Called us niggers," Nettie spoke emphatically. The shock value of the hateful words stopped everything as if the air were sucked from the room and everyone's lungs.

Dr. Yuell regained his voice first. "That's very sad and very inaccurate as everyone in this room knows. We are not the embodiment of someone else's hateful words. We are children of God and good citizens. Let's not forget that. You weren't hurt or anything, were you?" the doctor's voice turned to concern as he looked closely at Nettie and his daughter.

"They just sounded angry. Dr. Means took care of the rest," Nettie replied.

"Yes, Nettie, sometimes it's better to let the grown-ups handle things," Lady Dee said.

"Let them old peckerwoods rot in the sun. That's what we should have done," Nettie informed, getting her teakettle temper steaming.

"Nettie!" Mrs. Wilcox exclaimed angrily. "Where'd you learn such language? Right in front of the doctors here. I'll wash your mouth out with soap, I will!" Mrs. Wilcox leaned over to Nettie. "Now, you hush."

"Well, those people riled me up. Didn't mean nothing. Excuse me, sirs. Heard Grandpa say those words lots of times. That's where I learned it," Nettie said softer and looked a bit contrite.

"I thought the same thing," Ruth said trying to protect her friend from wrath in front of all these grown-ups. Lady Dee's frown furrowed even deeper. *Not a good sign.*

Doctor Yuell let out a big sigh. "Another example of living in tight places. Eh, Thurgood?"

Dr. Means sat back and folded his arms in his lap. "Seems so to me. Yes, seems so to me."

"Those words are *not* welcome here—either concerning the white folk or ourselves. Those words have shock value and vent emotion but they also demean us and make us appear less than we really are. We don't need to be ugly in return. I'm going to overlook what ugly words have been said here, knowing *full well* they will not be repeated again." Ruth could feel her father's gaze boring into her bowed head. "But if there should be any repeat of such foul language *on our part*, there will be a double portion of punishment rendered at that time. Agreed, Mrs. Wilcox?"

Mrs. Wilcox silently nodded in agreement. Dr. Yuell's face remained bland and serious as Ruth peeked at him as he finished his words. "Now, you girls can go."

"Sure hope someone lectures those white folks. They sure need straightening out, too," Nettie observed as soon as they caught their breath when they reached the grass. Ruth was just grateful she'd missed the lye soap and hickory switch whipping. "And thanks for sticking up for me, Ruth."

Ruth was shocked another time that day. Nettie was thanking her! That didn't happen very often. "Didn't know you had the gumption in you, being a doctor's kid and all. Thought all your doctor's-kid airs and refinements...and things would come bursting out. You defended me even though you didn't say one bad word."

ᘒᘓ

EMERGENCY ROOM AT 1:10 P.M.
CHICAGO – 1967

"It felt like I was being swamped in adult situations and circumstances." Ruth shook her head. "Lady Dee and my father always tried to think well of others and expect them to do the same." Ruth looked down at her hands. "They both wanted us to move slowly into the deep waters of people's darker sides and actions."

"But your parents also helped to right social injustices...when they could," Norma answered.

"Yes. I remember a time on All Saints' Day," Ruth recalled.

◐◑

ST. LOUIS – 1952

Dr. Yuell met Ruth as he left his office to go to the first of the two examining rooms. "I'm glad you've decided you can help now," he said with a wink. "Let me show you what to do."

"I li...like to help," Ruth thoughtfully stammered. "Leroy's helping down at the garage and Thelma's working at the animal hospital. It's my turn to help here." Nettie found a more public place for gaining spending money—working down at the corner beauty parlor.

As Ruth smilingly moved her father's examining stool, Dr. Means put his hand on the doorframe, "Looks like we have a natural here. Thinking of becoming a nurse? Perhaps a doctor, like your father?"

Dr. Yuell picked up the questioning. "What do you think, Ruth?"

Ruth was surprised and happy at the suggestion, always admiring people who knew what they wanted to do in life. "That would be wonderful, Father!" she gushed. "Can I keep working here?"

"There's one thing I can tell you, if you want to work in the medical profession, we'll try to help you," Dr. Yuell said to his daughter's enthusiastic whoop. Leroy wanted to be an engineer and Thelma wanted to be a vet. Ruth thought about nurse's training and a college education. Some families couldn't afford any formal education for their children beyond high school. Her cousins in Alabama couldn't get much education beyond sixth grade!

"I need some alcohol and vinegar," Ruth called. She'd help scrub and polish till dinnertime.

"You take your time, Ruth. I am going over to church," Dr. Yuell said as he went through the door.

"This evening's stew is in the covered iron pot in the oven," Lady Dee said. "Take the time you need."

◐◑

Nettie came running and pushed her way past Ruth. "Had to race back to tell you, Mrs. Bewyer's young cousin got in trouble with the police and it wasn't his fault." Her breaths were coming in hard pants. "Got into trouble for staying by the market parking lot too long. He was just sitting on the stair trying to open his gum wrapper. Before anyone knew what to do besides run for Reverend Fredericks, or Dr. Means or your father, a police car pulled up, put the boy in the police car, and took him away to the police station. Charged with loitering, I heard." Nettie looked to see if anybody was listening to the conversation. "Your daddy got him out. Seems like the head policeman's got a reelection coming and he wants to make sure people remember he's taking care of crime and not remember his second cousin Ely was arrested for running moonshine in Bishop Township."

"How do you know all this?" Ruth asked with wonder. The chief of police and his cousin were both white men. Ruth had only seen the man's picture in the newspaper.

"Found out at the beauty parlor. Mrs. Tate's maid, Belva, buys eggs from my Granny Wilcox," Nettie replied. "She says the policeman's stomach always acts up 'round election time and she comes by more often to get Granny's eggs to make him scrambled eggs with butter. Old guy picks on Negroes because we're the easiest target!"

Ruth hoped Mrs. Bewyer's cousin and her father were OK. She worried about them all afternoon.

Dr. Yuell looked exhausted when he got back home, only picking at his dinner. He went to his desk in the office and rested his chin on his fisted hands. Ruth sat pajama-clad, hidden in the shadows, willing him to feel better. Lady Dee came in with a fresh cup of coffee.

"Didn't get much done concerning the rally. Got the boy over to the Gillips' house. He'll stay there the night and then transfer to a train going to Cincinnati tomorrow. His people there will pick him up. I've called his folks and explained the problem. He still wants to go to school. So this is his next best chance. He's a marked man now that the police have arrested him. Now, more than ever, Reverend Fredericks agrees we've got to plan some kind of protest before the election or this will never stop."

"We should do something to protest their arrogance. But what?" Lady Dee's worry was clear in every word.

"We've got an idea for All Saints' Day. I'll check it out with the other elders. Think it will work. The police aren't fools. They don't want any trouble. Just to keep their sweet jobs and their badges. Let's go upstairs now. I'm tired."

Ruth stole away to her bed as they turned the evening lights out in the house, thinking she needed to ask God's forgiveness for eavesdropping. She sighed heavily as she pulled back the covers. Her father was often down at the jail trying to help people.

Negroes went to jail for a lot of things, but most of these arrests weren't right. The police goaded people into outbursts and pestered loud drunks and, sometimes, those sick-in-the-heads who heard voices or wandered around talking to themselves. "The whites get driven home nice as you please. The Negroes get thrown in jail. Plain as that," Nettie would say.

"I know," Ruth replied. Just being mean-spirited and using their authority in hurtful ways, which meant some innocent person was victimized.

"Remember when that white Rattley boy hit Sylvie in the arm with that sharp rock? Thought they'd never get it to stop bleeding. Needed six stitches," Nettie recalled.

"It was four stitches," Ruth corrected.

"Oh, I forgot. You sure?" Nettie asked. "Still they didn't do nothing to him!" The rest of the time was spent with Nettie going over the entire event in detail. Ruth sighed again at the recollection, rolled over, and fell asleep frowning. She'd just wait for All Saints' Day to see what her father, the pastor, and the elders had in mind.

❡❡

Finally, it was the day after Halloween—All Saints' Day. Reverend Fredericks scheduled a special assembly in the school auditorium for everyone to come and remember their friends and loved ones who had died. Refreshments were going to be served in the school cafeteria after the service. Ruth's list and the list of her family included Grandmother Bellamy this year.

"No one in the Wilcox family is dead but I'll come anyway," Nettie stated.

Everyone was dressed in their Sunday best. "Esther Spain is wearing her patent leather shoes," Nettie noted.

Dr. Yuell, Reverend Fredericks, and several others walked onto the stage. Ruth thought her father looked handsome in his brown suit, starch-stiff white shirt, and imported neutral tone silk tie he'd received as a gift two Christmases ago. His man-made onyx and gold-tone cufflinks peeked from his shirtsleeves and glinted in the sunlight coming through the hand-cranked high windows with the hand cranks near the ceiling.

"Ladies and gentlemen. Since it is such a fine autumn day and the attendance is large, I thought we should adjourn to the grass," Reverend Fredericks stated in his clear baritone voice. "Please feel free to take folding chairs with you, if you need to sit. The students will be happy to assist you." A general, confused murmur and whisperings came from some of the community but the Reverend started in the direction of the grassy lawns at the side of the school buildings toward the parking lot on the far end of the property. Mr. Wilcox and Lady Dee ushered Nettie and Ruth out of the auditorium in orderly pursuit.

Reverend Fredericks kept going until he got up on a log separating the school from the bakery parking lot. Students unfurled chairs and those choosing to stand formed an orderly group around the chairs to hear him.

"We'll be calling out the names of our loved ones who...," the Reverend started. Suddenly, the heads of everyone turned to see two patrol cars swooping swiftly down the street into the bakery parking lot. "Excuse me," was all Reverend Fredericks said as he leapt from the log and met the chief of police and a sergeant before the policemen could open their patrol car doors.

Several church elders, Dr. Means, and Dr. Yuell headed for Reverend Fredericks and the police cars.

"Watcha doing, Rev?" was all Ruth could hear the sergeant say as the crowd began shifting silently, looking at the scene and each other. The police chief glowered and chomped on a cigar in his patrol car. Ruth alternately held her breath and tried to see from her vantage point between trouser legs and swirling skirts.

"Is Dr. Yuell going to jail?" Nettie squirmed under the large-knuckled hold of her Grandpa Wilcox.

"You're stayin' here and stayin' quiet, Nettie-girl. This is God's work."

"Ah, Grandpa," Nettie replied with frustration.

Elim Treat, who, at six foot, six inches and an articulate debating team member, sounded like a radio reporter in his commentary, said, "Reverend Fredericks is gesturing to us and smiling. The police sergeant is gesturing and talking. They're standing about three feet apart. Reverend Fredericks is offering the sergeant a handshake. The sergeant shook it with a lightening fast quick grasp and release. Both policemen are heading for their cars..." Then Ruth could see the group, including her father, heading back to them.

"As I was saying," Reverend Fredericks laughingly began again. "We'll be calling out to loved ones and the dearly departed in this service of remembrance." Then he added, "I'd also like to add those names of those harassed, falsely accused, and hurt by the enmity between the races." There were audible gasps followed by polite words of encouragement with even a few male and female-voiced hallelujahs. No one had done or heard of anything like this before on All Saints' Day. "May I also include on the list the names of the people who have died without receiving justice by the laws of our land."

He proceeded to amaze the crowd by reading the list of lynching victims printed clearly on a page from *The Crisis* magazine. He concluded with the Lord's Prayer and the Benediction. After a moment of silence, the school principal invited everyone for refreshments in the school's dining hall.

Amid much smiling, dignified backslaps, and handshaking, Reverend Fredericks walked back slowly to the school. Men, women, students, and his family thought he had done a wonderful thing by talking about their abused and murdered brethren. But everyone wanted to know how Reverend Fredericks had gotten the policemen to go along with the plan.

"Reverend, you'd better tell the ladies and gentlemen here what you planned and, most importantly, how you managed to get the policemen to leave," Dr. Means smilingly suggested.

Reverend Fredericks smiled a wide, relaxed grin and said, "I'd been thinking how unfair and unjust it was to allow some policemen and other government officials to use and abuse our community to such an extent. Really came to a head with the incident with the Oklahoma boy. Not to mention all the horrors and abuses unto death by mob rule in our kindred regions south of here," he emphasized by hitting his index finger against the air. "We needed to remember those injustices are just like little deaths in a way, so we needed to get them out into the air. Maybe we won't be able to do it every year in this school setting but the experience was meaningful."

"But that still doesn't explain how you got the policemen to leave, Reverend Fredericks," Nettie interjected. "How did you do that?"

"Well, I've been down to the jail many times. The policemen know me. Know me well." Reverend Fredericks inhaled deeply. "I told them it was a beautiful day and the auditorium was crowded with the All Saints' Day ceremony. Said I'd decided to talk to you all from the lawn instead, as the only sunny place with a raised area so people could hear me and the other speakers. I specifically inferred they'd already made their department's point to the voters with the Oklahoma student leaving after the detainment and I left it at that.

"The facts and circumstances bore me out. We were within our legal rights to be at the school and on its lawn. I checked down at the county courthouse several weeks ago myself. Guess that hadn't occurred to them. I also reminded them having a pastor and elders down at the jail on All Saints' Day would be inconvenient to all our schedules, including three reelection speeches their boss, the mayor, had scheduled for this evening. Guess that hadn't occurred to them either. They couldn't take us all in their patrol cars. What were they going to do? Even shook my hand in a manner of speaking when I offered it. Not because the sergeant necessarily wanted to, mind you, but he couldn't very well refuse either. Might show some ill will against the Negro community...and they've always denied that."

"Won't want to offend us as prospective voters when we *all* can vote someday," Dr. Means grunted.

"From your mouth to God's ear," Mrs. Wilcox said. "I'm surely going to cast my vote against him."

"It's different further up north, I hear," Nettie said, wanting to tell Ruth her thoughts on the matter.

"Really?" Ruth asked as Nettie pulled her aside.

Nettie continued in a scholarly tone. "Sure. Mildred Newton visits her people in Detroit. They don't have separate things like some places here and father down south. Everybody can go and sit where they please." She paused for a moment for dramatic effect. "That's why I'm going to Detroit just as soon as I'm older."

"Really?" Ruth repeated the same word.

"Just as soon as I'm old enough or can get someone to take me." Nettie welcomed the shocked look on Ruth's face. "But don't you tell anyone or I'll know it's you that told and I'll bloody your nose."

"You won't bloody my nose, Nettie. I'm your best friend," Ruth retorted. Whenever Nettie threatened violence, Ruth knew it was a secret and she promised not to breathe a word.

"So you'll not tell a soul, living or dead?" Nettie asked, somewhat apologetically.

"Not living or dead," Ruth replied. Nettie spit on her hand and Ruth spit on hers and they both slapped their hands together and shook them hard. Nettie seemed pleased but as soon as she wasn't looking, Ruth wiped her hand on her dress.

"Well, we've had a victory today," Grandpa Wilcox said. "Let's raise our glasses...rather, glasses and cups, to things done freely and fairly." The group laughed, moved to clink glasses and cups, and drank just like actors did with champagne flutes in the movies. All Saints' Day could be a day of new beginnings, too.

❦

Reverend Fredericks preached injustices from the pulpit every Sunday. He, Dr. Yuell, and Lady Dee traveled all over the region trying to talk about breaking down segregation, Ruth knew.

"Aren't many places to eat or rest along the way and I've got to be careful," the pastor would relate. His dear wife Lettie had to get the family ready to travel, making sure they were self-contained so that her husband could go to the different churches and preach about desegregation and equality without worrying. It was like packing to go on vacation but they were only gone for the day!

One Sunday, Dr. Yuell and Lady Dee were going on a dual-purpose visit to speak and see outlying patients. Their box packing had already started.

"Got no other choice. This ain't Detroit," Nettie would whisper.

"What was that? Were you saying something, Nettie," Lady Dee said.

"Nothing. Nothing," Nettie replied sheepishly.

Not looking up, Lady Dee dipped her arms into the cardboard apple box she was filling. "Well then, you'll be a set of welcome hands to make sure the Yuell family's ready for tomorrow. Please hand me those rags on the table." Nettie dutifully got the rags. Ruth remained busy drying the cast iron frying pans Lady Dee used to fry the chicken for their next day picnic supper. The Yuells would picnic on the road between stops.

"Should I put them all in?" Nettie asked.

"Already gone over them for quilt pieces or making rag rugs. They're threadbare and too soft," Ruth replied.

"We'll need them for wrapping food and wiping greasy hands and faces," Lady Dee said while tweaking her daughter's chin. "Don't want to be caught short. Got the chicken?" Lady asked in half-question, half-statement fashion. "I've got enough for the water, lemonade, bologna, and bread. Got the mayonnaise."

The time she'd forgotten Ruth's favorite condiment, Dr. Yuell stopped at a market along the way and the white proprietor wouldn't sell him their last jar. Neither Lady Dee nor Ruth wanted such an embarrassment to happen again. The memory almost made Ruth give up mayonnaise altogether. Then, there was the time they had trouble purchasing gas. Thankfully, they'd always been able to get home, which was much more important than a plain bologna sandwich.

"Where we going tomorrow?" asked Nettie. Usually, Leroy, Ruth, and Thelma accompanied their parents on these weekend journeys but the Fredericks' cat and Mrs. Herman's dog were ready to give birth. Thelma was staying in the neighborhood just in case and had asked Leroy to help her with the heavy dog. Mrs. Whitley was coming over to answer the phone at the office and watch over them. Lady Dee asked Nettie if she wanted to come along to keep Ruth company.

"My father will travel to St. John's and Wilton City tomorrow," Ruth replied. "He's checking the car." They and her grandparents were lucky enough to have cars now, so Dr. Yuell could see patients who would have been impossible to see in the previous generation of horse and buggy.

"My father started out that way," Dr. Means regaled the family with stories about the horses, broken buggy wheels, and impassable roads. "But there were other dangers out there. Forget to be careful and you're borrowing trouble."

❧❧

On this trip, everything seemed fine until they got to Wilton City. People seemed tense and were whispering about someone disappearing. The tension hadn't troubled Nettie's appetite and she'd eaten two helpings of peach cobbler when Dr. Yuell said they'd been warned to start home early. Nettie refused to go to the bathroom before heading home. About forty miles from town, Nettie said she wasn't feeling well and wanted to stop. "This isn't a safe place and it's getting dark," Dr. Yuell said, giving a pointed look to his wife. "Can you wait a little longer?"

"Doctor Yuell," Nettie whined. "I'll get sicker if I have to wait any longer."

"I don't have any more rags either. Those are your Sunday clothes, too, aren't they?" Lady Dee fretted.

Ruth kept a rag to hold a gooey cupcake one of the ladies had given her back at their last home visit. Nettie's tears snapped Ruth into reacting. "Here, I've got this." Ruth held up the rag and sprinkled crumbs on both of the girls.

On seeing the rag, Lady Dee put her hands on her husband's shoulder. "Pull over and I'll take her fast while you keep a lookout." Dr. Yuell found a spot on the narrow clay shoulder, kept the car motor running, and Lady Dee snatched Nettie from the car. "Hurry now!" Lady Dee whispered as they both ran into the dimness.

"Hurry!" he urged.

Ruth recalled stopping by bushes and wooded areas before. But this was different because there was real fear in her parents' voices. They returned breathless as her father pulled the car back on the pavement as quick as he could, jostling the remaining containers in the car. "You feeling better, Nettie? Hope that's taught you a lesson." He looked in the rear view mirror. "Do what you're told."

"Will anyone go to jail?" Ruth asked. Someone had died, Ruth knew. Nettie still held her arms tight against her stomach, unable to ask about this latest news of racial problems.

Dr. Yuell kept looking at the road and replied after a time, "The ministers in the area are trying to speak with the authorities." Ruth knew what that meant, too. Someone white had done something to someone black; another name to add to All Saint's Day. Although there were several new Negro lawyers helping on several cases, Ruth learned there was little they could do about these indignities. With little recourse, Reverend Fredericks preached about the cases and the lawyers as well as the appeals being made and the possibility of using the Supreme Court of the United States. He and others sounded hopeful.

Even with a stomachache or whatever was bothering her, Nettie just had to get involved with the conversation. "Mrs. Brewer said her Eddie was arrested for no reason last summer. 'Just cause he's a Negro, he's guilty according to me,' she said the sheriff over in the next county retorted. 'That'll be $300 or he stays put.' Can you believe that! Sheriff said Eddie stayed around the restaurant too long. He was just sitting with his cup of coffee they had at the picnic table for the coloreds. Sheriff didn't know who he was, so he arrested him."

That was the last of the conversation in the car. All Nettie said in parting from Ruth after Dr. Yuell stopped the car was, "Now I know I'm heading for Detroit City. Don't want to be hustled into the woods ever again!"

CHAPTER FIVE

When Ruth didn't see Nettie in the next few days, she assumed Nettie was still mad at her or her family about the roadside incident. Then, Nettie burst though the screen door. "Some of the music students are going to practice the swing tunes they've been perfecting in our barn." She swiped an oven-fresh sugar cookie from the cooling tray on the Yuell's kitchen table. "As long as it doesn't stop the hens from putting down eggs they'll be welcome, my Grandmother Wilcox said." Nettie took another bite. "Grandpa Wilcox thinks the chickens like the music and I think your parents said they don't mind the music!"

During the weeks that followed, Ruth noticed Nettie was especially attentive when Albert Fowler played his trumpet. "He's just so handsome when he plays that trumpet. I swear, I think he plays like Louie Armstrong." After saying that, Nettie got real close to the side of Ruth's face, by her ear, wanting to tell a secret. "Don't mention to Mr. Fowler at church that Albert is playing his trumpet. He's sore against it and will beat Albert for sure! Swear!"

Ruth didn't know if she wanted to go along with Nettie's plan but she was not a gossip. All she could think to say was a warning. "You better not talk about swearing or Grandmother Wilcox's going to wash your mouth with lye soap again."

"You might be right," Nettie agreed with a frown, "but everybody says Albert's so good on the trumpet. Even Grandmother Wilcox."

Unlike her usually fidgety behavior, Nettie could sit for hours in the dusty confines of the barn listening to the music—mostly looking at Albert and pretending not to be looking. Now Ruth had to go over to the Wilcox house to see Nettie at all. Even then, Nettie groused at her.

"Can't see why you have to add to all the clanging and banging of chores with my grandparents when you don't have to?" Nettie complained. "All you have to do is sit here by me."

"I tried that," Ruth lowered her voice. "But all you want to do is talk about Albert or have me sit there to tell you if he's looking at you. I'd rather help do something more. You could help me, too."

"Got enough work to do. Don't need to do no more," Nettie snipped back. "I'm getting grown and there's other things to do besides work all the time."

Ruth didn't understand Nettie's words or her changing moods. She still gauged them both as being best friends. She just tried to understand the good and ignore the bad—assuming Nettie would regain her usual sunny composure.

ꙮ

Dr. Means's dear wife, Alma, died suddenly and unexpectedly from pneumonia and Dr. Means took a leave of absence from the practice to rest in Detroit. Her father needed help and Ruth volunteered.

"Dr. Means's sister-in-law, Mrs. Blaine, is caring for her two nieces and Dr. Means. The three of them seem like the only ones available to come back with him to St. Louis and help him in his grief," Nettie told Ruth. "Hear Mrs. Blaine's as mean as fire on a good day and twice as opinionated."

Ruth gave Nettie a sour look, thinking Lady Dee wouldn't like an elder person to be described in such a negative light.

"Now don't you give me any sour look. You know before dear Mrs. Means was dying, the only bad thing *ever* out of her mouth was about Mrs. Blaine... all her opinions and high-fallutin' ways. That's a sign sure as I'm standing here. Said the niece named Calli was just like her or worse!"

Ruth wanted to stop talking about this Mrs. Blaine and to catch up with her friend, starting with a trip to the movies. Her father had given her enough money for a hot dog and ice cream cone but she decided to add a nickel of her own money and treat Nettie to the movie instead. Besides candy, going to the movies was the only treat Nettie ever wanted. Nettie loved the movies. Never said why, but as the newsreel ended, she would squeeze Ruth's hand and twitch excitedly in her seat. Ruth was so glad she earned the extra nickel, so they both could go together.

"Come on, Nettie! Let's go before all the good seats are gone," Ruth yelled as she looked at her solemn face. "Are you sick or something?"

"No, not sick," Nettie retorted gloomily. "Who cares about the seats? It's been an awful spring and the summer's going to be worse. So much rain and all. Wish it would stop and the school year wouldn't end." This revelation surprised

Ruth because Nettie never really liked school and she'd *always* cared about getting good seats at the movies. *Why was she acting so strange?*

Nettie's pouty lip indicated trouble. "I'm years older than my classmates and it's holding me back."

So that was it. Ruth overheard Miss Viola, in an ominous tone, saying Nettie was getting "kinda' fast." Working at the doctors' office *had* taken time away from her relationship with Nettie. Ruth tried to sit and listen with interest but the monotony of Nettie's talking about community gossip and boys, especially her interest in Albert, tested Ruth's attention span. Nettie never wanted to listen about Ruth's concerns anymore.

Ruth knew how the older girls primped and mooned over the male students at school or talked endlessly about their boyfriends and beaus. "If I was in the right grade, it would be easier!" Nettie sputtered as real tears filled her eyes. "Albert will be with people in his own class!"

Ruth inhaled sharply. Here Ruth was mad about listening to all the gossip and Nettie not listening to her. This was worse. Nettie'd fallen in love, Ruth identified to her own chagrin! It seemed like Nettie was being wrested from her arms by some invisible flood and there was nothing Ruth could do to stop it. Ruth hadn't even seen it coming.

"So...?" Ruth prodded. *How long had she been so blind?*

It had all been Albert, Albert, Albert. The signs had all been there and she'd chosen not to pay attention.

"Is Albert your boyfriend?" Ruth asked, too concerned to be subtle.

"No," Nettie said to Ruth's short-lived relief. "Not yet. But we've been talking. Every chance I get."

Oh no. Ruth looked at her friend's shining eyes.

"I got plans," Nettie confided.

"What plans?" Ruth retorted.

"Boyfriend plans just as you asked. And if I can't get it done before summer comes, there's always time, I hope," Nettie said matter-of-factly. "Albert's got no one else so far."

Ruth frowned and bit her lip.

"Now don't go giving me a sour face, Nee-Nee. If it were you, I'd be happy."

Nettie was always the first at everything. She knew everything in the neighborhood. Tried everything. Answered every dare. Now, Nettie was "going discovering" without her into uncharted and, perhaps, dangerous territory.

"I'm happy for you," Ruth said without conviction. "Just don't want you to get hurt. Get too serious. Make a mistake." Her voice trailed off.

"You're thinking of the Douggins' girl, right?" Nettie asked.

Ruth hadn't been thinking of anything as horrific as what happened, two years ago, to the Douggins' girl, who got herself into trouble. There were whispers;

loud and persistent whispers about what had happened. Lady Dee had hustled Ruth out of the room whenever the subject came up. Between Ruth's deciphering the whispered pig Latin messages of the older girls at school and several overhead comments, the story was clear. Seemed the Douggins' girl had been seeing the son of a farmer in the next county. Her father became enraged when she told him she was going to marry the boy. Unfortunately, she was also pregnant. In his rage, he beat her, sent her down to her grandmother in Mississippi and said that was the last time he or any of the family was going to speak to her. To them, she was dead to the family.

"The boy who they say got her pregnant is not much older than Albert," Ruth whispered and looked up into her friend's eyes, "...and you're not much younger than the girl."

"I know. I know. Not going to do anything that stupid or nothing, but Albert's got a dream to play the trumpet. He calls it his horn," Nettie amended. "Can't go on using the one from the school. Needs one of his own. But he's got to save up to buy one. That should take some time. Plus, if I give him my savings, he'll be my boyfriend for sure!" How often had Ruth and Nettie counted their savings? Nettie had exactly $12.31 saved. She called it her "fortune."

"You mean you're going to use your whole fortune to buy Albert his trumpet!" Ruth cried.

"Don't be getting all excited," Nettie said angrily. "Just an idea. Haven't said anything to anybody except you. You think it's a bad idea, huh?"

"Nettie, it's the money you were saving for school...for...for the future," Ruth stammered.

"Well, sometimes the future's today," Nettie stated firmly, "and my future might be Albert Fowler."

The words sounded so final to Ruth. Ruth worried for her friend. *What was Nettie going to do?*

❦

As the school year ended, Albert Fowler left to visit family and Nettie seemed fine. "I'll see him when he gets back from vacation," was all that Nettie would say in a smug tone.

A wet spring yielded more tomatoes and beans for canning so Ruth set her mind to her regular chores and the family's spring cleaning.

"Remember, Ruth, today's the day for you, Leroy, and Thelma to start airing the house mattresses and starting in the offices," Lady Dee reminded them as she looked at the chore list. "We'll have a dinner picnic on the lawn as a treat after all the hard work."

"Time for father's and Dr. Means's offices...and we better get started," Thelma warned. "Dr. Means and his people are expected back soon."

Just after the Wilcoxes' rooster crowed, rivers of ammonia, vinegar, and homemade furniture oil and soap disappeared as the Yuells scrubbed, polished, and cleaned every inch of every room.

"Remember, we've still got time for berry hunting after cleaning because we're still in our raggedy working clothes," Leroy said.

Before they left on their berry hunt, they rubbed salt pork on their ankles and wrists. "Keep the bugs, chiggers, and ticks away," Nettie would say. "Renny Morris got an infection from a chigger and had to see your father and Dr. Means four times!"

After they had cleaned the berries and washed up, Lady Dee served a picnic supper on the back lawn. Dr. Yuell's dinner was in the kitchen because he'd been called away to tend to Grandfather Evers's flaring rheumatism.

"Only thing better would be if your father were here right now," Lady Dee said with a smile. "We'll be able to come and count the fireflies when the dishes are done and he might be home by then."

Ruth heard heavy footsteps behind her. Any hope that it was her father coming home from his house call faded as she heard a very deep, clipped woman's voice say, "Would you please tell Dr. Yuell and his family Dr. Means's sister-in-law, Mrs. Horatio Blaine, and her younger relatives need their assistance?"

Ruth pulled up her legs and twirled on her bottom to see a thick-bosomed square lady in a purple dress with a long black-beaded collar. The woman looked at her black cuffs in what seemed to be some displeasure.

Lady Dee didn't miss a beat as she gracefully pushed herself from the picnic blanket and extended her hand. "I am Dr. Yuell's wife and these are our children, Thelma, Leroy, and Ruth and a neighbor child, Nettie Wilcox." She turned to the children. "May I introduce you children to Mrs. Blaine and her nieces, I believe, which, as I understand it, are Calli and Bethany Winston."

"Please call me Meggie," the shorter, slimmer young girl said. Ruth thought the girl might be about her age. The other girl came out of the lengthening shadows. She was taller than Ruth but thickly built like Mrs. Blaine. "We've come here with Dr. Means."

"Bet that makes you Calli," Nettie said as she jumped to her feet.

"We don't bet on anything," the girl named Calli said in a nasal tone as she took a few steps closer to her aunt.

"We're a close, informal group here," Lady Dee said in a pointed tone. Ruth knew her mother saved that tone for when something wrong. "I'll be happy to fix you a pot of tea in the house if you prefer. Have you had any dinner?"

Suddenly, Sylvie called from the back of the yard in out-of-breath shouts. "Lady Dee. Come down. Granny Wilcox...bad sick."

They rushed from the blanket as Lady Dee called, "Thelma, see to the tea after you call for either your father or Dr. Means, if he's up to it. Send them over to the Wilcox house." Ruth turned to see Nettie well ahead of Lady Dee's lifted skirts as they ran. Ruth went to call Grandpa Wilcox so he might help to get his wife to bed or at least get her on a quilt or blanket until she was better.

"Hope she's not too bad," Leroy cried in a worried tone as they worked as fast as they could.

They rounded the corner of the house, dashed up worn plank steps and threw the screen door open to see Mrs. Wilcox on the floor. Nettie took on the task of holding Grandma Wilcox's hand and stroking her cheek, but she was still sweating and breathing hard from her run. Lady Dee arranged her clothes and body for easier breathing and felt for a pulse. Ruth got a blanket and covered Grandma Wilcox and sat Sylvie down on a kitchen chair she brought from the table. Thelma and Leroy got the dishes washed and watched the cook pots on the stove trying to keep things going. Ruth noticed one of the bootlace holes on her grandmother's shoes had grazed Nettie's arm. Fresh blood was smearing Nettie's cotton blouse.

Granny Wilcox's head was now cradled in Lady Dee's lap. Only the whites of her eyes were showing through slit-opened lids, reminding Ruth of the spaceman movie at the local movie matinee. Her mouth was slack and drooling foam and blood. Her body was as straight as a horse buggy whip. Ruth looked over at Sylvie. She was making rocking movements back and forth while alternately cooing and humming softly in the direction of Granny Wilcox's unresponsive head.

Ruth couldn't think of anything much to do except to take clean rags from the sink and wipe the foam and blood from Mrs. Wilcox's lips and use another to clean the floor. She glanced at Lady Dee and her siblings, who looked helpless and scared as she felt. "Looks like she's breathing better. We've got a blanket and here's something to pillow her head," Lady Dee said as she lifted the older woman's stiff arms.

Grandpa Wilcox came through the door looking concerned, helpless, and lost all at the same time as he headed toward his wife on the floor. Sylvie just kept rocking and sing-songing, not seeming to hear Lady Dee at all.

"Leroy, you go get Ellis to help Grandpa Wilcox and I get Granny Wilcox to bed. Ruth, please pull down her bedcovers, close the curtains, and light the lamp." Ruth's feet went toward the Wilcoxes' bedroom but her face was frozen on her loved ones on the kitchen floor. She didn't turn till the wood partition hid her from them. Time seemed to flow thickly, like when they poured the hot molasses candy from the pot to the butter-slick trays for Christmas treats. Ruth heard other running footsteps and the screechy screen door spring. Ellis must be there, she thought.

It took Leroy, Ellis, Grandpa Wilcox, Lady Dee, and Ruth to lift Grandma Wilcox. Her unresponsive body didn't seem to like the noise much because she started twitching. "Think it would be better to have her bed in the kitchen, Grandpa Wilcox? Much easier for her with this narrow door space and all," Ellis said as he wiped the sweat from his brow.

Grandpa Wilcox wearily raised his head, seemed to think a second about Ellis's suggestion, and then nodded. "We'll get it done."

"We'll help you when she's better," Ruth offered quietly, just knowing instinctively that Leroy and Thelma wanted to help, too. She looked for Nettie, who was sitting on the floor with her hand under the cover holding Grandma Wilcox's hand. *Was she still bleeding, Ruth wondered?*

They put the bed in the kitchen cove between the stove and the living room and got Granny Wilcox situated.

"She'll be quiet now," Lady Dee stated. "Thanks for coming so quickly, Ellis," she added while asking another question. "Do you have the time to get the animals bedded before you go home?"

Ellis softly said, "Sure," as he retrieved his bill-front cloth hat from his side pocket. Ruth had forgotten about the animals. Grandpa Wilcox had abandoned his evening chores. "Come on, Leroy."

"Go sit on the steps for awhile," Lady Dee ordered, looking keenly at her daughters. "I've got to talk to Grandpa Wilcox." Sylvie was still on the chair. Not rocking now. Not singing. Just sitting there, looking down at the floor. That hadn't happened before, Ruth thought. Before the screen door closed, Ruth watched Lady Dee put a blanket on Sylvie's shoulders.

Dr. Yuell spent most of the night at the Wilcox house. The rest of the family waited at home. Lady Dee, Ruth, Leroy, and Thelma wouldn't go to bed waiting for hopeful news. Everyone felt like they'd been up for days, tracking back and forth from the Wilcoxes' screen door a thousand times with no rest or food. Before Dr. Yuell passed the threshold, Lady Dee forestalled him saying, "Everyone's taking it hard." Lady Dee gazed around the room at its sad, tired occupants. "You all go up to bed now." Seeing the hurt look in the children's eyes, she added, "Let me see how Grandma Wilcox is doing. We all need some rest or we won't be able to help. The less commotion the better, and I'll let you go back over there as soon as I can."

Ruth went to the porch step and stared at her parents as they went on another trek to the Wilcox home. Ruth's insides were itching to go over to Nettie and Sylvie, but she was scared about not knowing what to say. She just sat there looking at the disappearing fireflies and listening to the sounds of dawn as she headed back home.

Both her father and Lady Dee returned home, grim-faced. Ruth left the step to meet them and could see her parents' sadness even before they spoke. "Grandma Wilcox's resting. Sylvie, too," her father said as they walked tiredly up the back porch steps.

"I'll get you a light breakfast and you can get a nap before office hours. Only scraps. No time to cook," Lady Dee said to her husband as she headed for the stove. "Want to wash up and have some?"

"Am hungry," Dr. Yuell admitted, "but not too much. How's my Ruthie?" he asked as he put his long arms out to hug her. He called into the bedroom. "Leroy, are you over there?"

"Yes, father. Thelma just finished our dishes and I'm going to get your slippers," Leroy replied.

"What's going on?" Ruth whispered, at his side.

"I'll tell you in a minute," Leroy whispered back as he gave the slippers to his father and brought the dress shoes to the closet.

"Father wipes them with a rag in the shoeshine box before he puts them away," Ruth instructed needlessly, wanting to forestall what she already knew.

"I know. I know," Leroy said irritably but his tone softened and he said without preamble, "Grandma Wilcox's dying. Sorry. It's true. Ellis talked about it when I went to help him with the animals." He took a deep breath and exhaled loudly, pursed his lips, and began again. "Something about her never taking care of her sugar diabetes," her brother said to Ruth's skeptical look, "but it's worse now. Problem with Sylvie, too, I think. Just sitting on the chair or on the floor like a broken doll; just rocking and moaning with tears falling the whole time. Almost took Lady Dee and Grandpa Wilcox as much time to get her up from the chair as Grandma Wilcox."

"How's Nettie?" was all Ruth could say.

"She held Grandma Wilcox's hand all night. Before she went home to her apartment, Mrs. Williams said Nettie was stretched out on the bed next to Grandma Wilcox on top of the blanket just talking to her quiet-like." Leroy gazed into his sister's sad eyes.

Leroy was only telling her the truth she already knew but her heart was resisting.

Poor Nettie. Ruth prayed. Her father called out. "Ruth? Leroy? Thelma? Will you come here, please?" Leroy looked at Ruth's face with a worried expression. All she could do was squeeze his hand reassuringly as they wordlessly went to the kitchen.

"Sit down, please," Dr. Yuell said as they suddenly felt like stiff strangers not knowing what to do.

Lady Dee put down her spoon. "They really have been so much help all night. We got all the work done here even with all the extra things with Grandma Wilcox's illness."

"Praise God. That's fine." He looked from Ruth to Leroy and Thelma; then back again. He remained quiet for a time, like when he wanted to think of some way to explain a punishment to his children. "Wish this could have waited many years in the future, but with Grandma Wilcox's illness...Can't be helped, though. I've an announcement to make and it can't be delayed. The church fathers and community know Grandpa Wilcox is going to need help, so we're going to take on the daily care of him and the girls because Grandma Wilcox is gravely ill." Dr. Yuell looked at Lady Dee and his children. "As you've seen in other cases in our community, when people need help, others take them in like they're blood family."

Ruth looked at her beloved father as if he were speaking some strange foreign language. Her eyes widened and she couldn't understand it at first, and then her brain quietly evaluated each word again. "So we'll be taking on the care of Grandma Wilcox...and Grandpa Wilcox as if they were our own and Nettie and Sylvie will be like you children...like your own sisters. They don't have anyone else as close to help them."

Thelma was her sister and Nettie was her best friend. *How could her best friend now become her sister? When people asked how many sisters she had, could she remember there were now suddenly three instead of one?* Ruth could only repeat names, it seemed. "Nettie? ...Sylvie?" she wheezed. "Nettie? ...Sylvie?"

"They'll live in their home but they're ours now." Dr. Yuell looked around the room. "Do you understand?" Ruth must have appeared the most confused because her father looked at her. "Ruthie, I know last night...this *is* a shock." With soft earnestness, Dr. Yuell tenderly grasped his daughter's hand and looked bleakly at Lady Dee. Lady Dee's reassuring smile seemed to energize him. He smiled back. "Why don't we talk more about this when we've had some rest?"

Ruth blinked for what seemed to be the first time since he started talking and looked at Leroy. Her brother got up and Ruth followed him out the door toward the big pine tree at the back of the yard. The coming daylight tried wanly to break through its lush evergreen branches. All Ruth could do was look at Leroy. He sat there a long time. Ruth just watched the pine branch shadows play over his profile as thoughts moved over his silent face.

"Know how you're feeling, Ruth. Everything has come out of the blue, like lightening in a clear sky."

Oh, Lord, help me. Ruth prayed silently, looking down at her shoes almost hidden in the dark. She'd infrequently heard anything poetic come out of her brother's mouth in all their years except when he read the Bible out loud at church or had recitation at school. This was a strange and surprising day. First, her father spoke things in a seemingly foreign language, and now Leroy spouted poetry. Maybe if she went to sleep real fast, she'd wake up and the strangeness would all be gone. Her brother spoke again. "This thing with Grandma Wilcox and Sylvie's got us all upset and wobbly."

"Can we help Grandma Wilcox? Sylvie? What about Nettie?" she cried angrily. "They're..."

"Hurting?" Leroy offered.

"Yes!" Ruth vehemently agreed as if her brother had guessed a hard word in a game of charades.

"Everyone's making sure things get taken care of and we need to help. Now let's go inside and get some rest," Leroy ordered. His face went from sullen to assured as he spoke. Ruth found comfort in that. The first comfort since she'd sat down at the kitchen table. Ruth mulled and tested what Leroy said in her mind. He was right. Father and Lady Dee would have to take over the care of the Wilcox family. It was the right thing to do.

"But we'll still do things like before?" Ruth asked.

"Just like when our grandmothers came to stay when they were alone," Leroy replied as his tone became laced with excitement. "Father says it's right. Church fathers say it's the right thing to do—can't get any plainer. You and I both know it would break Father's and Lady Dee's hearts not to have our full cooperation." Her brother pulled her down to sit in the moist grass. Ruth could barely see his eyes but the light of his words were unmistakable. "Read that speech on justice in my freshman civics class and got to recite it at seven churches. Remember?"

Of course, Ruth remembered. "Well," Leroy continued, "it's because we're trustworthy that's got us here. See?"

The truth hit her like a fireball. *What would she tell Nettie?* Her conclusion was swift and final. They were all going to be family right and tight and it was her job to help make the decision work for Nettie. It might take some doing, but it had to get done.

Ruth went inside and didn't talk to anyone. Her parents were back at the Wilcox house even though they said they were going to rest. Ruth still didn't have permission to go back over there from Lady Dee. A prohibition she couldn't disobey. So Ruth would buy herself some time and rest. She would do what she wanted to do earlier by shutting her eyes tight and telling herself nothing bad had happened last night. To Ruth's surprise, she slept through the morning.

"Time for your lazybones to get up," Ruth heard her father call as the coop rooster crowed in the distance. "Not too late for Lady Dee's flannel cakes and smoked ham, I think."

Before the flood of yesterday's memories poured in, Ruth's stomach growled as it sensed the wheaty fragrance and questioned this unexpected treat. She hadn't eaten since yesterday's dinner, she recalled, and not much of that because Mrs. Blaine and her nieces had come calling. "Come on now," her father called again with a laughing voice. "Let's eat or I'm feeding them to the barn cats." With a little sleep and in the daylight, things seemed better.

"Atta' girl, Ruth," her father encouraged as Lady Dee put the milk pitcher down on the table.

Leroy came through the door, yawning and rubbing his eyes. Thelma followed in his wake. "What's this all for?" he stated baldly.

"Well, son," their father began. "We got off to a bad start last night with the announcement about Sylvie and Nettie and their future. Your mother and I thought talking it over again, after a bit of sleep, would make it better. Checked on the Wilcoxes, just now. They're safe."

"Don't worry, father. We're OK, now," Ruth started, grateful the Wilcox family had gotten through the night. "Leroy helped me understand. Nettie and Sylvie are my sisters now, right?"

A fond look reflected on Dr. Yuell's face. "Well, praise God, Leroy. Thank you for your help." He placed his hand on his son's shoulder. "A doctor's not often at a loss for words, but for me, last night was one of those times." Dr. Yuell smiled ruefully. He turned to Ruth. "You sure about this, Ruth?" He looked deeply into his daughter's eyes. Ruth let him look, keeping her gaze clear and unwavering. Ruth felt her father needed her reassurance...and she was going to give it unequivocally.

"Ruth knows Grandma Wilcox is dying, father," Leroy said softly.

"I just didn't want to say it, either," Thelma added.

Lady Dee smiled reassuringly at her children. "Of course, not," Lady Dee said. "Guess it was shock to your father and me. We should have told you ourselves."

"Your mother and I have some ideas we'd like to share with you. See if they meet with your approval," Doctor Yuell looked at Lady Dee and smiled, "but first I think we need to say the table blessing and eat this lovely late breakfast before it goes cold." They said their morning prayers and table grace.

Leroy didn't need any prompting when they finished praying. "May I use the butter first?" he asked. Dr. Yuell smiled at him and passed the crock instead of answering.

Seems all the plans were for the Wilcox family. The whole Yuell family would get everything ready for them. Nettie, Sylvie, and Grandpa Wilcox would stay in their house but Lady Dee would take over the care of the house, their meals, and daytime schedules, leaving Grandpa Wilcox to work without being worried about Nettie or Sylvie. Ruth, Thelma, and Leroy would help, too, as time permitted.

Dr. Yuell took the hardest part. He told Nettie that Grandma Wilcox was dying. Grandpa Wilcox didn't have the heart to do it; just turned away with embarrassment as he cried silently. Sylvie didn't seem to understand much anymore. "Give her time," was all her father said.

Ruth certainly could see the wisdom in giving Nettie and Sylvie all the time they needed. The enormity of the changes had taken Ruth by surprise. Ruth would answer all Nettie's questions about them becoming sisters with all the love and care she had. Sylvie would get used to things, too.

꙰

"I've got to go over and talk to Nettie again," Ruth informed. So Ruth would tell Nettie everything was going to be fine because they'd be sisters.

"If you think this is the time, then go," Lady Dee said. She opened her arms. "Here's a hug for luck."

Ruth just told it straight, like Leroy had done with her, when he told her about the changes and them becoming sisters.

"What?" Nettie cried in a shocked tone so like Ruth's first reaction at the news but there was anger underneath. It seemed like Nettie was hearing it all for the first time!

"Don't worry. Don't worry," Ruth cried as her arms warded off Nettie's anger. "It's going to be fine." Nettie's fury moved her body forward and kept Ruth backing up to the kitchen wall.

Ruth kept talking, trying to make Nettie understand. "But I'm staying in our house. You...you can stay in your house with Sylvie and Grandpa Wilcox. I'll be here to help you as long...as long as you need me." Nettie's thundering look and rigid body told Ruth she did *not* understand. "We can even go to school together. I'll help with the chores and everything. I'll be here," Ruth grabbed Nettie's shoulders and started to shake her. "I'll be here." Nettie's anger went slack and she turned her tear-filled eyes to Ruth's face.

"Till it's all over?" Nettie asked quietly now. "Grandma Wilcox and all? You'll be here when she dies?"

"I'll be here when she dies. Promise!" Ruth stated in a firm voice far stronger than she felt. No one wanted Grandma Wilcox to die but Ruth knew this was the best plan for everyone left when she did.

Over the next several days, Grandma Wilcox's muscles were weak and her steps were at best wobbly the few times she'd left her bed. Nettie and Ruth acted like human crutches helping her to the porch for some fresh air. Grandma Wilcox had more attacks of chest pain, seemingly small ones now. She'd clutch her chest, seem to sleep for a long time after and wake up tired and a bit confused. The girls were there to comfort and baby her with smiles and hot milk, usually reserved for winter ills, not for full summer days. But Grandma Wilcox wanted hot milk and that's what they gave her in sips and spoonfuls.

One afternoon Grandma Wilcox seemed better, stronger in her legs and able to walk almost unaided to the porch. Ruth was going to read some Psalms to her and Nettie was going to sit on the small wooden chair next to her and hold her hand. They were planning on serving some fried chicken for dinner. Sylvie was getting better, too. Today she was more interested in her *Three Little Pigs* book and dinner plans than she'd seemed like anything since Grandma Wilcox got sick. "Granny be better soon," Sylvie said emphatically.

Nettie and Ruth looked at each other and said nothing. Ruth didn't want to spoil Sylvie's reborn cheerfulness by saying anything sad. Ruth felt funny, though, pretending everything was OK and all, but Grandma Wilcox did seem better today and that was a cause to celebrate. Savor every moment, Ruth thought, as she heard Grandmother Addison say. So she smiled at Nettie and Sylvie.

Ruth had just gotten through with Psalm 60. Nettie cleared her throat and started to talk conversationally, "Ruth and I are going to be sisters." Ruth sat there as if she'd been struck by the clear sky lightening Leroy had talked about as she watched Nettie try to smooth over the truth as Grandma Wilcox's mind considered and then realized what Nettie was saying. "Yes, Ruth and I are going to be like sisters. We've always talked about it since we're so close," Nettie amended as she saw her grandmother's dawning comprehension of her very fragile condition, "ah...to be, Grandma...like...just like sisters." Nettie kept talking and her grandmother's placid face melted into concern, like a cake in a hot kitchen.

Grandma Wilcox's eyes looked concerned and she said in a pitiful voice, "Sisters?" Grandma Wilcox gave Ruth a telling look, like someone who couldn't hold onto a rock and resigned herself to falling a long way. The tremors began. Just a little at first, then in giant waves as her chair, her body, and the hot milk all fell to the porch planks. Ruth tried to catch Grandma Wilcox as she went down. "I'm not! I'm not her sister!" Ruth cried, but Grandma Wilcox's eyes were gone behind her lids and she was shaking and moaning.

Ruth didn't see Sylvie but she heard her shrieking and crying hysterically, "Granny! Granny!" Ruth knew Sylvie must have seen Grandma Wilcox tip over but she couldn't help Sylvie now. Ruth saw the broken chair pieces wreathed around them and she swatted them away.

"Get Grandpa! Get Grandpa!" Nettie cried. Ruth threw more chair wood to the side and ran the steps alternately screaming, "Grandpa Wilcox," and, "Help!" all the way to the yard. Grandpa Wilcox came running and headed past her to the porch. Then, Ruth headed for her own house screaming, "Lady Dee! Lady Dee!" as she ran.

Lady Dee, Leroy, and Thelma came running with Dr. Means not far behind. "Get Reverend Fredericks and Miss Ella, Leroy," Lady Dee called. "Grandma Wilcox and her family need the Lord now."

Ruth turned around to run back with Lady Dee. The scene on the porch was like Grandma Wilcox's last attack, except Nettie held Grandma Wilcox's head. Sylvie was a rag doll again, Indian-sitting against the porch rail, the forlorn dead chicken meant for supper, lying forgotten in a gunny sack in her limp hand.

"How's she doing?" Lady Dee asked.

Nettie sounded scared. "She stopped breathing-like, just for a few seconds mind you, but she's started again." Just as she finished, Grandma Wilcox shook and strained so hard Grandpa Wilcox lost hold of her legs. Then she was quiet. Everything went slack. It was a moment before anyone moved. Grandma Wilcox was gone to heaven.

Everyone began crying, then. Nettie was draped over her head and resting her body on her grandmother's chest. Grandpa Wilcox was sitting down where he had been kneeling, arms resting on his knees, head down looking at the floor as his ribcage shook in grief. Lady Dee stood there with tears coming down her face and Thelma, who'd gone to get a blanket to cover Grandma Wilcox from the cold, had now come to cover her body. Lady Dee roused herself to catch one side of it as Leroy started to drape it by Grandma Wilcox's feet. Lady Dee stopped for a second to close Grandma Wilcox's eyes.

Sylvie just sat there as before, still breathing but with a glassy, unseeing stare like the pictures of the waxworks figures in the encyclopedia at school. No tears. No movement. Worse than before, Ruth thought. She started toward Sylvie and was forestalled by Lady Dee. Her mother bent down and whispered. "She's in shock, Ruth. Go get a cover for her. Best thing now." Her daughter's footsteps seemed to echo like hammer strokes as she walked from the porch. She picked up the quilt from Grandma Wilcox's kitchen bed.

Nettie looked up and saw Ruth come through the door. "Don't you be touching Granny's quilt. Don't you be touchin' it!" Nettie's anger startled Ruth, who stood open-mouthed and backed into the front door portal again. Ruth looked at Lady Dee. Ruth clutched the yellow and white quilt to her chest.

"That's all right, Ruth. Get another cover. Nettie doesn't want you to use that one right now." A look passed from Lady Dee to Dr. Means. He came to Ruth's side as Nettie's hate-filled eyes followed them into the house.

"She's just upset, Miss Ruthie," Dr. Means said softly as he put his arm around the girl's shoulder to lead her toward the house. "Let's put the quilt back and find something else before Sylvie gets cold. A lot of other people will be coming. She needs to get warm."

Lady Dee whispered, "She's gone, Nettie. Time to get up. Grandpa Wilcox's gone to pick out some clean clothes for the wake and Sylvie's going to be put to bed. She's feeling poorly. I need your help. The kitchen needs to be a kitchen again with everyone coming to pay their respects to your grandmother," she sighed with patience and then a bit sharper. "Nettie, where else are we going to put the people?"

Nettie's tear-stained, hateful eyes turned on Lady Dee this time, but thankfully she began to move. With some slow, jerky movements, like some invisible person was pulling on her, Nettie untangled herself from Grandma Wilcox's still, silent form. She walked unsteadily into the house. Nettie shook off Thelma's hand defiantly, glared, and continued unaided.

Nettie looked at the bed in the kitchen. Ruth made sure the quilt was replaced just like it was left. Nettie glanced angrily at Ruth, sniffed disdainfully, and entered the bedroom, turning impatiently. "You coming?" she called to Lady Dee. Ruth's eyes almost left her head and she inhaled sharply at Nettie's rudeness. Leroy and Thelma's expressions mirrored the same surprise. Lady Dee appeared not to hear Nettie as she walked into the room after giving some other instructions. Nettie pointed to where things should go and marched right back, straight-line, to Grandma Wilcox's body—this time not looking at anyone.

Ruth didn't have anything else to say most of that day. Just did what she was told. Better that way. She would mourn the loss and the wounds in silence. Grandma Wilcox's body went to the funeral home, Sylvie was put to bed, and the stream of covered dishes started to arrive at the Wilcox's doorstep.

There were so many questions in Ruth's mind as she thought of how to console Nettie. Lady Dee seemed to read her mind and she said simply, "Not now, Ruth. She needs some time alone to mourn in her own way. I think she'll let us know when she's ready. Pray to the Lord that it's soon."

❧❧

Funerals were always difficult but Grandma Wilcox's seemed worse. When she died the compass of the Wilcox family broke, too. Sylvie was still in bed. She wasn't interested in anything, even her book. Dr. Means and her father visited the home frequently. He came to the house that evening. After he examined Sylvie, he shrugged his shoulders and told Grandpa Wilcox, Dr. Yuell, and Lady Dee, "It's the worst case of shock without injury I've ever seen." All they could do was wait, he said, and pray for the best. "Can't take any more change." Several ladies from the church were taking time sitting with Sylvie, day and night, trying to talk to her and give her water but she just laid there looking lifeless with blank eyes.

Nettie took on another role. She became Grandpa Wilcox's shadow all through the wake and burial. Not talking or acknowledging anyone. She just held onto his hand or stood by his side the entire time either looking at the floor or into the pine casket. Every time Ruth tried to come near Nettie or talk to her, the hateful glare reappeared. Even Leroy could get right up to Nettie and she allowed it. That almost hurt more than Grandma Wilcox being dead.

☙❧

It was summertime. Nettie and Ruth should have been laughing, eating berries, and enjoying their free time together but Nettie still wanted no part of her friend. Sometimes Ruth went walking or picking berries with Leroy. Most of the time, she went alone. She didn't want to ask anyone else because she didn't want to affect Nettie's negative feelings further. *Could things get any worse?*

Ruth would see Nettie, but Nettie pointedly avoided Ruth. Ruth monitored Nettie's new routine but she didn't interfere. Nettie was trying to do all Grandma Wilcox's housework and help Grandpa Wilcox in the yard and the barn. Only time off she took was to pick wild flowers and put them by Grandma Wilcox's bed.

Lady Dee concentrated on putting together a schedule for helpers when Nettie would need to return to school when summer ended. "Ruth, there's one thing I do want you to do for me. You can bring the dinner over to the Wilcoxes's in about an hour when I get things ready."

"I'll go over there now and see if that's good for them," Ruth said, wanting to see Nettie too badly to wait. So far, the trips over to the Wilcox house had been fruitless. Ruth went several times just to see if Nettie would talk to her. This time Ruth crossed her fingers behind her back for luck as she walked on the worn path.

Nettie met her sullenly at the door. "Go 'way."

"I...thought. Can I help?" Ruth asked in confusion.

"Don't need no help. Now git. I got work to do before dinner and that's soon," Nettie stated loudly, banging and clattering anything close-by to reinforce the message.

"But Nettie," Ruth persisted, wanting to understand her rejection. "You've always helped me."

"You're more trouble than a traveling salesman. I said I'm busy, and I'm busy. Now go!" Nettie shouted as she tried to slam the door in Ruth's face.

"But you're my friend!" Ruth cried as she blocked the glancing blow of the worn wood.

"Get out of here, you cry baby! Your tears and bothering me are taking my time," Nettie retorted with hot eyes.

"I just came to tell you Lady Dee says dinner is coming in an hour. Did I do something?" Ruth asked, swiping away tears with her knuckles.

"You did *nothing*," Nettie stormed back. "You didn't tell them I could take care of things. You didn't tell them Sylvie, Grandpa, and me would be just fine without any of you." Nettie's face stayed contorted with rage. "Now everybody's putting themselves in our business and telling *me* what I should do."

"I didn't do that," Ruth pleaded.

"No matter," Nettie replied as her face relaxed but her attitude remained adamant. "This was a Wilcox affair and we don't need all the meddling from your parents and the rest."

"But Lady Dee has been helping ever since Grandma Wilcox asked for our help," Ruth offered.

"Grandma Wilcox is gone and now I'm the right-minded woman of the household," Nettie stated flatly. "Women about my age and younger are married down South. Everybody knows I'm smart and sharp and *everyone* should have left well enough alone."

"It's not you, Nettie," Ruth tried to explain. "Everything was already set up for us to be *family* and with Sylvie being sick and all." Ruth's reasoning evaporated. She was still confused by Nettie's talk about women, marriage, and being the head of the household. She knew Nettie loved Grandpa Wilcox and Sylvie... and Nettie was smart and all. But Ruth didn't know why Nettie was so mad about getting help from the Yuells and the community. This was what people did for other people when there was a death or a family needed help. Ruth tried another tack. "School will be starting soon, Nettie, and perhaps you could use some help then."

"Told you already I can take care of things, school or no," Nettie said, her frown returning. "Who says I need more schooling—like the baby classes I've been sitting in?"

Ruth inhaled audibly as she considered Nettie's stinging criticisms. "Are you that unhappy?" Ruth asked.

"Time to be a woman and find a man to get things straight," Nettie said. "Get everyone off our back." Nettie stared at Ruth and continued in a low tone. "And if you tell anybody, I'll whip you good."

"Why would you want to whip me?" Ruth whispered as the tears started again.

"Told ya. You didn't stand up for me and what was good for my family," Nettie spat.

Ruth didn't know what to say. Nettie was talking about Ruth and her family as if she didn't know them at all. "I'll be back with tonight's dinner," Ruth stated. It was all she could think of to say. Nettie closed the door in her face.

Ruth later sat on the back porch stoop looking over at the Wilcox home, trying to will an answer to come to her brain about Nettie's accusations and schemes. She was Nettie's friend and Nettie was talking about wild and dangerous things.

She'd keep everything to herself for a few days but if Nettie continued to talk about leaving school, being a woman, and finding a man, Ruth would talk to her mother and father about it.

☙❧

Several silent days passed. Anxiety like electric shocks went over Ruth's skin. Ruth knew she had to see if Nettie was thinking more clearly about the future. Lady Dee pulled Ruth aside. "Have you thought more about our plans to care for Nettie, Sylvie, and Grandpa Wilcox?"

Ruth had thought of little else. Nettie was cut off from her and everyone. Alone. Angry. Ruth couldn't get close enough to tell if Nettie was acting like a wounded animal or just turned vicious like Sylvie had turned blank. Her father and Lady Dee always said to think the best of people, so Ruth was torn by Nettie's strange vendetta against her and her loving memories of their friendship.

"I'm still sure but it hurts, Lady Dee. Getting up the courage to ask Grandpa Wilcox what he thinks is going on with Nettie. If Grandma Wilcox were alive I could ask her, but she's gone. Nettie won't talk. Tried many times!"

"I know. I know." Lady Dee gave a sad smile. "Sounds like you've done your best."

"It's just that Nettie won't talk to me...just yells and says hateful things," Ruth began, "so instead of hurting, she's mad. But no matter what, I want Nettie, Sylvie, and Grandpa Wilcox to be our family as if they were blood." Lady Dee smiled and patted her daughter's hand. "So I'm staying with your plan with all my might. I'm going out and tell Grandpa Wilcox, so he can tell Nettie." Ruth smiled suddenly and waved to her mother as she ran to the Wilcox house.

At least now Ruth had a plan. She'd wait and give Nettie more time. Perhaps Nettie would talk to her when she found out Ruth was still talking to Grandpa Wilcox and he went along with the plan for their future.

"Nettie? Nettie!" Ruth banged on the door, alarming Mrs. Pruitt who was watching Sylvie.

"Nettie. What's the matter?" Ruth heard the older woman say.

"Nothing. Stay sitting with Sylvie and read her book," she ordered, "I'm getting the table set and I'm behind." She turned back to her work and Mrs. Pruitt went back in the room with a shrug.

Ruth took a look at Nettie through the screen door and turned for the yard. "Since you're behind, I'll see if I can help Grandpa Wilcox."

Ruth would go to the yard and fill his water jar for him. A kind of peace offering to Nettie while she was busy in the house. He'd stop for a minute and maybe answer questions about himself and Nettie. Grandpa Wilcox's answers to her queries the last few days were punctuated by looking around, surveying the horizon or his yard, and then saying, "Doing passable," or "Getting by."

Ruth felt better than she had in days as she walked to the garden to find Grandpa Wilcox. Grandpa Wilcox was probably taking a break already, because there wasn't any movement or sound coming from the vegetable patch. Ruth turned into the garden to see him slumped, open-eyed on the ground. She rushed to his lifeless body and started screaming, then changed direction, running for help. Ruth forgot Nettie was mad at her. Forgot Grandma Wilcox was dead and Sylvie was in shock and just started calling them for help. Nettie came around the house and she pointed to the garden. "Grandpa Wilcox's over there. I'm going to get Lady Dee," Ruth called as she headed for her backyard and starting screaming again. "Lady Dee! Lady Dee!" she screeched. When Lady Dee caught her in her arms, Ruth cried, "It's Grandpa Wilcox. He's dead in the garden. Nettie needs you." Lady Dee must have headed to the garden as Ruth headed for her father's office. Ruth pulled the door open and started yelling for help until Leroy startled her and yanked her down on the cold tile floor. "It's Grandpa Wilcox," she cried into her brother's shirtfront. "He's dead."

Everything started going gray. Leroy was beside her.

"You can be quiet now," Leroy said gently. "Now you come sit over here on the office bench. Come sit by me." He gathered his sister in his arms and her body started shaking. Ruth wasn't cold or sick, just shaking like it was winter and she'd forgotten her heavy coat. But it's still summer, she considered numbly. Still summer.

After a while, Leroy picked her up and carried her across the room to the couch.

"I'm better now," she said.

"That's good," he replied.

"How's Nettie?" Ruth asked.

"Lady Dee called father, right away. Took her over to Mrs. Givens's house. Gave her some medicine to sleep," Leroy recounted. "See to things in the morning."

"Grandpa Wilcox?" Ruth persisted. Leroy went over to the sink.

"Here, take this water. Grandpa Wilcox's body's at the funeral parlor. Dr. Means said it was probably his heart, too. Losing Granny Wilcox and all was too much. Didn't suffer at all," Leroy said succinctly. "Now you keep resting. Suffered a shock yourself."

"I'm worried about Nettie. Won't talk to me. Angry all the time after Grandma Wilcox's death, and now with Grandpa Wilcox gone," her sentence broke into sobs. "I was going to have Grandpa Wilcox tell her I was staying her friend, even though Nettie was mad and all. Now who's going to tell her? I can't!" Ruth bawled.

"I'll tell her or someone else will. Maybe Thelma can try. Don't worry, please. Stop crying...or you'll get sick, too," Leroy said with growing agitation. "Please?" his tone turned pleading as he started to shake her. His tone stopped Ruth. Only her sniffling and hiccupping remained. *Plenty of people to tell Nettie.*

ೠ

Ruth wakened to dinner smells with a knitted afghan spread over her. She rolled over. "How's Nettie?" she asked as she sat up quickly and the blanket fell to the floor.

"Just checked on her myself," Lady Dee said as she put a spoon down and closed the lidded pot on the stove. "Dr. Means gave her enough medicine to last till morning. Then, we'll sort things out. Your father and I wanted to speak to you children first, though. Your father's making the funeral arrangements with Elder Brimley as well as helping decide what to do with the Wilcox place. We have to take care of Sylvie and Nettie now." Ruth hadn't even thought about the Wilcox property! There was no grown-up Wilcox to oversee things. *Where would Nettie and Sylvie stay?* All their people were gone.

Lady Dee saw her daughter's agitation and said, "Don't worry about Nettie and Sylvie. They'll be fine, I promise. Wait till your father gets home. We'll have some supper. After that, we'll talk. We'll see about it. Now, how are you, Ruth?" Lady Dee said changing the subject. "Let me feel your head. You feel feverish?"

As she finished, Dr. Yuell came home. "So glad to see you're better, Ruth," Dr. Yuell said as he pressed his cheek into his daughter's hair as he gave her a loving hug. "Finding Grandpa Wilcox must have been so sad and frightening. Nettie's resting and you need to take a rest, too."

"I have. I have," Ruth assured her father as she broke free of his embrace and looked into his warm brown eyes. "Lady Dee said you're working on the plans for Grandpa Wilcox and everyone else." It hurt too much to mention Nettie by name.

"That's right. Sad thing but we'll get it all settled," Dr. Yuell informed.

"Dinner's ready, but it's a tad bit dry being so late and all. Ruth, go call your brother and sister, please," Lady Dee asked as her father gave her another hug and looked at the stove.

"Smells good, Lady Dee. Don't you worry about the time with everything going on right now." Dr. Yuell turned to Ruth and said, "Tell your brother and sister, we're having a family meeting, so don't go too far after the dishes are done."

The late dinner passed in companionable silence. Nettie was sleeping and plans were being made. Ruth chewed on the okra and crowder peas with salt pork, praying her best friend liked the plans.

When the dishes were through, her father called, "Let's get started. Still have to meet with the Browns to take care of the Wilcox garden patch and the poultry. Come on now." The Yuell family members were all settled in a few seconds. "Your mother and I have been talking. Nettie and Sylvie have no kinfolk we know of to care for them as you children know," he continued while scanning their faces. "Their people left them. Can't find them. Have tried several times. So Nettie and Sylvie are alone," he paused again. "What would you think if we took them in *our home* as your sisters and let them both get a new start away from all the deaths?"

Ruth sprung to her father's neck. "Oh, thank you. Thank you! Nettie and Sylvie won't be alone or separated. Thank you!"

"Glad you're pleased with it, Ruth, even though Nettie's been so angry. What about you two?" Dr. Yuell said turning to Leroy and Thelma.

"I was worried they'd be all alone with Nettie trying to be all grown up and angry," Leroy said. "Now they have somewhere to go."

"Sylvie deserves someplace nice," Thelma remarked. "I've been teaching her how to feed the chickens."

"Would have rather had a brother but Nettie and Sylvie need help," Leroy added. "They'll stay in Ruth's room, right?"

"They will. They will." Ruth said as the possibilities of Nettie getting into trouble from taking too much on herself fell away. "I know they will."

"We haven't worked out all the details, but we wanted everyone to think about it first," Lady Dee replied.

"We don't need to think any longer. Sylvie and Nettie can move Grandma and Grandpa Wilcoxes' bed into my room," Ruth offered, not wanting the decision to change. "We can move the dresser onto the landing and we'll have plenty of room."

"We'll take a bed from the Wilcox house," Dr. Yuell said with quiet pride. "If Nettie agrees."

Everyone at the table knew how much Ruth loved the dresser from the time they moved to their new house. But she loved Nettie and Sylvie more.

The family awoke in the darkness to pounding and crying at the door. Dr. Yuell opened it to hear Mrs. Givens's frantic, breathless voice through the doorway. "Nettie's gone. She's gone," she called. "I checked to see if she was still sleeping and the bedding was made up. Went all over the Wilcox place calling for her and thought I'd better come to get you."

"Lady Dee, get me our lantern and get Dr. Means. Leroy. Ruth. Thelma. Get dressed and help me look for Nettie. She's not in her room at Mrs. Givens's."

Dr. Yuell ordered Leroy to check the Wilcox home and barn and Ruth was to go to the pens and garden. "When it's lighter, we'll go to the graves and the funeral parlor. Lady Dee, please call the church and get food started in the kitchen. Mrs. Givens, if Lady Dee has not heard from us in a half hour, tell Reverend Fredericks to start a search party. We'll need coffee, and if the search lasts...call the prayer circle, after its light. Nettie surely needs it."

"Thelma, go sit with Sylvie when she wakes up at Mrs. Givens's," Lady Dee amended. "Seems like it's going to be a long night."

They looked everywhere. With shaking fingers, Ruth lit the barn lantern and raced through the barnyard and pens trailing puffs of smoke and kerosene fumes. Some chickens remained sleeping while she startled others. Didn't matter. Nettie needed finding. Ruth's hot breath disturbed the cool, moist air and her feet were soaked with dew. *Where could Nettie be?*

Ruth walked into Mrs. Givens's bedroom where Nettie had slept. The bed was made real tidy-like while the covers on Mrs. Givens's couch remained unmade. *Had Nettie meant to leave intentionally?* Ruth looked at the well-scarred pine table on the side of the bed. *Had Nettie touched it?* Then, Ruth's eyes caught a whitish glint on the floor. She bent to find a medicine tablet by the bedpost. Then she crouched down to see another lying under the bed almost hidden between the headboard and wall. Mrs. Givens didn't take any medicine and these weren't the aspirin the older woman kept in the cork-topped glass bottle in the kitchen.

Ruth scooped up the tablets and ran to Lady Dee. "Lady Dee? Are these the pills Nettie was supposed to take?"

Lady Dee turned from her task of warming biscuits and said, "Let me see. Where'd you find these?"

"Under Mrs. Givens's bed," Ruth replied.

"Go get her. I'll keep them here." A sad frown got deeper on her mother's brow. Ruth got Mrs. Givens and the older woman agreed the tablets looked like the pills Dr. Means had given to Nettie.

"You mean the child wasn't asleep at all?" Mrs. Givens said desperately.

"Going over to the Wilcox place, Lady Dee," Ruth said urgently as she started for the door.

"Leroy's already been there a second time. What are you going to do, Ruth?" Lady Dee wondered aloud.

"Must see something, but I'll be right back," Ruth called. "Promise."

"Ten minutes," Lady Dee called, "Don't need to worry about where you are, too."

"Yes," Ruth called back sprinting across the yard.

Her heart fell as she saw the telltale floorboard was already loose. Nettie's $12.31 was gone. She went to check Nettie's clothes. Most of the few things she had were gone, too.

Ruth ran back to her family's house. Her throat ached with despair. "Father, she's gone," Ruth cried as desolation mounted in her chest. "Her savings and clothes...gone."

"What?" Dr. Yuell said incredulously. "Where would she go?"

"I don't know," Ruth cried, and then wailed, "I don't know!" Tears of fear and frustration poured from her eyes as she laid her arms and head across the cool tabletop.

"Of course, you don't," Lady Dee consoled as Ruth wetted her mother's dress front with her tears. Dr. Yuell announced it was time for him and Leroy to go to the police station. Ruth cried for Nettie's anger, Sylvie's loss, and for Grandma and Grandpa Wilcox. Now, she added her fear. *Where was Nettie? Where had she gone?*

Ruth's tears flowed through Grandpa Wilcox's funeral service and burial that afternoon. Ruth knew he was in heaven but Ruth couldn't help but think Nettie was alone somewhere here on earth now.

Two deaths in a summer and Mrs. Means gone, too! Everyone wondered at the meaning of it all. Not since the influenza epidemic had so many souls from one family gone to heaven. All Ruth could do was work, cry, and look for Nettie to come back down the street or into the room. She wanted to tell Nettie she was going to become part of the Yuell family. If only Nettie had waited.

CHAPTER SIX

The next day Ruth moped around the house, thinking every noise was Nettie as she raced to the office and kitchen several times. When she couldn't think of anything else to do, Ruth went over to the Wilcox house and sat there. Then she walked to the barn to see the poor chickens. They were alone now, too. The thought hit Ruth with blinding clarity as she planned to sit in the Wilcox house once more. The barn. The music. Albert Fowler. With an energy she didn't think she had, Ruth knew she needed to run to the school. Lady Dee saw her daughter race past the kitchen and followed her. "I've got to look at the school." Her legs started pumping as she ran. "Call Albert Fowler. Call Albert Fowler," Ruth shouted. "I've got to look for the trumpet!"

"What are you talking about and what do you know about the Fowler situation?" Lady Dee called, looking at her daughter with concentrated concern. "Have you been listening in on adult conversations? Come here, child."

Now it was Ruth's turn to look confused. As she stopped and loped a few steps in her mother's direction, she replied. "No, Lady Dee. I'm not a gossip."

"Fine. I believe you. Now come in the house and we'll get to the bottom of this," was all her mother said as they headed back to the house. "I'll let you and Leroy go to the school after we've had a talk with your father."

The Yuells and their children sat at the dining table. "Just wanted you children to know Sylvie's resting. We haven't been able to tell her about anything yet."

Ruth thought of Grandma and Grandpa Wilcox and Nettie. "Now what's this about Albert Fowler, Ruth?"

"Perhaps I should start by telling you something Mrs. Fowler told me in *strict* confidence," Lady Dee said with a grave expression. "This is adult information but these are special circumstances."

"Understood?" Dr. Yuell asked. He looked at each of his children, in turn, as each solemnly nodded.

"Albert and his father have had many disagreements about his interest in music," Lady Dee began. "He was unaware Albert was involved in the music practice at the Wilcox barn."

"A few nights ago, he found a jazz record collection under his son's bed," Dr. Yuell stated.

Leroy's eyes were big and incredulous. "Brother Fowler's always said in church that kind of music is the devil's music!"

Dr. Yuell did not directly respond to Leroy's statement. "There was a bloody argument."

"You mean they fought?" Thelma cried.

Dr. Yuell did not answer. "Albert has not been seen since and he might have wanted medical attention."

"That's why I wanted to go to the school," Ruth exclaimed. "Nettie changed even before Grandma Wilcox died. She talked of Albert and his music, so I wanted to check to see if the trumpet was still in the school band room. I think that Albert and Nettie are together."

"Trumpet?" Lady Dee cried. "What do you mean?"

Ruth sputtered before words came out, still trying to explain to Lady Dee and her father about her suspicions. "Nettie had a crush on Albert. Said she was saving her $12.31 to give him for a trumpet. If she's going to leave with Albert, perhaps she'll go for the trumpet. That's how we can find her."

Lady Dee seemed to understand now. "Take Leroy with you. We'll try to get a wider search going! I'm calling the Fowlers."

Ruth hadn't felt relief like this since they'd found Nettie was gone. Nettie was either between here and Albert or trying to get the trumpet. She'd be home soon. Ruth ran with Leroy all the way to the school stairs. The trumpet had to be there.

"Ruth. It's gone," Leroy said flatly. "The trumpets were in three brown cases with black trim and brass edges. Now there are only two."

"Perhaps one of the other students took one of them home," Ruth said, grasping for excuses.

Leroy looked into his sister's desperate eyes, saying nothing.

There was bad news at home as well. "Albert's gone," Lady Dee said glumly. "Left some time during the night. There's a note saying something about trumpet-playing and Nettie being with him." Ruth's heart sank again. At least Nettie was safe. Now there was Albert to think of, too. "Albert and Nettie are very angry at everyone." Lady Dee added, "I'm sure they're just upset. Nettie and Albert will be found. Let's have some lemonade. All we can do is pray and wait."

Dear Lord, maybe Nettie's deep losses were embalmed now. "Pickled" Nettie called it, Ruth remembered with little humor. *Maybe Nettie was trading her anger and heartache for a dream and adventure she was sharing with Albert, her trumpet-playing beau.* Ruth was happy for her but the Yuell family would have to pick up the rest of the pieces.

EMERGENCY ROOM AT 1:55 P.M.
CHICAGO – 1967

"Nettie never returned to St. Louis" Norma said sadly.

"Lady Dee, Father, Thelma, and Leroy were almost as sad as I was. I missed her whirling-dervish personality," Ruth confided, shaking her head. "The neighborhood seemed bland without her."

ST. LOUIS – 1952

The question of who was going to pay for the trumpet and the disappearance of Nettie and Albert were the first of many neighborhood questions passing through the front parlor of the Means home, with Mrs. Blaine and her two nieces in residence. Three afternoons a week, Mrs. Blaine started inviting prominent ladies in the community...and prominent gossips to eat homemade bakery goods while sipping from the tea service that came with all their belongings, lock, stock, and barrel from Detroit. "Things are certainly different here than they are in Detroit," Mrs. Blaine would say at least once every tea hour, according to those present. Usually this phrase punctuated a disapproving stance on some topic or another. Nettie, Albert, and the Yuells, by their association with the Wilcox family, in particular, were stained by the parlor gossip. With the added flames of Mrs. Blaine's tea parties, the Yuell family could only hope another scandal would head Mrs. Blaine and Calli in another direction.

Meggie Winston came over one afternoon to talk to Ruth and Thelma. "It's very hard coming to a new place." Meggie's statement reminded Ruth of the time when they moved from the Archer Street house and how alone Ruth felt. "Our aunt is having a hard time adjusting. She needs lots of company." Ruth hoped Meggie's verbal olive branch wouldn't make Thelma snort in an unladylike manner, but it seemed to Ruth the recipients of Meggie's aunt's malice were the ones to feel sorry for—not Mrs. Blaine herself.

"Calli and I have no place else to go, so we have to tolerate her while she adjusts," Meggie continued. "It might be a continual thing."

So Meggie was coming over, trying to make amends, and offer friendship? Ruth wondered how she should respond. "I remember feeling lost when we moved into this house almost nine years ago." She bit her lip. "Friends should be kind and say truthful things, don't you think?"

Meggie looked down at her lap and said, "That's what our dear departed father always taught us and I try to do that myself and not to judge others."

Thelma interrupted, impatient to see what point Meggie was trying to make. "So you don't like gossip but you can't do much about it?"

Meggie accepted this frontal assault in the conversation. "Yes," she replied softly.

"Then, we can be friends," Ruth replied hesitantly. "No matter what people may say."

"Thank you so much," Meggie said with a shy smile, looking into Ruth's eyes. Ruth realized she didn't think she'd ever seen Meggie smile before.

"Will you stay and help us with something?" Ruth asked impulsively.

"I will if I can," Meggie replied tentatively, trying to keep her tone light and still her shaking hands by putting them tight against her sides.

"Can you draw?" Thelma asked bluntly. "I can only do stick figures and Ruth's not much better."

"We're trying to make a book for Sylvie," Ruth began. "Her favorite book is *The Three Pigs* but with her grandparents dying and her sister...being away for..." Ruth didn't know what else to say. "She keeps asking about them, of course...and fretting, so we thought something like this might help ease her mind."

"What we need are some pictures to go along with the story we'll put in the back of Sylvie's *Three Pigs* book," Thelma said. "We've gotten the story approved by our parents. Basically, after the wolf leaves the brick house alone to the celebrating pigs, we're going to talk about another pig family. Just like in Sylvie's family, the Grandpa and Grandma pig go to heaven and the sister pig goes on an important visit over the hill. Then, neighbor pigs with parents and three piglets, just like us, want Sylvie to come and stay with them."

"I think we should put a few sentences in block letters on each page," Ruth offered. "We'll cut them the size of Sylvie's book."

"So you'd want a picture of two more houses matching the size and color of the book?" Meggie asked. "Then, we have to have a picture about the four pigs in the one house and with five pigs in another."

"You catch on fast," Thelma stated. "We've got some colored pencils here."

"Let me take a look at the book," Meggie asked. "If I can't do the job free-hand, maybe I'll be able to trace some things that might do."

"That's a good idea," Thelma said.

Lady Dee came into the kitchen. "Would you all like some sugar cookies and something to drink?"

"Thank you, Mrs. Yuell. I would really like that," Meggie said, smiling again. Ruth noticed Meggie's hands weren't shaking anymore.

Ruth looked at Meggie and then her mother. She really liked Meggie's smile.

❦

The last days of summer were bittersweet. More bitter than sweet because everything seemed to remind Ruth of Nettie and the glorious times she'd spent with her. Ruth had gone to the cemetery. All she found were the fresh mounds that held the Wilcox family graves.

Ruth couldn't help it but she still looked at every person of Nettie and Albert's age and size and got a bubble of excitement in her throat if she spied a couple fitting their description.

There were some small blessings. Sylvie was living with them and she seemed more comfortable every passing day, especially with the book additions she, Thelma, and Meggie had made to explain what had happened to Sylvie's grandparents and Nettie.

Sylvie was sleeping in Ruth's room now. *Nettie should be sleeping here, too!* With the three of them holding each other dearly and sharing sweet reminiscences in the bedroom rather than only Ruth reading fairy tales to Sylvie and tucking her into bed.

She'd have to begin again, Ruth knew, and finding Meggie in the midst of all the pain had helped, even though Meggie's waspish sister pretended to be sick half of the time and snubbed Ruth every chance she got. Mrs. Blaine would have put her fisheye on Meggie and Ruth's friendship if Dr. Means hadn't warned her off. No, Ruth didn't want any summers like this one again, please Lord! Ruth desperately prayed for the clouds to pass. *Let the sun shine again, Lord!*

"Do you think I can buy my pencils and paper tomorrow for school?" Ruth asked, helping her mother in the kitchen with the last of the dinner preparations. Dr. Means, Mrs. Blaine, Meggie, and Calli were coming as well.

"Wondered when you'd start asking about activities at school again," Lady Dee said as she turned her head and smiled.

"Can I invite Meggie and Calli to lunch if everything goes well at dinner tonight?" Ruth suddenly realized she'd missed feeling contentment for a long time. Seemed like forever.

Dr. Yuell looked at his daughter a bit overlong with apprehension. So much gossip coming out of the Means home added to the sorrow of Ruth's best friend running away. "Are you feeling all right, Ruth?"

All she could do, at that moment, was try to signal him with a reassuring look, a wide, happy smile, and a big hug in return for his comforting embrace. "I want to make the Winston girls feel more at home here," Ruth smiled, "but mother says always to ask you, first!"

"Please listen to me," she started earnestly. "I can tell you all, I'm not bringing the Wilcox sadness here anymore. I want Nettie found and she's welcome here if that's still fine with you." She took a deep breath, trying to find the right words. "But more than anything I want to be happy again. Missed it more than I even knew." Ruth stopped and squeezed her brother's hand tightly. "But I don't want to ruin our peace anymore," Ruth stated as she pointed around the room, "... or I'll make you sleep on a lumpy ticking bed!" Peals of laughter could be heard jingling down the street. They all laughed and the tension fell like a silent tree.

"What's all this I hear? Such gaiety in the early evening!" Dr. Means teased as he walked the last few steps through the door. He had his sister, Mrs. Blaine, and the nieces in tow. "What frivolity have you started, Dr. Yuell?"

"Just the usual," Dr. Yuell quickly quipped. "I am renowned for my edifying and therapeutic atmosphere, wherever I go." Mrs. Blaine and Calli stayed quiet and looked like they'd each just swallowed a lemon.

"Can I join in?" Meggie asked as she, too, came through the door. Her aunt and sister did not look pleased.

"Why, of course, Meggie," Lady Dee said as she went to the kitchen. "We're just putting some old business to rest. Miss Ruth says we're going to have to sleep on old ticking beds if we dare to spoil the good times she wants us all to have in the future." Catching the message of Ruth wanting them all to go on.

"Are you sure, Ruth?" Meggie asked hesitantly.

"We can," was all Ruth could think to say and not burst the bubble of good feelings they hadn't had as a family for a long time. "I'm hungry, are you?"

"That's good. That's good," Dr. Yuell said. "Got mounds and mounds of food. Much more than any one family could eat. So let's say table blessing and get to it," he suggested as he ushered them into the dining room.

"Very nice, although our rooms were bigger in Detroit," Mrs. Blaine noted.

"When I get the new draperies done, it will be nicer," Lady Dee confided into Ruth's ear, "but I haven't had time yet."

"This is all just fine," Dr. Means said. "All looks fresh and new to my eye."

"With several of our youngsters going to college soon," Dr. Yuell offered. "We have to think of other things than curtains."

"We've gotten all the extra work we can, father," Thelma said with a laugh. "Won't have any time to put our heads on those ticking beds if we try to get any more."

"Perhaps we could live above the garage and rent the house out!" Leroy hooted.

"Have you been raised to live above a garage, sir?" Mrs. Blaine asked pointedly. "That really what you want, young man?"

"What do you want me to say, father?" Leroy replied in confusion. "I was only joking, Mrs. Blaine,"

"Nothing, son. I think Mrs. Blaine misunderstood our family humor," Dr. Yuell replied, his brown eyes losing some of their warmth." He stopped for a moment. "We're trying...to do the best we can, committed to God, family, justice, and equality. The money and some of the things it buys doesn't matter."

"I'll raise my glass to that," Dr. Means said.

"Yes," Meggie agreed.

It was only then Ruth noticed Calli hadn't spoken. The girl's handkerchief was almost torn from the pressure of her hands. Calli got up from the table. "If you'll excuse me I think I need to go home because I'm not feeling well." She looked at Mrs. Blaine. "Will you come with me?"

Mrs. Blaine looked around the table with cold eyes and said in a brittle voice. "Certainly." Both headed for the door. "Please keep your seats. We'll see ourselves out."

"I'll stay here, Eleanor," Dr. Means replied sternly. "Seems like Calli has these unlikely spells like you had when you were a child," was all he said as he looked down at his plate. He seemed displeased by the memory. "I hope these don't continue." He cleared his throat and attempted to smile at the Yuell family. "Now where were we in the conversation?"

❦

Mrs. Blaine got her spite. There were persistent rumors the next few weeks about the financial state of affairs in the Yuell household and talk about their home being put up for rent. Ruth knew the information came directly from two of the three female occupants of the Means home but she didn't want to offend Meggie by saying so.

Ruth was glad not to have to renounce the speculation in front of Meggie. She only wished Meggie's sister, Calli, and her aunt could feel good about themselves and their community without having to make others look and feel bad.

"No getting around it," Dr. Yuell replied. "Thurgood's having a deuce of a time trying to corral Eleanor's tongue." He shook his head. "Wouldn't be so difficult if she and Calli hadn't seemed to take an instant dislike to us, it seems."

"I think we'll weather that storm just fine," Lady Dee said. "But it does weigh things down a bit when that woman and her niece put themselves so free to make nasty and cutting remarks."

"Thurgood's apologized many times, but he does need someone to take care of his home and manage his household," Dr. Yuell replied.

"I could have thought of a thousand other candidates," Lady Dee said as she turned off the kitchen lights.

Lady Dee had heard of the goings-on in Dr. Means's house. She didn't want to insult Dr. Means. But neither she nor her husband approved of the streams of gossip that flowed as freely as the tea. Both knew the Yuells were favorite targets of inquiry.

From what the Yuells had heard, Mrs. Blaine seemed to hold court and want only to dispense or mold the neighborhood gossip towards her way of thinking, while sipping or offering her herbal potions to Calli. To deaden the sting of her oftentimes venomous remarks regarding people and situations, Mrs. Blaine's habit involved speaking in the first person. "Mrs. Blaine would never allow such activity if she knew about it."

Another tactic was to take some current situation of which everyone was aware and describe it as if it were a story or fable. What really hurt was when Mrs. Blaine started speaking about the Wilcox family and Nettie. "It is such a sad time when family members flee their homes for disobeying their elders. I do believe someone should ask Pastor Fredericks to mention this topic in his future sermons from the pulpit so this does not occur in our neighborhood anymore. Such things blight our community and show poor character," Mrs. Blaine sniffed into her white lace hankie to a chorus of approving head nods and murmurs from her audience. "People condoning such behavior should be banned from our circle."

❧

EMERGENCY ROOM AT 2:20 P.M.
CHICAGO – 1967

"The Yuells tried to stay on the less sharp side of Mrs. Blaine's tongue but she never had a good word to say about us and always put our actions in a negative light," Ruth said.

"Why didn't you fight back?" Norma asked. "Mrs. Blaine and Calli were both shrews!"

Ruth tried to think of how to explain. "First of all, Dr. Means was my father's partner and Dr. Means talked till he was breathless, trying to get Mrs. Blaine to stop. Father and Lady Dee didn't want to demean themselves by entering into the gossip. They spoke the truth as they knew it, trying to meet wave upon wave of speculation regarding our family. Gossip doesn't survive on honesty; it runs on innuendo and salacious rumors pasted together with half-truths."

"How did things keep on going?" Norma made sure she had the time frame correct.

"I think my summer outing continued Mrs. Blaine's long-term career in speculating about our family: the drive I took with the Carters when I was in high school."

"That's the story about Stella and Eddie Carter?" Norma asked, her journalist's mind kicking in to make sure she was thinking of the correct anecdote.

"Yes."

∞

ST LOUIS – 1955

Ruth's afternoon excursion, a few days later, started out innocently enough. Stella and Eddie Carter had been married for two years and saved up enough money for a shiny, low-mileage used car. With the Yuells' permission, they drove Ruth and Dr. Deal's grandson, Orlie, out to the country on a Sunday afternoon. Both Orlie's and Ruth's fathers, as a dentist and a physician, respectively, had been working in the community for years and all the families knew each other well. Stella was past seven months pregnant but both Dr. Means and Dr. Yuell said everything was fine with both mother and baby-in-waiting. "This might be my last outing, so we'll make a day of it with a picnic down on my Aunt Ruth Ellen and Uncle Roy's farm. Please come along."

The sunshine had been bright with cool breezes. They'd walked around Stella's uncle's acreage and watched a new foal dance around the paddock and back-and-forth between the mare's legs while Eddie and Orlie helped to fix a rotted fence post. "You tired, Stella?" Eddie asked after the men washed up.

"Not tired enough not to eat another piece of Auntie's pie," Stella said with a laughing smile. "Then we'll give you the opportunity to drive the car on the roads here, Ruthie. All modern women need to know how to drive."

"Well, after the dishes are done, that's what we'll do before heading home," her husband replied after he kissed Stella's forehead.

Ruth enjoyed driving the sedan. It seemed like a battleship rather than a car as she tried to steer the green and silver beast. She drove carefully and seemed to use the brake more than the accelerator, praying she wouldn't damage the beautiful car. Orlie tried, too, with more bravery and flair than Ruth did but he'd been learning on his father's sedan back in the city.

The trip back to town started uneventfully until Eddie pulled the car over. "Think we're working on a flat. Walk over across the road there and sit in the shade. We'll only be a few minutes. I checked the spare before we left."

Ruth and Stella headed for the shade of the mature elm trees in a small grove bordering some cornfields. Ruth unfurled the picnic blanket so Stella could sit down. "We'll just rest over here," Ruth called to let Eddie know Stella was cared for.

Metal sounds clattered from the car trunk and ground near the car. Orlie helped Eddie put the car jack on the rutted gravel shoulder of the country road, putting the jack base on a solid footing as Eddie lifted the long metal brace from the trunk. Ruth didn't know if any of them saw the police car until the siren blared, startling them all. Ruth saw Orlie accidentally kick over the jack base. Eddie stood up and turned toward the sound.

"Hey, you there," the burly red-haired man shouted. Ruth squinted against the sun to see the khaki-uniformed man with the nightstick holster on one side and what appeared to be a gun on his other hip. "You got a weapon?"

At that, Ruth heard the thud of the tire iron brace hit the car fender and then the ground. Orlie kicked the jack base yet again as he moved to face the sheriff. "No, no," Eddie replied, making palms-up gestures with his hands in a side-to-side motion. "Just a flat tire. See." He pointed to the pancake-flat black rubber, now totally squashed against the tire rim and the dirt.

"Can't be too sure," the sheriff said. "I'm coming over there. Stay where you are."

At that, Ruth felt Stella's muscles move as if she were going to rise. Ruth's arms reflexively strengthened to keep Stella seated but Stella's body shifted from her grasp and she was on her knees and palms. The sight of her and Ruth must have come into the sheriff's peripheral vision because he reflexively reached for his holster while swiveling around.

Eddie's eyes widened and he lunged for the officer's body. "Don't! Don't!" he cried in rapid succession, hitting the sheriff's arm and forcing him to the ground. "She's pregnant!" he cried even louder, though all his energy was directed toward the lawman and his gun.

A loud gun crack erupted from the large black handgun. Ruth thought she heard the whistle of the bullet as it nipped off several of the tree leaves and buried itself into a low-lying beefy tree branch. Somehow, Ruth was on her side with her arms reaching for Stella. Stella in all the commotion had continued her rise to standing position but then fell over to her side as her body reacted to the threat of seeing the gun. Ruth's first reaction was to look at the scuffle on the other side of the road. Eddie, Orlie, and the sheriff were all dusty and bedraggled. Eddie had the gun and was pointing it to the ground and imploring the sheriff with his left hand, "My wife's pregnant and I thought you were going to shoot her and our friend, Ruth."

Orlie was between the sheriff and Eddie, holding the dirt-smeared arms of the short burly man. It seemed to Ruth like the man could overpower Orlie at any time. Perhaps he was wary without his gun.

"Stella, you all right?" Eddie called, his eyes not leaving the face of the sheriff.

Stella didn't answer. Ruth noticed her pregnant friend was on her side, holding her stomach. Ruth answered instead. *What should she say?* "Just stumbled a little in the commotion, I think."

"Put the gun down, boy. Before there's any more trouble," the sheriff said. His muscles appeared to tense and he moved to pull himself from Orlie's grasp.

"Here's what I'll do," Eddie offered, bending his left wrist and showing his palm. "I'll put the gun in the dirt and Orlie and I will go to the front of the car. All the tire-changing things are in the back. You go get your gun. We'll brush ourselves off, and then I'll go see to my wife." Eddie walked about ten feet, put the gun on the fringe of the grass and walked toward the front of the car. Orlie put his arms down and moved to the front of the car.

The sheriff scrambled faster than she thought any man of his size and stout gut could move, snatching the gun from the ground. He turned, pointing the gun at Eddie and Orlie. Ruth thought the man might shoot them. "You ain't going nowhere. Down on the ground, both of you!" He extended his gun-toting arm fully. "Now!" Sun glinted on the beads of sweat on his forehead. All his blood seemed to be in his face.

Stella still hadn't moved but she was moaning a bit. Would there be another errant bullet coming their way if she moved too quickly? "Stella?" she whispered. "Are you OK?" Ruth really couldn't tell because her friend's body ripe with her baby was facing the road. Ruth could only see her back and a bit of Stella's left collarbone. She looked at her friends across the road and the sheriff. She carefully crawled; pushing her knees close to Stella's back and looked over to see if her friend was injured. Stella looked like she was sleeping. Ruth bent a bit and cupped Stella's cheek. Her grasp became wet with blood. Ruth whimpered, wondering what to do. Eddie needed to know Stella was injured.

Ruth took a breath to call out when she saw the sheriff roughly push Eddie into the sheriff's car. When had the sheriff put handcuffs on them? Was that blood on his lip, she wondered or was she just seeing things? "Hey," she called out. "We need help."

Only the sheriff was there to look at her now. His pants were still dusty and one pant cuff was stuck above his white cotton sock. His eyes seemed beady but Ruth couldn't make out the color. "Send someone for you later." Ruth could hear Eddie's muffled pleadings in the back of the car to see his wife. The sheriff stuck his head down and looked into the glass. "Any more from either of you and you'll be getting a gag to shut your pie holes up or worse!"

"We need help!" Ruth exclaimed again trying to make the sheriff understand. The man just lifted his arm still holding the gun and shook his head. Eddie turned and craned his neck into the space by the back window. Tears fell onto his dusty and bloodied cheeks as they sped away.

❦

Ruth alternated between watching over Stella and trying to find a vehicle or anyone who could help them. Ruth kept Stella on her side, covered with the other picnic blanket, keeping her safe in the shade. After each unsuccessful attempt to look up and down the road or flag down the one truck and one car since the incident, she'd drop down to her knees and gently try to rouse her unconscious friend. Stella had only opened her eyes once. Ruth knew that wasn't good but she felt blessed when her friend opened her eyes like she was waking in sleep and smiled, then just as quickly closed them as if she were taking an extra Saturday morning rest and wanted to continue a pleasant dream. Ruth ripped her full slip from under her dress for a pillow for Stella's head and then retreated to the cover of the elm trees to take the rest of the ruined slip from her shoulders.

Ruth talked out loud to herself and the changing numbers of birds looking down from them in the trees. "Find some water! Find some water!" Ruth rubbed her shoulders and headed for the cornfield, wadding the slip material in her fist. The area was full of low weeds and ruts. Ruth spied a rusting barrel with a few drops of water left on its shaded lid. She swiped at it and looked to see that the water was clear on the white cotton material with a few pieces of bark she picked away with her fingers. Heading back to Stella, Ruth saw what looked like a wagon coming down the road. Water forgotten, Ruth waved the white cotton into the air. "Help! Help!" she called, running and waving the slip. An elderly black man with thick white hair under a battered straw hat and an even whiter beard pulled up on the reins of his two-horse wagon. "We've had an accident and my pregnant friend is unconscious."

The man looked serious and alarmed, saying nothing as he tied the reins to the brake. "Unconscious, you say?"

"There's an inch-long gash on her temple and it's swelling," Ruth said as if she was reporting to a physician like her father or Dr. Means.

"You out here alone?" the man asked. "We've got to get her to Mrs. Bailey."

"She's a nurse?" Ruth asked.

"No, she's a midwife and takes care of other things, including the sick stock when Mr. Beatty isn't around." Ruth's hands moved to put the moistened slip remnant on her friend's wound. She didn't want to rub the skin and start the slug-gish red flow to start freshly bleeding again. "We'll put her in this old blanket like a sling."

They rolled Stella onto the blanket as gently as they could. "I'll put knots in the ends so we don't lose our grip," Ruth offered.

"I'll climb into the back," the man said. "Then I'll hoist her head and the top part of the blanket on the count of three." Ruth didn't want the severe height of having to get Stella's unconscious body in the wagon bed but there wasn't any choice with the car keys gone and the tire out of commission. Stella was placed as gently as they could manage.

"It's about a mile from here and a block off the road," the man said wiping his brow. "By the way, my name is George and I live about another two miles in the other direction." George looked at the rumps of his two old horses. "You just hop up next to your friend and we'll get her to Mrs. Bailey."

"Just wait a second. I have to leave a note for her husband," Ruth called as she sped to the car. George deserved answers but she'd have time to answer all of his questions as long as he looked at the road and made his elderly team move as fast as they had in them. She scrawled the directions to Mrs. Bailey's house on last week's church bulletin from her purse and weighed it with a rock by the abandoned picnic basket.

☯☯

Ruth sat in the oil lamplight after washing the afterbirth and blood from her hands. She wanted to scream and cry and scream some more. As soon as the three of them carried Stella into the single-room farm shack's corner cot, the midwife announced, "She's in labor." For the next five hours, Stella's body tried to give birth and succeeded. The baby girl was dead.

Mrs. Bailey just shook her head. "About the mother. She's bleeding into her abdomen. All hard and black and blue." Her eyes misted even though she'd seen so many births and deaths. "Her people close?"

How could Ruth explain? Stella's husband was either in jail, at the worst, or flying around the countryside looking for them, at the best. The nearest relations were Stella's aunt and uncle on the farm southwest of here.

Mrs. Bailey wrote everything down. "Grady will go to the Smith place and use their phone. The Ellis place you say?"

Ruth nodded her head. If she talked more than a few words she'd cry for a long time and she couldn't waste the time with that now. "I'll go sit with her."

Stella died two hours later. Ruth and Mrs. Bailey got though washing her and her baby girl, swaddling the baby and putting her in her mother's arms.

The door flew open. Eddie was wide-eyed and looked as if he'd been shoveling coal in his picnic clothes. "Where is she?"

"Eddie," Ruth whispered. Huge tears broke the bounds of her eyelashes. Her look and the two soft syllables of his name must have screamed the truth. Eddie's hand shook as he raised it to rub his head while he turned toward the only other door in the tiny house.

"The baby?" he whispered. A lump so big came to Ruth's throat she felt she couldn't breathe. Stella and the baby were bathed in the stillness of death and lamplight. A deep groan and grief-panting filled Eddie's bass voice. The manly keen continued as Orlie burst through the door.

"Is she...?" Orlie said, more in a wish than for the truth.

Ruth shook her head, thinking she'd become mute, for sure and forever. She pressed air against her vocal cords praying she could say something from her stiff lips. "You...you stay with him while I get a wagon to drive to a phone. Neither of you can be seen on the road in this township ever again."

❦

EMERGENCY ROOM AT 2:40 P.M.
CHICAGO – 1967

"You want to stop for a rest?" Norma asked, pre-offering several tissues to Ruth as channels of tears fell from her friend's eyes. Norma's eyes were misting as well.

"Don't mind the tears. They just come with the story," Ruth replied as she gave Norma a thin smile of thanks and wiped her eyes and cheeks. "I want to keep going." She looked down at the notebook. "Still in high school and there's a long way to go."

Norma only signaled with a nod. She wiped her tears away with her hands and picked up her pad, ready to take more notes.

"The aftermath was hurtful far beyond the mourning period." Ruth stopped, trying to find the right words. "I'm a strong woman, raised never to speak ill of people, but I must say Mrs. Blaine was a spiteful woman with no cause. She never lost an opportunity to bring up the Carters' tragic story to put me in a bad light, it seemed. Father would talk to Dr. Means, and she'd stop for a time, but her ill will would come back like a bur under a saddle blanket, especially after the St. James family came to town. Think it all got started when Leroy and I were invited to Alice St. James's birthday party."

❦

ST. LOUIS – 1955

During an evening conversation, Dr. Yuell announced without preamble, "Got good news, dear. A renowned lawyer is moving into the neighborhood next week. He wants to get his younger children settled before school starts." Dr. Yuell recalled the name. "The St. James family."

The St. James family moved from Washington, DC, about the same time Sylvie moved into the Yuell home.

Meggie came over to share her excitement. "I have to tell you," she whispered. "Auntie and Calli are jealous as fire to know every detail about the St. James family coming to town."

"The who?" Ruth asked before she remembered her father mentioning the name.

"Mr. St. James is a lawyer and Mrs. St. James is a retired opera singer. Mrs. St. James toured many places. Can you believe she even went to Europe to sing?" The couple had three children: Devon was almost twenty, Alice was nearing eleven, and Cherie was a precocious age six.

"Just stay away from the older boy if you know what's good for you," Meggie said. "Calli's got her eye on him, even thought she hasn't even seen him yet."

"Thanks for the warning," Ruth replied. Ruth sat under a cloud of Mrs. Blaine's judgment about being with the Carters when Stella and her baby had died. Ruth feared the continued problems would affect her father's partnership with Dr. Means. Besides, Calli was as boy-crazy as Nettie, and Ruth knew where that had led her dear friend.

"Lady Dee. Do you know anything about our new neighbors?" Meggie asked as Lady Dee came to say hello.

"I met Mr. and Mrs. St. James yesterday when they came to deliver the family medical records to the office," Lady Dee confided.

Mrs. St. James had a touch of scarlet fever after her third child. Her doctor in Washington, DC, told her the rigors of traveling were too much, so she and her family settled down here in St. Louis in order to help with court cases here and in the South.

Lady Dee pulled open the oven door to look at the dinner cornbread. "They've invited Ruth and Leroy to come to their home for introductions and Alice St. James's birthday party tomorrow."

"I better not tell Auntie and Calli," Meggie whispered. "They wanted to be invited first!"

❧❧

The St. James family now owned the grandest house in the neighborhood: a huge gable-and-turreted structure with new grass-green clapboards, burnt brown trim, and windows topped with diamond panes in leaded glass. The front cement staircase only needed a red carpet for royalty to descend regally down its steps.

"A beautiful red roadster is driving to the front of the house," Leroy noted as they walked to the door.

Ruth now saw the car and driver: a tall, handsome young man dressed in suit-quality dark beige dress slacks and a cream-colored sweater over his white dress shirt, looking to all the world like a menswear advertisement. It was Devon St. James. He introduced himself and squired them on their first informal visit to the St. James home.

"Let me show you around, but mind the gift boxes," he said as he loped up the stairs and opened the door. "This is Leticia, our housekeeper." Devon called over his shoulder. "Sorry, I'm late, Letty," he smiled with more mirth than penitence to the thin, gray-haired woman. "And these bundles, coming too noisily down the stairs, are my sisters. Quiet now," he changed his tone to an admonishing whisper but neither of the girls looked penitent, though they did quiet their steps. They looked excited to see Ruth.

"Ladies, may I present," he started regally, "Ruth Yuell and Leroy Yuell. This is Mrs. Leticia McCloud, who runs this house like a major general." Devon gave the gray-haired, middle-aged lady a kiss on her head. "She's been with mother since she started her music career and stayed to manage us all as time went on. This is my sister Alice, who wants to be eleven already, although it's still four days away," he continued as Alice curtseyed, "and Cherie."

Cherie attempted a wobbly curtsey and jumped toward Ruth, "I'm almost seven. Will you play with us?"

A bit taken aback by the question, Ruth replied, "I'll do whatever your parents allow and playing with you sounds wonderful."

"Oh, good. I want to show you my dollhouse," Cherie announced. Cherie grabbed Ruth's hand and swept her toward the carpeted staircase. The cream and gilded wainscoting and carved stair railing caught Ruth's attention as her other hand was grabbed enthusiastically by Alice. "You're not going to make her play right now, are you?"

"Go ahead. Go ahead," Devon called.

"Go ahead, children. Miss Ruth has agreed to play, although she's a young lady, not a child. Just stay quiet and let your mother rest." Miss Leticia smiled up at the three girls, and then to Devon. "Devon's going to show Master Leroy the car."

"Father wanted us to have a nanny but mother wouldn't let him. Said she didn't have the strength to have another person living in the house with us and Leticia." Cherie continued her rushed movements down the hallway and through a door. "After Grandmother St. James went to heaven two months ago, it's been lonely. But then mother said we would make so many friends here in St. Louis, we wouldn't be lonely for long."

"Since I'm almost grown, I wouldn't play with dolls unless you'd like to do it," Alice said softly.

"I'd love to look at all the rooms in the dollhouse," Ruth replied truthfully. It was finer than anything she had seen since the storefront Christmas displays downtown. A tall, ramrod-straight gentleman walked into the room.

"Daddy!" Cherie cried. "Miss Ruth Yuell has come to visit and she likes my dollhouse."

"A pleasure, Miss Yuell," he spoke with a cultured, clipped speaking voice. "I'm Alexander St. James."

"He's a lawyer," Cherie informed.

He fondly looked over their heads to smile at Ruth. "That's correct. I'm a lawyer and I'll be working on some community and state projects with the help of your father." He cocked his arm and looked at his gold wristwatch. "I must leave you pumpkins for a moment. It's time for your mother to get ready." He then looked at Ruth and smiled, "You'll be meeting my wife in a few moments."

All the St. James family seemed to love to entertain as much as her own family and Ruth hoped she'd be a frequent recipient of the family's generous hospitality.

"It says here there are language and artistic qualities required in polite society," Alice recited as she looked among the English books retrieved from the bookcase in the library. "It says proper English young ladies were taught French, Latin, drawing, needlework, and manners, if I understand the books correctly." As Ruth listened to Alice's recitation, Ruth knew she'd learned manners from all the Negro gentlewomen at their church and guild gatherings. The Yuell family might not have had all of the pieces of forks, knives, spoons, and glassware in their cupboards but they knew how to place them, and when to use them. *Bet the St. Jameses had them all and then some!*

As far as languages were concerned, Ruth had learned French from Lady Dee and some Latin, Greek and German from her father's medical studies. Leroy and Ruth knew many Bible words and their meanings in these foreign languages, including verbs, adverbs, and adjectives.

About the needlework aspect, Ruth had learned to sew well and make most of her clothes. Lady Dee and her church sewing circle friends also taught her how to crochet but Nettie had been too restless to learn. Ruth felt a momentary pang as she thought Nettie missed the chance to be her sister and wondered what she would have said about all this grandeur. Cherie's exuberance reminded Ruth of Nettie. *Where was Nettie now?* Ruth prayed she was safe. She and Nettie had been like sisters except without the same blood. Ruth shooed the thought away as she saw the stunningly beautiful Mrs. St. James. Devon introduced them.

"Miss Ruth. This is my mother, Regine St. James." Ruth looked up to take the woman's pre-offered pink, manicured hand, bangled with bracelets. Her multi-chained and pearl-necklaced bodice came forward to softly brush the younger girl's extended arm. Mrs. St. James's grip was gentle. The woman seemed gracious, charming, and cultured, all at once; not like some packaged doll to just look at and dust on the shelf. Truly kind and approachable. *What an interesting first meeting with all these new people.*

"Your dear father, the doctor, is such a delight! It's wonderful for you to come over and meet the girls. They look as if they agree with my enthusiasm. We will enjoy music and laughing together. Your father has mentioned how much you love it!" Mrs. St. James exclaimed. "I've missed my music but my heart needs rest now and then. Bah, I say. I will rest but I won't stop singing. So you and my girls will have to carry on a younger St. James music tradition." Ruth was confused. It sounded to Ruth like she was doing the St. Jameses a favor.

"Your father says you speak some French and even Latin. That's wonderful. The girls will have such fun with you. You'll have to try your hand at needle-point," Mrs. St. James offered with the same fervor. "We'll talk of travel and politics and court cases. White America has to stop being held by the guilt of slavery. It demeans them and makes them hateful, but Alexander is working on all that. Aren't you, dear?"

"Working on what, pet?" her husband said as he stepped to take her hand.

"The Flipper case, for one, Alexander?"

"That's a hard one especially since his death in 1940. He tried to clear his own good name. It's because of the military courts. They have their own ways. Crying shame to strip a man of his commission; the very *first* Negro commission from West Point, mind you. Trumped up charges of embezzlement and all. Just keep going to the Army and Congress. Would help if we had more than just white politicians to listen to our arguments. A few are sympathetic, but they won't stick their necks out." Mr. St. James's baritone grunt followed. "He was a trailblazer in working in Washington, DC, in the Department of the Interior."

Ruth didn't want to stop the information with an unnecessary question. She thought she should just listen for now, rather than "put her foot in it," as Mrs. Givens used to say. A beautiful chime rang out as Mr. St. James finished speaking.

"A perfect C," Mrs. St. James informed as her husband escorted everyone to the hall. "Always a nice note to start a party. Now run along girls and show Miss Yuell the way to the garden. Alice, your birthday party has begun."

ଔଓ

The afternoon passed in a dizzying array of introductions, colors, and tastes. Alice had the largest and most lavishly decorated cake she'd ever seen, outside of Lula Bennett's wedding cake the bride's grandmother had baked and adorned with white sugar ornaments from the cake bakery by the railroad tracks. Ruth remembered singing "Happy Birthday" at parties and such, but never having all the little candles to blow out.

Bowls of fresh flowers adorned the serving tables and were placed throughout the house. Smelled like the best of spring as Ruth sniffed each one. Roses, lavender, lilacs, and large orbs of hydrangeas were artfully arranged and spilled all over themselves in other bowls.

"They're from the florist now, but Mrs. St. James's starting a cutting garden," Leticia offered. "She said when she settled down, she would have some flowers of her own, not just the store-bought bouquets sent from admirers. You like flowers, too?" She smiled. "Good thing, she always has them around, even in the winter. Takes bulbs, puts them in pots, and they grow indoors. We learned how to do it when we toured in the Netherlands before the war. She was just a baby herself but she always loved her flowers. Sends to New York for the bulbs, as I recall."

Leticia looked around at the refreshments trays, noting one tray of cookies needed to be replenished. "I'll get this household whipped into shape. I'm not happy I've had to allow untrained people in the house to help but with the unpacking and Alice's birthday party, I couldn't do it all myself." Leticia pulled a list from her lace-edged apron pocket. "I like time to make up my mind on household hires and references...just didn't have the time."

Ruth remembered learning to play croquet for the first time that afternoon with her very own shiny mallet with pretty blue strips on it that matched the ball she kept hitting.

"It's my favorite outdoor game," Cherie exclaimed.

All Ruth needed to do was picture Nettie's face on Cherie's body and Nettie became alive again. In playing this game, Ruth didn't quite understand the reason for hitting someone else's ball away from the hoops but Cherie did it anyway.

"You get too much glee out of hitting the balls away," Alice cried as her yellow sphere flew away into the new rose bushes.

"I'll help you, Alice," Ruth called and chased after her retreating back.

"I'll tear my dress if I chase after it," Alice cried again. "I can't continue without my ball."

"Here, take my hammer," Ruth said, remembering too late the correct term was "mallet." "You can use my ball while I get yours." She headed for the bushes and looked around for something to fish the ball away from the thorny branches. There was a small shed behind the last row of flowers. Ruth headed there looking for something long enough for the rescue. "I'll get something from this shed. You go on," Ruth called as Alice left with the blue mallet to return to the game. As Ruth opened the door, an imposing, handsome man in workingman's clothes faced her. She drew in her breath in fright. *What was he doing there? Was he one of the new hires Mrs. McCloud mentioned?*

"Came in here looking for something, as you did, missie," the man announced with a growl and tried to block her entering the shed interior. "Delivering some food." Ruth's eye caught the retreat of flowered chiffon as she remembered a tall, lovely girl in a dress of the same frothy material, who had come with her parents to Alice's party.

"Just give me the rake, please. I'm rescuing Alice St. James's croquet ball," Ruth stammered, ashamed at what she had interrupted, knowing this was a long, long way from the kitchen. "Got to hurry."

❧❧

Everyone seemed pleased to see Ruth and talked about how much they liked meeting her father or looked forward to seeing him again. "Your father is an important asset to the community," Mr. Grayson said proudly. "We've got many ideas." Almost every night at the dinner table and in evening conversations, her father and Lady Dee explained about the plans to push forward many educational initiatives and court cases destined to gain desegregation.

Ruth tried to help clean up the scattered plates and dishes Miss Leticia and her helpers were clearing. Bessie Lee was one high school-age helper and Lee Ann Rhodes was the other.

"We all can help, too," Mrs. St. James said, as she held a plate in each hand.

"Of course, we'll help," Mr. St. James said, "but not you, pet. You'll sit here and order us around as you always do, so you don't get too tired." He ushered his wife to a large shaded lawn chair. "Now, stop that pout, dear," he continued. "If you keep pushing yourself, you won't be able to go to church tomorrow. You'll hate that, I know. So behave."

Mrs. St. James feigned displeasure but stayed in the chair. "Well, if you really insist, Alexander."

All too quickly, it was time to go home. Ruth walked down the sidewalk humming and treasuring the present she'd gotten at the party, cupping the cellophane bag of white sugar-coated almonds in her hand. She'd ask permission to put them in Lady Dee's cut glass candy dish when she got home. Ruth knew her father liked a sweet before bedtime.

Why hadn't she said anything about seeing the man in the shed? Such news would certainly have caused some stir but Ruth didn't want to ruin Alice's party or jeopardize the identity or reputation of the unknown girl. There was only the brief glimpse of a dress. No use throwing mud without reason or proof.

Ruth was interrupted by a honking horn and looked up to see Devon with Leroy in the passenger seat. "You slipped out too quickly. I thought your "thank you, kindlys" would last another half hour." Devon saw the stricken look on Ruth's face and amended, "I was just kidding. You were very polite. I'm supposed to drive you home, according to my father."

"I...I didn't know," Ruth replied self-consciously. She looked at her brother. "I couldn't find you and Miss Leticia thought you were already home."

"Well, he isn't and that's all the more reason for a ride," Devon said as Leroy swiveled to open the roadster door from the inside. "But I have to hurry. I've got to get back to the house." Ruth rushed over and sat quickly on the leather seat. "This is a welcome break from the rest of the chores." They all burst out laughing at Devon's candor. "Here we are," Devon said as he leapt from the driver's side door to open her door. "I'll take you to the steps...and, by the way, thanks for helping today, Ruth."

Lady Dee must have seen the car pull up because she opened the door before they got to the porch. "Hello, Mrs. Yuell," Devon said smoothly, "My father asked me to drive Leroy and your daughter home from Alice's birthday." He extended his hand and after a few brief pleasantries was gone as quickly as he came.

"Seems like a nice young man," Lady Dee observed. "Did you have a good time?"

Leroy talked about the car. "The motor purrs like a huge cat."

Ruth swallowed her laughter. She talked excitedly about the St. Jameses and all the people she had met, the food she'd eaten, and asked about using the candy dish as she and her mother finished dinner preparations.

Her strategy was rewarded as soon as her father spied the treats in the cut glass bowl. "Are those candy almonds I see? Did you have a good time at the party, Ruth?"

"Oh, yes, father. It was quite a time," Ruth replied. "I've been telling Lady Dee but I've still got lots of questions."

"Questions?" Dr. Yuell repeated as he grabbed a carrot stick off the relish tray as Lady Dee swatted at his hand.

"Lots," Ruth confirmed. "Mr. Ray from the NAACP dropped his daughter off at the party and he said you and he had lots of plans. And Mrs. St. James said her husband and you were making plans, too?"

Dr. Yuell began to speak carefully but with great feeling. "You know we're equal under God and everything else, Ruth." He gestured with the carrot, emphasizing his words as if he were using the pointing stick at an imaginary blackboard. "We're going to try to keep changing things for the better. It's neither right nor proper to let things go on as they have been."

"You mean the separate thing," his daughter offered.

"Yes, Ruth. The separate thing can't go on. We want to change things peaceably by changing the laws and regaining the things we should always have had without interference." Ruth nodded. "Can't say it's going to be easy."

Ruth saw a flicker of fear in her mother's eyes. It wasn't necessary to talk about the lynchings, murders, burning, and bombings. Ruth knew working for change might bring violence.

"Father, I know about the burning, the church over by Aunt Sarah and...about the Klan," Ruth spoke softly. Her mother's lips thinned with tension.

"Guess you are almost grown," her father began. "Seems you were just a baby a few years ago." His face looked sweetly wistful. "We've talked about the court cases time and time again. There will be resistance in the courts and in the streets. We have to be strong about it. We'll have to pray just as hard as we organize our forces for change."

"So Mr. St. James is going to lead in the courts and Mr. Grayson is going to lead in the streets?" Ruth asked. "That leaves you...helping the pastors leading their congregations, I guess."

"Yes, Ruth. That's right." The serious mood seemed to lift a bit. "Lady Dee's going to do her best to keep things running here and help with all the other concerned ladies in the community, too."

"I...I could help more around here," Ruth offered. It seemed like everyone was making pledges and sacrifices, so, she thought she should, too. "Sylvie can learn new things too! She's always eager to help."

"That's so fine of you to offer your and Sylvie's help, but your education is important to you...and to us."

"Ruth. Thank you for being thoughtful. Wish everyone saw it that way," Lady Dee chimed in with a soft smile.

"What do you mean, Lady Dee?" Ruth asked both in pride and confusion.

Lady Dee spoke carefully. "Well, some people are afraid of changing. Afraid of how the white folk will react and all. Afraid of bad things...I guess," Lady Dee's voice became heavy and trailed off. Ruth could think of who might be talking against them. Mrs. Blaine.

"But if we interest enough people to get laws changed, everybody, Negro and white, will be better off in the long run. Understand?" Dr. Yuell concluded. "We've got to be happy for the doubter as well as the believer. That's what freedom is all about."

"I'm with you, father...and you too, Lady Dee," Ruth smiled, not letting the fear gain any stronghold. "I can do my homework until you need me? OK?"

"You're a young leader in the demonstrations we've planned," her father offered.

"You mean I will get to protest with you?" she cried joyously.

Dr. Yuell nodded.

"Where's Leroy?" Ruth asked, wanting to share this moment with her brother.

"He's gone over to the high school," Lady Dee replied. "Took Sylvie with him."

"Leroy said he'd be back for dinner. Better get here or cut more carrots before I eat them all." Dr. Yuell made the prudent decision to look sheepish before grabbing another from the dish. "Would you cut some more carrots for me? Talking about all the things we're doing together...with God's help, makes me hungry."

"Leroy and Sylvie better get here quickly, dear, or I'll have to go back to the store," Lady Dee stated dryly.

"I'm here. I'm on time. I haven't done anything wrong," Leroy said as he walked through the door. "Honest. Sylvie can vouch for me." The other three assembled family members all laughed as his worried expression turned to bewilderment.

"Spoken like a young man telling the truth," Dr. Yuell teased.

"A college student," Ruth corrected. "Right, Leroy?"

Figuring he wasn't in trouble with all the laughter, Leroy ventured in questioning tone. "What's going on here?"

"We're just having a civil rights discussion," Ruth offered.

"Discussion," Sylvie parroted.

"That's a pretty serious subject. Why the laughter?" Leroy persisted.

"If we can't laugh sometimes, Leroy, it's not worth living," Dr. Yuell said.

"My tummy feels good when I laugh," Sylvie said.

Lady Dee smiled at Sylvie. Trying to be more informative, she added, "It was a serious discussion and it is going to be serious work. Your father and I were discussing your roles as young leaders."

Dr. Yuell looked at his daughters and son and back to Lady Dee. "It's time for you to join us as full partners in this. We're all adults now and we just used humor to lighten the tone a bit."

"That's good. That's good," Leroy repeated as he came over to hug his sister. "That was some party at the St. James house." Sometimes it was difficult to know what Leroy paid attention to and what he didn't, but everyone seemed ready for this change of subject. Leroy grabbed some celery. "Devon St. James has the coolest car!" he exclaimed.

"Using slang terms, are we, Leroy?" Lady Dee inquired. "Does Mr. St. James keep his car in a freezer?"

"Lady Dee," Leroy pleaded, "I know when to use proper English. I want to fit in."

"I don't think your English teacher would be pleased but if you promise to wash the car as you promised yesterday," Lady Dee emphasized the word 'yesterday,' "...and keep your school marks up, we'll discuss your wishes further. Need

I say anything about a high grade in English class?" his mother glared meaning-fully. "Then, and only then, will we consider letting you get away with a few minor linguistic oddities."

Leroy smiled as he hugged Lady Dee, grabbed a carrot stick and headed for the garage. "I'll do the car tonight after supper. I'll just go and get things ready now."

Leroy was out of the door as Lady Dee called, "Be sure to change your clothes before you start!"

CHAPTER SEVEN

EMERGENCY ROOM AT 2:55 P.M.
CHICAGO – 1967

Ruth remembered Regine St. James was never like other more paltry hostesses of the neighborhood. *How could she make Norma understand?* She was the consummate party-giver, making sure Leticia had children's treats as well as a complete high tea set out for the whirl of visitors, business associates, and Negro community leaders who passed through the doors of their home almost every afternoon. Before the afternoon festivities began, Alice and Cherie would concentrate on homework. Cherie would usually be the first up from the table, needing to expend some of her youthful energy. Leticia at some point would cry with loving exasperation, "Sweet child, some day you'll cause me to drop the sandwiches or cakes, I declare! You're always dartin' and dancin' around my feet like that."

Norma shrugged, relieved Ruth hadn't mentioned the woman's son, Devon, again. "She had her music, her family, and her church," Norma replied honestly, wanting Ruth to take the lead on what she wanted to talk about next. They were on treacherous ground.

"I know you want to talk about Devon, but I've got a few more important things I want to say before that," Ruth said. Norma almost jumped, thinking how closely Ruth was to her thoughts. "My church and the beginning of my demonstration training is important to me and my upbringing...being a change agent for my community needs attention before anything else." Ruth closed her eyes to think of how to express the information. "Think I'll start talking about how important the church and Pastor Fredericks were in the course of my life."

"Don't you think people are aware of how the church has led the movement of non-violent change for civil rights?" Norma asked.

"Perhaps, but from my way of thinking, *real* positive gains for the Negro race in this country weren't a sure thing by any means. Desegregation was a hard and dangerous journey. Still going on today. Needs repeating. This non-violent philosophy really started with the prayers of generations of oppressed people. The church kept everything peaceful."

Norma looked at Ruth passively. *So Ruth was going to skip over the subject of Devon?* All Norma could do was take down what Ruth was saying now, knowing her friend had promised to talk about that painful time. Norma took a breath and looked down at her notes.

Ruth looked at the ceiling of the cubicle. Ruth wanted to emphasize the importance of the church in Negro spiritual and civic life in her conversation with Norma. People didn't know how blessed a thing it was for white and Negro citizens that bloodshed had been spared. "Just think of the bloody French Revolution!" *A very good thing the American Civil rights movement started at the church door.*

"In the pre-Civil Rights era the church was both a place to worship and a town hall of sorts to get community work done. Truth was there was no representative government for most Negroes. In the South especially, the church was the only place where Negroes could really gather in large numbers on a consistent basis to meet each other at all. Putting their gifts and skills to work beyond the confines of his church community in St. Louis, clergymen like Pastor Fredericks acted like unofficial alderman, representatives, or senators of their congregations, trying to: meet the needs of their parishioners, move toward legal equality measures, and take care of skirmishes with the white community." Worship, solemn ceremony, and talk of civil liberties blended into Sunday as long as Ruth could remember.

❀

ST. LOUIS – 1960

Reverend Fredericks started the announcements, frequently calling all the church members to help with concerns in their community, asking the lady leaders of the church circles to watch over the needy people within the congregation, and then turned his remarks on the larger social and legal issues the congregation was undertaking.

"Now, Mrs. Whitehead, you have all the meals and helpers lined up this week for Sister Elliot? How's she doing?" he would ask from the altar area.

"Much better, Reverend. Thanks for asking. No more meals or visits are needed at this time. She's asking how the plans are going to publicize how badly she was treated at the prescription counter and how her health was affected by not being able to get her medicine."

"Glad you asked, Mrs. Whitehead. We have every right to impress this fact on the white owners and the public. Please pray for me in our deliberations with the store owner."

After announcements and a sermon hymn, Pastor Fredericks would begin to preach. There was a special cadence, rhyme, and rhythm to his speaking, as if he was talking in time to a metronome no one else could hear. He'd also use his voice to send or emphasize his ideas from a whisper to a roar and back. His words would soar with strength to a piercing baritone height and then crash like a brick avalanche thundering into its bass depth. Movement also punctuated his message. He might leave the pulpit to stand alone, move, or gesture. Other times, he would emphasize the words with cat-like strides and sudden stops. This was not carnival or circus, but an orators' tradition; using all the ways he and his predecessors teach and guide.

Ruth was amazed by the poetry of his message and the vast recall he had of Biblical settings, people, and situations. Reverend Fredericks used them to illustrate and strengthen each part of his sermon. Everything he said was generously wrapped and tied with Biblical references. "All you need to know is in here," he'd say as he patted his well-worn Bible, "...all you need to know." The pastor loved to preach and welcomed preparing a word from the Lord for the congregation. "I've been waiting a long time since God's calling to get my own church. God's word has never failed me and it won't fail me now. I'll just preach till the Lord takes me home," he said with a satisfied smile. "It's a blessing to be able to present the richness of God's word in the context of our needs, experiences and everyday life. We were born free and deserve to live free, too. Never mind the drunks, the ignorant, or the bigots," Pastor Fredericks would say. "Maybe we're only all free on Sunday thus far," he continued, "and maybe only within the confines of our black neighborhoods and church walls. But here's where we start...and stand."

"The police, city officials, or whoever would usually meet with Negro pastors." Dr. Yuell once observed, "They understand the role of the pastor. Know there won't be any trouble because Negro pastors are sworn to peaceable standards just like their own white pastors. Know pastors are fair and base their judgments on the Bible. Most of those white folk don't have much more education than high school. White folk can't stand to be intimidated by their own race's professional people, not to mention a Negro professional person. Some white folk don't even want to admit Negro professional people exist. So Negro pastors go first to smooth the waters and drop anchor in the truth of the matter."

Reverend Fredericks would spend untold hours with a particular problem or concern, thinking everything was said and done, and then someone new, who was white, would come into the situation and turn things upside down. "Just keep praying, everyone. Got to get some power under the law," he kept on saying, "but we're working toward it with no bloodshed and that's good. We'll talk to these issues at church every Sunday till it's done."

◐◑

EMERGENCY ROOM AT 3:30 P.M.
CHICAGO – 1967

"So, we were working on the local level and had some success, most notably the Montgomery Bus boycott." Ruth looked at Norma to make sure she understood the progression.

"The most successful Supreme Court case of note in the early '50s, in my estimation, was the Brown case," Ruth remembered. "Pastor Fredericks described the court's opinion when it was read in the chamber. He talked about the stunned silence and a mass inhaling of breath. 'Would have loved to sit there; one of the most amazing things ever brought before that august chamber.'"

"Her name was Linda." Ruth hoped she recalled the young girl's name correctly. "We'll have to check to make sure. Her father, Oliver Brown, wanted her to be able to go to her neighborhood school in Topeka, Kansas. When he went to register her for the school year, he was told his daughter would have to go to the Negro school across town. That's what all Negro children had to do. Go only to the Negro school. Her father filed a lawsuit called *Brown vs. the Board of Education of Topeka*."

Ruth saw Linda Brown's picture in a black-and-white photo in a magazine, dressed in what looked to be her Sunday church coat. She stood very straight and serious with her hands clasped behind her back in front of a dark brick school reminding Ruth of her own elementary school, or was it in front of some trees? Ruth remembered being dragged into the dark trees and she shuttered. Ruth had to concentrate on telling Norma all the important things. Other people had suffered and she had to get control of herself. *Did Linda know what the lawsuit meant?* She looked so small and so young to be carrying such an important issue on her slight shoulders. Ruth tried to keep her mind focused and remember the rest as she wiped a tear from her eyes.

Ruth remembered her father say Mr. St. James sounded so excited in recalling his feeling after the ruling. "'Separate but equal' was finished in education. It's what we'd been waiting and praying for. Carter was brilliant in his presentation. The justices could have set a timetable for integration. That would have been even better but at least we had this ruling to build on. We fanned out all over the country with challenges for the schools just as soon as we could. Little Rock became one of the first challenges and we were hopeful, our own time in St. Louis would come—soon." Ruth frowned at her statement.

Progress was painfully slow. State courts across the country were slated to hear challenges based on the Brown case but legal stays, continuances, and other roadblocks stymied immediate implementation of the law. Negro students' educational experiences were caught in the middle. "This logjam altered the path of my college education."

"Was it about the time you started practicing for the protests?" Norma asked. "You did mention you wanted to talk about your church and practicing for demonstrations."

"Things I got involved in were still years away. The media started publicizing things with the efforts to start protests like the lunch counter sit-ins about 1959 or 1960, but a few unpublicized things started before then," Ruth replied, "...and it wasn't easy."

Norma lifted a questioning brow but said nothing.

Ruth looked at Norma and down at Norma's notebook. "If you want an example I can remember a time when I was back from college in 1961."

📽

ST. LOUIS – 1961

Meggie asked Ruth if she could volunteer to be in one of the local protests. "I've been thinking and praying about it."

"Me too," Sylvie repeated enthusiastically.

"Meggie, just ask Dr. Means and your aunt for permission and inform Reverend Fredericks," Ruth replied, not realizing what verbal fireworks she and Meggie's conversation would set off the next afternoon.

"I will *not* have my niece endangered in such a way, sir," Mrs. Blaine railed at Dr. Yuell. "You, sir, might be a strong proponent of such activity for your family members, but I must say I find it highly suspect such well-bred girls are being recruited by your daughter, Ruth."

"As Ruth relayed to me yesterday, Meggie asked *her* about participating in the proposed demonstrations, Mrs. Blaine," Dr. Yuell replied in a cool tone.

"That's what Meggie told me also, Eleanor," Dr. Means agreed.

The lines between Mrs. Blaine's eyebrows became more prominent. "Be that as it may, I am most concerned about the safety and well-being of Meggie. She has fragile sensibilities."

"Pastor Fredericks has declared any teenager who prayerfully considers the situation and has the permission of parents or guardians may participate," Dr. Yuell replied.

"I will give Meggie *my* consent," Dr. Means said with a definite air of finality.

"Me too," Sylvie said.

Mrs. Blaine's face became more pinched as if her brow would totally disappear into her eye sockets. She looked at Sylvie, and then Dr. Means. "We will revisit this after dinner, brother," was all Mrs. Blaine said as she turned to go out the door with no goodbyes.

◕◑

Meggie, Sylvie, and Ruth attended all the practices and meetings together.

The teenagers and adults set up chairs in the fellowship hall for the soda fountain stools and tables in a fort-like row to simulate the counter. There were chalk lines on the floor to show them where the doors and cash register stand stood. They said a prayer together, then everyone lined up outside the make-believe outside door of the "drug store" and slowly walked in precise lines.

Ruth and the others passed many grueling hours of being silent and stoic in hours of cruelly abusive taunts and heckling, no matter what insults were hurled, stated, or whispered; to speak very little, if at all, and not to laugh or berate their opposition. They were to ignore the blazing hatred in people's eyes and not wipe any spit from their clothes and faces; movement might be interpreted as aggressive behavior.

At times, the "demonstrators" were either blindfolded or told to keep their eyes shut to make them feel even more vulnerable. "You this and that," other volunteers would cry using the worst racial epithets.

Sometimes, the trainers flicked sugar water on them to add to the authenticity. "Makes it seem like when they start spitting on you. Don't want you being surprised or anything," Ida Wenn whispered unnecessarily.

Ruth would sit there while the itchy-wet droplets fell from her face and down her bodice. "Concentrate and focus. Concentrate and focus," a male voice commanded. "Don't retaliate. That's what they want; to give them a reason to snicker and be even more violent. Don't want to give them any reason at all, in turn, to say we're uncivil."

◕◑

On the day of their first demonstration, church and community volunteers met at the church at one p.m. in their neat and tidied Sunday clothes. Jittery participants, including Ruth and Meggie, practiced the routine a last time.

Everyone gathered for prayer, hoping no violence might erupt from civilians or police answering the call to intervene. They became silent. *Like soldiers going to battle.* Not the Boston Tea Party or a momentous war campaign but a small step against wrong.

Their efforts were to integrate an all-white drugstore lunch counter—walking in two lines towards the doors of the drugstore. More people were placed at the beginning and ends of the line for protection. In the front of the line, the clergymen planned to talk to the soda counter personnel and, in the back of the line, other volunteers were taught to be reinforcements, to take any blows and act as a safe path for retreat.

As expected, there were many insults and catcalls with marked resistance by the drugstore management and the local police. "Stay close to me, Sylvie. You, too, Meggie," Ruth tried to whisper.

During the brief scuffle, Mrs. Brown's blue straw hat lay squashed beyond repair in the front door of the drugstore. The beefy arm of a disgruntled police sergeant, called away from his Sunday dinner, knocked it from her head as he reached to close the drugstore door. Ruth was pushed from her position momentarily and several other young men and women got jostled about as other policemen "encouraged" them to leave or else be arrested.

They were never allowed to enter the soda fountain area. No soda on that Sunday but no burning crosses, tragically-beaten protesters, or vigilante visits after the demonstration either. They'd made their point.

◉◉

EMERGENCY ROOM AT 3:50 P.M.
CHICAGO – 1967

"I'm glad to have those stories in the mix, but I don't think we can avoid other stories any longer," Norma said flatly, "or my notes will get all muddled."

"You want to talk about Devon?" Ruth asked needlessly.

Norma only gave her a baleful look and looked down at her notes.

"Where to start?" Ruth struggled to find the right words. "After Devon drove me and Leroy home from Alice's birthday party, he remained on the thin fringe of my acquaintance as we inched slowly into friendship."

◉◉

ST. LOUIS – 1955

Devon immersed himself in his own concerns with a graduation trip to Europe and then leaving for law school. In Devon's chance conversations with Ruth, these public meetings were all done politely, without emotion, as Ruth faced her studies, church, her own burgeoning civil rights activities, and looking at college prospects.

Thelma, Leroy, and Ruth's friends joined other visitors who squeezed and darted through the numerous lanky, ambling bodies, legs and arms as they talked, laughed and studied. Sylvie loved all the company and gleefully handed refreshments to everyone. Lady Dee and Ruth were baking double and triple batches of what used to be adequate amounts of cookies!

"Got a powerful group of children out there," Mrs. Purdy laughed as she opened the kitchen door. "Dr. Yuell might need to increase his fees to pay for feeding everyone."

"Don't worry, Adelaide. Remember, the St. Jameses and others feed the five thousand of us, so to speak, during all their afternoon soirees, too. The children are having fun here. Just be grateful others pitch in and...progress doesn't wait on the school calendar, does it?" Lady Dee replied as she began to smile. "Easter's next week, too. With last week's rain, I could barely get supper done with all those extra bodies inside the house."

"But not the St. James family?" Mrs. Purdy announced.

"No," Lady Dee replied. "Mrs. St. James isn't up to entertaining right now. You know how Mrs. St. James cuts her schedule when she's not feeling well. Pastor Fredericks told me she's cancelled all appointments." Lady Dee reported. "I'd better go to the store tomorrow to get extra baking supplies or we'll be facing some sad, empty stomachs out there."

"Got to go." Mrs. Purdy looked at her watch. "Milton needs his supper."

Dr. Yuell didn't say anymore until Mrs. Purdy was walking down the sidewalk. "Mrs. Blaine's been taking her venom around the neighborhood and to the St. Jameses' door again?"

"I don't know for sure, and you know it's impolite to make such assertions, Edgar," Lady Dee replied. "Mrs. St. James's health has been frail of late. You told me yourself...and the children are within earshot."

"I'd wager a dozen of your cookies against a stone, the gossips have Mrs. St. James all riled again. What was it the last time?" Dr. Yuell wiped his hand on his brow. "Oh, I remember. Mrs. Blaine told her that I'd said something about her health."

"Oh, yes. To think Eleanor would intimate you would break patient-doctor confidentiality is *absurd*." Lady Dee banged the cookie tray onto the stove rack. "The only things you mind are your integrity and your own business, which is more than I can say for some other people." She looked at him balefully. "Always seems like she wants to get Mrs. St. James in a fight against us. But I won't be saying another word about it."

"That's the truth, but when that kind of sludge comes to my door, as it sometimes does, I get near mad as fire," Dr. Yuell said with feeling. "Just let me know if the message and the person spreading it need to be dealt with...again."

Lady Dee balled her fingers in her apron, hoping to avoid a confrontation between her husband and Dr. Means about his sister-in-law and her tongue.

๏

EMERGENCY ROOM AT 3:55 P.M.
CHICAGO – 1967

"OK, Ruth," Norma replied, "but I might have popped Mrs. Blaine."

Ruth smiled at Norma's comment. "Our parents bred us to the bone to be polite."

๏

ST. LOUIS – 1956

Ruth would be ready for college in the fall of 1957. "Doesn't look good for integration of some schools, Ruth. Yet. Mr. St. James told me so yesterday. State courts won't have it. Set up all kinds of roadblocks. But you've got other choices. Praise God. There's the school in Ohio and the one in New York and let's see...," Dr. Yuell said as he sorted through the paperwork. "Where's the one from Michigan?"

"Here, father," Ruth said as she handed him the brochure. "Is that the one you're also suggesting for Eddie Banes?"

"Ah, yes. This school in Michigan. Looks good. Looks very good." Dr. Yuell looked over the brochure. "You looking at the one from Chicago?"

"You got your church auxiliary correspondence done, Ruth?" Lady Dee wanted to know before she started her next task.

"Yes, mother," Ruth replied as she looked from the oven and called to the dining room where Mrs. Purdy and Lady Dee were sitting.

Mrs. Purdy considered the information and asked, "I see. Is Leroy enjoying his basketball play over at the college?" Leroy's high school coach had accepted a post at the Negro college in Acadia, and Ruth's parents had agreed Leroy could try out for the team, if his grades stayed strong.

"What you going to do with Ruth?" Mrs. Purdy asked, knowing her activities were now being scrutinized.

"She's thinking about colleges," Lady Dee replied.

"College? Haven't gotten any fine young buck you want to marry yet, Ruth?" Mrs. Purdy laughed as she bent her head to call into the kitchen.

"Everyone in her group of friends plans on going to college too, Adelaide," Lady Dee interrupted.

"Love don't care about college. Eh, Ruth," Mrs. Purdy called to her again. "Know of two girls who are getting married before the ink on their high school diplomas is dry."

This banter continued as Ruth became of marriageable age. The full blast of inquiries about the Yuell's daughter's feelings and activities were high on the list of neighborhood concerns. Through some rite of passage, Ruth became more privy to the "women talk" of the ladies in the neighborhood. "What are you going do about that, honey lamb?"

Ruth breathed deeply and sighed as she formulated her answer. "I'm going to college."

"That's all fine and good. But who's going to pay for it?" Mrs. Purdy harrumphed.

This retort seemed like gossip and Lady Dee's face darkened as she replied pointedly. "Adelaide."

"Well, it's an honest question. Two children in college and one almost going... is a lot of expense."

Ruth felt compelled to enter the discussion. "I'll keep working for a time."

"Well, I see. Finally, going to service, eh?" Mrs. Purdy remarked. "Service" was a well-known term for going to work as a maid for the white folk, but Ruth's job was going to be in a local restaurant. It seemed paid babysitting was calculated in the neighborhood as play, not work. Keeping precocious, lively children occupied on the average of four evenings a week seemed like work to Ruth, plus it was also her duty to keep up with the whirl of plates and cups, visitors, and discussions in the Yuell home when she wasn't babysitting. "Mrs. Daily is asking for help down at her family restaurant. I'll be starting as school gets out."

Ruth's work opportunity brought loud discussion within the family but she wasn't going to share those facts with Mrs. Purdy. Truth be told, there *was* going to be further financial strain of three children going to college. Thelma had many semesters to go before she was finished with all her veterinary work. Leroy was working hard but the family still needed to supplement his expenses. A Negro doctor's salary was more meager than his community status indicated.

At first, Lady Dee announced she was going to take a domestic job to meet the financial challenge. Ruth and Leroy were aghast at the possibility. "You can't, Lady Dee. You can't!" Leroy cried as his dessert fork clanked on the table. "I'd rather stay out a year and work myself before I'd let you. Father, tell her, please!"

Dr. Yuell looked at his wife and said, shaking his head, "I told you, Lady Dee. Told you this would be his reaction."

"I get a job," Sylvie announced. Ruth finally found her voice.

"I agree about Lady Dee *not* going back into service. That's not right!" Ruth emphasized, her voice rising.

Lady Dee let out an audible sigh. "Plain as day, really. We have to pay cash money for everything. Our budget is not big enough to go around."

"So the only answer is for you to be a domestic? I don't believe that. Who's going to do all your church and civil rights work. I can't. I can't help at the office as much as you do. Neither can Leroy. Father can't do anymore, either." Ruth and her brother looked at their parents accusingly. "Besides it's time I get a steady paying job. College is coming for me, too. With all the experience I've gotten with babysitting and helping here at home and at church, those should count for something,"

"You sure, Ruthie?" Dr. Yuell asked.

"If you'll do that, then I'll ask Hank for some more hours down at the garage near campus," Leroy offered.

"Lady Dee and you deciding this and all, without talking to us first. We're almost grown. Can't say it's going to all work out but at least we...I must try something. Lady Dee did enough working for other people before we were born. It's our turn now." All of Ruth's parents' arguments to the contrary couldn't shake her. Then Sylvie started to cry.

"Don't you think we can do it?" Ruth wailed, distressed. "Can't you see I'm serious?" Lady Dee unfurled her hankie from her apron pocket and got up to put her arm on Sylvie's shoulder.

Ruth dried her tears and kneeled before her father. "Don't you see? I'm just trying to help," Ruth reassured her father as she raised her arm to grab Lady Dee's hand. "I'm just trying to help."

So now, they were trying to explain their decision to Mrs. Purdy.

"I hear Eleanor Blaine is looking for some party help," Mrs. Purdy offered.

"Yes, Dr. Means mentioned his sister-in-law needs help with an all-day Ladies' Aid Society event," Lady Dee replied, hoping she and Edgar made the right "charitable" decision in asking Ruth to help out.

御

Ruth's working for Mrs. Blaine was big mistake! Her mouth sat in a thin angry line as she walked home from her first, and last, day of work there.

"I'm so sorry," was all Meggie could muster when she got home from the all-day Ladies' Aid Society local convention. Mrs. Blaine was out of earshot, wrapping her new purple hat in tissue paper.

Ruth should have known it wouldn't work, but Dr. Means personally asked Ruth to help with his sister's preparations for a garden party. With the meeting taking her and Meggie from the house and Calli having her "headaches and miseries" for two days, Mrs. Blaine required help. From all Ruth could see, Calli was well-recovered because Calli kept her running up and down the stairs and in and out of the house like a trained animal from her lounging position either on her bed or the downstairs couch!

Calli barked out orders from Mrs. Blaine's list with a sharpened pencil in her hand. Seemed like Mrs. Blaine was trying to get a week's worth of work out of Ruth's hide in a day! First, there was the pile of eight all-cotton tablecloths and sixty-four napkins Mrs. Blaine wanted pressed. "Be sure you get the tissue paper between the folds on each table hanger," Calli called. "Auntie can't abide wrinkles."

Then, polishing the three tea sets Mrs. Blaine needed and the assorted serving pieces and sets of silver. Most of the pieces were almost black, the tarnish was so heavy. "Are you sure you're working fast enough?" Calli called as Ruth wiped her perspiring brow. *The only thing working on Calli was her mouth.*

"You'll have to skip lunch to polish the downstairs furniture properly," Calli called. "I told dear Auntie you should do the upstairs, too, for the price we're paying, but she's a kind woman and only wants you to concentrate on the public rooms."

"Kind" was not a term many people used when referring to Mrs. Blaine, but Ruth wasn't going to give Calli the satisfaction of a fight.

Calli seemed to have a gift at turning any piece of information into a tantalizing morsel of gossip, like the snake turned Eve and Adam toward the forbidden fruit. Fighting with Calli would end up in words pressuring her father and Dr. Means. Both men had struck an uneasy truce, since the incident Pastor Fredericks mediated regarding the false rumor accusing Dr. Yuell of talking about Mrs. St. James's medical records in public. Ruth didn't want to be the one to break the peace.

Meggie and Calli were sisters. She shook her head. *How different in personality and demeanor these two young women turned out to be!* If Calli and her penny-pinching aunt wanted to pretend they were high-flying rich folk for a day, Ruth wouldn't grouse. Better than having hard feelings between her father and Dr. Means.

"I need my lunch now or my headache might get worse," Calli called. Ruth wondered if suggesting Calli stop all her shouting from upstairs might help to ease her pain. "I'll come down there to have it on the couch. I need the meat to be cold... with mayonnaise on the bread and the crust to be cut off."

After making Calli's lunch and bringing it on a tray to the couch table, Calli looked at the plate and sniffed. "I think I'll get into bed and take a nap." She got up from the sofa and grabbed her magazine. "I want lemonade instead of milk when you bring the tray upstairs." Calli hesitated on the stairs. "I left the list you need to get done on the sofa table."

For the rest of the afternoon, Calli sat in unavailable and disinterested splendor in the middle of her bed surrounded by the fashion magazines strewn around her pink bedspread like thick paper rose petals.

"I'm so sorry," Meggie repeated again as she and Mrs. Blaine returned from their meeting.

Ruth checked off the last task on the lengthy list. Now it was time for Ruth to play party maid. For two hours, she handed out tea, dainty sandwiches and desserts as Mrs. Blaine alternately called orders in a refined tone or found fault with Ruth's work.

More apologetic words from Meggie were interrupted by Mrs. Blaine. "I'll have my brother bring your pay over next week." The older woman straightened her dress cuff. "Before you leave, will you put fresh water on to boil. Poor Calli needs hot compresses."

Meggie saw the rage build in Ruth's eyes and grabbed her friend's wrist. "I'll get it, Aunt Eleanor. Ruth's going to have to leave after doing such a fine job today."

Ruth was glad the woman didn't say a word more. As she walked home, Ruth knew she would never step foot in that house as a domestic helper again without an explicit order of her mother and father. Once burned, twice shy.

◠◡

As Ruth, her mother, and Mrs. Purdy readied Ruth's two older white blouses and dark skirts together as her work wardrobe, Leroy called from the porch. "Devon St. James is here!"

Mrs. Purdy's turnaround speed belied her matronly girth. "Well, Devon. Welcome home. How was your trip?"

Leroy whispered into his sister's ear. "Did she wheedle out all the particulars about our working?"

"Not yet. But I'm sure she will," Ruth smiled up at him.

"And this, as you know, is Miss Ruth," Mrs. Purdy intoned as if this were her own parlor.

"A pleasure to see you all. It's been a long time away," Devon said in a deep, soft voice. Ruth looked into chocolate brown eyes with amber glinting in the kitchen's afternoon light. His face reminded her of an actor who played opposite Dorothy Dandridge in the movie she'd seen several weeks before. Long years of church manners saved her from discomfort. "Would you like a cup of coffee?"

Dr. Yuell came in a short time later, peppering Devon with all types of questions about law school, Europe, and the feelings of foreign citizens about current civil rights issues. Mrs. Purdy would have no more and lanced into the conversation with a question more to her liking. "You got another girlfriend yet? You let the Hardy girl get away."

"I have been away..." Devon began and left the phrase hanging with embarrassment.

"A lot has happened," Dr. Yuell offered. "There are a lot of important court cases coming up for us. That's why I wanted to know about any improvements in international affairs."

"Heard that white woman, Mrs. Daily, is trying to get herself up in the world. Probably work you to death for your pay. The police have shooed them away but watch out for some unsavory characters hanging around there." The woman looked speculatively for a reaction on Ruth's impassive face. "And that St. James boy sure is a looker. Real good man getting through with college and law school. Anybody could do worse."

ॐ

Ruth's prospective employer, Mrs. Daily, seemed to be fond of chewing her gum in an exaggerated, snapping way behind her ruby red painted lips. Trying to get this job in a white establishment meant Ruth would have to explain why she had Sylvie in tow. "I wouldn't have brought her to the interview except there's a family emergency. My sister's been kicked by a horse at veterinary school and my mother has gone to care for her."

"I work good, too," Sylvie said proudly.

"So you both want work?" Mrs. Daily asked, looking confused.

"I work hard," Sylvie reiterated, this time more loudly.

Ruth didn't want to lose this job or make Sylvie feel bad. "I have references, as you can see. My sister is also very dedicated and works hard," Ruth said, turning to Sylvie to smile at her.

"Reason I'm asking is my afternoon dishwasher quit to go to New Orleans and left me in the lurch. If she can take care of those dishes over there, I can get aprons to cover her clothes. If you start today clearing dishes, I'll pay you time and a half. You bring your sister to wash dishes and she'll get a dollar," Mrs. Blair offered. She brought a dollar bill out of her tight black pants pocket and gave it to Sylvie. "You wash dishes for me?"

"I wash dishes!" Sylvie exclaimed as she headed for the sink.

"Don't get your dress dirty," Ruth called as she sped to grab an apron for Sylvie.

"I've got a dollar, so I work," Sylvie looked at the mountain of cookware, dishes, and silverware piled around the deep wash and rinse tubs in the kitchen. Ruth wanted to get Sylvie away from the sink, give the dollar back to Mrs. Daily, and ask her some more questions about her job when a tall, muscular man came around the corner. The first thing Ruth saw as she struggled with Sylvie was the man's coal black chest and arm muscles straining against the arctic white cotton of his short sleeve T-shirt.

"If we don't get some pots, we'll only have the fry surface left," the man grumbled.

"I'm getting help right now," Mrs. Daily replied, trying to find another apron and two hairnets. "You know what we need. Can you do it?"

Ruth looked at Sylvie, remembering the promise of extra pay. "We can stay until five, if I call my father."

"Fair enough. Right, Belma?" the man said. "I'm not doing the dishes and cook...or you can find yourself someone else."

"Now don't get all riled, Jace," Mrs. Daily retorted. "They're right here and starting right now."

"That's all I needed to know," Jace replied, setting his amber eyes to admire the young woman and her older sister, who seemed strangely happy to be facing the pile of dirty, greasy plates before her.

"You'll clean the tables and help out in the kitchen," Mrs. Daily told Ruth. "Jace will tell you everything you need to do. He's Jace Prue, my cook."

Ruth nodded at the terse introduction. "First tell me how you want Sylvie to clean and stack things and in which order so I can get her started," Ruth replied. "She's a very good worker but she may need my help at times."

"Yes, good," Sylvie said, plunging her hands in the water. "Too cold for dishes."

"Give me a few minutes to get the sinks set and I think we'll be fine," Ruth countered. "Sylvie's done very well at helping with church functions without any trouble."

"I work at church," Sylvie smiled. "I work at church, Ace. I work at church, Dolly."

"You mean Mrs. Daily," Ruth corrected.

"We'll see how things go," Mrs. Daily said, picking up the racing form she'd abandoned on the card table at the back of the kitchen area. "Don't want any breakage."

"We understand," Ruth said. "Give me a few minutes and I'll start clearing tables."

"Mrs. Dolly and Ace will help," Sylvie said.

"Mrs. Daily and Mr. Prue, Sylvie," Ruth remarked, trying to have Sylvie remember her manners—and the correct names.

"Mrs. Dolly and Mr. Ace," Sylvie replied at the two people she'd named.

"She simple or something?" Jace whispered to Mrs. Daily.

"She's my sister!" Ruth wasn't going to have her sister belittled for a job.

"Simmer down," Jace replied. "Just trying to understand."

"We let anyone call us almost whatever they want," Mrs. Daily remarked, trying to take the sting out of the situation. "We're respectful here."

Jace nodded his head. "I'll change the water if she needs. So...so will Belma."

"Fair enough," Ruth said, rolling up her sleeves and accepting the hairnet from Mrs. Daily.

◖◗

Ruth and Sylvie came home tired and a bit bedraggled. "I wore the wrong shoes," Ruth said. "I only thought I was interviewing today but the owner needed me and wants Sylvie to come in every day I'm scheduled."

Sylvie hadn't stopped smiling the whole long afternoon as the dirty cookware disappeared and were replaced by more organized work surfaces.

"I helped show Sylvie where everything goes. She's doing fine but she's calling Mrs. Daily and Mr. Prue, Mrs. Dolly and Mr. Ace. They don't seem to mind," Ruth said truthfully as she shrugged. "I defended my sister."

Dr. Yuell smiled and brought his hand across the table to squeeze his daughter's fingers. "I know you did."

"I got a dollar," Sylvie said, pulling the mashed bill from her pocket.

"I got regular pay and a half today for starting right away," Ruth said, "and if Sylvie can continue, she'll get paid, too."

"You can keep up your school work and your activities?" Dr. Yuell asked. "It's not easy being a supervisor." Ruth knew he was referring to taking care of Sylvie at work as well as doing her own.

"Its fine," Ruth replied with love and confidence in her voice. "Everyone at the restaurant understands the situation. We'll be fine." What she didn't say was she recognized the short order cook at Mrs. Daily's diner. Jace Prue was the man who she'd caught in the St. James greenhouse on the day of Alice's birthday. There was no look of recognition in his eyes and Ruth was more worried about Sylvie breaking dishes or denting pans. *Jace Prue and the greenhouse were light years ago.* Ruth wanted to rest and think of things other than the diner. "Tell me how Thelma's doing."

Dr. Yuell smiled. "She'll be fine with a few days rest and some heat on the thigh bruise. Told her she should be a human doctor. Haven't been kicked by any of my patients yet!"

CHAPTER EIGHT

Several days later, Dr. Yuell was scheduled to speak at the local NAACP meeting. "Lady Dee, is my blue shirt pressed? Oh, should I wear my white with the pinstripe?" the doctor raced toward their room. "Where are my cufflinks? Sylvie, have you seen my cufflinks?!"

"Don't you remember Lady Dee's gone to get the preparations going at the auditorium and Sylvie's over at the Henderson's?" Ruth informed.

"You must help me then," her father said. "Where's my shirt? Where are my cufflinks?"

"Your white shirt is downstairs in the hall closet. The cufflinks are in front of mother's jewelry box on the dresser. I'll get them for you, if you'd like."

Ruth walked down the stairs slowly, smoothing the shirring of the full shirt of the purple dress she and Lady Dee made for the occasion. Ruth was startled when she looked up to see someone sitting in the parlor.

"Sorry." Devon St. James rose from the couch. "Didn't...didn't your father tell you that I was coming?"

"No," Ruth smiled. "He's busy getting ready."

"*My* father wanted to make sure *your* father got through his morning appointments, so I came over here to see if he needed assistance." Devon offered his hand. "It's always nice to see you, Ruth."

Ruth took it and held it for only a second, wondering why their relationship had become so formal, when her father yelled from the stairs again. "Your mother's put out two ties. Which one should I wear?" Devon and she laughed as Ruth went to the stairwell. "I wanted to wear the blue one but there's two here now."

"Excuse me." Ruth felt nervous for some reason. "He's really excited," she said unnecessarily.

"Perhaps I can go up and help," Devon offered. Ruth thought a moment, headed to the hall closet for the white shirt, and handed it to Devon.

"Thanks," Ruth said as she watched his form disappear up the stairs.

"I think this selection looks well," Dr. Yuell said, preceding Devon down the stairs.

"What?" Ruth knew she needed to make more polished remarks. Her father had always prided himself on encouraging women about their intelligence and praised them for it. Ruth mentally shrugged it off as neither of the men seemed to notice.

❧❧

Dr. Yuell's speech went well, a rush of well-wishers talked enthusiastically about him speaking at future events. Devon faced a barrage of questions as well. "How's law school going, Devon?"

"Fine. Fine. My last year," Devon replied. "Dad says I should take advantage of getting some legal experience in the time between."

"That sounds like good advice," Leroy replied.

Ruth remembered one of their friends, Walter Brill, who wrote to say he was going to a previously all-white college in Boston and then, hopefully, to law school in his father's footsteps.

"If I'd had the chance, I'd have gone north to school," Dr. Yuell said as everyone enjoyed the coffee after his speech. "I'd have come back here but the education is good and the opportunities...could really have made an earlier impact."

"That's what I plan to do," Devon said. "Get a fine education there and come back here...to change things."

"You're next in line, Ruth. You considered what you're going to do?" Reverend Fredericks asked.

"I'm thinking about which college or university I should select, Pastor Fredericks, but I haven't decided," Ruth looked at Devon instead of the pastor.

Devon's gaze never wavered as he made a few more comments about education in the North. As the crowd began to thin, he asked the Yuells if he could drive Leroy and Ruth home in the family sedan. Leroy took the back seat. Quiet settled in the car. Leroy was still smiling, leaning his head back, and closing his eyes, pleasantly exhausted from all the excitement from the afternoon.

Ruth was nervous and sat with her side almost plastered against the passenger door, feeling half-scared and half excited and not knowing which emotion to push down and which to welcome.

Ruth noted all kinds of women flocked to meet Devon at the luncheon. There were all kinds of questions about his family, his trip, and his educational plans. They'd smile and he'd smile. They'd talk and he'd answer. He was as easy with them but he seemed stilted in his conversation with her.

The first sound besides the road noise was Devon's heavy sigh. "Ruth, I've got to start work along with finishing my classes in the fall. Leroy's in college and you'll be following after that. You're going to college, right?" he asked.

"She'd better or Lady Dee and father will be fit to be tied," Leroy interjected with a smirk from the back seat. "But she'll only be seventeen when she graduates and could work a year to save more money."

"I haven't narrowed my selections," Ruth retorted, stung from her brother's remark. "As you might recall, I've just finished my junior year."

"Heard what your father said. I wanted you to know its hard being first and all, but it's worth it," Devon replied.

"First?" Ruth said, again not knowing exactly what he meant.

"Guess I'm not explaining myself very well. I mean, the first to do something. Like my father was the first Negro from my family to break the color barrier and go to a previously all-white college," he replied patiently. "It's been a challenge. For me, too. They tried to ignore me but I did my work as well as they did and I'm hoping it counts for something. Trusting it does."

"Sounds good," Leroy interjected. "Hope when I get my degree, I'll help break up all this 'separate' stuff. Our families talk about it all the time. With all the soldiers from the wars and all, tasting freedom and working with the whites, changing things can come if we keep going to college and laying the foundation."

"So you'll get a chance to go North to school?" Devon asked.

"I'm looking at my options. I just don't know which school," she replied defensively. "Why does it matter to you?"

"Think you should go North if you have the chance," he continued. "You're strong enough to take their guff. Smart as any. You'd do well up there." Ruth didn't know whether to be happy with his encouragement or angered by his foisting his opinion on her. They were home and since Leroy opened her car door, she was only obligated by good manners to thank Devon for the ride and not continue the conversation. But as she was walking up the steps, Devon called to her, "Don't forget what I said."

Ruth fumed as she entered the house, flinging her purse on the couch with a soft thud and the clasp opened with the pressure.

"What's gotten into you, Ruth?" Leroy asked as she sat down to jam things back in her handbag. "You're treating Devon like he was a stranger or something—not like someone you've known for years."

"All these people want to tell me what to do...and they're not even kind about it. Don't ask what I think or what I want," Ruth groused. "It's happening more and more."

"Touchy. Touchy," Leroy said as he raised his hands in a defensive gesture. "People know I'm set in college and now they're just starting on you as the next in line, that's all."

"But even Devon St. James thinks he can tell me what to do," Ruth grumbled.

"He gave you a lot less advice then Mrs. Purdy does every time she comes over. She doesn't even care about your brain or potential. Just wants to marry you off so she can say her matchmaking was responsible for the coupling."

Leroy was right. People always had opinions. Questioners plagued Ruth the entire summer until she developed some thicker skin and pat answers to dissuade people's curiosity. Ruth *was* also getting to marriageable age so ladies of the congregation continued to pepper her with advice and stories about what and whom she should consider as husband material.

"Just listen. You don't need to say anything," her parents remarked when she complained. So Ruth listened. Mrs. Purdy, Mrs. Jackson, and Mrs. Applebee extolled marriage as if the examples of her parents and grandparents weren't adequate to impress her of its institutional virtues. Often, her thoughts strayed to Devon St. James.

"How you getting on?" Jace Prue asked as he handed the BLT on white toast with fries over the slick silver order shelf separating the kitchen from the dining floor. There was a lull in the early dinner crowd at the diner.

Ruth smiled, hoisting a dirty dish container. "OK, I think." Then she thought a moment. "Mrs. Daily isn't displeased. Is she?"

"No, now don't get going. She'd tell you loud and long if she was," Jace said with a glint in his eye. "Whites don't *ever* mind taking a piece out of our back sides, whether they're right or wrong."

Ruth didn't know what to say. Mrs. Daily treated them fairly and the waitresses on the floor gave her a dollar from their tips if she watched the floor while they took their breaks but she couldn't have any *closer* contact with the customers.

As if Jace was reading her mind, he said. "They'll even let you pour a refill beverage and wait on the tables but don't except anything more." His head tipped to one side, and then the other, as he bent forward, looking more deeply in Ruth's eyes. "The clientele is still too skittish."

Ruth felt uncomfortable. *Was it by this man's nearness or the truth of what he was saying?* His penetrating gaze held her attention.

"Nee-Nee. Need more water," Sylvie called. Ruth felt grateful for the inter-
ruption to get away from Jace and the conversation.

Ruth told Meggie about the incident at the diner. "I don't know anything
about him."

"Sounds like a bad boy to me," Meggie said. Ruth couldn't hide her surprise.
Meggie usually wasn't so bold in her assessments. "I know I don't say much,
Ruth. There's always so many words flying like arrows around Dr. Means's house,
it's dangerous to have too many opinions around Calli and my aunt." Her lips
thinned. "Don't like to talk mean about them, but they'll bludgeon you just
about to death with words to win an argument or get you to come over to their
side."

Ruth smirked at Meggie's fully accurate assessment of her aunt and sister,
sounding like a detached bystander and not an occupant of the household.

Meggie hesitated and continued, "You say he wears tight T-shirts and rolled-
up jeans, right?" Ruth nodded her head. "Sounds like he wants to be noticed, and
perhaps not in a good way."

"Think he knows he's good-looking," Ruth agreed.

"Was there any other incident besides him looking at you that one time?"
Meggie asked.

Ruth thought hard for a minute. She was so busy when she worked at the
diner: doing her refills, cleaning and pickup, watching the tables for the waitresses, and keeping an eye out for Sylvie. Ruth shook her head, not knowing
whether the greenhouse incident was relevant. They were talking about her observations at the diner.

Jace Prue's friendliness could just be macho bravado and she didn't want to
cause any problem because of that! There was plenty of that going around in the
halls of school between girl and boy students. The only problem was that Jace
Prue was a man—and he advertised it.

There were plenty of women, including the waitresses, who bantered with
him, sometimes in explicit sexual terms. Talking about impolite things Ruth
didn't want her parents to know about. She needed this job to keep Lady Dee at
home and out of service.

"You got a boyfriend, Missie Ruth?" His deep singsong voice sounded like a cat-
call. Ruth kept silent and mimicked the looks the waitresses gave him.

"They're only trying to include me in their game, I hope is all," Ruth said.
"I can't ask if that's all it is or I'll be as harassed as you are with Calli and your
mother."

"Guess you're right," Meggie replied. "It could mean you're heading yourself for more verbal punches if they want to start making fun of you."

"Remember when Ed Davis starting calling Vilma Deels a prude because she wouldn't kiss him after a month of going out together," Ruth replied. "She said the months of ridicule seemed like years and it was all she could do to ignore it and hold her head up like it didn't bother her." Ruth looked at her friend. "The diner is an adult environment—not school.

"The money's decent and so are the people most of the time, Meggie," Ruth added, "and I don't have to tell you how pleased and excited Sylvie is at having a paying job."

"She told me several times, your father took her down to the bank to start a savings account," Meggie said with a smile. "She's certainly proud of her blue passbook."

Meggie was being kind. Sylvie was so proud; she'd probably told Meggie dozens of times about her job! Sometimes, when she was helping her mother and Sylvie change the sheets, the small blue book would flutter from beneath Sylvie's pillow. "She's asked lots of times about interest, her money, and how it accumulates."

Meggie's eyes got bright. "Why don't you let me come over some afternoon when you're working and I could see what's going on?"

Ruth looked at her friend for a moment. "Do you think it might help?"

"At least I could hear what's going on and we'd know better what to do."

"It's a touchy thing, Meggie." Meggie knew the diner didn't have many Negro customers at all.

"I know it's mostly segregated clientele, Ruthie." Meggie had another plan. "I'll just come by the back door to give you something and get a glass of water." She looked over at the wall. "I'll take my time and look at a schoolbook or something." She stopped again. "You say there's a step in the back to sit on, if I can't get in?"

The next afternoon, Meggie showed up just as planned with the excuse of giving Ruth some papers for a school assignment she had forgotten to give her friend at school. There was no sexual bantering, nor did Jace Prue say anything out of the ordinary about Ruth or anyone else, even though Meggie spent twenty minutes staring at her history book and dawdling with her water glass until it was warm.

The only repercussion from the visit came from William Bennis mentioning to Calli that he'd seen Meggie on the back step of the diner the previous afternoon. Calli immediately went to their aunt with the news. Meggie knew something was wrong when she entered the dining room for dinner. The skin on her neck prickled. There were no serving dishes on the table. Her uncle's chair was empty, so no one came to her defense.

"Your sister talked to William Bennis." Her aunt gave a dramatic pause. "He said he saw you sitting on the back step of the diner on Logan Street yesterday afternoon." There was another pause and an intensifying of her aunt's glare. "Would you mind telling us what you were doing at the diner?"

Meggie wished she could wipe the smug look from her sister's face. Meggie wondered why Calli liked to place her in such a negative light. It was almost like the same look Calli displayed when she ate a favorite dessert or talked about her latest boyfriend. "I forgot to give Ruth Yuell some information for the youth rally at church. It was Sylvie's and her workday at the diner so I delivered the pages to her there." Meggie prayed Calli hadn't checked any deeper into the situation.

"You couldn't have dropped them at her home...or Dr. Yuell's office?" Calli asked.

Meggie made sure her face stayed neutral. "I had to speak to her about what I felt our intentions for our project should be before she started her work on it." Meggie thought she should sit down, trying to put an end to the conversation. She willed herself to relax and smile as if nothing had happened.

"That was a kind gesture and I'll tell William Bennis," Calli replied. "Perhaps we both can go down to visit Ruth at the diner sometime."

Meggie didn't realize that "sometime" was going to be the next day but Calli accompanied her sister to see Ruth the next afternoon. Ruth was just wiping her brow. Sylvie needed a clean tub of rinse water because a dirty, greasy pot had fallen from her hand and fouled the tub. The first thing she saw was Meggie's familiar penny loafers. Her welcoming smile curdled when she spied Calli. "How nice to see you...again," Ruth faltered.

"We thought since Meggie was here yesterday, we'd both say hello today," Calli announced.

At the same time Jace was going from the cooking aisle to the back room for some supplies. He spied the three teenagers near the back door. "Introduce me to these two other lovely young ladies?" Jace said expansively with an appreciative eye. Ruth made sure he wasn't glaring at them in a suggestive way. She wouldn't stand for that, job or no job. "I just finished baking some cinnamon rolls but a few got too done. Still good to eat, though. Would each of you like one?" he asked.

"It's not time for my break yet," Ruth replied warily.

"I'll have the girls cover for you if you don't take too long." Jace ducked into the kitchen and brought out three rolls wrapped like hot dog buns at the carnival instead of on plates. "Hope you enjoy them."

"Can't do this anymore, now that Calli knows," Meggie said with a sour whisper. Ruth nodded as she ate the warm pastry and looked at the door. Jace was gone. She'd have to get Meggie and Calli on their way and thank Jace later.

☙❧

"You feeling well?" Dr. Yuell asked with a frown. He was somewhat startled but he managed to hide it as his daughter ignored his enthusiastic perusal of her college information sprawled across the dining room table.

"I'm fine. Maybe I need some fresh air and to walk a bit," Ruth replied. "I'll be out on the stairs if you need me." Ruth walked slowly out the screen door. She'd never felt so alone. When Nettie had been gone for several days and hope faded she'd ever return—the same sinking feeling was in the pit of Ruth's stomach now.

Ruth became so engrossed with her feelings, she hadn't noticed someone in a car had seen her come out of the house and pulled to the curb. Devon's voice startled her and she jumped as he said, "You OK?"

Ruth laughed nervously after the fright, "Do you always sneak up on people like that?"

"Ruth, I parked the car and came up the walk. I wasn't sneaking around!" Devon said incredulously.

"Ruth. Who's out there?" Dr. Yuell called as he heard voices.

"It's just me, Dr. Yuell. Devon St. James." Devon called through the door.

"Devon. Good to see you. Just helping Ruth with these college things." Dr. Yuell took off his new reading glasses.

"How's it going?"

Dr. Yuell didn't need any prompting as he began to talk about all the choices and all the exciting opportunities.

Ruth was happy and enthusiastic, but scared, too—the empty feeling in her stomach interfered with the joy. She'd never been away from home for more than a few days.

After Dr. Yuell's lengthy, exuberant talk with Devon, Devon turned back to Ruth. "Would you like to go for an ice cream? Would that be acceptable to you, sir?" he asked Ruth and Dr. Yuell in turn.

"Sounds like a nice idea on a warm night like this," Dr. Yuell remarked. "Go ahead, Ruth, if you want."

Ruth didn't know if she wanted to leave or not, but she heard herself say, "Yes." She left silently to get her purse and check her hair. *Why had she agreed to go?* She didn't want any ice cream and she certainly didn't want any more lectures about college, which was exactly what had happened the last time Devon had talked with her.

They drove in silence for awhile. "I've wanted to talk to you in private. I wanted to apologize for trying to be so bossy about going to college...but I didn't take the opportunity."

His apology startled Ruth as much as when he came to the house that evening. She savored being irate as she listened to others talk about him. His time at college and his successes were chronicled while others sang his praises about how kind he was to his family and friends. Ruth resisted such accounts as she hid her anger. "Why now?" Ruth asked.

"Don't know, really. Just saw you so alone and sad-looking there and remembered I wanted to apologize. Pulled over and I'm sitting here now," Devon smiled. "Timing's not too good, though, with you checking over your college entrance papers. Thought you might take a spoon to me when your father started talking about college." Ruth smiled at the image of taking some physical punishment out with Lady Dee's big worn, wooden spoon.

"You're lucky. I could have done some damage if I wasn't a properly raised child," she teased in return. Sobering Ruth continued, "Picking a college isn't easy."

"Where are you considering?" Devon asked after they ordered their sundaes.

Things couldn't be all bad with a treat of a chocolate sundae. Ruth told him about every option. He listened quietly and asked probing questions.

"What do you want to study?" was his next query. She'd told him with conviction and enthusiasm about her nursing and degree goals, even the pressure of being the daughter and granddaughter of doctors, college graduates and community leaders.

Ruth found herself looking into Devon's face and saying, as she slid into the car seat for the ride home, "You know Lady Dee's so excited about me graduating!"

"Oh! A future nurse to go along with her father being a doctor," Devon joked.

"Yes," Ruth laughed. "In part, and because we'll all have degrees!"

"It's a long road to get an education," Devon replied. "Your father talk about it much?"

"We love to hear him...and Lady Dee talk about how they managed to meet and all. He'd just come back from out of town," Ruth stopped as she realized she was rambling. She looked down suddenly, feeling embarrassed.

"Would it be all right if I asked your father for permission to ask you out sometime again?" Devon asked.

Another surprise! First, his apology, then being easy to talk to again, and now, asking to go out with her. "That...that would be nice." *Had this conversation turned from just a sundae-trying-to-make-a-person-feel-better situation?* The sinking feeling gave way to flutters.

Dr. Yuell came through the door and Devon said goodnight to them and headed for his car.

"Were you expecting Devon this evening?" he asked.

"No, father. He came by to apologize for trying to tell me what to do...about college. It was a while ago," Ruth said.

"I see," Dr. Yuell replied. "I've given Devon permission to take you to dinner on Saturday. That is what you wanted, wasn't it?"

"Yes, father. Thank you," was all Ruth could say to the riot of emotions piled on top of the decisions she needed to make. "Father? I know I want to learn all I can about...about nursing. I can't do that here." Her tone became mournful. "I need to find out what I can do."

Dr. Yuell seemed to sense his daughter's discomfort. Love and concern flashed from his eyes as he grabbed Ruth in a tender hug. "It's natural to be wary of the unknown. Isn't that right, Lady Dee?" Lady Dee came through the screen door.

"You talking about college, dear?" Lady Dee asked.

"Just telling her we'll back her no matter what she chooses." Dr. Yuell released the embrace.

"It's my biggest decision," Ruth began slowly. "I have an ambition to be a nurse. I keep looking and keep getting excited...and scared," Ruth gulped, and then smiled. "I've had a lot of advice, especially from both of you and...I'm thinking of accepting the offer from Chicago." Her parents looked at each other. Ruth rushed on. "I want to learn the latest techniques! It's a superior program; better than anything else we've researched." Ruth stopped for what seemed like a long time. "Chicago."

❦

When does love begin? Ruth didn't quite know with her love for Devon. Perhaps it sprang from his cool reasoning and confidence, which calmed her anxiety.

Devon was older in years and attitude than Ruth's other friends and beaus. Seemingly light-years ahead of Ruth and her peers in his knowledge and experience. He frequently came by to say hello and encourage Ruth before his attention was taken away by others. Ruth thought she saw irritation in his eyes that quickly disappeared as he was led away. *Was it just her imagination or was he really interested in he*r? The teasing of her friends intensified her internal questions.

"Seems like Devon's been around you a lot since he got home, Ruth," Nellie Sanders teased. "You been sneaking out to see him?"

Just stay calm, Ruth, she heard her father say in her mind. *People like Mrs. Purdy and Mrs. Applebee are just baiting you, wanting to get information.*

"What did you say, Nellie?" Ruth asked, pretending not to hear her question.

"Nellie asked you about Devon, Ruth. Interested in him?" Clara Beal asked more succinctly. They both looked at Ruth expectantly. Besides, she saw Calli Winston was now paying particular attention to the conversation.

Devon was a handsome man and an attractive escort, but he seemed far beyond her reach. She was just college-age, not old enough to really be accepted into Devon's crowd or participate in more sophisticated entertainment choices. She wondered if Devon, like a number of the college men, visited the saloons down by the tracks. Reverend Fredericks preached against these places. If Mrs. Daily's diner was one block instead of two blocks from the saloons, Ruth wondered if her father would have given her and Sylvie permission to work there.

Besides, she'd be away in Illinois and all those other girls at law school and in the neighborhood were always available. To admit too pointed an interest would lead to more teasing and ridicule, but to be too heated in her denial would surely raise other questions. Ruth's debating skills kicked into gear, obliging the point of his overall appeal but diluting the impact on her interests and her life.

"He's been telling me about his collegiate experience. I can use all the advice I can get. Have you asked him anything about you going to Memphis, Nellie?" Ruth asked trying to deflect their interest.

Nellie stared at Ruth's face to note any change in her reaction as the tall, pretty doe-eyed girl replied, "You know perfectly well I have, Ruth. Saw me ask him last Sunday after church. Hear Mae Claxton's got the inside track with him. Keeps inviting him over for dinner as many times as he'll come. Besides, her mother and Mrs. St. James are in the same ladies' sewing circle. Probably got their heads together on that one."

Clara continued the barbs. "Yeah, she sure got her wiles going on with Devon, 'What do you think of this?' and, 'Devon, what do you think of that?' No secret what she wants."

"You're right about it, Clara," Nellie laughed. "She almost dragged Devon away from Ruth at the Millers' party. Surprised to see him or Mae there. What do you think brought him, Ruth?"

"How about you, Missy Calli?" Clara said, not afraid to bring their gossip nemesis into the conversation since everyone knew Calli was interested in any marriage-age man in pants. "You've lures out to Devon but no bites yet?"

Calli's eyes turned cold as she looked at Clara. "I don't know what you're talking about." Calli turned and walked to the refreshment table.

All Nellie could do was laugh. "Bet a quarter, that's not so. Even bet a full dollar!"

On a hot, muggy night, promising rain, the Yuell children planned a simple gathering of teenagers and college friends. Eddie Fry asked permission from Dr. Yuell to open his car doors and sit on the seats to visit with friends. "Only in large group gatherings, Eddie. Must be more people in there than just you and a girl," Dr. Yuell said. "Don't want anyone getting the wrong impression of our fine young people."

As always, no detail was too small or insignificant. Ruth didn't know if anyone, let alone a sophisticated college student like Devon, would abide by the strictures of her parents' concerns. Boyfriends and boy visitors abided with all her father's pronouncements, observed in the fishbowl of community interest. Being a doctor's daughter definitely added to the challenge of being a teenager.

Ruth saw Devon making his way through their house into the kitchen where Esther Witman was helping her serve lemonade to all their friends.

"Hi, Devon. You want some lemonade?" Thelma questioned brightly as she continued to replenish cookie trays. Ruth jerked herself back to her task, not wanting Devon to see how awkward she felt in his presence. "Why'd you come so late?"

"Had to work late on some paperwork for my father," Devon answered. "Couldn't come over here until I got the job done."

Ruth relaxed a bit knowing it was work, and not someone, who attracted his time and attention. *Was she being foolish?* Ruth's hand shook and the lemonade pitcher spilled a few drops on the smooth tabletop. Ruth hoped Devon didn't attribute it to her thoughts of him and his presence there.

Neither of them got to find out as Dr. Yuell entered through the screen door. "Esther, is your father home? I must speak to your father immediately. Is he home?"

"I think he's over at the Shepherds' house, Dr. Yuell. I'll go call mother and ask." Esther headed for the parlor.

"Devon. Will you come with me, please?" Dr. Yuell asked as Ruth walked a step toward him as he headed for the door. Dr. Yuell shook his head. Ruth was stung as both men left to go down the back stairs, feeling like a ballroom dancer being abandoned in the middle of the floor.

Esther returned quickly. "Wonder what that's all about? Daddy's at the Shepherds', just like I thought. I'll go and tell your father. What's he doing with Devon? Give a nickel to know."

Ruth hadn't even wondered what was going on. Her thoughts were on Devon and trying to keep from spilling the lemonade. But now she saw her father did look worried and stern; something must be wrong.

Devon opened the screen door. "I've got to leave now. Say goodbye to every-one for me. Sorry, we didn't get to talk. Hopefully, later...," his voice trailed off as Nellie Bolls entered the kitchen.

"What's this with your father huddling with Devon out there? You know what's going on, Ruth?" Nellie asked loudly.

"No." Ruth returned to wiping the table. "He's got something to do, I think. Business is never done, I guess. Devon said something about helping his father."

"Came down to the stationery store for some paper stock. Waited on him myself," Samantha Mills offered as she grabbed two cookies from the plate.

"Paper? That all?" Nellie said, obviously deflated. "Why would he come here for that?"

"Getting late, Nellie. Still got chores to finish or are you going to walk?" Samantha said as she looked at her watch.

"Don't want to walk alone," Nellie replied, losing interest in her inquiry. "Going to be able to get everything done so we can meet tomorrow?"

"Yes. If we hurry now, we're fine. If I break curfew, my daddy will put his foot down faster than anything." Samantha grabbed two more cookies and lifted her arm to push at the screen. "Great cookies, Ruth. Thanks for having us. Come on, Nellie."

∾

Thelma helped Ruth clean up. Now, Ruth couldn't concentrate, thinking instead of her father and Devon with their serious-looking expressions and tired lines on both their faces.

Ruth hurried into the living room to see Lady Dee with the mending basket at her feet. This was a bad sign. Her mother frequently grabbed the mending basket when she was worried. "Father's stopping by the Shepherds' looking for Mr. Witman." Ruth waited a moment and added, "He asked to talk to Devon St. James. Alone."

Lady Dee jabbed at a brown sock hole. "I know I don't have to tell you to keep this confidential but Wilbur Garber is being detained at the jail and Calli Winston is in danger."

"What?!!" Ruth cry-whispered as she dove for the chair next to Lady Dee and grabbed her mother's arm. "Meggie must be frantic!"

"Some unfortunate thing or another." Lady Dee laid the sock over the sewing basket. "As far as I could interpret from the phone call from the jail, Wilbur found out there was going to be a talent scout or something at the Moonglow Tavern. Took his saxophone and Calli down there tonight and the place got raided."

"Are they safe?" Ruth inquired again in a whisper.

"It's all rather suspect, if you ask me. Sadie Thompkins, the owner, called from the jail. Which was kind of her, considering her call to our home was the only one she'd get to make. They need bail and all. Knowing how your father feels about saloons in general...with all the carousing going on in those places." Dr. Yuell frequently and loudly let everyone know his feelings about drinking liquor, throwing money down the drain, the evils of loose living, and the health implications.

After several long hours, the headlight flash of the family car in the driveway ended their conversation. "Ruth, pour a cup of coffee. There's a pot on the stove." Lady Dee went out the door.

Dr. Yuell wearily grimaced as he sat down at the head of the kitchen table. Lady Dee folded his suit jacket as he rubbed his face with splayed fingers. "It's been a long day. Lady Dee said she told you about Wilbur and Calli. Haven't sorted it all out in my mind, but we've done all we can tonight. See you got me some coffee. That's good. Real good. Been a long day for you, too.

"Don't like to talk about a situation without all the facts," he began, "but I think this incident has got something to do with the labor negotiations down at the hotels." Dr. Yuell, several pastors, and prominent citizens had been working with the NAACP and the hotel workers to get better pay and working conditions at the hotels in the region. "Some pressure to call the whole thing off. Reverend Siddell is leading the initiative." Dr. Yuell folded his hands around the mug in a nervous gesture. "Miss Thompkins got several calls at the saloon about a week ago saying a talent person was coming from Chicago. The information seemed to check out and all. She advertised, putting up fliers in her place asking for people to come and tryout for prize money, a chance to go to Chicago and get a break in the music business. Tonight was the night."

Ruth remembered hearing snatches from her friends or at the church, she couldn't quite remember. But with the mention of the Moonglow, she didn't pay any more attention. She wouldn't be going; not with her parents' strict and abiding rules concerning the place. "Guess Wilbur thought the chance was too tempting. You know there are a number of upstanding people who want music careers."

"I think people were lured over there to be jailed," Dr. Yuell concluded. "Seems police who conducted the raid were asking for certain people *by name*, including all the pastors and officials in the NAACP. Even us." Lady Dee and Ruth both inhaled sharply.

"Us?" Lady Dee questioned.

"Seems so to me," Dr. Yuell replied. "Miss Thompkins didn't give too much away in her call. Said the police were right there by the desk, which was strange. Whenever there's been trouble, the guards make the calls. Some like to be a bit smug when they're reporting trouble. Not this time. Miss Thompkins said there were 'two nice policemen and three detectives' standing all around her." Dr. Yuell shifted in his chair. "Usually they're all at home or asleep this late, after business hours. They were the ones giving her the names and asking her if anyone in the holding cells were related to any of us. Started asking her about names as soon as the exits at the Moonglow were all covered."

"Where's Calli?" Ruth asked. "Did they get her or anyone else?"

"No, not really," her father replied to her questioning face. "When the police started coming, Miss Thompkins thankfully pushed Calli into the room where the performers dress. Hid her under the vanity skirt of the makeup table. Told her to stay there all night if need be and not make a sound. When the police asked her what she was doing ducking in there, Miss Thompkins said she was going for bail money. Got the message about Calli to one of the patrons and he filled me in after they let him go. She was just calling to see if I got the message. That's where Devon St. James came in."

"Devon St. James?" Ruth cried. "He was there?"

"No, no," Dr. Yuell laughed, lightening his mood as some of the tired lines disappeared from his face. "I couldn't find anyone to help me and this was an emergency. Had him go over to the Moonglow to get Calli out of there. Could make a cover story by saying Devon and Calli were out for a movie show and a soda or something rather than her being with Wilbur and getting arrested at the Moonglow."

"Are they safe?" Ruth asked tentatively.

"They're fine. You can ask Meggie tomorrow. But only in private, you hear?" Dr. Yuell warned sharply. "Gotta' keep this quiet. Could still blow up if people find out about it. Devon's real smart, though. Got stopped by some police who pulled into the Moonglow parking lot. Told them he was working for the lawyer and picking up some stuff to pawn for bail for Miss Thompkins. Guess he found an old area rug and wrapped Calli in it. Walked it right past the policemen and put her in the car."

Both Ruth and Lady Dee startled, and then all three of them started laughing. "Wish we could tell this story to everyone but it might get out. Devon was very cool under pressure." The laughter left Dr. Yuell's face and eyes. "Another strange thing. They had a reporter and photographer down at the station. When has a raid of a Negro saloon ever gotten much press attention? We're going to have to be careful. Pressure's on to break this thing about the hotel workers. No burning crosses or their white satin witch hats yet, but our opposition still means business."

"Why can't they just treat us decently and fairly?" Lady Dee remarked.

Dr. Yuell just shrugged and answered, "Only the good Lord knows." He got up from the chair. "It's late and I've got to get up early. There's an emergency meeting of the Hotel Steering Committee set for tomorrow."

"You both go ahead. I'll finish cleaning up here. You want the sewing kit in the hall closet, mother?" Ruth asked as her thoughts cascaded over Devon, the police, Calli, and the Moonglow.

"Don't be too long, Ruth. Are the doors locked?" Lady Dee called in a tired voice from the stair landing. "Make sure, you hear?"

"Yes, mother," Ruth called back. Now Ruth knew the threats her father alluded to were real as she walked over to the kitchen door, locked it, and rattled the knob to hear the reassuring sound. There was the threat of trouble but what about Devon? *How was he? Was he still in danger?* She'd find out in the morning.

Ruth tossed and turned, picturing the scene: how Calli had hunched down under the table waiting to be rescued and how Devon talked to the police.

Unanswered questions kept Ruth awake as well as how she could contrive to see Devon tomorrow and find out.

❧❧

The next morning didn't go much better and Ruth's irritation grew. Meggie was home taking care of Calli, who was "with a cold," Rulene Reynolds told Ruth when she dropped by to talk of plans for her birthday party. Fortunately, it didn't appear Rulene knew anything of the previous evening. Ruth rubbed her tired neck muscles.

Rulene had remarked, "You're looking peaked, too, Ruth. If you've got any germs around, don't you go breathing any of them on me. I don't want getting sick to spoil things!"

"I'm not. Just did some mending with Lady Dee last night after the party. Guess I stayed up too late." Ruth related this plausible part of last night's happenings, unable to gain any more information before it was time for her and Sylvie to get to work.

❧❧

After a busy day at the diner, the end of the day couldn't come too soon. Ruth walked home on leaden feet hoping dinner preparations would be uncomplicated and she could disappear to her room for an early night. Her parents, hopefully, would attribute her fatigue to her workday. Ruth was thinking of her "excuses" when she noticed someone sitting on the kitchen stairs.

Devon saw Ruth and Sylvie as they rounded the cement walk to the driveway and walked to greet them. "I didn't know if it would be proper to pick you up at the diner so I waited here."

"Are you OK?" Ruth asked. He looked just fine to her in a long-sleeve white shirt and khaki slacks. He must have finished his work and changed to more casual clothes, unlike the coat and tie when he was working with his father.

"He looks good," Sylvie said, not knowing the pretext of the question.

Lady Dee called. "Sylvie. I've got some fresh cookies and milk for you."

Sylvie smiled as she headed up the stairs and turned back to speak. "Cookies."

Ruth felt so grateful her mother would allow her some time alone to talk to Devon and find out what happened.

"Your father told you?" he asked. "Guess I paid more attention then I thought in my literature and world history classes. Saw the carpet in the dressing room... thought of the story about hiding someone in the rug." Devon smiled brightly and laughed a bit. "Heard Mrs. Delbart at the high school teaches that story in class."

"Yes. That was really clever. Too bad you can't tell Mrs. Delbart. She still has one or two students falling asleep every year. This might really give her some hope," Ruth giggled. "She told us Cleopatra was a beautiful Negro woman who probably looked like Lena Horne."

"I was told Cleopatra looked like Lena Horne in a similar class in DC," Devon laughed in reply.

"That's nothing. William Bents got sent to the principal for saying Mrs. Delbart had taught so long she probably knew Cleopatra."

"I talked to your father and he asked me to help find Calli. Thought that would be OK. Didn't think the police would still be there. Calli was still under the table. Told her I might have to leave her because the police were nosing around. Calli wouldn't let me leave her alone because she was so scared. Said she'd heard steps two times after the raid and muffled voices but no one calling her out by name, so Calli stayed put. Smart thing, too. With the story about the raid plastered all over the paper this morning."

"The paper!" Ruth recalled. "Father mentioned a reporter and photographer at the jail."

"They took lots of pictures at the Moonglow. Broken flash bulbs all over the place. Must have been tipped off, like your father said. Had everybody against the wall. Like a lineup. Very professional-like," Devon concluded. "The article went on about 'criminal elements' and 'troublemakers' in the Negro community. Real shame but it would have been worse if Calli Winston or anyone else's relative working on the Hotel Steering Committee had been arrested."

"So how did you get Calli in the rug?" Ruth asked.

"It wasn't easy. Believe you me," Devon laughed and shook his head. "I pulled off her shoes and put a towel over her face. Didn't want any sneezes or falling shoes to give us away. Told her to be quiet and not move until she heard the trunk shut and we were at least several blocks away from the Moonglow. Rolled Calli up, went out to open the trunk and told the police I'd found a rug and a few other doodads and jewelry I was going to pawn for Miss Thompkin's bail. Picked Calli and the rug up and dropped it in the car trunk and drove away. Didn't think I'd be able to pull it all off if I'd had to put down the carpet and pick it up again in front of the police. I didn't feel nervous until we were to the Meanses' house."

"How's Calli?" Ruth asked.

"Knows she put her uncle's reputation at risk by going to the Moonglow with Wilbur. The Hotel Committee could have been affected." He looked at his leather-banded watch. "My parents are concerned about last night," he said quietly. "*Quite* concerned about how close I came to getting arrested."

Ruth wondered how the St. James family could think anything so brave was bad. "Oh."

"There were reporters and my father is on the Hotel Committee. If I would have been caught or Calli didn't do as she was told ..." Devon's voice trailed off. "My father told me to say nothing to my mother or Letty."

Ruth's brow creased. *Did that mean that the St. Jameses were angry with her father? His actions?*

"Father is having Mr. Meiers's carpet company get the carpet back to the Moonglow now," Devon said quickly. Mrs. Thompkins is out on bail. There were no charges, really. None of them broke the law." Ruth nodded in understanding. "But I did want to ask you if you'd like to go to the music concert over at church next Saturday."

Ruth's heart raced to her throat. "That would be nice."

"I was hoping for your company. Tell Dr. Yuell I'll come by later to ask him personally. Must go now, Miss Ruth," he said formally as he started for his car at the end of the driveway. Ruth suddenly didn't feel tired anymore. Her usual inclination would have been to tell Meggie, but this time it was different. She wanted to pillow her feelings to herself. Sharing would ruin it, like letting perfume evaporate from its bottle.

Dr. Yuell gave her permission to go to the church concert and out for ice cream after the program, even though it was a Saturday night—if there was another couple in attendance. He amended the entrenched habit of everyone going to bed early because Sunday morning preparations usually started before the sun. Devon promised not to keep her out too late. "We'll be going with Meggie Winston and her date."

Dr. Means was also on the alert, making it clear to Meggie she could *not* be seen without at least one other couple who he deemed acceptable.

"Aunt Eleanor took Calli down in the basement and yelled at her for two hours. Then she told her to zip her lips and never to say anything about the Moonglow again! Never seen Calli so quiet," Meggie said. "Even I feel sorry for her. Calli can't go out for two weeks and no boys can ask her for a date for a month."

When Devon came to pick up Meggie and Ruth on Saturday, Ed Shepherd, Meggie's escort, was already in the car. Meggie sat in the back seat with Ruth and Ed sat up front with Devon. "If I hear any different information, about the destination or any other couples involved, there would be no more dates," Dr. Means warned.

Even Devon, as a grown man, listened to Dr. Means's instructions and promised to abide by them. It seemed like a church oath, as the young people solemnly looked into the doctor's stern face as they stood in the living room. Ruth wondered about two things: if Ed had any questions concerning Dr. Means's harsh rules and if Calli was listening from her bedroom.

"Tell you, Ruth. Don't know what I was more scared about—whether the police were going to find Calli or what my uncle was going to do when he found out," Meggie whispered. "Thankfully, Miss Thompkins hid Calli or she'd be in bigger trouble for sure. All those church biddies clucking their tongues like Mr. Bekins's chickens in their coop."

"Aunt Eleanor hasn't talked about it. Calli really let her down, I guess," Meggie said. "If this gets out, she'll be answering for her household instead of the other way around and she doesn't like the fact one bit!"

"My father would have me restricted to home till I was old as Mrs. Delbart!" Ruth whispered back.

"Everybody'd be talking for months. Some people don't let you explain. They think the worst—adding to their list of gossip to chew on for years and years. Being a doctor's niece makes it juicier for all of their speculation. If Calli's name and face were spread all over the paper, Uncle and Aunt Eleanor would about die of mortification. All Calli wanted to do was see Wilbur play his trumpet and win the prize." Meggie shook her head. "Sounded good and innocent at the time. Don't you think? How were they supposed to know the police wanted to catch some Negro leaders or associates to discredit the hotel thing? Even Miss Thompkins was fooled. Advertising it and all. Doesn't seem fair. Can't even tell anybody about Calli's adventure except you. Not fair at all."

"It could have been much more serious," Ruth offered. At the same time, Ruth frowned, remembering Mr. St. James voiced his concern and told Devon to say *nothing* to his mother or Letty. *Would this incident come between the beginning of a relationship she and Devon could build?*

The double date ended too soon. Devon opened the car door and escorted Ruth to her door. Ruth was just about to thank him for the evening as she heard him say, "Would you like to go to the church supper in three weeks? I hear they're having a fine spread, honoring Mrs. Willetts's many years of service to the church."

Just as Ruth was about to speak, Dr. Yuell stepped through the doorway. "You have a good time?"

"I did, Dr. Yuell. I was just asking if Ruth could accompany me to Mrs. Willetts's service dinner in three weeks. My family should be home by then. Of course, I was also going to ask your permission, too, sir," Devon concluded formally.

Ruth marveled at his composure as he smoothly transitioned from talking to her to asking her father for his consent. Other beaus hedged, stuttered, and stammered to the point of having her father complete their thoughts. "Let Ruth and I think about it, Devon. Ruth will get back to you before you leave for

Washington." Ruth smiled at Devon knowing her father's response was his way of saying yes but not wanting it to appear too easy.

"I understand, Dr. Yuell," Devon replied as he looked at Dr. Yuell and then turned again to Ruth. "I had a good time this evening. I'll be calling you before we leave, if that's all right with you and your parents. I've left Ed in the car too long and have to get him home. Dr. Yuell. Miss Ruth." Nodding to each of them, Devon strode down the driveway to his car.

Dr. Yuell held the door open as he said, "Got you home by nine p.m. Was he polite and abiding by Dr. Means's rules?"

"Yes, father," Ruth replied.

"Well good, then. If you want to go out with Devon in three weeks, I'll talk to Lady Dee. Tell him tomorrow if you like. Make sure all your chores are done here. If that's done properly, you can call Devon and tell him to pick you up at five-thiry. Think that should be enough time." Even if it wasn't, Ruth wouldn't have said anything. She didn't want to say a word to ruin it.

CHAPTER NINE

After Mrs. Willetts's dinner, ladies in the community started asking pointed questions about Devon and Ruth. Lady Dee deftly explained Devon and his family were dear family friends and he was just catching up with her daughter and the family after his trip from Washington, DC. She also reminded them, just as pointedly, that Ruth intended to go to school in Chicago. That effectively stopped speculation and even sank Ruth's more romantic hopes as she remembered all the other eligible girls always flitting around Devon. Then, there was Henry Bascomb and the July Fourth dance. Henry had been a leading man in Ruth's paltry girlhood dreams before Devon. Ruth stood for long hours of fittings for her pink tulle-trimmed dress thinking of dancing with Devon instead of Henry.

Before leaving for the July Fourth dance, Dr. Yuell came to Ruth with a small florist box. Ruth had seen it in the refrigerator and thought her father had bought it for Lady Dee. "I must say you look handsome in your dark suit," Ruth said with a smile.

"Thank you, Ruth. I do hope I can please Lady Dee in my escort efforts this evening. She's as beautiful as the day I met her." Dr. Yuell whispered, "This isn't from me but another secret admirer."

Ruth looked questioningly into his eyes. "Devon?" she whispered.

"Yes." He kissed Ruth's cheek. "Devon asked me if I would allow him to buy this for you. He was very persistent about it," Dr. Yuell smiled appreciatively. "See what you think." Ruth looked at the two delicate pink roses and daisies in the leaf-edged cluster in the mirror. She hadn't saved her prom corsage but she vowed these flowers would be dried and pressed as a treasured memento. Her cheeks grew hot.

"Why?" was all Ruth could think to say.

"Well," Dr. Yuell took a deep breath. "It's a special time for you and Devon wanted to know what I thought would be an appropriate graduation gift. He's been thinking about it for weeks."

"Graduation is over. He wanted to give me a gift?" Ruth looked at the reflection of the corsage in the mirror. "You won't tell him I acted so foolish, will you?"

"Guess I should have asked you about it first, Ruth, but I thought you might prefer the surprise. Think it's too personal?" Dr. Yuell frowned. "Did I make a mistake?"

"No. No. Of course not!" *What to say?* she wondered. "It's lovely. Lovely of him to want to do it. Lovely of you to help him give me a graduation gift."

"Looks pretty with your dress." Dr. Yuell seemed reassured. "It'll be time to leave in a few minutes."

This was such a puzzle! The corsage meant he must think of her, too—perhaps only in a friendly sense, but strong enough to ask her father for permission to give her a gift.

Jealous thoughts replaced the hopeful ones. *Had Devon sent corsages to other family friends who graduated, too?* Ruth hoped not, deciding to see what happened and pray a little for her corsage to be the only graduation gift Devon sent to anyone. Ruth lifted her collar to capture the fragrance and walked quickly down the stairs.

Ruth accepted each of Devon's subsequent invitations. She mentally kicked herself several times each hour as she thought of him because her life had no room for love. Her future was in Chicago, helping to break down racial barriers. She knew she was being a fool but she couldn't help herself.

Chicago was a long way away from St. Louis and four years was a long time. Ruth remembered what Devon said about taking advantage of the opportunity. *How could she regret something Devon had encouraged her to do?* She wouldn't disappoint Devon, her parents...or her community!

Devon seemed to sense her tension. "You're wondering about Chicago, aren't you?"

Ruth looked up, angry at her failure to cover her feelings more effectively. She thought she had been hiding it so well. "What do you mean?" Ruth bumbled for words trying to save her pretense.

"You're telling me you haven't thought about it? About us?" Devon's smile took the sting out of the volatile question.

Forgetting all about the feminine strictures about being secretive and coy, Ruth replied, "I've thought about it many times every day."

"I have, too," Devon stated quietly. "You've got all your college years ahead of you. It'll be a wonderful thing...getting to go up north and all."

"What are you trying to say?" Ruth asked shakily.

"Just thinking many envy us the chance to go, that's all, Miss Ruth," Devon replied honestly.

"I've never thought of quitting or not going to Chicago," Ruth said flatly. She still didn't have any answers. "Guess I'm just nervous...about a lot of things."

"Won't you feel proud when you graduate?" A smile returned to Devon's face. "That's the way I'm going to feel when my sisters and you graduate. Alice wants to go to college near Washington, DC, but Cherie's another question. Hope she'll be getting offers to go north, too. Told her I'd take her myself." Hope replaced some of the fear when Ruth heard him mention her name in his family litany.

"You'll be proud of me?" Ruth hoped to keep her romantic ideas intact.

"What are you fishing for, Miss Ruth?" Devon asked. Embarrassment made her look away. Ruth wasn't any better at being coy than she was at not being honest. "You asking about us?" he said so softly. Ruth looked into his questioning eyes and Devon said it again. "You asking about us?" Ruth couldn't speak. She only nodded, and even then, just barely. "Well, you don't have to ask," Devon continued gently as he lightly grasped her upper arm to turn her toward him. "Thought you knew." Ruth sadly shook her head, her lips pursed and turned downward.

"Guess I'm going to have to make it plain, then," Devon stated matter-of-factly. "I apologize for not saying something but I truly thought you knew. Haven't seen anybody else for weeks now. Thought you were comfortable being mine." Devon pulled Ruth close and brushed a kiss on her forehead. "It might take four years but I hope we have a future. I'm willing to wait till you tell me either way."

"Yours?" Ruth pulled her head away. "I had hoped but I didn't know. Are you sure? Yours?" she asked again, getting things straight in her head and reassuring her heart.

"You really didn't know? Well, I'll make it plain again and any other time you ask me. You are the young woman for me." Ruth breathed a sigh of joy and relief. "I love you. Let's just take things slow."

"Oh, Devon. I think I've loved you for the longest time," Ruth began.

"There's a big world out there, Miss Ruth, and four years is a long time. Things might change for you...and I don't want to hold you back from finding them," Devon stated as he cast a serious look into her eyes. "It's the truth. Please believe me. You go to Chicago. We'll keep in close touch but you've got to have your chance to experience life without thinking of things back here gumming up your chances."

"I've been looking into trying to graduate college in three years instead of four."

"You'd do that for us?" Devon asked.

Ruth could only nod as she watched Devon's head slowly descend toward her face.

He gently pressed his fingers to her lips and his gaze changed to warm kindness. "Believe me. No more about it now. We've settled things, for now, I hope. I'll be talking to Dr. Yuell about it in the next few days."

"Have you spoken to your parents?" Ruth asked.

"I'm a man now. Making my own decisions," Devon said with feeling. "Let's go for some ice cream."

ෛ

"So Devon thinks your feelings might change after you've gone to Chicago? Your father said much the same thing, one time," Lady Dee replied to her daughter's shock and dismay. *First Devon? And now her father?* "Don't go getting all upset, Ruth. It's really an honorable thing to do, on Devon's part. It's just, in your father's case, he had so much schooling ahead of him. He was just being honest and practical about the scrimping life of getting an education. Got my head out of the romantic clouds thinking if I wanted to go through that with him. Till death do you part is a long time on the mature-thinking side of it."

"You're telling me the good part of the story?" Ruth asked incredulously.

"Well, yes. I guess I am. I was completely committed to your father. Didn't think for a moment that he didn't love me. Just thought both he and I should be blessed sure before we kept going in our courtship." Lady Dee talked without rancor as she continued to peel potatoes. "Devon went about it the wrong way with you, I guess. Devon's a grown man ready to marry but somehow his heart has chosen you. You're just starting in college soon and he's going to have to wait a long time. He's back here with the rest of his professional life on his mind, but little social life now, since he's pledged himself to you. Every biddy in town and back is just itching for him to look at or talk to another girl and report it to me or you. You'll be free as a bird according to everybody, experiencing things for the first time. It will be lonely and hard for him, too, but in a different way."

"I've never loved anyone before Devon," Ruth gulped as her eyes started to sting with tears.

"I know." Lady Dee wiped her wet hands on her apron and came to hug her daughter. "He's doing everything he can to let you know he loves you and still let you fly away like a little bird from the nest. It's scary to let your little birds grow up. But we have to let you, no matter how much we love you. It's God's way."

"So you're telling me Devon's right?" Ruth asked.

"You said it," Lady Dee replied as she got back to the potatoes, "...and I can see by the look behind your eyes you're getting to know it, too."

"Yes, Lady Dee. Thank you so much." Ruth's heart seemed to be more settled now.

☯

The summer of 1957 flew by with lightning rapidity. Even though Devon and Ruth tried to spend every available hour with each other, it was never enough.

Ruth's going to college up north was being mentioned in tandem with the *Brown vs. Board of Education* ruling, the Montgomery bus boycott, and the push to desegregate Central High in Little Rock, Arkansas—as a great achievement and something to cherish. The excitement and enthusiasm of others in the community concerning her going to college in Chicago included many, "Do it for us," and, "Do us proud, you hear?"

"See," Devon said. "You've been offered a chance. I'll still be here rooting for you and praying for you."

Ruth straightened her backbone even though the journey on the horizon seemed like traveling to the other side of the moon; she was relying on Devon's words and Lady Dee's assurances concerning Devon's maturity and commitment. Ruth wondered if Miss Rosa Parks felt like she did, eager to help the Negro community but just more than a little bit scared about how things would all end up. Ruth's fears were the leaving home, leaving Devon, and going all the way to Chicago, Illinois.

Reverend Fredericks kept on talking and negotiating with church and government officials as he participated in organized planning to start protests at a bus station south of the city as well as several lunch counters and a train depot on the Arkansas border. The white citizenry remained recalcitrant, at best, in what changes they would consider. "We seem an endless ocean apart on some issues, as if they'll never consider restoring any privileges or power to us."

What would happen was the question on everyone's mind. *Would all the progress be swallowed up in hatred again?* Were the cracks in the wall of prejudice filling in, yet again, and denying them justice after the Jim Crow laws? Would the northern colleges suddenly decide educating Negroes was passé and decide to plop Ruth back in Missouri?

"Don't forget. You promised to write and call," Ruth reminded Devon more often as the day of her departure came near. "Often. Very often." Ruth knew asking for expensive phone calls was an extravagant request but she wanted to hold on to the hope she'd be able to hear his voice, at least a few times before she came back for

Christmas. It seemed like a hundred degrees in the shade and she was already pining for getting back for Devon and Christmas!

"I know. I know," Devon smiled. "By the way, I've got some things to celebrate Christmas early this year. You wait here while I go out to the car." Devon held two gaily-wrapped parcels with frothy bows. "Alice wrapped them for me."

"This is *better* than Christmas," she cried as she rushed to open the door. "Put them on the table by the chair," Ruth said breathlessly. "I want to see everything!"

Ruth plopped down in excitement, forgetting her lady-like manners. The first was a large box, larger than any gift Ruth recalled receiving, besides the new winter coat she'd gotten two years ago.

"Here," Devon interrupted. "Let me cut the binding." He smiled, deftly splitting the cord with a few twists of the knife and his wrist. Ruth grabbed at the shredded paper. Gold and brown gleamed against the wrapping paper. She looked questioningly at Devon as she pulled the paper away. "A leather thesaurus and a dictionary!"

"What's so exciting?" Lady Dee called as Ruth just dove for Devon's neck for a hug as she realized his generosity.

"Devon gave me these leather-bound books," her muffled cry rose from his collar.

"What fine books!" Lady Dee brought her hand to her mouth. "Devon, that's so generous." Her mother, for once, looked as incredulous as she.

"I couldn't," Ruth said as her sense returned. "They're beautiful but it's so extravagant. I...I can't accept them."

"You're not going to hurt my feelings, are you?" Devon asked. "Have to promise to write every chance you get for all three years you're away."

"No, I'd never intentionally hurt your feelings," Ruth replied simply as she raised her right arm to portray a mock swearing ceremony. "*All* three years."

"Glad you like the gift. Now open the other one," Devon stated.

She'd forgotten about the other present in her excitement. Ruth turned toward it then back to Devon and Lady Dee in her confusion. "Oh, I can't. I just can't."

Ruth heard Lady Dee's laughter. "Better stop teasing her, Devon." She turned to her daughter. "Ruth, you'd better stop sputtering before Devon leaves in a huff for our ungraciousness."

"Better do as Lady Dee says," Devon admonished, still smiling.

"Go ahead, Ruth," Lady Dee encouraged. Ruth hesitantly went back to the chair still wondering why there wasn't a Christmas tree in the window and pine garland on the stairs. She'd never received two gifts, when it wasn't Christmas. Ruth closed her eyes and put the second smaller box on her lap. She slowly pulled the paper from the smaller box. It was a silver bracelet. Made of unbreakable links, Ruth thought. Tears came down her teenage cheeks. Devon rushed toward her.

"If I would have known it would make you cry, I would have chosen another gift," he said with fake pouty lips as he grabbed Ruth's shoulders, making her giggle. Ruth wiped the tears with shaky fingers.

"You sure are spoiling her, Devon. I better get back to the kitchen, although I'm sure Dr. Yuell would understand a little burned meat for leather-bound books *and* a beautiful silver bracelet," Lady Dee said wistfully.

"I'll cherish these," Ruth called to Lady Dee as she left. "I will, Devon. These are the most beautiful presents I've ever gotten but I asked you over here about something else." Ruth began wanting to get an important issue off her mind. "I don't know if you'll understand."

"What won't I understand?" Devon's smile evaporated and his mood changed to wariness.

Ruth plunged right in not knowing how else to say it. "I don't want you to see me off at the train," she said with her eyes closed tight against his reaction.

"Is that all, honey? You had me scared for a minute. Faced all kind of potential problems in the split seconds the smile faded from your face. Your seriousness gave me a start." Devon relaxed again.

"You...you...mean, it's OK?" Ruth asked with relief. "I'll just be trying to be brave and trying even harder not to cry, and then, I'll start to cry. I just know it. I don't want to leave you. I'd like to pack you in my suitcase and take you with me. I'll be embarrassed and you'll try not to be sad. Can we just say goodbye in private and I can cry all I want?" Ruth gulped away the impending emptiness she felt already. "You know I'm honored to go to Chicago. You know I'm going to do my very best to represent my family and our community but I can't help it if leaving you is making me feel sad. We're going to be apart till Christmas," Ruth rushed through the words as the tears started to flow again. "See. I can't help it," she said as she left the chair and headed for the handkerchief in her purse. "I don't want to be embarrassed at the train station. My eyes just don't know I should be happy."

Devon hauled Ruth into his arms. "I understand too well, Miss Ruth. I'll be crying, too. Sometimes there are invisible tears. The invisible kind no one can see."

❦

On that late August morning Ruth left to go to college, she'd gotten into the car, sighed, and put her head back against the backseat cushion of the family sedan. So far back, the back of her close-brimmed straw hat touched her neck. Ruth opened her eyes to stare at the gray cloth upholstery. Her hands trembled a bit. Ruth watched the morning shadows of the late summer trees racing with the sunlight. She congratulated herself for not crying. Ruth's silence hadn't been from strength but basically because she'd been crying for days in Devon's willing arms. They'd said goodbye that last night after a quiet dinner at the restaurant in the neighborhood, bittersweet like flat champagne in a fancy bottle, though she'd never tasted any wine in her life. That would have to wait until she was twenty-one, when Devon said they could share a taste together.

Devon teased her into agreeing to continue her driving lessons during Christmas vacation. Something he'd demised to take her mind off of today. "You're going to have to be able to drive a car to be independent."

Leroy tried to keep the light-hearted mood going. "You both lived through it," Leroy joked. "Can't think of anything better to find out about another person, then to risk life and limb teaching them to drive. You got enough insurance, Devon?" Ruth tried her best but so far she'd only had the courage to drive down a few side streets in the neighborhood.

Devon reminded her of their verbal jousting and Ruth's nervous white-knuckled grinding of gears and floor pedals. Devon's car was certainly different than driving the family sedan. He was doing his best to distract her from her fear and the impending loneliness. After a few more awkward words, they shared a final long embrace and she waved until Devon was out of sight around the corner and hidden by the houses and trees.

Now Ruth sat in tense silence next to her father. Lady Dee had chosen to say goodbye at home. Like her daughter, she was unable to stem the flow of embarrassing tears.

Dr. Yuell remained a bit stiff and nervous, too. Ruth thought of Devon talking about crying invisible tears. If her father's conversation and actions said anything, he was weeping invisible buckets. Ease and camaraderie fled with their anxious behavior. The older man asked his daughter mechanical questions, repeating himself several times, about the snack money Lady Dee already had given her in front of him at the house and if she had the baggage tickets for her suitcase and steamer trunk. Ruth dutifully opened her purse after each request to show him the money or the stubs. Then he asked if Ruth had her train tickets. After showing him the envelope, Ruth finally said she was all set and she was going to miss him and be fine in Chicago. He seemed to relax a bit but some edginess remained.

The minutes till boarding dragged as Ruth nervously looked at the station clock every thirty seconds. "Ruth? We've got a few minutes for prayer," Dr. Yuell said in a quiet voice. Ruth suddenly felt very small as her father held her hands and talked quietly to his daughter and their God. Those soft words, echoing in the station, felt like a solemn benediction to her teenage life in Missouri.

After the station master's call, the last familiar thing Ruth remembered seeing were those same fatherly hands waving her into the future and into God's hands as he stood on the wooden platform.

The train strained on the tracks, seemingly not wanting to leave anymore than Ruth did at that moment. Finally, the engine gained control and momentum, taking her away from St. Louis. Silent tears could come now. Ruth had been brave for her father and managed to stick to it. She flailed all her anxiety, fear, and trepidation from her aching right arm as she waved goodbye to her father's receding figure held in dark silhouette against the train station wall. The pain from those aching muscles helped because it took Ruth's mind away from her loneliness. She waved long after she could not see him. Truthfully, several seconds longer than that. As long as Ruth kept waving, she felt less afraid. She could concentrate on the action and the pain and not her thoughts.

Ruth opened up her pocketbook to retrieve two things: a starched white handkerchief her mother trained her to carry for such moments for sneezes and tears, and a folded page of letter stationary from the St. Jameses' family graduation gift. One tear dripped on the paper and she swiped it away, not wanting to leave any marks on the expensive paper and several more fell into the dainty linen hankie folds.

Ruth took a deep breath, calmed herself, returned to an erect lady-like posture, and forced her gaze forward as if to see her road ahead. Ruth was going to write Devon, vowing to chronicle her experiences to him as best she could, whenever she could. "You won't feel so lonely that way because I'll be there right with you mixed in with the writing. You can talk to me on paper and tell me everything."

> *Dear Devon,*
>
> *My trip is a solitary one. A "pretty far ride for a teenage girl," as Miss Purkey would say A light-year's trip for a girl like me. I'm tired from dreading the goodbyes and thinking about my college future in Chicago. My trip will come in several stops and stages. We'll be stopping in Cairo, Illinois, and Springfield, I think. I know you went over the schedule with me but not much has been sticking to my brain recently. Don't worry, I'll be fine. We can face the challenge of three years!*

Her pen stopped. Ruth knew she'd had lots to share.

❦❦

Without fanfare, Ruth miraculously entered the integrated world. People had talked about it, even going as far back as Nettie's confidences, and told her how some things were different in Chicago. Suddenly, she was on an integrated train car, in an integrated state, and in an integrating society. Integrating, as Devon and her father would say, because the citizens of both the north and the South would discover, there were many visible and invisible barriers and layers between segregation and true integration. But that didn't matter to her at this moment. She savored the freedom as if it were a tangible thing because she could sit in any coach car on the train from the first to the last if she wanted. There should have been a brass band. She felt she could stand right there in the aisle and shout!

Ruth wanted to share this experience with someone! She felt sad that Devon, her parents, or siblings weren't there to share this victory. Ruth wanted to run through the train car with profound elation—just like she and her siblings, Leroy and Thelma, ran down the street at home when they were children. Ruth wanted to jump on the plush seats because she felt the same joy and abandon when she and Nettie bounced on their beds at home and at the Wilcox house.

Any faded green seat had only to be vacant and it was hers for the price of a ticket. Any one at all! No colored-only waiting rooms. No "Coloreds only" signs. No mop bucket for a restroom—just the promise of a wide-open, shining wood, metal, and porcelain bathroom with pine-smelling toilet stalls.

Ruth tried to memorize the look and the feel of things so she could remember them. Bring them back when times got lonely or tough. Something to help when she was tired or when silly people called her racist names. Exhilarating moments felt like diving into a cold river on a scorching hot summer's day. *The heat leaves but now what was a body going to do with the cold?* Her heart was beating fast. Ruth squeezed the handle on her purse. Ruth didn't have to do anything this minute. She'd just sit back and enjoy this ride, to be replayed and relived from the store-houses of her heart and mind.

ᏋᎧ

Besides leaving her parents and Devon, explaining her need to go to college to Sylvie had been the hardest. Ruth fell back to the story of the Three Pigs. Meggie helped her with the additional story they would tuck in the back of the book. The cardboard and colored paper book cover was rounded on the ends; exposing its tattered, repaired pages of the original story and the pages Ruth and Meggie had written and illustrated to explain the deaths of her grandparents, Nettie's disappearance, and her coming to live with the Yuells.

"How old is Sylvie again?" Meggie asked as she outlined Ruth's character for the new book pages.

"We think she's thirty, perhaps older," Ruth replied, cutting some pages to fit into the book. "We celebrate her birthday in June because Mrs. Wilcox's correspondence with the people involved before she died indicated that's when she was born." She measured the book again to make sure the new story would fit properly. "My father got a birth certificate registered but it took quite a bit of time. Her people didn't stay long enough to get the proper documents, I guess."

"We didn't have to do book pages when Thelma and Leroy left," Meggie noted as she took a red pencil from its box.

"She was close to them and loves them both," Ruth began. "But I think Sylvie's sadness is because I was the closest to Nettie."

"Haven't heard anything from her, have you?" Meggie said in more of a statement then a question, knowing full well her best friend would tell her anything as important as finding out about the girl who had fled the neighborhood at the time Meggie arrived with her aunt and sister.

"No." Sadness flickered in Ruth's mind. "I can see the fear in Sylvie's eyes when I tell her I'm going to Chicago but I'll be back for Christmas vacation. "It's hard to explain about needing to go away and going to school since I've been in school all these years and haven't had to leave home at all."

Meggie put her hand on Ruth's wrist. "Even though it hurts us all, it's for the best and you've got to go."

Ruth nodded her head. "Alice St. James is going to supervise taking Sylvie over to the diner twice a week on Tuesday and Thursday so she can continue to do the dishes and earn some money."

"Is the St. James family happy with that?" Meggie asked.

"Devon and Pastor Fredericks asked her...and Mr. St. James approved it," Ruth replied. "Their driver and Alice will pick Sylvie up at the house and bring her home after the dinner crowd dishes are done."

"Sylvie will do well...and so will you," Meggie said with authority to reassure her friend.

Ruth knew every word Meggie said was true but it didn't help to see Sylvie's sad loam-brown eyes. Ruth wanted to sound sure and strong. "Thanks, Meggie. You helping me with this book will make things better for both Sylvie and me. "

Now, that Sylvie was taken care of, Ruth thought of other people outside her family who encouraged Ruth to go to Chicago. Ruth remembered Emma Stone who sat, rain or shine, in the fourth pew on the left hand side of the church. Mr. Stone had died years before. Her son, Allan, was in Cleveland now and her daughter, Gloria, was in a Negro college in Tennessee. Allan sent what little he could spare from his paycheck to help Mrs. Stone pay for the daughter's college expenses, but his contribution wasn't enough. Mrs. Stone expanded her sewing business to make ends meet and accepted a position with a white family whose home was close to the Negro neighborhood.

Her white employers, the Clovises, weren't kind people. The reason they lived so close to the Negro community was they had been dirt poor themselves. After coming into some inheritance money, they had fixed up their house, razed the chicken coop in the side yard, and hired Mrs. Stone as their housekeeper. She cooked, cleaned, and watched the husband's elderly father, a heavy drinker, who dipped snuff and whose disposition was mean as a snake. Her duties began at sunrise and ended long hours later when the elderly man was safely home.

Everybody in both neighborhoods knew about the money and the grandfather's alcoholism, two subjects they politely ignored now that the eyesore of a home had been cleaned and repaired.

Grandfather Clovis spoke in a grating bellow that echoed with humiliating clarity outside the home's paper-thin walls, spitting verbal fire or tobacco juice anywhere but into the spittoons. Mrs. Stone was told this senior member of the family had an "illness" unrelated to her duties of gathering and discarding the large collection of empty liquor pints and moonshine jars. The elderly man roamed in and out of the house until the edge-of-town bars opened or his moonshine deliveries arrived.

Drunk or sober, he enjoyed calling Mrs. Stone racist names and spat on her shoes or cotton stockings when he was angry. With a gleeful leer, all he would say, if he said anything at all was, "Guess I missed the spittoon."

When there was trouble down at the bar or he landed in someone's lawn or flowerbed, his family answered the phone messages by dispatching Mrs. Stone to bring the old man home. Mrs. Stone would walk to wherever he was, check to see if he was injured or bleeding, and slowly help the inebriated man get back to the house. Thankfully, he got drunk early so Mrs. Stone could go home and wash the tobacco stains from her white cotton stockings and shoes before sitting down to her quick dinner and sewing chores. Neither Grandfather Clovis nor his family ever thanked her much for her efforts to help. Mrs. Stone never complained. Being in church on Sunday, getting paid, and knowing she was helping her daughter got her through it all.

"How I love Sundays, knowing my Gracie is worshiping at her college. Sundays lighten the ache and washes some bitter tastes away." Mrs. Stone would always add, "You have to be strong to put up with such things if we're going to educate teachers and lawyers and sheriffs to make this thing right. We're strong. Have to be—to go on to victory."

CHAPTER TEN

EMERGENCY ROOM AT 4:10 P.M.
CHICAGO – 1967

"OK, so I've got the story about your leaving St. Louis, your train ride, Sylvie, and Miss Stone," Norma smiled and looked in her bag for another pen The one she was using was beginning to drag and skip. "So you were heading up from St. Louis?"

"Seems I got there a few days early," Ruth replied.

CHICAGO – 1957

It was late afternoon when Ruth reached the university. She wearily paid the cab fare to a nice Negro cabby named Ben with four children and seven grandchildren, none...lucky enough to go to college. "Mighty fine thing, you coming here. Yes, mighty fine."

He brought Ruth's trunk and suitcases all the way to the service desk and patted her on the shoulder with a departing "good luck" as he waved away any tip money.

"You must be Miss Yuell." Ruth turned quickly to see a trim pageboy-coifed girl in a light blue sweater set direct a questioning expression at her. Ruth nodded and looked in her lake-blue eyes. "Glad you're on time. I'm Rita. Let's see," the girl continued, as she started moving into the hallway leading from the room without sharing her last name or giving Ruth a chance to acknowledge her. "Miss Dowling will see you tomorrow morning at nine a.m. after breakfast. See the windows to the right? That's it. Be prepared to be poisoned at least once a semester at our cafeteria." The girl smiled and kept moving. "Don't worry. It takes a bit of time to adjust. Then, there's getting your books and finding your classes. Just the usual. Bet you want to take your shoes off and shower. It's this way."

Ruth felt lost, but she kept her expression bland. Rita left as quickly as she'd come with a smile and a few last words. "Gotta get back to the main desk. I'm the only one there. Leave at four-thirty. Think you'll be alone here tonight. Maybe tomorrow, too. According to the schedule, but it's not an official one, other students are due here day after tomorrow." After a whirlwind of looking here and there and rapid-fire information, the girl handed Ruth a schedule, something blessedly concrete to refer to after Rita left.

The door to the hallway was left open. Ruth heard Rita's echoing footsteps as she sank to the bed—not knowing how long she sat there still wearing her coat and hat with her purse resting in the crook of her arm.

Ruth jumped hearing footsteps coming toward the room. Slower this time and punctuated by a persistent squeak. She hurried toward the dimly lit hall and saw the macabre shadows of what seemed to be a head and a lengthy triangular shadow. A stoop-shouldered man in a worn blue baseball cap was coming down the hall dragging a wobbly handcart with her trunk and suitcase on it.

"Usually have more people to help with these things. Sorry for the wait, miss." The man's conversation abruptly halted as he stared at her. "Well, I declare. You're colored," he said baldly. "You're one of the very few persons I've seen like me on this side of the business," he said to Ruth with a laugh. "You're not one of them foreign students from Africa now, are you? Trying to dress American and all?"

"I'm Ruth Yuell from St. Louis, Missouri," Ruth enunciated clearly as she extended her hand. She hadn't taken her gloves off yet.

"St. Louis? You from St. Louis?" the stooped man continued to lug the unsteady cart into the room. "Just watch yourself, miss. Must get this cart fixed before tomorrow. The boxes will be flying when the rest of them start coming." He changed the subject back to St. Louis. "Got a cousin in St. Louis. Homer Jeffries. You know Homer?" Ruth quickly considered the name and shook her head. "Thought everybody would know Homer. He's such a talker and all. Been there all his life."

"I don't think I remember a Mr. Homer Jeffries," Ruth said this time.

"Right nice fella. But I'm forgetting myself. Surprised to see a colored girl here, I guess. Name's Ennis Dell." His hand shot from his side again to grasp hers. "Been here since '17. Came up from Louisiana. No hope down there at all," he said as he swatted the air disgustedly. "Mind if I sit down?" he asked as he pulled the desk chair into the small open empty area. "Still can't believe you're here. Been talking about having colored students stay in the dormitories. Your name's Ruth, you said?" Ruth nodded again. "Right nice name. You're going to have to have somebody show you the ropes around here. Get off on the right foot and stay there. I'm your man. My wife and me both.

"You see some differences up here but not so different," using a conspiratorial tone. "Just like I tell my Clara. That's my wife. We got six children. All grown and gone since this past April. Got three grandkids, too." He quieted his voice. "You can go far but not too far, if you get what I mean. Use the toilets and all that. But they don't welcome you much. Remember that," Ennis got up quickly. "Yep. Not that friendly about things." He headed down the halls without a farewell.

Ruth called after him. "Goodbye, Mr. Dell, and thank you." She closed the door and headed for the closet. Ruth unlocked the trunk to give it air and retrieved her toiletries and robe from the suitcase. It seemed like she was the only one in the world on this side of the echoing hallway. Since the cab, there had only been Rita-with-no-last-name and Mr. Dell. Ruth wondered if anyone else was going to visit tonight, feeling glad she hadn't eaten the wrapped slices of pound cake Lady Dee had handed her for the train ride. She'd been too anxious to eat. Now it seemed like they were going to be her dinner.

Ruth hung up her coat and checked the shelf above for dust not wanting to get her hat dirty. Motes flew against the pale yellow closet light. She retraced her steps and placed the hat on the bed. Maybe there was something there to clean the shelf. Ruth certainly didn't want to use her bath towels for cleaning! The bathrooms were down the hall just at the beginning of the wooden hallway they'd entered as Rita led her to this room. As Ruth walked toward the bathroom, she heard an astonished intake of breath and the sound of water spilling.

"My lands, girl. You startled me!" a thin, gray-uniformed lady said in a rush as she scrambled to her feet. "No one supposed to be here till tomorrow afternoon. Ennis didn't say anyone was here. I'll fix him when he gets home. You 'bout scared the life out of me. You speak English, don't you?"

"Yes. Yes. I'm Ruth Yuell," Ruth said. The woman's petite figure could only have been five feet tall as Ruth helped steady her. "Ennis, er, Mr. Dell, brought my things up to the room. I'm so very sorry I startled you."

"No harm done, child. Just some water here." The lady wiped her hands on her bibbed apron as she extended her hand. "I'm Clara Dell, Ennis's wife."

"Mr. Dell mentioned something about having to fix the handcart and not expecting any students till tomorrow. I just came in here looking for something to clean the closet shelf. My hat..."

Mrs. Dell cut Ruth off. "Land's sake. They weren't supposed to let any students over here until tomorrow. They've got no more sense then a mule at a tea party, I declare. The last hall to be done in the whole place and they set you there! Well, we'll just fix that. Gonna do it right now and finish the rest so you can unpack in a clean place. Don't want one of our own to get the wrong idea about this dormitory. Right clean and tidy all the time." Mrs. Dell headed for the door and started pushing a cleaning cart hidden in the shadows. "You from around here?"

"No. I'm Ruth Yuell from St. Louis."

"Well, welcome Ruth Yuell from St. Louis," Mrs. Dell restated with a smile. "Let's get your new home cleaned up." They worked together for about twenty minutes. Mrs. Dell tried to shoo her away several times, telling Ruth it wasn't right for a student to clean her own room but Ruth helped anyway. "I appreciate the help but only when we're alone. OK? If it gets around I'm having students help me and all, there might be trouble."

"Trouble?" Ruth questioned.

"You know," Mrs. Dell said as if Ruth already had the answer. "Being lazy. Not working for my pay. Getting too friendly-like with the students.... " No, Ruth didn't *know*, until Mrs. Dell mentioned it. "You're a student here now. Can't be both." At Ruth's confused look, Mrs. Dell continued. "Didn't anybody tell you that you can't be too helpful or friendly? It's like being in the Army. There's the officers and the privates, yeah!" Mrs. Dell frowned as she continued her explanation. "You're the officer now. I'm like the private. Don't want to mess with the rules and all or we both might end up in trouble. Finished here now. You eaten supper?"

"A...no," Ruth replied.

"Bet you're just tired," Mrs. Dell replied as she patted Ruth's hand. "I'm going to see if there's something I can get till breakfast tomorrow. Think I saw some sandwich things in the icebox downstairs. I'll be back in a few minutes." The only sounds were Mrs. Dell's soft steps and the cleaning cart wheels.

First Mr. Dell, and now Mrs. Dell, telling her things and giving her warnings. *Could Ruth really get the Dells in trouble by treating them as she would anyone else?* The thought scared her. *Did she really understand what to do and how to act?* Panic wiggled from her stomach to her throat and waves of loneliness engulfed Ruth's emotions. She smelled the freshly made bed, like the towels at home in St. Louis.

She could do it and do it well! She'd gotten over the shock concerning Stella and her dead baby and willed herself with God's help to go on. She laid there for awhile and prayed about it.

"Put the soiled towel and the glass on your shelf," Mrs. Dell instructed as she delivered Ruth's makeshift dinner. "There's a doughnut downstairs for the morning if you're the first one down there. Maybe I should have brought it up. Wasn't thinking, I guess. Too used to being almost alone, except for Ennis, all summer. The cooks come back day after tomorrow."

The ham sandwich wrapped in a hand towel and a glass of milk tasted good along with the pound cake from home. As she ate, Ruth weighed and recalled the cabby's positive conversation and information from the Dells.

Ruth knew she was on the tip of a new frontier—not only for her but for Negroes as a race, as well. Ruth and the four other students going up north to the all-white schools talked for hours about how to behave in the face of challenges and adversity. Ruth had gotten carried away with the train ride and all. She'd let her good sense go out the train coach window, being too excited and energized! The new surroundings added to her lack of composure. Even though the university wanted her and recruited her, this was all new territory with pitfalls, she was sure. She wasn't being wise, gauging situations for things to go wrong, which could cause a mistake. She'd now rely on the demonstration training, which taught her to be careful. This easy freedom had surprised her for a moment and misplaced those hard-learned lessons.

Ruth turned off the desk light. Time for bed in this new world. She'd have to be more careful.

∞

The next morning, Ruth was up early as she showered, got dressed, and retraced her steps. Breakfast had been sparse. Just as Mrs. Dell said, a stale doughnut sat on the commercial kitchen counter. No milk to be found. The coffee pot was clean and dismantled. There was nothing else except a mummified brown lettuce leaf at the bottom of the huge icebox in the cafeteria kitchen. The sound of the huge silver lever clashed and Ruth jumped as she continued exploring for something else to drink. She ate the doughnut hurriedly and washed the sugar from her throat with lukewarm water from a glass in the mammoth cupboard on the side of the sink. It had been too early to stay in the empty waiting area, so Ruth returned to her room. Perhaps she could use the ironing board she'd seen hanging on the wall in the utility room to tidy her clothes until Mrs. Dell returned.

About an hour later, Ruth heard Mrs. Dell calling her name in the hallway. Ruth unplugged the iron standing on the wooden board. "I'm coming, Mrs. Dell."

The older woman turned toward the voice. "Child, got a note for you from Mrs. Dowling, who's the boss around here."

Ruth opened the note telling her to come over to Harrell Hall in an hour.

"It's over across the street and the third building on the left," Mrs. Dell said. "You got your freshman map?" Ruth was grateful for the information but she had already memorized the layout of the campus they had provided in her new student packet.

"I'll finish a few more things and get ready, Mrs. Dell," Ruth replied, being more formal as Mrs. Dell instructed the previous afternoon.

"Know you'll do us proud," Mrs. Dell said with a smile and a swift pat on Ruth's arm.

ର୍ତ୍ତ

"Miss Yuell. I'm Miss Dowling. Miss Patricia Dowling," the thickly built woman with a talc-colored complexion said as she gestured for Ruth to take a seat in the leather chair opposite the worn wooden desk. Ruth wondered if she ever got any sun on her face. "I'm the Head Administrator for the college. Miss Osborn will be here later this afternoon." Ruth remembered Miss Osborn's name at the bottom of the letters her family and she had received as she prepared for her trip to Chicago. "Unfortunately, there was a mistake in the arrival dates for you. The rest of the outside students won't be here until tomorrow."

"Outside students?" Ruth asked.

"Yes. Late this summer, we've decided the integration program needed more personal time before the greater influx of students. You'll be able to fit in here, I'm sure. You've chosen an ambitious course of study in your application to accomplish in three years," she looked at Ruth with a thin smile. "So you can stay close to the dorm and just walk around the campus until Miss Osborn returns to explain the rules and regulations."

"Where do I eat?" Ruth inquired, not knowing where to begin with the other information.

"That is a problem. The kitchen staff doesn't return until tomorrow. Supplies begin to arrive today, though. I'll check into that and have a message sent to your room. Now you must excuse me, I'm late for another meeting. Good meeting you, Miss Yuell," she said as she whisked past Ruth in a quick pace. Ruth only had enough time to avoid the smoky half-glass door and see Miss Dowling's orthopedic-shoed stride take her from the office and toward the ivy-covered, multi-storied buildings featured in the campus brochure.

Ruth certainly wasn't going to continue to stay in the dormitory cowering until the other students came, fighting boredom and waiting for snatched meals from heaven knows where. As Ruth got her purse and white sweater to explore the campus, Mrs. Dell returned.

"Guess you met Miss Dowling. She's something, isn't she? Saying this and delegating that. Means well, I guess. Least of all, she thought of meals for you. Ennis and I wondered what she was going to do. But even if she didn't, we brought you something for lunch. Would have brought back dinner, too, need be." To think after only after a few hours the Dells were thinking of food for her. It made Ruth feel better.

"Bessie, the domestic over at the administration office told me you are one of three Negro female students in the dorms they put over here. One's from Africa. Could have been four of you, but the girl from Arkansas decided to get married. Can you believe that?" Ruth was taken aback of how similar this unknown girl's life had paralleled her own. *What if Devon had wanted her to stay?* The other part jolted her into awareness.

"One of three?" Ruth cried. At the time of recruiting, the administrators had promised there would be "many more Negro students from around the country" that school year.

"Sure enough. Can't remember where the other girl is from but there's one riding over from our neighborhood but she doesn't count in the dorm tally. Been in school together since last year. The churches are helping her with bus money and a few dollars toward books, but she lives at home. You're one of two out-of-the-area from the United States. There are four young men. Two from here in Chicago, I think, and one from northern Indiana. The young man from Indiana lives in the dorm and plays football, I think my husband said. Don't know about the other as I recall. Think he's from Africa. Does that help you any?"

Ruth felt gloomy at the small number of Negro students. It took all her concentration not to laugh or be offended at the wide-eyed stares and backward glances coming her way when she walked around the campus or stopped people to ask questions as she referred to her small campus map.

Ruth felt like an exhibit at the zoo but they'd get used to seeing her on campus. Ruth was going to graduate from this institution of higher learning, she promised herself. Due to circumstances, she might be one of three Negro out-of-state female students but they certainly weren't going to be the last, if she had anything to do with it.

Everything was the same except for the skin color.

She wasn't alone, Ruth reminded herself. Her family and her community encouraged her. The Dells and that cabby, too. If those considerations failed to rally her, there was always Devon. She could write to him and pour out everything, including her feelings. He'd promised to listen, understand, and write back.

"See you at classes," Ruth would say to the kaleidoscope of friendly, thoughtful, amazed, and hostile faces.

Now she had to tell Devon she was one of two American Negro female students dorming there this semester—perhaps the year. *Wonder what he would say if he were here? Bet he'd laugh at the rock-hard doughnut part and Miss Dowling's razor-thin conversation with her orthopedic-shoed gait.*

Mr. Dell was there on Ruth's return to the dorm. "Oh, almost forgot, Miss Yuell. Here's a letter come for you. The postman almost snatched it away but I told him you were a new student here, a day early. There's more for the other students coming, too. Strange-looking lettering and paper so thin, almost like toilet scrap. Can you believe it! I knew you'd want your mail."

Ruth was thrilled. A letter from her father or Lady Dee, she guessed. Ruth's mouth opened in surprise when she saw Devon's handwriting. "I knew you'd be happy for it!" Mr. Dell laughed. "Nothing like a letter. I'll just let you get to it. Your chicken sandwich will be waiting by the front desk when you want it. Bought a Grapette, too. Don't let it get too warm. No, sir. Nothing like a letter."

Ruth waited till the door closed and rushed to the bed to sit down. She tore the envelope open with shaky fingers.

Dear Ruth,

Hope you are well and don't think I'm too forward in writing this letter before you've gone. There were things I wanted to say, not scare you, and not change things your last few days in St. Louis. As you probably already know, things up in Chicago are better in some ways, different in others, and the same in others. How do I make myself clear? I read once in a book that theater and movie people can make water in scenery look like fathomless lakes from only an inch of water or two on top of glass. That's what it was like for me in my first years at college. Had some freedoms I never dreamed of having in Washington, DC, or St. Louis but it only went so far. Had to feel my way like a blind man half the time, the waters were deeper and freer in some places and just hard as glass in others. Don't know what else to say.

Be sure and write any time you need to—and don't hold anything back. Maybe I can think of something that happened to me to help you. So you can enjoy the deep waters and swim instead of gulping water. Perhaps it will help to share the pain when you rap your knuckles against the glass. I know I needed somebody but I didn't have anyone dear to share these things.

Know you don't have much money for phones. But we can write and "talk" to each other in letters. Will that help you? It will help me. Will you help me? Make me worry less about you and know that you're thinking of me. Sorry if that's selfish, but I know that I needed to say these things. Do you? If you do, you'll write back about your experiences. Please write.

Hope you had a good trip up to Chicago.

Sincerely,
Devon

"He knew I'd need him," Ruth said aloud as she quickly reread the letter twice again. "Knew I'd feel isolated or be isolated."

Devon wanted to be so positive and reassuring when they were together. Still, the phasing, intonations, and times he brushed against subjects and didn't really answer her questions about his experiences in the freer atmosphere of his university. Ruth remembered how much Devon's answers frustrated her, saying there were some things she'd have to experience for herself.

Guess he'd had a point. *Would she have come here so willingly if she knew she was one of only two Negro female dorm students?* With Devon at her fingertips, there would be no more awkward silences now, only truth.

☙❧

After the bologna sandwich and Grapette soda for lunch and a cold fried chicken dinner with snap bean salad and a glass of milk, Ruth went to mail her first letter to Devon. The envelope contained five pages of tiny writing on both sides of the vellum paper, telling him everything—good and bad. She also told Devon he was right about the depths of the water he'd mentioned. Some hazards were real and some were fake, but she would cope.

On her way back to the dorm, Ruth noticed a Negro girl walking around in the dusk, looking lost. Ruth tried to touch the girl's shoulder somewhere beneath the girl's thick, straight black braid. The girl jumped, gasped, and turned at the same time.

"I'm sorry! I'm sorry!" Ruth apologized urgently, putting her hands palm up.

"Sizemore," the thin Negro girl said slowly in a Southern accent. "I...," the girl swallowed. "Sizemore." She pointed to her official-looking papers like the ones Ruth received.

"That's the building right here." Ruth pointed to the dormitory building that had been both her two-day home and makeshift meal prison. "Sizemore is over here." The girl looked in the direction of the dormitory, taking a few hesitant steps. They got up to the door with the pitted brass sign that showed in four-inch block letters that this indeed was Sizemore Hall. "See?"

"Sizemore at last," the chocolate-skinned girl replied slowly with a lessening of the tension in her face. "I mean...a...yes," she said. "Haven't slept for days on the bus."

Ruth tried to capture this progress. "You look tired."

"Yes," the girl replied more strongly. "I've been looking for the dormitory. The white cabbie dropped me clear on the other side of campus...and I carried my two bags. One at the time and going back for the other one." The young woman blew at her bangs. "Hop-scotching from there to here."

"You're going to live here?" Ruth asked again, thinking this girl must be the other Negro student assigned to Sizemore. There was no one here now. Ruth wanted this stranger to know she was safe and in the right place. The girl stopped warily again. Ruth tried another tack. "Ruth Yuell," she smiled and offered her hand in welcome. "I'll carry one of your cases. Just follow me."

The girl squinted her right eye and lowered her brow before saying, "Ellie Beal. No one but me." They walked in silence up the stairs and over to Ruth's hall.

"No sheets. No food till tomorrow," Ruth said as she went to the room across the hall, the one she had read on the girl's papers. Ellie Beal looked at the bed and bare pillow as if satisfied, took off her coat, and laid down on the bed. She covered herself with her battered tweed coat Ruth now realized was a few sizes too large as the girl snuggled into the mattress. Ruth got the extra blanket Mrs. Dell had put there for her use. "Just a blanket," Ruth said. The girl looked startled as she felt the edge of the blanket as Ruth took the battered coat and hung it in the closet.

"Good," she said. "Thank you." The girl closed her eyes and snuggled under the blanket and Ruth could no longer see her face. She intended to offer her the last of the chicken she had in her room but the girl seemed sound asleep. Ruth shook her head and tiptoed out the door to get ready for bed.

๛

Upon waking up in the dorm room, Ellie seemed busy eating everything in sight. Last night's chicken was gone. "This bread and butter is good."

"Want some cereal?" Ruth asked slowly. "I'll take you down to the cafeteria kitchen."

When they got there, Ruth got out the cereal and bread loaf from the refrigerator.

"Haven't had much food lately since the rain was scarce down on the farm," Ellie said as she gestured away from her body. "Who is this?" she said, as she pointed to the athlete on the cereal box.

Ruth looked at the box front, but before she could answer, a medium-height Negro lady in a dark blue business suit walked up to their table. "Excuse me. I'm Miss Eunice Osborn and I hear you arrived a bit early, Miss Yuell."

"It's a pleasure to meet you, Miss Osborn," Ruth replied politely, looking at the woman with brown clay-colored skin. She felt on more solid ground now; ready for this introduction. "May I introduce Miss Ellie Beal? She arrived last night." Ellie lifted her head and stopped chewing.

"Yes, I thought that was the case, Miss Yuell," Miss Osborn smiled. "Good morning, Miss Beal. You're from Alabama, correct?"

"Good morning," Ellie replied, trying to clear her mouth as she began to pull her plate and bowl closer to her. "Milltown, Alabama."

Miss Osborn pushed the cereal box, milk, and bread closer to Ellie and said, "Excuse us. I need Miss Yuell." Ruth and Miss Osborn walked in silence over to a set of chairs in an office by the front door. Ruth was back in the leather chair with Miss Osborn behind the desk. "I hoped to be back sooner to greet you personally before you began your stay here. Things have worked out satisfactorily so far." The crisply dressed woman pursed her lips and looked at Ruth with an intense expression. "The university has worked very hard to come up with a protocol for allowing more Negro and foreign students to come here. This program has not been easy to implement or without its naysayers. So things will be scrutinized quite carefully during the course of your enrollment. Do I make myself clear?"

Ruth nodded her head.

"Good. I hope we can get to know each other better over the course of your education. Should you have any questions, don't hesitate to call me. I'm most anxious the program succeed and be expanded." Unlike Miss Dowling, Miss Osborn came around the desk and shook Ruth's hand. "When Miss Beal is through with her breakfast, will you please send her in here?"

"Of course, Miss Osborn," Ruth replied.

Ruth returned to Ellie, whom she discovered had eaten the rest of the cereal in the box plus a half piece of toast from Ruth's plate before she was called away.

⚭

"I'm Norma Reed from the Bronx," the medium-height, red-haired girl with milk-white skin and freckles over her nose said while putting her traveling bag down in the third room. She came over to shake both Ruth's and Ellie's hands. "When's dinner?"

"About five-thirty," Ruth replied. This white girl didn't seem phased by having Negro dorm mates.

Perhaps she thought they were maids. So she tried to clarify the situation. "I'm Ruth Yuell. I'm studying nursing and English literature in a three-year program. I've got the room on the end." Ruth turned to Ellie. "This is Ellie Beal. She's a nursing major from Milltown, Alabama, near Birmingham and lives in the room next door." Ruth saw only openness and frank inquiry in the depths of the Reed girl's eyes.

Ruth, Ellie, and Norma told their stories and gave their outlooks on everything and every topic, sliding into friendship from that moment. "I've been interested in equal rights since I watched the *Brown vs. Board of Education* ruling at the Supreme Court. Didn't think much about it before then, but I do now," Norma said in her now-characteristic, straight-as-an-arrow way. "Only signed up for elementary education with my journalism major because my parents said they wouldn't help pay for college if I didn't have a *real* job to fall back on when I graduated." Norma wrinkled her nose. "They don't think I'll be able to get anywhere as a female journalist and they don't want to support me beyond age twenty-one or so...and I'm hungry."

All three girls began to laugh.

⚭

EMERGENCY ROOM AT 4:50 P.M.
CHICAGO – 1967

"I remember," Norma said with a laugh. "That's exactly what I said."

"You didn't seem scared or anything," Ruth remarked. "I always wondered about your calmness until I discovered the bigger city aspect of life and saw all the different ethnic and racial groups here in Chicago. I had never experienced such diversity before."

"And I'd never experienced the segregation and repression you'd experienced. So we're even," Norma said.

"So I'm getting too sentimental?" Ruth smirked. "I'll try to be objective... and not too melancholy as I keep talking about the three of us and our college careers."

"Your honesty...and sarcasm are duly noted," Norma said. "Why don't we start with how you first felt being in classes."

⚭

CHICAGO – 1957

Ruth, Ellie, and Norma attended college classes for a few days and things settled into a comfortable routine. Some incidents had been laughable, as when Mrs. Dell found Ruth and Ellie the second morning in the dorm kitchen, "Two of you! Don't that beat all!"

Everyone who was white, with few exceptions besides Norma, was so reserved at first. People were polite and informative but elicited no warmth and exuberance, reminiscent of her family and friends back in St. Louis. People weren't unkind, necessarily, but cool and distant like their fast-moving bodies getting to the next class or their clipped sentences and replies to questions. Ruth's verbal friendliness and embraces her parents and grandparents taught her were greeted with polite, lightning-fast helloes at best or with people pointedly trying to avoid her at worst. It was almost as if people's upper arms were glued to their sides, only allowing their limbs to move their forearms from elbow to hand for a handshake or wave. Smiles were also rationed like wartime gas tickets, but Ruth vowed to look in people's eyes and try to connect there. Gone was the Southern stricture where Negroes could only look at the ground when they were talking to white people. That was a welcome change.

Prejudice was still there, though. At busy times on campus, Ruth was a rock in the swift-moving river of humanity. Many people changed direction, stared, or shunned Ruth, passing like angry silent ships steering clear of any contact. Ruth told Devon she wished she could see the scene from a helicopter or hovering balloon, watching the people glimpsing her and running away. People might want to avoid her but at least they knew she was there. She wasn't going to change course—ever.

Other times, Ruth's interracial experiences seemed too artificial and fussed over—like back home with Mrs. Buzby, always wringing her hands as she looked in the oven at her coconut cake pans, trying to make sure they came out perfect. Ruth knew the university wanted their progressive integration efforts to be successful, but she saw the worry on their faces. Sometimes, Ruth felt like a laboratory animal being poked, prodded, and given endless rules and blind mazes for the price of tuition, room, and board by dispassionate university officials. Ruth didn't mind helping people understand her race's plight, but she wanted more say in the situation, too. They were dealing with her life and she wanted her voice to promote racial understanding in a more personal way.

Ruth remembered the first time she'd seen the joyous faces of the Negro lawyers on the television talking about the *Brown vs. Board of Education* case when she was in high school. Ruth would never forget where she was. Meggie had found her coming out of her last class for the day. "Come on! Come on!" her normally well-mannered friend yelled excitedly. "Thurgood Marshall is on the news. The principal brought his television!"

During the first month Ruth was in college, another vitally important event was broadcast from Arkansas, many miles away from her campus. "We've got to get down to the Student Union," Ellie called from the bathroom. "So don't put your sweater down. The news is going to show Little Rock!"

◐◑

Everyone tried to squeeze in to see the dim gray light of the television screen in the lounge. Someone said, "Give Ruth some room. She's been talking about this!" Ruth swallowed and moved forward, seeing the steps of a school building similar to a newspaper picture. Then Ruth frowned, hearing chanting and taunting voices of angry white protesters, all yelling and shouting as hatred stained their faces. *Nine Negro students against all that venom!*

Fear sliced through her. The Arkansas governor, Orval E. Faubus, was on the screen answering questions. *What was he doing? Trying to keep the Negro students out of Central High?* Ruth prayed he wasn't.

Was anyone injured? Ruth bit her lip as unbidden tears started to form in her eyes. *Had those poor students or anyone else been hurt?* They were her age or perhaps a year younger. The idea surprised her. Ruth gulped in an anxious breath and nervously clenched her hands. They seemed like such scared innocents looking at the ground, or with bewildered glints in their eyes when they stared straight ahead. Just trying to be brave against an angry, hateful tide! They were people she would call friends if she lived there!

The Central High students were walking in the way she and other demonstrators learned in the training sessions in St. Louis, for the sit-ins and the demonstrations that were sure to come. Yes. Yes. Trying to remain calm, look dignified, and not rouse the anger of the crowd. But sometimes the Central High students' furtive glances looked so hot-scared and bewildered, like icing melting on a warm cake. Ruth looked at those celluloid images which were several hours old and prayed anxious, fervent prayers. *What was going to happen next?*

Ruth was so far away. Her father had always said school integration was going to be difficult but the strength of the undeserved hatred Ruth saw on the faces of the mob took her breath away. She felt the urge to rush and help them. Help them all. *Were they OK?* There seemed to be no help or no mercy for the Little Rock students. *Keep going!* Keep going, her brain cried as Ruth saw the students walking along. Then, all she could see were the faces of the reporters talking.

Television changed it all and it was an ugly, ugly picture. The unjust hatred unleashed toward these Central High students in the news reports showed the "battlefield" in living rooms across America, night after night. The hatemongers, white parents, students, and people protesting school integration were difficult for Ruth to look at, but she knew now, at least, they were finally in the light of truth on the pictures broadcast on the television.

Not, as before, in just an occasional image in the newspaper or sad stories buried in back pages near the bottom of a page, but savage images while people were eating their dinner, getting ready for bed, or fixing their morning breakfast, saying more than a thousand sermons. *Would the lessons of peace, perseverance, and setting a Christian example on one side withstand the onslaught of hatred from the other?*

Ruth dredged her mind to remember every detail of her family's conversations about the Little Rock school situation. First, Negro students couldn't attend classes there. Not even to consider it as a possibility. Period. All Negro students were sent to Dunbar High School several miles away, if she remembered what her father and brother said. She recalled pictures of Central High's rolling green lawns, impressive stone facade, and mature leafy trees as the integration images from the television returned to her mind. Usually the all-white Central

High had been a quiet place when students weren't there. Negro students were only allowed there to have their high school football games in the high school stadium. Nothing more. Not one thing more, until those nine students braved those crowds. Ruth tasted blood from where she had bitten the inside of her lip.

Ruth thought Arkansas might be different from the Deep South. Hadn't Reverend Fredericks mentioned some race-relations progress made under former Governor Cherry? Ruth didn't see a wit of progress on the television screen. The white commentator's voice sounded scared and urgent.

Ruth felt the fear of the Deep South Negroes as if the Arkansas border had been dragged to the lynching fields nearer the mouth of the Mississippi River. Hate seemed to scar those angry white faces. Ruth was afraid for those students and the Little Rock Negro community. *Would the whites start burning houses like they did in Florida years ago? Would violence spread to other cities?*

Fear snaked through her as she remembered the informal history lessons she learned about the burning of Rosewood and the 1919 and 1938 race riots she'd studied in high school. Ruth remembered Martin Luther King's house had been bombed during the Montgomery bus boycott. *If she and her family continued to be active in the movement toward racial equality, could violence visit them on their shady, peaceful street? Would anyone protect her family?* Ruth prayed everyone would be safe.

Please, protect them, Lord. Please, don't let anyone be hurt. Please, don't let anyone die. I don't want to go to another funeral, Lord. Keep me and my family strong. Amen.

ଔଓ

As the days unfolded the Little Rock police, U.S. Marshals, and Army soldiers, looking like they were dressed to go to war, came to Little Rock. The huge show of military and police force behind the nine students, the presence and support of leaders of the black community and other civil rights leaders awakened a tide of public opinion.

It was a near thing but Ruth's prayers were answered. With God's help, they would overcome. Ruth would leave the fate of their critics to Him.

ଔଓ

One crisp late October afternoon, Ruth was summoned to Miss Osborn's office.

"Hello, again, Miss Yuell," Miss Osborn greeted from behind the desk. "You've adjusted well, I hear, and your grades are excellent. Congratulations." Miss Osborn looked pleased. "The Fall Reception is coming."

Ruth was going to comment on the heavy vellum invitation she found in her mailbox but Miss Osborn was intent on talking.

"You will be escorted to the reception by Thomas Wills, a second-year law student."

"I could ask Jimmy Barrett?" Ruth indicated, "We can also find Ellie an escort."

"Isn't he a white student from Cincinnati, I believe?" Miss Osborn asked in a disapproving tone.

"He lives near Boston," Ruth replied.

"That won't be acceptable, Miss Yuell. We want to make sure we make the correct impression...and Miss Beal won't be attending. She needs to improve her grammar and academics, so you need to help her with more tutoring." Miss Osborn looked down at her file. "Mr. Wills will be in the guest area at your dormitory at six p.m."

"So you're telling me you *require* a Negro law student to escort me rather than a currently-enrolled white student?" Heat rose from her neck to her face as another question tumbled out. "Why is Ellie excluded? She's always working on her studies and doing her very best."

Miss Osborn got up from her chair and left the room, saying distinctly over her shoulder as she went, "Mr. Wills at six p.m. sharp. Miss Beal can and will do better before any invitations will be forthcoming. Good afternoon, Miss Yuell."

Ruth sat there for a few minutes—now knowing definite boundaries within the polite university society which could *not* be broached. Ruth felt the sting of her elbow inadvertently hitting the tabletop, bruising the skin. She'd go and write it all to Devon, she thought, as she groped in her handbag for her handkerchief. She wouldn't shed angry tears. *What would Devon say about this? Would he be angry for Ruth or Ellie? Would he surmise Miss Osborn had gone through the same experiences or worse in her own effort to gain social equality?*

Ruth didn't know the answers. She only had questions.

When she knew Miss Osborn better, Ruth vowed to ask. Until then, her parents' admonitions about minding her elders and her own feeling she skated on very thin ice would find her dutifully waiting for Mr. Wills on Saturday.

Ruth also vowed to increase her hours helping Ellie. Her new friend from Alabama deserved to attend the parties, too.

Now, by Miss Osborn's rapier-edged admission, dating presented an awkward arena for the university. It didn't matter as much to Ruth now because she was Devon's "girl" but Ruth felt she should have been informed beforehand of these restrictions so she could voice her objections in an organized fashion. Ruth expected some differences in the college social life but definitely not to the extent of the dating segregation voiced by Miss Osborn.

So this was the knuckle-rapping Devon described in his letters and more? More like hitting a brick wall. In her university life, there would be many official activities that required a male escort. *Would Miss Osborn consistently arrange black male escorts to accompany her?* Ruth had not met Mr. Wills. There were only two black male students living on campus, a young man from Indiana and a foreign exchange student from Liberia. If Miss Osborn picked her escorts, she needed to get busy and look for some other candidates. Three years was a long time.

CHAPTER ELEVEN

Ruth clenched her jaw and went to the Fall Reception with Mr. Wills. He was nice, polite, and more philosophical than Ruth. "Listen, Ruth. The meal is free and if we cooperate, we'll get what we want. I don't know about you but it's been hard to get though all this and a little cooperation from the administrators is just what I need for these last two years in law school. So I'll sit here, be polite, and smile. What about you?" Ruth didn't have a quick answer. She couldn't fault his personal logic but these "dates" seemed false, like rehearsing an opera or play in the arts and literature class. It wasn't so much interaction as staging.

"Yeah," Thomas continued. "The Montgomery situation is old news in some quarters and Central High might just be the same. As far as I can see, even with the notoriety about the Till case, because he's buried here, some of the steam has gone out of the civil rights movement." He dipped his head and whispered. "Most of the students and faculty here are still slobbering over the sad stories of the foreign students and refugees who are still flooding into this country—from Korea this time. What'd you think? I talk about our ancestors coming over in slave ships in the last century or Till getting killed and they can trump me with their own personal horrors. If they're looking for a way to cut down on the Negro program and put in more foreign students in those admissions openings, I don't want to be the reason."

"I don't agree with your assessment about our fight against segregation," Ruth asserted. "Do you know they wouldn't let my dorm mate Ellie come tonight because she doesn't have high enough grades, in their opinion?"

"No. But what other choice do we have? Either we cooperate or we scare them off. I call this our academic underground railroad. Can't let this opportunity dry up for us! Do you want them to tell us to pack up and leave?" Thomas lead Ruth to the dance floor, hiding the severity of their conversation with a relaxed face and neutral expression. "Now smile."

"What about the forming of the Southern Christian Leadership Conference this year?" Ruth whispered, her stubborn streak getting the best of her.

Thomas's eyes glared back as he kept smiling. He said nothing.

But Thomas gave Ruth something to consider. Her parents, siblings, and Devon would be so disappointed if she were asked to leave the university because she caused too much trouble...and the program terminated. Miss Osborn's thin-lipped, clipped answers to Ruth's questions proved as much. *Forfeit a whole college scholarship for resisting a few managed dates? How would she be able to explain her actions?*

She'd only been asked to cooperate, help out Ellie, and have several arranged dates with a Negro law student. Still, Ruth chaffed to gain more independence and choices while she was in college, or why had she come here at all? Ruth didn't want to live in fear of what she could or couldn't do. That would be like exchanging fears from the life-threatening satin-peaked hats and robes of the Klan to the life-altering, nameless, faceless administrators who ruled her scholarship; a harsh comparison indeed.

They were all there tonight with their spouses and academic colleagues, as she looked over the banquet tables. Were they all falsely congratulating themselves for being so broadminded in their integration efforts, and then running their Negro students' academic and social lives like chessboard pawns? Ruth was going to have to find broader expression starting with more Negro friends or she feared losing herself in this seeming unknown maze of dos and don'ts.

❧

Thomas was right about one thing, the stories of the refugee students were wrenchingly sad, but those close to home seemed even sadder. Ellie's was one of the sad stories; a near-tragic one.

At first, Ellie lived a solitary life at the beginning of classes. She always worked on her studies.

Ellie didn't talk much about her experiences at first. Perhaps it was her apprehensive nature. Neither she nor Ruth adopted the cool, sophisticated style Norma and other girls projected so easily. Norma could be as caustic as she wanted without thinking a thing about her words or actions. Ruth and Ellie held back. However, slowly but surely, they were able to speak of light-hearted girl talk; spiced with Ellie's extravagant gestures. Suddenly, Ellie would catch herself, like the pull of an invisible string or ringing of some silent bell only she could hear. She would abruptly turn sober, excuse herself, and go back to nestle with her books, leaving Ruth and the other girls to shrug or look confused.

"You OK?" Ruth asked. Had Ruth said something to offend her?

"No. Nothing. Enough. Got to work," Ellie would say as she flipped her hair behind her ear and turned to her mountain of books again.

Ellie was almost indefatigable in concentrating on her studies. She'd sit for hour upon hour leafing through her class work, along with a huge Webster's dictionary next to her textbooks, trying to read and understand the words in her assignments. She'd always try to work out the concepts herself before coming to Ruth's room to ask for help. Neither of them had a social life since arriving at school, if one discounted Ruth's arranged dates. They spent their time studying, trying to get good grades, and beginning to talk about their disparate lives at Ellie's pace.

Ellie revealed her life story, starting slowly. The process took several, painstaking months of gaining trust and finding people who were sympathetic, not cold and judgmental. Once she got to know people, Ellie blossomed. She started to talk more freely beyond the confines of her dorm friends.

Ellie's animated face, adroit, lithe body, amazing spineless onyx hair, liquid brown eyes, and lovely Southern accent aided her sorrowful storytelling of segregation and poverty resembling ballet.

Ruth remembered Ellie's first meal with her when Ellie talked of having little food to eat. Unlike Ruth and her family, with friends and neighbors who filled their lives, all Ellie's blood relatives were dead, as far as she knew. She didn't know her mother's or her father's names. Her grandmother forbade their names be mentioned in her home after they left. Ellie was too young to remember even if her grandmother had talked about them.

Unnamed acquaintances said Ellie's father fled into the Army when he found out he was going to be a father. Her near-term pregnant mother returned to her family's home and left shortly after the birth. That left only Ellie's grandmother to care for her. Then, Ellie became an orphan toddler found crying in her dead grandmother's shanty. A sharecropper heard her and he and his wife took Ellie in. That was all she knew.

Instead of stories about relatives, friends, and neighbors, Ellie told of helping to work a near-played-out farm with her adopted parents, the Beals. "I was lucky," she asserted.

"At least you lived," one dispassionate bureaucrat told Ellie when she tried to get a birth certificate. She'd traveled by foot seven miles with no shoes to a one-room schoolhouse with a leaky roof and few books. The teacher who taught all six grades said Ellie was "bright and sharp." The teacher, Miss Milner, got her pastor interested in seeing Ellie get an education beyond the pittance in funding the

Alabama school system allowed for Negro students. Ellie wore hand-me-down clothes and shoes from the pennies, nickels, and dimes that nameless sponsor families and congregations scraped together, making sure Ellie and other deserving Negro students had the chance for higher education in the South.

Nothing fancy for Ellie. No store-bought holiday or birthday gifts. Just a few dollars spending money for an occasional treat or haircut...and this treasured college educational experience, which Ellie had dreamed about for all those years.

Beneath Ellie's beauty, deep invisible scars hid from view. Ruth soon guessed nights were Ellie's worst time. There were knocks on her door in the middle of the night or early in the morning. "Can I sleep here, please," was all she would say. She'd be tousled and sleepy in her pajamas, robe, and slippers, carrying her pillow and blanket over to the floor by the window. "Please," Ellie would say from the muffled cocoon of her blanket. No matter how much Ruth urged her, she couldn't convince Ellie to take off either her robe or slippers. "May have to go," she'd reply. At first, Ruth was hurt and puzzled until Ellie told her of the occasional mob or midnight rides of the segregationists where she would be woken from sleep and moved to the storm cellar for safety. *Had she been forced to leave her slippers? Had she lost her robe? Had Ellie ever been threatened or touched by angry white men looking for trouble?*

When the time seemed easier than in the dead of night, Ruth told Ellie, "I'm sorry. Sorry for things that happened."

Ellie shook her head. "I won't go back to Milltown without an education. I'm going to make sure segregation ends down there, so others...won't have nightmares."

The bulk of Ruth's college friendships were drawn from the people Ellie entranced with her endless tales of subsistence and survival. Besides Norma, there were Ellis, Belinda, Thomas, and Jane from Illinois; Connie from Ohio; and Jack and Eleanor from Michigan. They all spent hours talking about human rights, and ethnic and racial injustice. Soon, Ellie put herself out to be Ruth's co-champion for racial justice.

Even when students and their friends were enthralled with her story-telling, she would ask Ruth to tell her impromptu student audiences and their friends about Ruth's segregation experiences as well. "They took from me. They took from Ruth," she'd say. "They even kill. Just kill for the maniac pleasure of it." Her efforts told everyone her stories of living in daily fear in the South. "Skin is the story. Only our skin." She'd point to her arm and struggled for words to describe the situation. "We are killed for one thickness of cells. It's wrong, very wrong."

Their white classmates' ideas of Negroes were slanted—in tragic and laughable ways. Some viewed Ellie's and Ruth's race as: servants, tap dancers, or variations of Paul Robeson singing "Old Man River." They had a lot to learn and both young women had a lot to tell.

Ruth and Ellie cried through retelling the tragic story of Emmett Till. The unfolding of his story had local interest because he was buried in the Chicago area and international publicity because of the circumstances. Hadn't the news article said he was visiting his relatives in Mississippi and perhaps had "forgotten his manners" regarding behavior with white citizens because he was raised in an integrated state? He'd allegedly whistled at a white woman and been killed. Killed for whistling.

One uninformed white classmate of Ruth's said Till must have been a thief or a lawbreaker. He wasn't. Not at all. Ruth tamped down anger at the constant disparagement of her race, emphasizing the injustice of such stereotypes as well as the injustice of racism. "We Negro citizens should be treated equal with you under the law of the Constitution of these United States."

Ruth closed her eyes and remembered the graphic picture of the open casket funeral they published in *Jet Magazine.* Mrs. Till wanted everyone to see her son's shot and beaten head: thrown in the Tallahatchie River before his corpse was retrieved and brought to burial in Chicago. She wanted everyone to know there was no need for his death or for him to have been bothered by anyone at all, let alone killed, for that matter. Some of those who listened to Ruth and Ellie wavered, at best, or seemed unconvinced. This shameful, horrific story didn't have anywhere to fit in their audience's preconceived notions.

What had Thomas said? That the steam had gone out of the civil rights movement? Not according to Ruth or Ellie. They just kept on talking whenever they could. Ruth was grateful for any and all opportunities, trying to explain segregation and civil rights and walk the tightrope of the controlled environment at the university.

❧

There must be other Negro students who could help them get their points across, Ruth thought. She went out searching for some Negro students on campus and found none—other than the girls who carpooled to classes and left quickly each day for their jobs. Mrs. Dell advised her to try the smaller college campus about six miles away if Ruth and Ellie really felt they needed more Negro friends. "All my people are too young or too old."

Ruth took the bus over to another campus one Saturday while Ellie worked on a literature assignment. Ruth heard a, "Hey girl, where you from?" assail her ears. Ruth turned around quickly to see two college-age men and a girl laughing as they walked closer. "You're not from around here. I'm Lukas and this is Ben and Clara."

"I'm Ruth Yuell. It's a pleasure." Ruth she extended her hand.

"All right and proper." They looked at one another and smirked. "Dead give-away. You're not from here. We're going to get some Cokes and fries and we'll tell you how to act up here in the north."

"I don't know whether to be pleased or offended, Mr....?" Ruth let the question linger in the air trying to show some oft-taught backbone to this insult. "St. Louis is not so far away."

The young man didn't seem to mind as he tilted his head, "Well, you got some spunk, at least. Shaking hands and all...is real Southern. Get some more 'city polish'. Come on now for those fries. I'm getting hungry." With that, Lukas, Ben, and Clara became Ruth's first real Chicago Negro friends.

Ruth recalled the easy laughter over fries and Cokes as her new friends laughed and chided her about her too-proper diction and manners.

Well, perhaps she could teach them a thing or two, Ruth thought with a smile as she checked her mail box and spied the thin white envelope. She tore it open.

Dear Ruth,

Sorry people don't seem to be listening. I know I liked to hear the war veterans talk about their combat stories. I'm trying to think of some way to encourage you. It is so hard.

White people don't seem to understand or they take their personal freedom for granted. My so-called "freedom" lasted for only a day, too. Thought things would be different until the administrator came and talked to us. First thing he said was when it came to dating or even talking to white women; we couldn't cross that line or risk getting expelled. He made it very clear that if he caught us talking to them or getting within ten feet of them we'd be on the next bus home. I didn't cross him. I didn't want any trouble. Still don't. Was that brave? Yes and no. I missed making a stand again but I got to stay around and to make my presence known.

I wasn't going to hurt anyone. I didn't want anything from anyone, other than friendship and respect AND to be known as one of an increasing number of qualified, capable Negro professionals in this country. I asked myself, was I going to be a short-term warrior patting myself on the back for a raging fire of short duration or was I going to burn slow and sure? Guess my lack of immediate action is the answer. You're doing the same. Aren't you?

Osborn sounds like my administrator—both Negroes trying to keep the momentum of civil rights going by making sure nothing bad happens under their responsibility. What would you do? What would I do in the same situation? I know I've thought about it and I must say I would probably do the same thing. Everything is so fragile in our efforts, so far. Let's talk about it when you get home for Christmas.

What I should be asking you about is how you're doing and are your studies going well? Shouldn't be asking you to singlehandedly accept and understand why these negative things are happening. I should be asking you what good things are happening at school. I shouldn't be asking you if you're still missing me as much as I'm missing you. I should be asking you about your pre-nursing classes. All I know is you're doing the very best you can.

Have to get back to work. My lunchtime before my next meeting is almost over. Miss you.

Sincerely,
Devon

Do you still think you'll be able to finish in three years?

∾

EMERGENCY ROOM AT 5:00 P.M.
CHICAGO – 1967

"I wanted to get back to St Louis to see Devon and my family at Christmas but I *also* wanted to know I'd done enough to promote civil rights," Ruth explained. "I guess it was good from a personal humility standpoint I hadn't overestimated my personal accomplishments during my first semester. On the contrary, I really was racked with guilt I hadn't done *enough* and people would be disappointed in me."

"What?" Norma asked incredulously. "I never knew."

"Exactly," Ruth replied with strength. "Acting strong on the outside, and keeping the doubt at bay." A stress wrinkle puckered the bridge between Ruth's eyebrows. "Some doubts were eased and others spread at Christmas."

∾

CHICAGO – 1957

Finally, Christmas was coming. *Praise God*, Ruth thought as she stepped on the train platform to return to St. Louis.

Desegregation plans. Her parents' letters were filled with the details of their efforts. "The time is now," Dr. Yuell said enthusiastically again and again in his letters. Ruth longed to be with him as he talked about going to meetings, especially for the integration of the schools.

One person could make change happen, Dr. Yuell constantly reminded Ruth. One Negro person sitting at a white lunch counter. One Negro soldier unselfishly saving the life of a white comrade. One beloved Negro daughter going to college in Chicago. "Praying 1958 will be a banner year in our efforts everywhere," Dr. Yuell wrote in his last letter before Ruth started back to St. Louis.

Most of the local school efforts met stiff resistance. "Speaking with others who want to stand up for change? Slow work, Ruth. But then, things fall like

the walls at Jericho, sometimes. That's what I'm always hoping and praying for."
He had written to his daughter about the prominence of Dr. Martin Luther King,
Jr., with his brilliant, ringing prose and calm, effective manner, during that fall's
Central High integration in Little Rock. Dr. King emerged as an effective and
even-handed leader of the community and church coalition down in Alabama; and
now in Arkansas and fostering a growing national prominence. Dr. Yuell met Dr.
King at several meetings talking about the success of bringing the various Negro
church denominations together as a strong force for civil rights. "The Southern
Christian Leadership Conference just started and Pastor Fredericks said the orga-
nization already shows great promise for our efforts in the South."

At the university, there were only a few handfuls of people other than she,
Ellie, and the refugee students, who seemed committed and willing to work stuff-
ing letters and raising awareness about injustice. Others, like the Negro athletes,
would come and express interest but were unable to help because of their practice
schedules. "Philosophy to some. Life to others," Ellie observed sagely as they
looked at the mountains of letters for anti-segregation and international refugee
causes in front of them on the table.

What had she accomplished, Ruth asked herself, as the final miles home
passed by? Ruth's bursting exuberance and dreams for making change when
she left for Chicago hadn't pushed the limits or boundaries of convention. She'd
itched to light a small blazing fire of change, if just a little one. Ruth couldn't
claim one ember.

Ruth's grades were fine, which would please everyone. She was accepted as
an equal in her dorm and in her classes. She'd managed many normal-feeling,
giggly moments with the students in the dorm as they talked about every subject
under the sun. The differences of skin and culture melted away with time and
perseverance. *Was it illusion or was it real? Could she tell anything, for sure, in these
short months?*

No demonstrations or media interest at her university. No inroads from her
activities in Chicago. She had talked to students and faculty about Negro concerns and enthusiastically argued for full, unequivocal rights for Negroes in every
discussion. *Was that progress? Could she have done more?*

Ruth squirmed in the train seat. The formal receptions and her mandatory
attendance at them all, she mused, picked up the former thread of her thoughts.
She needed to concentrate if she was going to be able to really tell people what
she'd been doing with "all that time" at school. Nothing acutely extravagant
like looking at the barricades at Central High School, as she'd seen on the grainy
television set in the dorm sitting room. She could just hear the questions flying
fast and furious from her friends and neighbors, making them seem like seasoned
newspaper reporters trying to find every iota of material, similar to the interest

last July for Sophy Barner's wedding all the way over in Memphis when she married the AME bishop.

Miss Osborn indicated she was pleased with Ruth's attendance at university functions. She'd successfully made her own way in the fight for her race by being strong and being herself. *Those things would be attributed to her upbringing and community, wouldn't they?*

Other semester-long acquaintances showed interest in her efforts. She'd stood on her own two feet and even managed to convince Lukas and Clara to come to some of the civil rights lectures and even stay to stuff a few envelopes. She'd work on Ben and Thomas to participate more after she got back from the Christmas holiday.

On most days the only people she knew with black skin were Ellie and her own reflection.

Ruth worried about Ellie. Thankfully, her father said he would send the money for Ellie to come down to St. Louis but Ellie said she couldn't have the Yuells spending family money on her. About the same time as the Yuell's letter with the offer arrived, the Dells volunteered to have Ellie stay for Christmas.

"Want to stay and have some extra time to study," Ellie reasoned. "I'll save the fare to Alabama to be able to pad my savings for next year."

Miss Dowling and Miss Osborn did their best to place students, who had no other place to go, or no money to get there, in private homes for the holidays. All the rest of these 'orphans' were housed in a dorm across campus. They'd have a decorated tree but no gifts and only cold lunches and suppers. *What would it be like without even having someone and someplace to go?* Ruth couldn't imagine as her longing to go back home became a physical ache within her.

The Dells talked with Ellie on work breaks, promised to fix all the traditional foods and invite her to all the holiday church services. Ruth breathed a sigh of relief, knowing the Dells would take good care of Ellie. And Ruth hoped she could report lots of progress made in her community's efforts since she'd left at summer's end. "The Dells say we'll go to church on Christmas Eve and go caroling," Ellie said. "It will be fine. Go home, Ruth, and we'll spend time together before next semester's classes and you'll fill me in when you get back."

The train was coming close to St. Louis. Outside the window Ruth recognized the barns and farmhouses near the river...and then the Mississippi.

She'd already spent hours on the train, and there would be almost a full day of travel on the return trip in order to be at classes on the Monday after Christmas vacation, Ruth grumped in her mind. She wasn't even home yet and already she was thinking of her leave-taking. At least all this fretting about her civil rights work kept her mind off of Devon. *What if he wasn't there? What if his feelings had changed?*

The train was slowing and Ruth looked at all the eager faces trying to find her family. Ruth smiled as she saw Leroy's head bobbing among the colorful sea of anxious and happy people. Ruth located Lady Dee with a colorful corsage of small Christmas bulbs and greenery on her red coat lapel, and then, her father joined her mother from behind, guiding her elbow along the platform as Ruth waved from the train car steps and came down to the platform to hug them.

"Lady Dee asked me to check if the train was arriving on time," Dr. Yuell said as he rushed to give his daughter a hug. "Then, Dr. Means stopped me to ask a question and we were almost late. How are you doing, Ruth of mine?" he smiled.

Lady Dee looked more worried and assessing. "Are you doing well? Seems like years since I've seen you. Spent more hours on my knees praying for you and looks like the good Lord answered my petitions."

"I didn't leave work early to let you have all the time with her," Leroy good-naturedly intoned as he patted Lady Dee on the shoulder. "Let me get in a hug, too." He squeezed Ruth tightly. "I've missed both you and Thelma. Get a chance to hug her in a few days."

"Got to tell you...Devon sends his regards," Dr. Yuell interrupted. "He's sorry, but he's got a few more hours at work and then there's running the office festivities for his father. He'll call you as soon as he can. Let's get out of the cold. No use catching a chill and ruining the holidays."

"We've got early dinner and your father even took off early today. Imagine that," Lady Dee said with a bright smile. "But it won't last long. There's a party at the McDougals for all you college folk." Ruth hoped for some rest but she couldn't object. It would be fun to kindle some Christmas spirit now.

"Peace won't last at all," Leroy added, whispering. "There's the Christmas baking, good dishware to polish, and the church to decorate, as always. If you still want to go Christmas shopping, Ruth, we'll have to put it in the schedule, too. Thought I heard Lady Dee mention several other doings. Better get your needs scheduled before too long or you'll get bowled over!"

Leroy was right. From the moment Ruth finished dinner to near Christmas Eve, a wave of social engagements, holiday chores, and church program rehearsals engulfed them. There had only been a few, fleeting phone calls from Devon and one brief meeting at church between his work and going to his mother's Christmas tree decorating party—limited to only family members.

Although Ruth felt frustration in not being able to see Devon, most everything else looked and seemed so welcoming to her. She loved the excitement of being home—talking to everyone at long last without Miss Osborn's...and the university's restrictions. Everyone was as happy to see her as she was to see them.

One thing was certain. Everyone *did* want to know about what Ruth had done from the moment she left St. Louis until the moment she returned home. Many would ask with concerned eyes and crinkled foreheads, "How's it going?"

Others would query, "Are they treating you right?" They talked to her like she was someone important. Ruth didn't feel important. Just the same girl covered with flour when she was making biscuits or the same girl struggling to understand Deacon Richards's chaotic hand waves and signals to close the doors against the cold winter wind at church.

People said Ruth was doing important work. They sought her out everywhere to ask questions and give her encouragement. They paid rapt attention to her explanations. They "oohed" and "aahed" as she explained what she thought were puny and paltry anecdotes about going to the college receptions, sitting in an integrated classroom and getting to know Negro students from another college campus. Mrs. Sanders called her brave and Mrs. Engalls patted her hand and said she was so proud Ruth did so much in so little time. Ruth was amazed.

Other of Ruth's peers experienced similar reactions. Some had less to tell but the community appreciated all their anecdotes with similar enthusiasm. William Bessie said with his studies and long football practices most of what he saw besides his classrooms were his room and its ceiling before falling into exhausted sleep. "The other freshmen players stared a bit at first. There were some racial slurs. Some looked to see where their locker was in reference to mine. Some were grim-lipped, but so was I, trying to be brave and not make any mistakes in my play. Some people are still cool to me and others are downright mean, looking to purposely bump me in the hallways or knock me down hard on the field when they can. Maybe they always will, but I've done my work on the field and done what the coaches have asked. I've earned my right to stay there. It seems enough so far. No time for much else. Fighting off loneliness but I made it through with a few friends I've been able to make," William concluded matter-of-factly with a shrug. "I'll let you know when I get back in the summer." His weekends were spent trying to catch extra rest to recover from games and the bruising daily practices. Besides going to classes and the laundry room to wash his clothes on Sunday, those were about all he had to talk about concerning his college experiences.

"Same for me," Doug Wilbur said, reaching for a Christmas-decorated sugar cookie. "But I'll tell you this. These white people don't know how to cook. The cafeteria food is bad. Not a chitlin in sight or a green to speak of on the table. Thought I saw a pan of collards and it turned out to be overcooked green beans. Don't get me wrong, they're fine but green beans and peas seem to be the only vegetables they give us to eat."

"Do they cook them till they're dead and almost bluish like they do on my campus?" Theodore Carvel asked. "That's the way they do it at my school. If the loneliness didn't get me, their food would! I'm going to eat until I bust, while I'm here at home," he said grabbing for the cookie platter. "Coaches keep telling me to gain weight but I don't have money for restaurant food. Can't eat all-day-long-boiled vegetables like that...or trying to digest their hard-as-leather meat. Just can't. Not enough salt, butter...and no amount of chewing makes it worth eating." Ruth smiled at Theodore's story. Here she was worried she hadn't done enough work toward equality and they were talking about vegetables and not even getting out of their dorms, which helped Ruth feel better.

Ruth's words and feelings meshed with theirs. In their eyes, there was the look of knowledge, understanding, and sympathy with what she was going through. They knew how she felt about the loneliness, even if the athletes spoke more about the food. She'd only had Devon and her parents' letters to comfort her in those fragile fall days in Chicago. Now she could listen to her friends who'd "gone north" and know she wasn't alone in her feelings and observations. They all knew how it was to feel the loneliness, joy, and the pain of being on the frontlines of these college integration efforts.

The joys of the north—being able to travel, speak freely, and go to public places without restraint—also brought the tension of coldness, lack of receptivity, and even hatred, emanating from racists and bigots who seemed as plentiful there as in the South. "Just doing it in quieter, littler ways," Theodore mused.

These other students also knew of the sadness and loneliness of people *wanting* you to make a mistake or expressed surprise when Negro college students conversed in proper English without using words like "dees" and "doos." Ruth and her compatriots compared the incidences of congratulations given from white students and faculty when they acted and spoke in ways that the whites hadn't anticipated were within their intellectual grasp. Others were incredulous there really were Negro professional people. Ruth and her friends laughed at some incidents and sighed in frustration at others. "Some think we're supposed to be dumb as stumps, but they're the ones who have no manners or grace in their approach to us," Doug noted.

Ruth shook her head knowing what everyone said was true and prayed all that would change—soon. At least, praise God, they all had this time of Christmas to rest.

ଔଈ

Ruth tossed and turned under the covers the previous night, squeezing her eyes tightly to quiet her mind. Her heart ached to see Devon. Ruth turned over and hit her pillow hoping to find a soft spot because she had to be sharp for all the activities yet to come. She awoke feeling tired.

As Ruth fixed the breakfast coffee, Leroy came down the stairs into the kitchen. "You looking a bit peaked, little sister. You OK?"

"Just getting used to being home, I guess," Ruth said, not wanting to refer to Devon. "I'll be fine."

"All this hullabaloo about being in college too much for you?" he inquired.

"No. Nothing unlike all the other Christmases. Right?" Ruth reached for two cups in the cupboard.

"Well, that's true. Remember back when Mr. Montrose's mule got out of the pen and ate the church Christmas tree Deacon Jones stored at the altar entrance," Leroy recalled. "All his shooing and flailing?"

"As I recall the animal ate most of one side," Ruth laughed at the memory.

"Yeah. Lord knows, the mule had a good meal on that pine tree. Good thing the congregation didn't see the chewed part staring at us from the altar side. What did father say?" Leroy asked.

"I believe I said something about needing a few more ornaments and no one would know the difference," Dr. Yuell said as he strolled into the kitchen. "Couldn't afford another tree. Those were hardscrabble times, you've got to remember. The church tree was probably the juiciest meal the old mule had come across in many a day and he wasn't passing it by, Christmas or no Christmas. So we did the best we could. Made a good memory, didn't it?"

"How about the time the shellacked board got into the wood pile and it burned Mother Yuell's biscuits?" Leroy said.

"Oh, yes. The Anders boy was helping out. Wasn't he? A city boy who'd just moved with his family, as I recall. Didn't know how to check the kindling. Had to teach him how to stack it in the stove. Mother Yuell was a bit put out, with the smoke and all...and only two days before the holiday," Dr. Yuell recalled.

"But the Anders family came over with biscuits and helped to clean the smoke damage. Didn't they?" Ruth replied. "I was just a baby then, right?"

"Yes, they did. Brought over a mince pie so delicious, I can still taste it. Gave Mother Yuell the recipe. We'll be eating it for Christmas dinner. Won't we, Ruth?" Leroy asked.

"I've been stirring the crock and trying to keep you out of it," she replied dryly as both her father and Leroy laughed. "You've been under the cheesecloth more than the stirring spoon."

"Mrs. Dolly and Mr. Ace are making mince pies," Sylvie said, walking into the kitchen with a wide smile. "Pumpkin, too." She looked around at everyone. "I love pie."

"Are you working over at the diner for the holidays, Ruth?" Leroy asked.

"Mrs. Daily can use the help, especially the early afternoon closing when they've scheduled their Christmas party," Ruth replied.

"Have you seen much of Devon?" Dr. Yuell asked, abruptly changing the subject. "Said he wanted to talk to you about something."

"Yeah, Ruth. Have you seen Devon?" Leroy asked with equal interest.

"I know you think we might be prying...." Dr. Yuell left the question hanging in the air.

Ruth stared at both of them before she answered. "Why, no, not much. I've been so busy with holiday chores and Devon's doing the same, plus working at his father's office with staff leaving for the holidays and...the office Christmas party. You know that," Ruth emphasized, looking into Leroy's eyes, and then, to her father, "And so do you, father. I told you we were planning to get together after the pie baking this evening."

"You got your present for Devon picked out?" Leroy asked as Dr. Yuell playfully punched his son in the shoulder.

"Now you leave Ruth go on that. Bad enough the holiday time has been so busy. Hard on all of us, at times. Right, Ruth?" Dr. Yuell's smile faded. "Are you sure you're feeling good? You look a bit anemic to me."

"Asked her the same thing myself, father," Leroy responded quickly. "Told her she looked peaked."

"And I told him I was fine," Ruth retorted to Leroy, and then, looked more kindly at her father. "I told him it was just the pace of things before coming home. Probably by the time I get settled, I'll be getting ready to go back to Chicago. You know how those things go."

"Well. You just take care of yourself," Dr. Yuell chided. "I don't need any more patients."

"Just like you take care of yourself." Leroy rolled his eyes. "Your schedule just gets busier and busier."

"Know you're right there. Know you're right. But I get energized when I'm working on things like the school desegregation efforts and emphasizing changes needed from the school board." Both Ruth and Sylvie stayed quiet as Dr. Yuell pinned his attention on his son. "The white community isn't going to just let us come into the schools without us prodding them every step of the way. Matter of fact, they try to shift and renege on just about everything all at the same time."

"We know it can't be easy, father. You'd rest some if you could, wouldn't you?" Ruth asked.

"Thanks for your concern. You too, Leroy. The other people involved have about the same load. We're all trying to help in every way possible to get things moving. We want more opportunities for everyone in our community." Dr. Yuell smiled. "But this season is just for praising the Lord and remembering His birth. Now let's move on or we'll all be behind in our schedules."

Dr. Yuell went to his office and Leroy went to work, both promising to be home early to eat before they all headed to church together. Ruth got the flour and baking supplies out as planned and started on more Christmas cookies. Sylvie got out the mixing bowl. Ruth daydreamed about Devon as she mixed the dough.

Ruth saw Devon at the Christmas play rehearsal that evening. "After tonight, Ruth. After tonight, we'll have some time." Devon smiled but it didn't go to his eyes. "The pre-Christmas rush will be over here. You go with the others now." Devon widened his reassuring smile. "We'll have a bit of time."

"Think I want to attend Reverend Fredericks's informal lecture on our local civil rights activities. Will you have some time to accompany me?" Ruth asked as they walked to his car.

A cloud seemed to come over his face. Devon tried to hide it but Ruth thought she had seen something in his look. "How about we talk about it later? Being able to see you is good but not being able to talk or spend time together...."

"Must be like Lady Dee feels when father's gone all the time," Ruth interrupted.

"Yeah, it must," Devon agreed. "But its a little bit harder knowing you'll be going back to Chicago all too soon."

"I know," Ruth replied as Devon's sister, Alice, called for him to hurry or they'd be late.

"See you soon. Don't forget. I want us to open our presents after you get though with your last pies," Devon called as he pulled the car from the driveway. "Call me at the house and I'll be ready."

Ruth pulled her sweater up around her throat as she turned to hear Deacon Brown calling her to close the sanctuary doors. Ruth felt instantly alone as she pulled her sweater collar tighter on her neck, waved, and watched the car disappear. Having to wait to see Devon alone till this evening, coupled with the continuing, intrusive whirl of people's well-meaning questions about the relationship, only made things worse. Ruth just replied truthfully to their inquiries with, "I've got two years and a semester more of college."

The mental exercise of "he loves me, he loves me not" started when she returned home to the evening pie baking. She rolled out more piecrusts into circles. Lady Dee wanted the mince and apple pies to be the last of the baking, so Ruth cut the shortening into the flour and added the ice water to start the crusts. Devon loved her. He said so in words and his letters. Ruth loved him, too. She had said it so many times.

He'd been faithful. Her friends kept a watchdog eye over Devon and thankfully reported he hadn't been spotted in any other female's acquaintance. Ruth couldn't think of the future without him. He said the same about his future with her. Concrete plans would come when they could talk, Ruth reassured herself.

She'd see him tonight.

☙❧

Devon seemed nervous when he got to the Yuell home. It had been dark for hours. "May I see your daughter in private, Dr. Yuell?"

Ruth's father raised his eyebrow a bit and thought for a second. "Lady Dee mentioned she needed me to layer sweets in the Christmas cookie tins. I'll just be in there if you need me." Dr. Yuell folded his paper and walked to the kitchen.

"Is there something wrong, Devon?" Ruth asked with questioning eyes.

"I've been trying to tell you and trying my best to get out of what I'm going to have to tell you," Devon began. "It's going to be really hard but...we're leaving tomorrow and I won't be home till it's almost time for you to go back to Chicago."

Ruth's mouth gaped in what she thought afterward was a most unladylike fashion. "Leaving?"

"I know," Devon replied sadly. "I was dumbstruck when my mother mentioned it."

Ruth tried to hold back tears.

Devon shook his head sadly. "Seems one of her foreign music teachers is in the States for a short time and wants all her former American students to have a recital in New York City a few days after Christmas. Mother's afraid of flying with her heart condition." He looked into Ruth's sad eyes. "I'll take the train with her and father is talking about taking the girls on the plane so they can have some semblance of Christmas in a hotel."

So Devon and she were only going to have a few hours this entire holiday to see each other, Ruth determined, as she tried to swallow against the lump forming in her throat.

Devon tried to put his arm around her, but Ruth couldn't help but be a bit stiff with disappointment. Devon read and felt her body language. "I knew this was going to be a shock, so I've kept it from you." He shrugged his shoulders. "Have been trying to get out of it but my parents are adamant. I have to help care for Alice and Cherie since Letty isn't feeling very well."

Ruth thought over what Devon had said, trying to look at it from his parents' point of view as a chance for a reunion and recital in New York City. Ruth knew she was being selfish but she held onto the hurt until it melted away under the heat of reason. "It's sad, I know. I had such hopes," Ruth began, "But your mother's music...."

"Exactly," Devon said with exasperation. "It's an unfortunate time but not an unreasonable request." Devon shook his head. "Everyone else in the family is thrilled with the prospect. Rockefeller Center. The Statue of Liberty. Fifth Avenue. Broadway."

"Keep talking, Mr. St. James, and my sadness will turn to envy and there won't be any forgiveness from this quarter," Ruth said, trying to regain her composure and holiday attitude.

Seeing the fond light return to her eyes, Devon relaxed a bit and looked toward the kitchen. "That deserves a hug at least," he whispered. "No stolen kisses in my only girl's house."

The words "only girl" warmed Ruth's heart. "Shall we invite my parents in and open the presents?"

"I'd love that," Devon said, hugging Ruth again.

❦

After cookies and hot chocolate, Ruth smiled because Devon was wearing the tie and clasp she had given him. She lifted the silk in her hand and he brushed the hair from her ear. "You like the scarf?" he asked. Ruth dropped the tie silk and gathered the necklace from inside her sweater collar.

"I'm wearing the beautiful necklace, too," she added. "See?"

"Glad you like it," he replied in a whisper. "Wear it when I get back from New York."

❦

With Devon's absence, Ruth was able to assuage her loneliness and fill her time with extra shifts at the diner. "Thanks." Mrs. Daily wiped the sheen of sweat from her forehead with the end of her white cotton apron.

"You're welcome," Ruth replied. "Helps me buy a few things before I go back to college."

"You're staying for the party. Aren't you?" Mrs. Daily said.

"I was hoping to," Ruth replied gratefully. "It will be fun to see everyone in their holiday finery and to catch up on things without being interrupted by customers."

The diner Christmas party promised to be fun. Ruth would see everyone and Sylvie could give them the homemade bath salts Lady Dee and Ruth helped her make as her gifts for her co-workers. Jace got a new handkerchief and Mrs. Daily got bath salts and a few pieces of Lady Dee's delectable pralines.

"You know Sylvie's been talking about the party for weeks!" Mrs. Daily replied. "She's a dear soul."

Sylvie rushed in. "You call my name?"

"Yes." Ruth looked at Sylvie's happy face. "Mrs. Daily said you've been looking forward to the party."

Sylvie brought her hand up. "Mr. Ace made me a cookie."

Ruth walked over to inspect the gingerbread man and smiled, "His arm is missing."

"Mr. Ace said I had to take a bite to see if I liked it," Sylvie said. "He's giving me one to take home."

"Several," Jace said while wiping his hands on the apron. "A whole plate full if you stand underneath the mistletoe with me, Miss Ruth."

"She's taken, Jace," Mrs. Daily said. "Now, don't you go fooling around with Ruth."

"I'm never fooling," Jace said with a smirk.

"Cookies are good presents," Sylvie said. Ruth led her sister back to the dishes. She didn't want to have to fend off Jace Prue. She was Devon's and his being away for Christmas hurt enough without her having to give any further explanations.

◌◌

Ruth got through the days without moping too much for Devon. The church celebrated with Christmas carols and the children's reenactment of the first Christmas, playing the angels, shepherds, and the Holy Family.

Christmas Day dawned clear and a bit colder than usual. Underneath her winter white coat and wool headscarf, Ruth wore the sweater set her parents had given her and Devon's scarf and necklace. Ruth felt so pretty that morning, thinking of the fine young man who had gifted them to her. She hoped Devon wore the necktie and tie clasp she bought him for his Christmas present to his mother's recital. *Was he thinking of her, too?*

Reverend Fredericks told the congregation about the birth of Jesus being a new beginning for the world just as the changes and inroads made for Negro civil rights was a new beginning for their community as well. After the Christmas morning service came the annual Christmas breakfast. Everyone felt happy with ringing laughter and chinaware clatter filling the fellowship hall smelling of fresh pine boughs, biscuits, and cured ham. Ruth volunteered to wait tables and clean up after the festivities to fill the time till Christmas dinner.

In the late afternoon and evening, before and after their huge family dinner scheduled with a menu of all the family favorites, Ruth and her family entertained visitors, served refreshments, and cleared dishes in a happy bustle of laughter, more clattering plates, and exchanging small gifts with good wishes.

Ruth didn't want to be alone till Devon returned, so she kept busy at the diner, helping her parents, and getting things ready to get back to school. She wanted no interruptions when Devon returned.

◌◌

Devon called four days before Ruth was scheduled to leave for Chicago.

"Can't wait till tomorrow. You sure we're going to get some time to see each other?" Ruth said doubtfully, frazzled every time the phone had rung the last few days.

"Starting tomorrow, I promise. We're at the station and the conductor assures me I'll be home tomorrow," Devon stated emphatically, trying to erase the exasperation he heard in her voice. "Told my family I needed some time with you since you're leaving soon. Made it clear."

"So we'll be together tomorrow night?" Ruth asked hesitantly, not trying to sound too uncharitable.

"Be there at seven. Ice cream with the girls so you can see them before you leave, and we'll have some time after to see each other," Devon promised. "We've all been running these past few weeks. Must go now," Devon concluded with a smile in his voice. "See you tomorrow night. Seven o'clock. Right?"

"Right. Tomorrow," Ruth emphasized and laughed as she put down the receiver. Ruth looked at the front door. It was only one more day.

∾

Ruth woke up from a dreamless sleep as the next day finally arrived. All she had to do was get through the day until early evening.

Lady Dee wanted to get the Christmas decorations put away. "Don't want the tree to get dry. Bothers your father's sinuses. Starts coughing and all. Fire hazard besides." Leroy wasn't too enthusiastic about the chore and Thelma was tending to several ill puppies and kittens overfed with Christmas treats in the neighborhood.

"They're so cute, people think they should give them 'people food'," Thelma said giving a skyward look with her eyes as she left to help train the new animal owners. "That's when the trouble begins."

So Ruth volunteered to put everything away while Lady Dee went to church to help the Women's League finish the interim cleanup of the church after all the Christmas activities.

Any diversion was welcome to keep her mind occupied and make the time go faster. Ruth could sit and look at all the childhood ornaments she, her twin siblings, and Sylvie had made before wrapping everything in tissue until next year.

Ruth was only somewhat successful in tamping down her nerves. She started to fidget in the afternoon and only pushed the food around her plate at dinnertime as her appetite fled. She looked at the clock too often, after finishing her evening chores and sat craning her neck at each car coming down the street. Finally, the

St. Jameses' highly polished sedan pulled into the driveway. The bright flash of its lights passed from the ceiling to her father's armchair.

"You ready?" Devon called as he entered the door but stayed on the threshold. "I need to stand here, Dr. Yuell. Alice and Cherie are waiting in the car, if you don't mind."

Dr. Yuell smiled and Ruth spoke, "I'll just get my things." She passed the closet door to check her hair and lipstick, making sure Devon's scarf and necklace were in place. She grabbed her coat to ward off any further interruptions as Devon helped her with it.

"We're going for ice cream. Then I'll drop my sisters off and I'll be showing Ruth some of the photographs I took in New York City. Does that meet with your approval, sir?" Devon asked.

"You go on and have a good time," was all her father said, as Devon ushered her through the door. Ruth greeted Devon's sisters sitting in the backseat as she smelled the car polish and looked in the dim light at the pristine interior. The Sunday-clean metal shone in the streetlight. Ice cream and looking at the holiday pictures, Ruth thought. *Finally being alone with Devon, to really talk to him for the first time since September.*

"Can't wait to take Sylvie to work at the diner," Alice said from the backseat. "She loves working there."

"And I like the vanilla ice cream," Cherie added. "Mrs. Daily always makes sure my scoops are extra big when I'm allowed to come along."

"Extra large, Cherie," Devon corrected.

Ruth didn't remember what kind of ice cream she ordered. Most of it melted in the bowl. She just remembered holding onto Devon's strong hand under the tabletop. Everything was fine as they alternately talked with Devon's sisters while sitting next to each other and exchanging furtive glances.

"Well, hello Miss Ruth. Miss Cherie. And how are you, Miss Alice?" Ruth looked from Devon's face to see Jace standing next to their table. *What was Jace doing out of the kitchen?*

"We're fine, Mr. Prue," Alice replied.

"See you're enjoying some ice cream," Jace said. He'd donned a casual shirt over his usual uniform of tight sleeveless undershirt and blue jeans. "As sweet as the gingerbread I gave you, Miss Ruth?"

Ruth's brow creased and she was silent a moment trying to think of what Jace was talking about. "Oh. Oh. You mean the two gingerbread men you gave to Sylvie?"

"And a plate more promised to you, Miss Ruth, from under the mistletoe," Jace retorted. "Been spending a lot of time here since then...."

"You were under the mistletoe?" Alice asked with a stricken look.

"No such thing," Ruth replied, even though the teasing look in Jace's eyes indicated there might be more information to share. Jace usually left her out of his suggestive conversations. Ruth had *never, ever* given Jace Prue a reason to say such things; she'd always acted like a proper young woman. Ruth took no time to set the record straight. "Sylvie got two gingerbread men from Mr. Prue. There was nothing more." Ruth shook her head and pinned Jace with an icy glare. "Shame on you, *Mr. Prue.*" This was thin-ice territory, especially in front of Devon's younger sisters. "Mrs. Daily is motioning for you." She hoped Jace would go away so she could get back to talking to Devon and his sisters.

"See you then, Miss Alice. Miss Cherie. Mr. Devon." Jace gave a jaunty salute with his right hand to his brow as he turned. "Christmas gingerbread is a fine treat."

Ruth and Devon dropped his sisters off at the house and then walked back to the car, blessedly alone. As Devon opened the passenger door, he escorted her to the door. "I've sent them upstairs. Want to see the pictures?"

Ruth breathed in the cool, crisp air of contentment and a belated Christmas present of them being together. Finally, alone.

Ruth didn't pay much attention. She just reveled in being alone with him.

Devon scanned the room. "Don't want people to talk and say we're trying to make out or doing anything we shouldn't," he stated. Ruth loved him for his concern for her reputation.

Devon walked across the room, escorting Ruth to an overstuffed couch. After a few thready, nervous words asking if she was comfortable, Devon swallowed audibly. "Do you really have to work at the diner?"

Ruth hadn't known what to expect in their first private meeting in so long as his words sank into her consciousness. "I haven't thought about it much, except I make some needed money for college and they treat me well. A valued employee." Ruth didn't know what else to say.

"I see," Devon replied. "Mr. Prue seems to be talking to you with a good deal of familiarity."

"I'm sorry about the lack of his manners. He shouldn't have talked so low with Cherie and Alice present."

"I wasn't talking about Cherie and Alice," Devon said with heat. "His talk with you made me uncomfortable."

"I would have asked for a formal apology but I didn't want to say much more in front of the girls. His conversation was totally unexpected...and unwanted.

He usually keeps me out of his sordid talk. I've told him to several times," Ruth recounted.

"He seemed to give some indication that he's after you," Devon said.

"No such thing, as far as I know," Ruth replied, still incredulous at what had set Jace off into his rant. "Perhaps it was seeing you with your sisters and me." Ruth shrugged her shoulders. "I don't know what he meant by it...and I certainly set him straight before he went back to the kitchen." She looked in Devon eyes. "Has he spoiled this evening?"

"No. No. I was just curious," Devon said. His light words didn't match the concerned look in his eyes. "Let's look at the pictures. I've got some good ones of the Statue of Liberty I might frame."

They spent about an hour looking at the pictures and making shallow conversation. "I've wanted to talk to you about so many things from my letters and experiences, Devon." Ruth reached out for Devon's hand as he placed the final pile of pictures on the sofa table. "Your letters helped me more than I can say."

"Yours too, Ruth," Devon replied. "But if you don't mind, can we do all this another evening? I guess I'm just tired after helping father take care of all the details and my sisters during the trip." He squeezed Ruth's hand and kissed her temple.

"Fine," she stammered. "If that's what you need." Ruth closed her eyes to savor the fleeting feel of his lips on her skin.

They drove back to the Yuell home. "I've really wanted to see you in the worst way, Ruth."

"Me too," Ruth said with as much enthusiasm as she could put in her voice.

"I want our relationship," Devon faltered, trying to find words. He pulled up into the driveway, escorted her to the door and gave her a gentle hug and kissed her lips.

"That's my dream too, Devon," Ruth whispered. She watched him pull away from the curb. *Why had this kiss been cold instead of the warm feeling and embrace she had hoped for?* They'd have to talk it all out when Devon felt better. There were still three days till she left for Chicago again.

❧

"Sorry, I have to leave so early, Ruthie," Dr. Yuell said as he snatched a piece of toast from the white china plate on the table the next morning. "Chicken pox in the neighborhood."

"Chicken pox, this time?" Ruth knew colds, flu, pneumonia, and other infectious diseases affected people before, during, and after the holidays. So far, Dr. Yuell and Dr. Means had been spared extensive bedside duties. "Needed to tell you. Cherie St. James came down with it in the middle of last night. Dr. Means was there to attend to her." Ruth's appetite fled as she considered how fretful she'd been as a child with the chicken pox.

"A bad case with high fever," Dr. Yuell said as he swallowed a bite. "Dr. Means prescribed Mrs. St. James leave the premises because of her heart condition. She, Alice, and Devon have gone to visit family in Joplin."

"Devon's gone?" Ruth asked with alarm in her voice.

"Yes," Dr. Yuell said, not wanting to upset his daughter more than necessary. "I know you wanted to see more of him this holiday."

That was an understatement. After the misunderstanding of last night, Ruth had wanted to clear the air. "Joplin?"

"Yes," Dr. Yuell replied. "When Cherie is no longer contagious, Alice will return with Mrs. St. James but, from what I'm hearing, I'm afraid Devon will be returning to do work in Washington, DC, directly from there."

Ruth looked thunderstruck. "Washington?"

"He didn't get a chance to tell you?" Dr. Yuell asked.

Ruth tried not to feel like an afterthought. First, it had been Devon's other work responsibilities, the office Christmas party, the family-only tree trimming party, and the trip to New York. Now, there was the misunderstanding at the diner and Cherie's getting ill with the chicken pox. The words of commitment when they were together were right but they didn't have enough time together to reconnect their lives and thoughts; too many things, people, and events were keeping Devon and her apart.

Devon was gone and he hadn't even shared his news about going to Washington, DC! *If she was his girl shouldn't she have been one of the first to know? Where was he going to be in the summer? Would they have any time then?* Sadness ached within her. Things felt so undone.

CHAPTER TWELVE

EMERGENCY ROOM AT 5:10 P.M.
CHICAGO – 1967

"I'd never been in love before and I felt like a person who'd lost the rule book," Ruth said, thinking of all the excuses she'd made. "I hid my confusion and hurt in studying and helping others."

"You spent a lot of time writing letters to him," Norma noted.

Ruth nodded, not saying anything in reply.

CHICAGO – 1958

Ruth sincerely tried to explain herself and her feelings in her letters to Devon's new Washington, DC, address. All the vellum paper was gone in an effort to tell Devon how dear he was to her. It was a blow Devon wasn't going to be home for Easter. Since Devon was living in Washington, DC, the St. James family decided to visit friends there.

"Cherie has been a trooper in her recovery from chicken pox, which stole a good deal of her Christmas and New Year's. She deserves a proper holiday," Mrs. St. James told Lady Dee. "Besides we have to find Devon another suitable residence while he's doing work at the Capitol. His roommate and fiancée want the apartment as their first home after their August wedding." From one of the half-dozen brief letters Devon had sent since Christmas, Ruth knew the law firm had asked him to continue his work in Washington, DC.

So Ruth waited until the summer. Ruth's college year was finished several weeks before Devon was expected home for a visit. She'd hurriedly packed her things and said goodbye to Ellie, Norma, and the rest of her dorm mates.

"I'm going into an apartment with Mary Beth Harris in September," Norma said before she left. "So that will leave you and Ellie with a new face next year."

Ruth was sad to see Norma go because she was an open, discerning white girl who had grown into a good friend and champion of the Negro students on campus. Ruth wondered if she'd be seeing much of her when she returned to her immersion in white culture again. *Was it only a one-year lark for Norma?*

"You have fun," Ruth replied, both as an encouragement for the summer and her adventure in independent living. Ruth's parents were adamant. Ruth must reside in the dorm for at least another year. "Come over when you get back and see us when you're settled."

"You're sure in an all-fired hurry to get out of here," Ellie observed. "Been packing for a week. Know you want to see Devon and all in the worst way...."

"Want to get back home and get settled before going to work. My family has made inquiries for other positions for pay but nothing's come up yet," Ruth replied, wanting to get away from Jace Prue to put Devon's objections to her work and proximity to the man behind them. "My parents, Mrs. Blaine, Calli, and Meggie are going to Philadelphia and Leroy and I will be taking care of Sylvie while they're gone." Ruth put a folded sweater in the suitcase. "Have to work as much as I can to save enough money, so I can take some time off to care for things when my parents are away."

Ellie was well aware of all the Yuell siblings and Ruth's parents' activities. Both girls loved to talk of their hometowns of St. Louis and Milltown. "You are still planning to welcome me to St. Louis when we head back here at the end of summer?"

"Already got the approval from my parents and the welcome mat will be out from the train station to our home," Ruth replied. "Be happy to have your company on the way back here."

"I'll be happy for the company, too, but I'll miss you until then," Ellie said. "My first train ride!'

"I'll miss you too, but I can't say I won't enjoy the time at home," Ruth noted putting her blouses on the top of the sweaters.

"And one young beau?" Ellie asked.

"Think that goes without saying," Ruth replied. "Wish I had a nickel for every time I've thought, said, or written Devon's name since the holidays. My tuition for the rest of my college education would be paid for in full."

Ruth's train trip home seemed to take forever, like she was traveling to some place far away like California or Florida instead of St. Louis. Ruth fought strong, troublesome dreams she couldn't remember in the morning light, which occurred with increasing rapidity. Sometimes, Ruth's bedclothes looked like they'd been tossed about in a storm. Seeing Devon eye to eye would settle things and put everything behind them—and soon.

Dr. Yuell and Leroy picked Ruth up at the train station. "Your mother is getting things ready, Ruthie. We'll be home soon."

"Sylvie's at work at the diner. Alice and the St. James driver will have her home soon." Leroy picked up Ruth's suitcase and wedged it next to the small steamer truck.

Ruth only had a few moments to kiss her mother when she saw the St. James car pull to the curb.

After welcome home hugs, Sylvie ran up the stairs and into the house.

Alice gestured to Ruth. "Told Devon he'd better get home soon and straighten things out with you," she whispered.

Ruth frowned, because she didn't know the rest of the St. James family had known of the strain the last time she and Devon were together. *Devon had been talking about these matters at home?*

"Men. They're so thickheaded sometimes." Alice looked coy. "Jace Prue doesn't want you." She stopped for a moment. "He's looking at someone else."

Why would Alice St. James want to talk about Jace Prue and the dust-up at the diner? Just as Ruth was going to ask Alice about their strange conversation, Sylvie ran down the walk. "Lady Dee has cake! Lady Dee has cake!"

"I'd really like you to join us," Ruth said, wanting Alice to explain herself and her remarks.

"Can't. I've got my music lesson and I'll be late if we don't hurry." Alice looked at her watch. "But thanks anyway. See you soon." Alice reseated herself in the back of the car and waved.

Ruth turned back to her sister. "Chocolate," Sylvie said with a bright smile.

◑◐

"I'm sorry, Ruthie," Dr. Yuell said for what seemed like the hundredth time that summer. "Devon is working on an important brief for the North Carolina litigation." He shook his head again, looking into his daughter's sad eyes. "Just have to keep busy and the time will go faster."

Dr. Means came to the house the morning after Ruth got home for summer vacation to tell her Devon was still in Washington. "Mrs. St. James and Cherie are in Cleveland visiting Leticia's family and Mr. St. James and Alice are the only ones home." Ruth guessed this was Dr. Means and her parents' polite way of telling Ruth she would have to wait a few more days or weeks before seeing Devon. Ruth knew she was being unfair about her building anger concerning Devon's absence but she wanted to spend at least a few days of summer with him.

"You talked to him and he says he'll be back in three weeks, right?" Dr. Yuell asked.

Ruth pressed her lips together, thinking about her father's words and wondering how to reply. "In time for us to go to Mary's summer party."

"Hopefully, things will go well and he'll be able to get back here..." Dr. Yuell said as he put his arm on his daughter's shoulder. "When you look back on this time, it won't seem so bad." Her father was trying to tell her to be strong but what she felt was lonely as her summer plans seemed to slip away.

All she could say in reply was, "I'm trying to look at it that way."

❦

"Now you have all the emergency numbers?" Lady Dee asked with a tinge of fear in her voice.

Ruth patiently replied for the fourth time in twenty minutes. "There's one list near the kitchen telephone and one on the sofa table."

"Do you know about the Hendersons?" Lady Dee asked.

"They'll be home the entire time you're at the convention. All Sylvie, Leroy, and I have to do is go across the lawn, ring their bell, and they'll be there to help us."

"Lady Dee, you've about wore the children out," Dr. Yuell said with sweet exasperation. "They're responsible people and have answered all your concerned questions."

Lady Dee nodded at the sense of her husband's statement. "Dr. Means will be home on Friday but your father and I as well as Mrs. Blaine, Calli, and Meggie will be staying a few extra days at the conference."

Lady Dee repeated the itinerary over and over again and Ruth listened with smiling patience. "I know. Sylvie goes to work on Tuesday and Thursday, although Mrs. Daily might need her for the Saturday evening group that's coming to the diner." Ruth thought for a few seconds. "Leroy will drive her and pick her up in the family car if she needs to work that day. I think that's it—except for you to stop worrying and have a good time."

"Wish you all could come," Lady Dee said.

"I know. I know," Ruth comforted. "I'll miss Meggie but this is her first chance to get a travel holiday, since she's in college downtown."

"Won't be much fun with Calli stepping on her tail," Leroy interjected.

"Leroy! Please watch your language...and we must avoid speaking against Dr. Means's family," Lady Dee exclaimed. "We must be Christian in the toughest of circumstances."

"I'll mind my tongue, but you know its true," Leroy said. "Calli never takes a breath with her mean stories about everyone in the neighborhood, especially us. She should be a journalism student rather than studying to be an elementary school teacher. She could give Randolph Hearst a run for his money with her own private brand of yellow journalism." Leroy looked like he tasted something sour. "She's as bad as her aunt. Not any better."

"I don't want to talk about this subject now," Lady Dee said with a deep furrow in her brow. "Mind your manners now and when we're gone."

❀

"Got to work late at the garage this evening, so don't hold dinner for me. George Haskell needs a major engine overhaul before his sales trip to Mississippi," Leroy said as he wolfed down his dinner before he headed toward the door. "I'll pick Sylvie up at eight-thirty p.m. but I won't come in the house when I drop her off. So be waiting."

Ruth nodded, thinking Leroy spent all his extra time at the garage. He was determined to pay off all his college loans as near to graduation as possible.

"On a Saturday night?" Ruth put out another plate and got a clean tea towel from the drawer. A bit of wax paper under the towel might not keep his food warm but at least it wouldn't be dried out when he got home.

❀

After dinner, while reading one of her next semester's English literature assignments, Ruth made sure Sylvie was tucked into bed. Ruth worried because Sylvie had eaten little and seemed distracted at the dinner table. Ruth remembered Sylvie had the chicken pox the same summer as she and Nettie, but it didn't hurt to be careful about her sister's health. "Good night, Sylvie." Ruth stroked her forehead and turned out the light. Sylvie gave no answer in return. "Let me know if you're not feeling well." If Sylvie wasn't better in the morning, Ruth resolved to call Dr. Means.

Ruth went to bed. She'd only been in bed a few minutes when Sylvie came into her room babbling disconnected words and crying. "Alice at diner. Ace. Dark."

At first, Ruth thought Sylvie had a fever, so she felt her sister's forehead—bone dry and cool.

"What are you saying?" Ruth asked, muzzy with fatigue.

"Alice with Ace," Sylvie cried fretfully.

The realization of what Sylvie was saying bolted Ruth upward while fumbling for her nightstand light. "Say it again! Are you sure?" Ruth scanned Sylvie's eyes as her sister repeated the words. "I'm going to talk to Leroy. Get dressed in your play clothes." Ruth kept her voice calm as she watched Sylvie give a teary-eyed nod.

Ruth wakened Leroy, who groused as Ruth had until the meaning of Sylvie's sparse words became clear. "We've got to find her," he said, heading for the chair where he'd tossed his work clothes. "You get dressed."

They all met in the kitchen. "Got to see if we can get Alice out of there," Leroy offered. "Don't have many options. Pastor Fredericks and his wife are away. Did the oil change on his sedan before he and his wife went to Melville."

"Call anyone else and there's bound to be so much talk, it'll take months for it to be over." Ruth ran her hand over her forehead. "Mrs. St. James hasn't been well. Dr. Means won't be back for hours." Ruth tried to think of what to do. "We're just going to have to go over there and see what's going on." Ruth didn't want to make Sylvie upset by outright doubting what she had told them. "We'll be together." She closed her eyes and prayed this was some misunderstanding.

Ruth already discarded the idea of going to the St. James home. If Sylvie was wrong, the embarrassment of Ruth and Leroy accusing Alice St. James of such behavior would flare back to affect her family, not to mention her relationship with Devon. On the other hand, if Mrs. St. James had one fault of late, it was listening to gossip. Her vulnerability had increased as her health worsened.

Ruth heard Mrs. St. James mention many, many times of late. "People who are touched by scandal should leave the neighborhood." If what Sylvie was saying was true...and the truth got out. Ruth's hands shook on the drive to the restaurant. *What would these unsavory facts mean for her and Devon, not to mention the local civil rights issues spearheaded by Mr. St. James and Devon?* Devon helped her father spare Calli from scandal. *Shouldn't she do the same for Devon's dear sister?*

"It's one-thirty in the morning," Leroy said, putting down the flashlight he was using to look at the clock. "How can we explain that?"

"I don't know yet," Ruth answered truthfully. "If you turn off the headlights and we park the car in the alley across the street, we shouldn't be seen."

"What are we going to do?" Leroy asked.

"Don't know that either, other than a teenage girl isn't supposed to be in a man's room alone after dark," Ruth replied, trying to keep her breathing calm. "We'll have to figure something out."

"Say that. Man's room," Sylvie offered. "Go." Sylvie pulled at Ruth's sleeve.

"Yes, we're going." Ruth looked in Sylvie's eyes. "But you must, *must* promise to sit on the back step of the restaurant and wait for us." Ruth looked at Sylvie again. "Promise?"

Sylvie nodded her head. "Yes. Go."

"I think it would be best if I go and talk to Alice first. If I go talk to them, they might listen to reason, especially Alice. She knows how dear she and her family are to me. It might take away the sting of being found out. Understand?"

"You've got five minutes, and then I'm coming in," Leroy replied forcefully. "Five minutes. You hear?"

Ruth nodded and opened the car door.

Ruth walked slowly up the drive to the side buildings at the diner to search for Alice. There was light coming from Jace Prue's room. The door was open. Ruth found Alice in Jace's bed. Jace was on top of her.

"Alice, you have to come with me," Ruth said in a monotone, shocked to actually *see* Alice in such a compromising position.

In a few bumbling seconds, Prue had an old blanket around his waist and a shame-faced Alice was covered in a sheet pulled to her chin.

"What you doing here?" Prue spat.

Ruth didn't speak to him. She bent a few times to pick up Alice's scattered clothes and threw them at her. "Get dressed. Don't leave anything behind."

As Ruth heard the sounds of the girl getting out of bed and into her clothes, she stepped between the diner cook and Alice. Prue was quick in getting his pants on and lunged at Ruth as she handed Alice one of her shoes. "I said what are you doing here in my room?"

Ruth threw Prue's hand off her shoulder, ignoring the question. "Leroy's in the car and he'll take us home, Alice," Ruth ordered, changing her posture and averting her gaze to Devon's younger sister. "We won't say a word about this."

"Alice is with me, now," Prue said. "She ain't going no place."

"Leroy's in the car and he'll take us home," Ruth repeated, looking at Alice, trying to give a good impression of how Lady Dee would sound in similar crisis circumstances. "Now go."

"Fucking people," Prue screamed as Alice, in rumpled clothes and clutching jewelry in her clenched hands, fled the room into the night. He grabbed for a drawer in his wobbly, age-scarred dresser. Ruth saw him swig from a bottle of what appeared to be liquor while she tried to make her escape.

Ruth scrambled out the door and bumped into Alice. Ruth grabbed the girl's slim arms and shook her. "You know what a scandal will do to your family. Don't say a word and get to the car! The alley across the street. Now!"

Ruth turned to Prue to reason with him. "It's the first time I've been in your room...." Prue brandished a gun, making Ruth freeze in her tracks. He hit her, venting all his anger with an open palm. As Ruth's knees buckled, Prue grabbed Ruth by the throat. There wasn't enough air in her throat for anymore words to come out.

Prue'd been drinking a lot. Ruth could smell the cheap liquor as he changed his hold and stuffed her neck in the crook of his arm in a chokehold. Ruth felt his chest turning in concert with his neck as he scanned the area for witnesses or trouble. Ruth's shoes were gone from trying to stop the dragging and her legs shook as she tried to regain her balance to stop the painful ripping of the skin on her heels and feet. "Go get Alice," Prue bellowed to some unknown person. Ruth tried to crane her neck to see and all she could hear were heavy footsteps, running away from them. *Who could that be?*

"Don't you make a sound or you're dead," he ordered angrily as he shook her and applied more pressure on Ruth's neck. "I'm not alone," he warned. Ruth continued stumbling and crying as he hit her again and told her, "Shut up." She tasted blood and felt what seemed like hot metal as Prue's gun scraped her face. He continued to terrorize her, bumping the gun barrel time after time on her left temple. Its hammer-like pounding made Ruth dizzy with pain.

Suddenly the path changed from gravel to grass. Ruth noticed they were behind a row of garages with connecting fences. Some light peaked though the weather-warped boards. It was a long way to the houses, she thought frantically. *Would anyone hear them from the long expanses of lawns and backyards to this alley? Was she going to die there?*

Prue turned Ruth around and threw her down, like an angry child's doll thrown to the dirt, slamming her shoulders, forcefully and painfully, to the grass. Her head bounced like a hollow ball against the hard turf, dazing her. Her legs flew in the air and crumbled. She felt shame, unable to cover herself.

Darkness and shadows swam before Ruth's face. Ruth tried to find the edge of her skirt to pull it down, embarrassed to have anyone see her upper legs and underwear. Blood, hot as fire, bloomed on her cheeks. Prue's entire weight fell on her, like the collapse of a giant wall. He straddled Ruth's body, placed his thick forearm over her neck and put the gun to her chin, etching scrapes as he did. Ruth felt his heavy breathing and the path of his hot-liquored breath on her neck as he alternately scanned the area to see if anyone had heard or seen her kidnapped struggle.

Ruth prayed.

She thought she heard footsteps again and saw another man's silhouette, a shadowy face, but she looked around and he was gone. *Where was Leroy? Had he seen this other man?*

Prue slapped her for her inattention, "Listen, you, do what I say or you're dead."

Ruth called out over and over in a voice she didn't recognize as her own say-ing, "Stop!" and, "What do you want me to do?" after he slapped her several more times.

Prue lifted his weight a bit and pulled roughly at Ruth's clothing, trying to get her upright. Ruth heard the cloth rip and the buttons fly. Ruth followed his orders to pull down her garter belt. Her shaking hands were clumsy and Prue slapped her again. She felt an empty, screeching feeling of violation take over her body. A cold stillness like black ice invaded her mind.

Only a husband on his wedding night was supposed to share such acts with his beloved bride. Her virginal innocence was gone and she was bleeding. Prue forced Ruth to kiss and hold him as he hit her and raped her. No reason prevailed. No one came to help. It was just Ruth and this evil man in a dirty alley smelling of garbage.

Ruth didn't know how long she was there or how long it took to get on her feet. She only recalled her mind's inaudible silent scream of pain, fear, and revulsion, punctuated by Prue's grunting and heavy, angry breathing. After he finished, he just slugged her and said dismissively, "Now you get outta here and don't look back or I'll kill you. Don't say anything to anyone or I'll kill your fam-ily. I've still got the gun." Prue stumbled away.

Somehow, Ruth got up from the cold, dirty grass patches and gravel. Things didn't look right. She felt miles away from the diner. Her skirt and sweater were torn. There were cuts and scrapes on her hands. They were filthy and bleeding.

Ruth ran as best she could: staggering, weaving, and falling. She thought to just get away and told herself if she didn't look back she would be OK. She had to run. Saving her life dictated it. So she looked straight ahead and willed herself to stay upright. Her legs alternately felt like jelly and logs on fire.

Ruth tried to think. She could help Alice better if she could run. So she would run, not look back, and make sure Alice was gone. Try to find Sylvie and Leroy and drive for help. *Run on your legs and run to the car. That was running, wasn't it? Those actions would get everyone to safety, wouldn't they?*

In that blessed haze of shock and unreality, she headed for the light at the end of the alley and didn't think of the rest.

❧

Ruth heard a sharp intake of breath and almost fell again as she saw Alice's face swim into view. Ruth couldn't be sure because her vision was a mix of fun-house mirrors and looking through what she could only think was stained glass. "Is that you, Alice?"

"It's me, Ruth," Alice whimpered. "Oh my God! What did Jace do to you?"

"You've got to get out of here," Ruth ordered, but her lips were too swollen to speak clearly so she repeated herself again. "I've told you twice now. You've got to get out of here. Leave here, forget everything tonight, and don't say a word!"

"Let me help you!" Alice cried, trying to keep them both upright. "I should have stayed here but you said to run. I thought I saw someone coming after me and I ran halfway home but you were still here...and I had to know if you were OK."

Ruth fell against the bed. *Dear Lord, she was in Prue's room again!*

"We've got to get out of here," Ruth ordered.

Before Alice could get Ruth situated on the bed, Prue burst through the door.

"What did you do to her?" Alice shouted.

"She got what was coming when she busted in," Prue slurred, the neck of a liquor bottle in his left fist. "You said you didn't tell anyone, you little slut." Prue put his hand around his back and pulled the gun from the back of his waistband. "Should kill you both and your families."

"Oh God, Jace, no. I...I thought you loved me." Tears streamed down Alice's cheeks. "You said to bring my jewelry and we were going to run away together." She lunged toward Prue with blind fearlessness. Betrayal and lost love whirled in Alice's mind.

Ruth tried to raise herself, but she fell back yelling helplessly, "No. No." The gun exploded and a wind of hot sulfur filled the air. Tiny dark spots of blood hit Ruth's face. Ruth closed her eyes and swallowed, trying to push down the nausea in her throat. A sweet smell on her face was making her sick.

❧❧

"Ruth?" Someone was shaking her shoulder. Ruth didn't know what time it was. Another watery "Ruth?" followed as Ruth tried to stay conscious and talk back to the voice calling her name. It was Alice. Ruth had to get back to Alice.

"He's not moving," Alice whispered.

Ruth tried to right herself as if nothing happened. An explosion of pain ripped through her head but she had to get back to Alice. Had to think of what to do. "Are you OK?" Ruth thought she saw Alice nod hesitantly. "Seen Leroy?"

Alice only shook her head.

Where was Leroy? He said five minutes! Where was Sylvie? Alice was there and Ruth had to keep her safe. It was difficult to speak. "You've got to get home. Say nothing. Run home again...and stay."

Ruth braced herself to look over on the other side of the bed. Her gaze was drawn, like an invisible string, to the open-eyed, dead face of Jace Prue.

"He's not moving," Alice repeated.

"He was crazy," Ruth said. "Run home and say nothing. You've been home all night."

"You're hurt," Alice said.

"I'll be fine," Ruth insisted, trying to get her lips and mouth to work. *Did Alice understand what Ruth was saying?* "Go home. Go to bed. Say nothing! I've got to get this done." Ruth raised herself from the sitting position. First things first. There was the gun. Ruth wiped it on the old, threadbare coverlet but her fingers were clumsy and slick as the gun fell to floor with a loud thud. She had to find Leroy and Sylvie. Ruth groped her way along the outside wall of the diner, fighting pain coming from everywhere in her head and body. Ruth's steps were unsteady but she got to the diner window and saw it was still dark from the inside. Ruth headed for the car. She found Sylvie in the backseat of their family car, sitting with Leroy's head cradled in her lap. Leroy was moaning and his head was bleeding from a now-sluggish wound. *More blood.*

"Leroy hurt," Sylvie said in a tiny baby-like voice with eyes as big as sunflowers as she rocked back and forth.

"What happened?" Leroy asked in a whisper, trying to sit up.

"Just lay there and keep your eyes closed. I'm driving us home," Ruth said as loudly and distinctly as she could while she got in the driver's seat. "Save your strength." She got behind the wheel of the car, still wondering about the tiny spots on her face. Ruth wished she'd had more driving lessons but there was no one there to get them home with Leroy bleeding in the back seat with Sylvie. "No one was back there but me. Understand?" *Where was Jace? Where was Alice?* She was having trouble holding on to the steering wheel because she was shaking so badly. Another question floated across Ruth's mind. *Where was Devon?*

◕◔

That early summer night after the rape, only three thoughts pounded in Ruth's throbbing head: she had to get help for Leroy, she had to stay calm, and no one could find out about the whole story. She vowed to tell her parents, the police, and anyone who could help them everything she knew, *except* to implicate Alice and the St. James family. Sylvie was in the backseat, holding Leroy's head as he drifted in and out of consciousness while Ruth drove home. *How had he gotten back there?*

Ruth careened crazily into the driveway, landing on the lawn as she slammed on the brakes. Dr. Means had just gotten back from a late night call and was up and out of the office in an instant. He saw Ruth staggering toward the Yuell house from the family's crookedly-parked sedan. Ruth collapsed on her way to the door; pieces of her panties, garter belt, and hose hung tattered around her legs.

Dr. Means got Ruth onto the house porch somehow. "Leroy and Sylvie are in the backseat."

"Where, child?"

"In the backseat," Ruth repeated as distinctly as she could.

"Don't move, Ruthie." Dr. Means ran to the car after he folded his jacket into a pillow so Ruth could stay on the porch till he could move her. The doctor found Sylvie still cradling Leroy's head like it was a priceless crystal globe. Dr. Means opened the car door and examined Leroy's head and neck. "Can you move your fingers and toes?"

"Yes, sir," Leroy said, his voice muffled against his sister's sweater, not losing his manners. "My head hurts like thunder...and I think I'm bleeding some."

"Yes, son," Dr. Means replied in a concerned tone. "Think you can try to get up?" He reached for Leroy's shoulder. "Stay still, Sylvie, till I can get a hold on him." Dr. Means moved more fully into the car interior, seeing Leroy would need some stitches. "If you feel bad, just lay down again."

"How's Ruthie?" Leroy asked weakly.

"I doctored her on the porch and Mrs. Henderson's coming across the lawn now. She'll be safe now."

❧❧

Why didn't I know my underthings were there until now? Ruth turned to cover herself with her hands.

From then on, Ruth only remembered seeing black and white shadows around her. Some loud sounds like piercing voices and shouts flitted into her mind and were ignored by her disinterested brain. At least she was home. *Were those sounds from her mother, her family?* No, they were in Philadelphia. Ruth didn't remember at times as she called out to them. She couldn't focus.

What were they doing and what else had happened? Dr. Means wondered as his skilled hands and mind turned to healing.

Suddenly, Mrs. Mobley, another family neighbor, was there. "Been a ruckus down at the Daily diner," she cried brokenly. "Jace Prue is dead."

❧❧

Ruth's body flailed like a broken marionette as Mrs. Henderson tried to take off Ruth's clothes to tend to her wounds and the dirt. She'd fought Prue, but she didn't need to fight Dr. Means or Mrs. Henderson, she reasoned, but her body couldn't stop itself. "Don't touch me! Don't touch me!" she cried to the memory of what Jace Prue had done to her.

"We'll clean what we can now and leave the rest," Mrs. Henderson whispered. "It's all right now."

A warm washcloth cleaned Ruth's face. Ruth rejoiced to get clean but turned away when there was pain. Mrs. Henderson hummed spirituals and cooed, like the pigeons in the rafters of the Wilcox barn, Ruth thought.

Dr. Means called Philadelphia and told Lady Dee and Dr. Yuell to rush back to St. Louis.

ƏƏ

The police came at four a.m. They wanted to talk to Miss Ruth Yuell.

Dr. Means let them open the door to her room but nothing more.

"I won't let you talk to her. She's terribly beaten and in shock," Dr. Means said. "I'm her father's partner. Their son's in one of our examining rooms. Room Two. He needs some stitches for a terrible gash in his head. You'll have to come back later after I've given them proper medical attention."

"She looks half dead, too," Ruth thought she heard a strange voice say.

With grave-black humor, Ruth thought that her heart didn't have the good sense to stop beating.

ƏƏ

Mrs. Henderson went back upstairs to be with Ruth and coaxed her from her clothes, which were now more like bloody, dirty rags. Ruth was too tired to fight this time. The older woman bathed her like a corpse and gave her pained, sympathetic looks sitting with her dear friend's daughter, not knowing what else to do.

"Leave the light on," Ruth heard herself say—her first sentence in some time. She needed someone there, or at least a light on, to ward off the terror branded in her mind as if her brain refused to remember anything else. Blessed shock took over.

For the first time in her life, Ruth slept for many hours. Ruth dreamed of Lady Dee helping Grandpa Wilcox when Grandma Wilcox died and she, herself, trying to help Nettie and Sylvie when Grandpa Wilcox passed away. *Nettie was still gone, too.*

ƏƏ

Mrs. Henderson went home to feed her cat and Dr. Means had gone back to the office to get fresh bandaging supplies. Ruth woke and struggled to get out of bed.

Every bone in her body hurt and what didn't hurt seemed bruised or swollen. But Ruth had to leave her bed and talk to Leroy. Ruth couldn't get her lips to move. She tried to enunciate clearly but it was difficult.

"Leroy. Are you awake?" Ruth asked, thinking she sounded like she had a mouth full of food.

"Yes. But only speak in whispers. I can't open my eyes or I'll be sick again," Leroy whispered. "Can't keep anything down but I don't want any pain shots." He held his body unnaturally rigid, trying to overcome the dizziness and pain.

Ruth tried to be clear and concise but her mind seemed fuzzy and far away from the pill Dr. Means had given her. "Can't say Alice was there. We'll say Sylvie was there instead."

"Oh, Ruthie. Are you sure?" he whispered. A tear came down the side of his face toward his hairline.

"I'm sure." Ruth patted his arm and wiped away the tear trail with the edge of the sheet.

"I'll keep your secret." Leroy sounded distant and painful in her ears as she crept back into her room unnoticed.

With that promise, Ruth knew she could let go for a time.

☙❧

The story was in the afternoon newspaper, all neat and descriptive in four paragraphs on the front page. It described a Negro man named Jace Prue who died from a gunshot wound to the chest. Ruth, Leroy, and Sylvie's names were mentioned along with the word "murder."

☙❧

The Yuells rushed into the house and ran up the stairs without taking off their coats.

"She's still deeply affected," Dr. Means informed. "Leroy's a bit better."

Dr. Yuell gently shook his daughter awake to break her shock-like state and told Ruth to listen. "Jace Prue did something unspeakable and you fought to save the life of you and your siblings."

"It was bad," Ruth whispered in a chant. She parroted the same pitiful phase over and over like a broken recorder trying to make her mind accept the truth.

They just held her. *What could they say?*

Ruth heard her father talking to Lady Dee in the hallway. "Let's give it one more day and pray she's better in the morning," Dr Yuell whispered in worried tones. "I've held off the police. She's got a concussion just as bad as Leroy's."

Funny. Ruth felt like a rock now but she didn't know rocks could cry. Tears came down her cheeks like the water from the desert rock under Moses's wooden staff. Just like the Sunday school teachers taught and Reverend Fredericks preached from the pulpit. But if she remembered her Bible reading correctly, striking the rock for the water kept him from the Promised Land.

CHAPTER THIRTEEN

EMERGENCY ROOM AT 5:20 P.M.
CHICAGO – 1967

"I've got to stop," Norma sniffed. Even if Ruth was her friend and she'd promised to write everything down, Norma needed a rest...and some time to recover from the facts of Ruth's rape. "You can't expect me to go on...without... without getting more tissue!" Norma claimed between attempts to calm herself and blow her nose. "I thought I could be objective and keep going, but knowing you makes it impossible!" Norma gave her nose a healthy blow, and then grabbed tissues for her eyes as her abandoned pad rested on Ruth's hospital covers. "Just give me a minute. Just a minute!"

Ruth caught her friend's red nail-polished hand. A luxury Norma foreswore in danger areas, not wanting to make herself a target with the vibrant color. "Let's just keep going, Norma. My journey's only half done."

Delving into the excruciating facts of a rape and Prue's death involving her dear, sweet friend, Ruth, was a huge challenge. *Would she have said "yes" several hours before, if she had thought the whole thing through?* Norma looked into her friend's sad, memory-misted eyes.

Norma took a few deep breaths, blew her nose one last time and picked up the pen and pad. She looked at her friend with a straight gaze. "Only for you, Ruth. I'm doing this only because it's you."

Ruth started talking again about events several days after the rape and death. "The second and third day after the diner incident, Leroy was healing and trying to help Sylvie and I recover." Ruth bit her lower lip. "I wasn't proud about having to lie but Leroy agreed with me in his brief bedside visits. There was nothing else we could do."

❀❀

ST. LOUIS – 1958

"Just like you've been saying, about the necklace and Sylvie," Leroy whispered, making sure no one listened to their furtive conversation. He pointed to his head swathed in the bandages hiding the nine stitches needed to close his wound. "I don't even know who hit me in the head!"

Unfortunately, Sylvie wasn't much better than Ruth. Although Sylvie had seen nothing of the fateful night's events, she had no context for the situation except to know Jace Prue was dead like her grandparents—enough to shatter Sylvie's nerves. Sylvie reverted to one of her rocking-and-moaning states. "He young," was all she could say with her fists tight against her chest. *What could they tell her concerning the real facts of the horrible situation?*

Almost as soon as Ruth woke up, Sylvie was in her room needing solace. Thelma, Dr. Yuell, and Lady Dee tried to comfort Sylvie but Sylvie gravitated to Ruth and Leroy for comfort and attention—comrades in a situation Sylvie would never fully comprehend. Just like the time Nettie disappeared. Ruth now knew the depths of misery, but she needed to pull herself together to help her sister.

"Don't go into it. Don't go into it," was all Ruth could whisper from her battered, swollen lips. "It's over and we're safe now."

"That's right, Sylvie," Leroy said as he dry-swallowed his next dose of aspirin.

"Just going to find a...my...lost necklace." Ruth lied to everyone. No use anybody else being guilty if her story fell apart.

Leroy said nothing. He just closed his eyes against the plaguing, dull ache in his temples.

So Ruth and Leroy shut the door and threw away the key on their own needs for the sake of their sister, Alice St. James, and their community. They'd been given only forty-eight hours: one day to rest and one day to comfort Sylvie. They needed to be down at the police station the following morning.

❀❀

Unbeknownst to the Yuells, the police had a theory—a very wrong theory. They thought Jace Prue had been killed by another jealous boyfriend or lover of Ruth Yuell. Even though there was no information or a shred of evidence, they adopted this enraged-boyfriend-pushed-too-far analysis for every interview. They secretly theorized that, after killing Jace Prue, this unknown boyfriend slapped

Ruth around to "show her who was boss," enacted revenge sex, and knocked her avenging brother unconscious. To cover her and her family's standing within the community, Ruth had concocted this rape-self-defense story. They were sure if they kept on pressing her, she'd tell them the truth. All they needed was to spread this story around her neighborhood and squeeze her with some rough interrogations. Eventually, she'd confess everything and save them time and needless paperwork.

Their interrogations followed their plan. One of the detectives' hands settled on Ruth's bruised shoulder during an extravagant gesture. "Get your hands off my daughter!" Dr. Yuell shouted out in bitten-off, clenched-jaw precision after a few minutes of outrageous questions. "Look at her! She was the one who's been assaulted and you are treating her like she's some criminal!"

Ruth's hand flew to cover her father's, fearing the police sergeant's sneering demeanor would become even more pronounced and they'd both be in trouble. Her cheeks heated with mortification as she considered her life had been shattered by fifteen, perhaps twenty, vile minutes of fighting against being raped. Ruth couldn't speak against her drought-dry throat. She tried to concentrate on what she was going to say, while gazing at the sad-looking cracked paint on the interrogation room walls.

Ruth watched strong men wither under her father's patented look of physician indignation but this was 1958 in St. Louis, Missouri. A definite sorry place to be when the sergeant was white and Ruth and her father were Negro!

The sergeant's smirk stayed pinned in place as he shrugged, dropped his hand from the Ruth's bruised shoulder, and sauntered to the head of the scarred maple table, making no apology. He hoisted his leg onto one of the worn wooden chairs, squinted, and pointed at Ruth as he shouted in retort, "We got a Nigra man shot dead in a house over on Sullivan Street in the wee hours of the morning a few miles from your home, which seems fishy to me, and the taxpayers deserve an answer." The man kept chewing a seemingly thick wad of gum as he continued. "This report here says you've been in a scrape *before* down in Madison Township. Something about another woman and her baby?"

Ruth couldn't let the accusation hang in the air. "That was when I was fifteen," Ruth croaked, as salty tears scalded the cuts on her chin. "Stella and her baby were victims of neglect. Not by my hand." Ruth dared not say anything about the Madison Township deputy, although her tongue burned to tell this blowhard sergeant everything. Her father had already shouted at him. *If she alienated these white men by a second outburst, would there be any justice for her?*

"So at age fifteen and now, you're saying?" the detective retorted.

One double-chinned detective asked in a slow, smirky drawl, "Do you have any other boyfriends?" He was wearing a too-short tie and tight-waisted trousers unnecessarily fastened with suspenders.

Ruth answered, saying, "Jace Prue was a cook at the place where I was employed. He was never, *ever* my boyfriend." The detective didn't blink an eye and repeated the question. Ruth was always shocked when her vehement denials didn't seem to matter to the police. She always stayed quiet, not wanting to mention Devon's name.

Dr. Yuell always staunchly defended his daughter every time the questioning got ugly. "What are you implying, officer?"

"Oh, nothing," was the example of a reply Ruth recalled a thin, pockmarked detective saying. His words were respectable, but his sing-song tone wasn't.

"Maybe you liked it. Ya like the rough stuff? You make up this story, missy," they questioned in a ribald tone.

"To my mind, no white woman coulda driven a car in your condition. How could a bashed-up Negra woman with no driver's license, let alone with no drivin' experience, get herself home? I don't think Nigras have that much intelligence," one detective mocked and the others' faces held the same contempt. Ruth was either covering something or the killer had driven her home and fled, which implicated Leroy as a liar and conspirator as well.

Ruth gritted her teeth and felt the pain of her facial injuries.

"Sounds too uppity to me," one detective finished sarcastically.

"Your rude inferences insult my daughter, my other children, my wife, and me," Dr. Yuell stated in a steely tone, staring at the detective with hot, angry eyes. It didn't matter Ruth was a doctor's daughter and a good student who had been invited to attend a college in Chicago to promote racial equality. They ignored her fresh scars of savage brutality. They'd seen it all before.

The detectives talked about it amongst themselves, sometimes as if the Yuell family wasn't in the room, trying to enrage them into implicating themselves. "This kinda of stuff happens in the best of families," they theorized. "This gal does seem uppity—this Chicago stuff and the trouble in the other county a few years ago. She sounds like a troublemaker. Maybe she's a radical or someone with a secret life and wild ways. That boyfriend or lover of hers might be from Chicago and long gone by now." They'd have to check all this stuff out. "There are lots of Negroes in Chicago." Yes, they'd have to check it all out.

Ruth closed her eyes. At least they weren't sniffing in the direction of Alice St. James.

Dr. Yuell, incensed by the questioning, repeatedly defended his daughter. "Just look at her clothes", he said, showing them Ruth's ruined shoes and the tattered material that had been her skirt, which the police kept in paper evidence bags. Evidence didn't mollify their skepticism.

"They don't look too torn up to me," a thin, pasty-skinned detective with a fresh crew cut replied. "That sweater's just stretched and torn in a few places—not very bloody."

"My son's got a concussion and stitches on the *back* of his head," Dr. Yuell continued. "You've kept his bloody clothes, too." *How much blood would be enough?*

On her father's behalf and in her own defense, Ruth showed them the choke-hold marks and swollen bruises on her neck and face; brutal evidence of the horror she endured. That, too, wasn't enough for the authorities. Ruth could see they clearly perceived her as guilty rather than innocent.

"Tell us one more time." Ruth would repeat her previous answer to the same question again. The detectives would write a little and look either skeptical, bored, or both. They brought up what they thought were the inconsistencies and asked questions until they were tired of Ruth and her answers. In these small battles, Ruth won.

"Call for you, Farley," the slightly muted voice called from the other side. "This might take some time," the disembodied voice added. The sergeant grunted and left without a glance as his hideous words hung in the air, leaving both father and daughter bathed in the yellow-white fluorescent light within the walls of the sickly green painted room.

Ruth sat, trying to remember all the terms concerning her injuries from her current nurse's training in Chicago. Perhaps such information would quell the sergeant's suspicion when he returned. Ruth knew her father could help her if she forgot anything and this would distract him from his own simmering rage. Ruth started her dispassionate clinical litany of a severe concussion, lacerations above and below both eyes, on her cheeks and chin, cut and swollen lips, two stitches near her brow, and five by her collarbone, ticking off each injury in her mind. Purple-black searing bruises wreathed her ribs and her hips as well as bruises and deep lacerations on her back, arms, knuckles, elbows, and feet. In other words, she was a black-and-blue beaten nightmare who needed to be home instead of sitting there on an old wooden chair.

Ruth's father moved his long, slender fingers planted over her knuckles. "Look at me, Ruth," he ordered in low tones. "You have to remember to be strong. Let's try to mix the bitter with the sweet. You're completely innocent of any of this and we'll fight to make it all right again. So let's try to lift ourselves with prayers and memories of what's gone on before." Ruth looked down at their lightly clasped hands. So much of the last few days whirled in a cotton wool jumble of nightmares, daylight, and conversations that couldn't seem to stick in her brain. "While we're waiting, let's tell some stories," Ruth's father continued as he smiled for the first time since they entered the police station. "Which ones would you like?"

The promise of stories relaxed Ruth's tight expression. Ruth only hesitated a moment, trying to enunciate against her raw, swollen lips. "Let's start at when I was born and talk about you working to be a doctor. Let's see how far we get."

Dr. Yuell was glad he got to see his daughter trying to relax in this grimy police station smelling of stale cigarettes and burnt coffee. He'd just have to continue with his storytelling till the detectives arrived. He bit his lip and wondered what would happen next. "Just close your eyes." Dr. Yuell had to keep his daughter's mind off of her self-defense killing.

📖

The peaceful mood Dr. Yuell tried so hard to establish was shattered by the explosive intrusion of the police sergeant into the interrogation room. *Did the job make him so ill-mannered or had he always been this crass and bitter?* The medium-height, beer-bellied man almost spat, "Give me the full names and addresses of your high school, college, and the place where you live."

"Do you mean the addresses of my daughter's high school, *university*, and the home where we've resided for almost fifteen years?" Doctor Yuell asked with cold politeness.

"Yeah, that's them." The sergeant slammed the door behind him in rude dismissal before the Yuells could say anything more.

"Don't worry about the time, Dr. Means is talking the house calls," Dr. Yuell said, trying to keep Ruth calm. "Alice St. James has a cold and has been in bed the last few days. Leticia says she's acting quite fretful and might need a sedative."

Now, Ruth's unease turned to true anxiety. "How is Alice?" She tried to blot out the thought of Alice being ill or letting anything slip. Alice had to hold on to her story of being in bed at home the night of the shooting. *Please don't say anything. Please don't say anything*, Ruth prayed. *Get your mind off of it and calm down. Think of something else.*

Ruth shut her eyes against the fresh pain. *Her family's plans for widespread civil rights couldn't be affected, could they?* "You work too hard, father," was all she could think to say.

The Yuells were working on desegregation plans for all the grades in all the schools in the country someday. Any possible problems to her family's work seemed unfathomable. *Was this incident going to affect her community?* Ruth closed her eyes and remembered the Moonglow. How Ruth hated thinking her situation might cause some trouble...and that Alice might be compromised.

Several large, thick, well-worn books were plunked unceremoniously in front of Ruth. "See if you can do anything with these," the detective said in a tired voice.

There were endless mounds of books with even more endless angry faces staring back at her in the shiny black-and-white photographs. Ruth needed to find the face of the other man who had been there that night. The police had a gun, a dead man, and her. All she had besides her story was the seconds-seen face and description of an unknown man. *Please, Lord, show me the face of the other man!*

Ruth had an inkling of recognition of the man in one of the pictures in the green mug shot book but she needed to have more time as she considered her memories and the occurrences in the alley. She'd keep her peace until she was sure in her accusations. Ruth knew what it was like to be falsely accused of something.

"I'll come back later with more. You'll need to get done with these. Then, we'll see what's what." He wasn't any kinder than the rude men who'd already trooped in and out of the room. A solemn, solitary tear ran down her cheek. Ruth's hand dashed it from her face.

Ruth was about to mention the familiar-looking face when she saw her father had something to say and, by the looks of it, it was important.

Dr. Yuell struggled for words when he knew they had privacy again. He was having a difficult time himself and it wasn't because of the rudeness of the police. "I need a moment, Ruth. There's another subject to discuss." Dr. Yuell's lips compressed in a tight line. "Didn't want to say anything so you could get a good night's rest and concentrate on the pictures, Ruth, but I've got something to tell you. It's not easy to say. Just best to get it out before we go home."

"What?" Ruth couldn't think of anything else to say. *What else could happen?*

"The St. James family doesn't want you around their house for a while," her father began as he put his hand up. "Mrs. St. James is not well and they're not going to have afternoon gatherings for a time."

Ruth took a shocked intake of breath and covered her mouth with her hand.

The St. Jameses had sent some pastries over to the family when Ruth and Leroy were recovering, but that had been the extent of their condolences. The exception was Mr. St. James recommending another attorney to help the Yuells if she and Leroy needed legal assistance.

Not hearing from Alice, Ruth could understand, but not a kind word from Mr. or Mrs. St. James or Cherie? It was too painful to think about Devon.

Devon hadn't called. Not one word. Their last conversation had been several weeks before when he promised they'd attend Mary's summer party.

"Devon came back in town but left just as quickly." Dr. Yuell's voice was flat.

Ruth's last thread of hope revolved around Devon waiting until the investigation was over before he came over to visit, wanting to spare his and his family's reputations. *But by his own actions and words they'd been boyfriend and girlfriend for almost two years. The letters, the phone calls—what were they?* Ruth had hoped they'd be able to talk away their estrangement...but now the break was complete.

Dr. Yuell and other emissaries made discrete inquiries regarding the stonewalled silence, and then, the St. Jameses announced they were leaving for a stay in Washington, DC.

Dr. Yuell looked at the drab green paint on the police office wall as if there were words printed on it to make Ruth better, under the situation. "I've talked about it with them but they feel, *wrongly* I might add, that things need to be more settled in this investigation." Dr. Yuell shook his head and looked into Ruth's eyes. "I don't know what else to say except I am dismayed and *extremely disappointed* in them and their actions."

Ruth sat there like she'd been slapped by an invisible hand. This time it wasn't from Jace Prue, but the St. James family who she had loved, trusted, and... now protected. *Wouldn't Devon know such silence would make Ruth appear guilty when she was innocent?*

It was like a knife wound to Ruth's soul.

Dr. Yuell shook his head again. "It would be different with Mrs. St. James, I think, if Letty were well and hadn't had her stroke. Regine is so fragile and scared for her own health...and now with Letty...." He looked down at the table. "Can't pretend it doesn't hurt, Ruthie," her father continued with a pained sigh. "We're concerned for you because the two of you had become close...or was I misreading the situation?"

"No. No," Ruth replied haltingly. "I thought we had 'forever' feelings. Promised to one another." She thought the entire St. James family had regard for her. Without even hearing her side of the story, they'd cut her off from their company. The same rote numbness that took over after she knew Jace Prue was dead, took over now. Ruth's face felt hot, then cold. She wished she were close to her bedroom so she could pull her quilt around herself.

An edgy silence descended on the interrogation room; all that was left was to concentrate on getting the police to believe her story.

The same detectives, a thin chain-smoking man with even thinner brown hair and a perpetual bland look, accompanied by the angry, fat sergeant named Farley and another equally rotund white sergeant with a grease-spotted, garish tie entered the room. The thin detective thumbed through what Ruth guessed was her statement about the night of the shooting and her answers to the questioning so far. "Why don't you continue from the point where you get to Mr. Prue's room?" he asked dispassionately.

Ruth swallowed against a throat that suddenly seemed too small. If she was going to get things behind her, she was going to get *everything* behind her: Jace Prue, the shooting, Devon, the gossip, and the rape. Ruth looked each one of the detectives in the face. "I'm not going to say another word until I can tell you about the rape." Ruth took a deep breath. "You're always talking about *him* but you never say anything about me. What he did to *me*." Big silent tears came down Ruth's cheeks. "This will be my last time here until you do."

The detectives looked at each other. One shrugged. The other nodded.

"I was looking for Sylvie. We'd checked her room and she was gone. I suggested we drive to the diner." Ruth wanted to keep her version of the story straight. Innocent lives depended on it. "At dinnertime that same evening, Sylvie discovered my gold necklace I let her borrow to wear was missing. We looked everywhere in our home and found nothing. I'd told her we'd go to the diner when Leroy got home from work. I'd forgotten he'd said he was going to be working late. I apologized to Sylvie when it got past her bedtime and promised her we'd go to the diner first thing in the morning. She was sad but I thought I'd been able to calm her," Ruth continued, hoping she'd be able to remember the whole string of lies she needed to tell. "Leroy got home, and before going to bed he noticed Sylvie was missing and he woke me up." Ruth tried to appear thoughtful. "When he told me she was gone, we checked the house and the yard. I told him about the necklace and we went over to the diner."

"Go on," the detective said in a monotone voice.

Stick as close to the facts as possible, Ruth. Hide Alice St. James in the shadows. "Mr. Prue's room was in the back of the storage area and garage of the diner. The light was on. I walked up to the door." Ruth looked at her parents and her voice weakened. "Sylvie was there. Her blouse was off."

Farley broke in. "Why wasn't your brother with you?"

"It was late at night. I thought Leroy could just stay in the car with the motor running. If Sylvie was there, I only expected she would be there looking for the necklace. Thought we'd be out and gone...." Ruth looked at the detective, shrugged and her voice thinned. "I didn't think Mr. Prue would take advantage of Sylvie."

"Is that when you killed him?" Farley shouted.

"No. No. It wasn't like that," Ruth cried.

"This is, I promise, the final time I will warn you." Her father's icy fingers and snarling words startled her. "If you continue to accuse my daughter of crimes when she clearly is a victim, our conversations are over and, as my daughter said, you will be speaking only to our attorney."

"OK, Farley. You can leave," the detective sighed. "I'll call you if I need you." The heavyset man unfolded his arms, which rested on his ample paunch. All he did was grunt in reply and leave the room.

"I didn't have time to comprehend..." Ruth stammered a bit and continued as moisture beaded on her lashes. "Sylvie's like a child and he *knew* that."

Ruth gulped again. "I handed Sylvie her blouse and told her to go to the car and tell Leroy we were leaving." Ruth's voice began to rise and thinned like a balloon in a higher atmosphere. "I turned toward the door to follow her and a rough-skinned hand hit my cheek. I saw a gun." Ruth remembered something huge and black with shiny glints of icy gray. "His arm grabbed me in a choke hold around my throat as I was dragged out of his place into the alley. I fought to breathe and my ears started to ring. I tried to scream but no sound would come." Ruth recalled the choking; the harsh, gurgling sound in her throat as no air came to her lungs while Prue's muscled arm dragged her through puddles and bumpy pavement. "He threw me to the ground and I hit my head."

Ruth lifted her hand to her throat, indicating the now-yellowing bruises splotched over her neck and collarbones as well as the red, healing scratches from the gun butt. Ruth closed her eyes, recalling the receding streetlight becoming reddish in her sight as she was dragged backward by her neck into the alley. "Prue drummed the gun barrel against my temple as I struggled to see where Leroy and Sylvie were. If they were hurt. If anyone would help me."

"I saw someone else, a man, near the tool shed and I tried to raise my arm to get his attention. Prue barked at him to go away and he left." Ruth closed her eyes thinking about this lost opportunity; a survivor's grief when a rescue boat or plane went away.

"Prue alternately kept vilely cursing and telling me, 'Shut up, I told you, or I'll shoot ya,' over and over again. He kept ranting, 'I'm tired of you fucking people!'"

Ruth's cheeks now flamed at the profanity.

"I fought with everything I could muster but he was too strong. If any of you policemen have daughters, you must know what this means. He raped me in the alley against everything I tried to do, say, or fight against. May I have a drink of water?" she asked, hoping to buy time and keep her alternative story straight.

Ruth's story for the police would have to go in a different direction...again. Ruth took a few quick nervous sips. "I kept hearing him yelling at me. He kept ranting about killing me and my family if I said anything about the rape." Ruth swallowed and the pressure hurt her chest because she was going to tell them a lie that she'd killed someone...taken the life of Jace Prue.

"So, when he rolled from me, I saw an opportunity and started to get away. I don't know where. It was dark. There was blood running down all over me and I was staggering. He caught up with me as I staggered into a room where there was a light. I saw the gun in his hand pointed at me...I lunged...I fought...and then it went off."

Ruth stopped again to wipe her eyes. *Keep Alice safe. Keep Alice safe.*

"Tell us again about the other man you say you saw," the police asked.

"How could you see in the dark?" one detective sniped, taking another tack since the bruises were more than evident.

"The streetlight filtered through slats in the alley fence," Ruth replied softly and calmly. Ruth tried to recall every tiny detail, scene by grizzly scene, to the smallest point. She tried to shut out the scalding shame in her mind. She gathered a few last threads of strength to keep her promise to protect Devon's family foremost in her mind.

"I saw his picture in the mug shot books. I can identify the other man," Ruth shouted loudly. "Bring the green book over here and I'll show him to you." Ruth quickly found the face she recognized the night of the shooting.

The detective, Farley, and several other men in shirts, ties, and gun-toting holsters looked at the picture. "We'll let you know," was all they said.

∽∞∽

"I just can't understand it," Lady Dee said, her hands striking the dinner potatoes with exaggerated force. "Things have gotten so ugly with the police and the gossiping."

"Thinking the same thing. First off, we should have put Eleanor and Calli in their place long ago and thrown away the key." Dr. Yuell shook his head in sadness. "Our actions and thoughts were concerned about Sylvie, Nettie's leaving, and the deaths in the Wilcox and Means families, we didn't get a chance to keep Eleanor from getting dug in...and it was too late."

"Yes, she also got herself so well entrenched...in the St. James parlor."

Ruth knew it all. Thelma filled her in when they got home from the police station.

"I've got to talk to you," Thelma insisted. "Let's go out and sit in the backyard." Ruth followed her sister without question. "No easy way of putting it. Mrs. Blaine has had plenty to say about our situation," Thelma said without preamble. "But being involved with the death of Jace Prue was just too much! She said it probably started when you got uppity after skipping the seventh grade!" Thelma rolled her eyes. "I told everyone the truth of the matter."

Ruth shook her head. "Calli saying the same thing, too?"

Thelma just looked into her sister's face. "Why do you even bother to ask? That old meddling busybody should be thinking about her niece's mess at the Moonglow instead of us. She better watch out or she's going to tar Dr. Deal's grandson, Orlie, with the same talk. He was there, too!" Thelma frowned again. "Wonder if the neighborhood dentist will get better treatment?

"First Lady Fredericks put a stop to it at the Women's Bible Guild meeting by retelling your whole story and the truth of it. Proud of Meggie, too," Thelma continued. "Meggie's quietly taken your side in every instance, incurring the wrath of her Calli and Mrs. Blaine and their killing looks. Meggie always politely sets the record straight to anyone who asks about her relatives' constant innuendo against us concerning the killing and your part in it." Thelma nodded her head with satisfaction. "After the guests were gone, bet she had a tussle defending herself against her sister and aunt's wrathful tongues."

୧୨

The questions in the white community were political. Wasn't Dr. Yuell the one who was trying to get Negro children into their schools? How could white children be expected to associate with the Negro children if a doctor's daughter was involved in a killing? Did anyone suspect a doctor's kids were so wild? This was the second incident involving the Yuell girl, hadn't the police said? Were the Negroes, and Dr. Yuell, hiding something about his daughter?

There was no stopping the hateful flood coming from the Negro and white communities. The anonymous calls and letters started a few days after the newspaper story. People said they were going to get Ruth and she would pay for her illicit behavior. Others said they knew something was wrong when a Negra went to school up in Chicago, calling it an unnatural thing.

Besides rallying their friends and associates to tell their family's side of the story, there was little to do. "I don't care what anyone says. God knows what happened and that is all that matters. May God have mercy on all the loose tongues out there," Dr. Yuell said. "The truth will win out."

Ruth wished Nettie had come back home. Even though Nettie made gossip an art form, she'd say something funny, at low times like these, to make Ruth smile. Then, Ruth could feel better, even if the situation was bad. "Can't be sitting here being polite and all, Nee-Nee. Gotta talk it up! Lies travel around the world before truth gets its boots on."

୧୨

Feeling she had no inner resources left, Ruth sat there and gave the task to God. Ruth hung onto Him by what she felt, at times, seemed like a fraying, fragile thread. God would have to knit that thread into a rope to pull her through everything or she knew she'd fall, like the scenes in the movies where a person falls off a building and gets smaller and smaller before they disappear. Ruth prayed what seemed like a thousand times a day, "Help me grow stronger."

For now, all Ruth felt she could do, until her battered face looked presentable, was sit quietly, pray, walk around the yard, or lose her troubles for a time in mundane chores. Remember all the family stories and assuage her guilt feelings as a person who had been given more time on this earth to live—even if only for a minute at a time.

Somehow, in a still, small place within her, a prayed-for inner strength slowly emerged as her physical injuries healed. The first step had been confronting the detectives and making them listen to her story; the truth and pain of a woman being raped. *She was the innocent victim.*

❦

"You'll be going back to the university in a few weeks," Lady Dee reminded Ruth.

"If the police let me," was all Ruth could reply.

"The college has called," Lady Dee said as she squeezed her daughter's shoulder. "The dean told us the university will delay judgment until they speak to the administrators and their own legal counsel."

Dr. Yuell nodded his encouragement. "Your lawyer, Mr. Maynard, said we have to make the authorities here and at the university in Chicago act in a respectful manner."

Would they believe her?

❦

"Nee-Nee sad?" Sylvie asked, her face drawn and crestfallen. Ruth was more than sad. Ruth was stuck in all these relationships and polite alliances of love and loyalty. She didn't want to push Sylvie into a silent shock episode like she had when Nettie ran away or put a wedge between Dr. Means and her father because of Calli and Mrs. Blaine's vitriol. Even with Devon's betrayal, Ruth didn't want to harass the St. James family because Alice could break down and the smear campaign could spread to them. Most of all, Ruth didn't want to stop the community's desegregation progress, although it made her mad as fire that Alice had put herself in such a needless, compromising position...and left Ruth to take the burden and figure out what to do with all this!

No one talked of rape in that day, either. It was only a whispered word among women and a reviled word to the world. Her parents and Leroy agreed publicizing the graphic truth of her rape, if she wasn't ready, was not necessary. Ruth held the untreated pain squarely on her own bruised shoulders; this unpardonable invasion left her alone in the silence and the shame.

Ruth patted Sylvie's arm and tried to smile. No, Ruth didn't need Sylvie falling into another of her brooding, rocking spells.

❦

Ruth missed one Sunday service because she "looked a fright," as Mrs. Purdy might describe it. The next Sunday, Ruth was well enough—and her face presentable enough—to go to church. When Ruth looked in the mirror, her first impulse was to stay home, again, because the healing wound on her brow and hints of facial swelling still bore evidence of the attack. Backbone trumped vanity. *You are not guilty of anything, Ruth. So you can't act guilty.*

Ruth tried to keep her head up, and act cordially as she greeted people. "You know we want to keep talking to everyone to set things straight," Dr. Yuell said, patting her hand. By sitting in the front pew, as always, Ruth hoped to show everyone she was innocent. As eyes bored into her back, Ruth returned questioning looks and whispered comments with straight posture and as kind of a smile as her healing mouth could muster. Staying plastered against her mother's side for moral support, Ruth listened to Pastor Fredericks's sermon.

"I've been thinking about how each of us in this church community relies on a power from above and a wisdom greater than our own. God created the world, our world, and everything in it. One of His creations was the wind. Sometimes it is kind, and sometimes it is cold." He stopped for a moment to collect his thoughts. "We do not know why or how, but it seems life sets us against the great power of the wind of misfortune and pain. But God, our heavenly Father, is in the whirlwind to see us through. Cutting a hole through everything and taking us with Him. Many of our birthright and heritage stories have been lost to death and disease like autumn leaves in punishing winter winds. We know about the innocent blood spilled on the ground and in the sea. Moans and cries on the breath of our forefathers come to us on the wind."

Reverend Fredericks looked from his congregation to his hands and back again.

"Slave traders kidnapped our ancestors, and men with sinister motives stole money from others. Kept us from reading and writing but the oral storytelling tradition continued. We learned those stories in hidden whispers, in secret, and in the dead of night after bone-wearying days. Sometimes written on thin hide shards or scratching them with dry sticks in the drier earth, seen in firelight while the slave masters made our ancestors toil the nearby soil every day." The pastor stared at the people in the pews. "And God was in the night wind. He saw them through." The church was so quiet, not even Emma and Samuel Thomas's colicky baby cried out.

"The ancestors of these old cheekbones have walked against the wind." A loud "Amen" escaped from Elder Manly as he, too, recalled the story of the Cherokee Trail of Tears in his mind. "They refused to ride into exile to Oklahoma. They walked, under appalling conditions, all the way from Carolina to Oklahoma."

"Walked all the way," Quentin Best exclaimed.

"Walked all the way," Celeste Engels repeated. "My great-grandmother was one of them!"

"Yes. Yes. They walked and cried all the way to Oklahoma." Reverend Fredericks returned his gaze to the congregation. "There were others out in the wind. Have you children heard of the Buffalo soldier and the cowboy? There were Negro soldiers helping to fight the wars, settle the West, and keep people safe. Remember those heroic black faces up there looking down at you. Now let us pray to the Lord who sees it all and is in the whirlwind with us." A rousing chorus of "Amens" followed Reverend Fredericks's words.

"But we must also talk of the ill winds; those that come from our mouths." Pastor Fredericks walked to the pew where Mrs. Blaine and Calli were sitting. Then he rested his gaze on several other of the notorious gossips in the congregation. "We need to uplift and sustain our community as the Lord commands us." He walked over to stand before the Yuells but he did not look at them. "Troubles come to the community through no fault of our own. I have been disappointed by the gossip and smears on blameless families and people. We must stop this behavior at every turn!" He stomped his foot with indignation. "If you don't have something good to say, shut your mouths, stay home, and stop sipping tea and spreading venom...or I'll have to start naming the names of the offenders!"

Calli's intake of breath could be heard for several rows and she squeaked as Mrs. Blaine poked her in the ribs. Dr. Means stifled a smile and stared straight ahead.

Pastor Fredericks concluded with, "You just pick up the pieces and go on... and *all* the church community will stand by in full accord. Let God hear us...*in full accord!*"

❧

A month after returning from Philadelphia, Meggie had to go help a sick aunt in Virginia. "I solemnly promised Aunt Emily," Meggie sniffled. "I've given my word...and there's no one else." Those were code words to say that Calli didn't want to go.

"You have to go then, honey," Ruth lied, trying to shove unkind thoughts from her mind. Ruth knew she was going to dearly miss her friend, but the money Meggie made was going for her education expenses. It would be unspeakably selfish to deny her friend the trip and those resources. Ruth felt alone. Till Ellie came for them to return to school, there were no friends to talk to and no girlfriend small talk to lighten Ruth's mood.

She didn't want to hear the damnable whispers that she might have brought on herself! If she was supposed to steer this roller coaster from hell, not one more word about it would come from her. Until she decided differently. Ruth kept praying for her period to come. When that prayer was answered, she gave another prayer: one of thanks.

೦⊃೦

The only thing left for Ruth was school. If she wanted to continue her education, she needed to get back to Chicago. On time. No excuses accepted or her scholarship would be lost, the administrators informed them and Mr. Maynard.

In God's care, and with parental wisdom, the Yuells decided to send Ruth back to college in Chicago to escape the lingering brunt of the gossip and the police's caprice in dealing with the Prue case.

So the Yuells used this strident decision to their advantage. "If the police had any evidence of wrongdoing, they wouldn't let our daughter go anywhere. Not only that, but the university officials were welcoming her back as well." Dr. Yuell and Lady Dee simply added, "Ruth and Leroy are innocent and time and the facts would prove our case."

೦⊃೦

Ellie's greeting at the train station was less festive than Ruth had planned at summer's beginning. Lady Dee explained the events of the past days over the phone to Ellic's family.

"Oh, Ellie," Ruth said with a long, strong hug.

"First things. You are going back?" Ellie asked with clouded eyes. "Please?"

"Of course, I'm coming back," Ruth retorted. "What makes you think I wouldn't?"

"Oh. Because," Ellie's nervousness showed as she talked in curt, clipped sentences and dropped her hard-learned sentence structure and phasing. "I was just packing...to come...when your mother called."

Without warning, tears started falling down Ruth's cheeks. All she could do was gulp large mouthfuls of air. She couldn't speak as silent sobs racked her body. Leroy quickly guided Ruth and Ellie through the station and back to the car.

"Keep walking. Keep walking. I'll go get the suitcases," Leroy commanded in a low voice. Ruth headed blindly for the car, at a trot, embarrassed at her outburst as Ellie followed helplessly in her wake.

"When we get to your home, I'll hang up the clothes I'll use till we catch the train. Then we can talk. Me...I'll talk first," Ellie said as she scooted in the backseat. "We'll let Leroy chauffeur us like the white family I babysat for this summer." Ellie kept up the mindless chatter and Ruth composed herself, seeing just a few of her brother's troubled glances into the rearview mirror as they drove home.

After greetings at the door, Ellie excused herself and pulled Ruth in her wake to hang up her clothes as if she were in her own home. Ellie started to put her green dress on a hanger. "I have learned a lot," she began, "and earned some good money. Took care of three children this summer. Read them books and played with them. Cooked some. Watched them day and night for their parents. Child books. Fairy tales. Mother Goose rhymes, too."

The rest of that day and the next morning till they caught their train was spent in companionable silence. *It was so good to feel the presence of a true friend.*

❦

"Please," Ruth said. "Just let Leroy take us to the station this afternoon. It's been a hard summer and we need to leave things with calm and not tears." She didn't want to mention Lady Dee crying most of the day before they left.

Dr. Yuell put Ruth's face in his hands. "You know we love you, so I'm not going to fight your wishes. We're so proud of you, getting through...everything. We'll do as you say."

"You're going to make me ruin another hankie," Lady Dee said, dabbing her eyes and trying to smile. "How did we get such wise children, Edgar?"

There had been some wise words and over-long hugs on the porch of the house, until Leroy beeped the horn and pointed to his watch from his place in the driver's seat.

Ruth felt as gray as the weather but at least she'd regained the ability to talk. The tears wouldn't stop, though. While they talked on the train, Ruth confessed everything to Ellie about Jace Prue's death including the part about Alice St. James, the rape, and Devon's abandonment.

Ellie alternately hugged her friend and offered clean handkerchiefs. "Just resolve to leave your emptiness behind...and don't give up, just like you've always said," was the only advice she could think to give her heartbroken friend.

Ruth was not going to give up on herself. She was a survivor like her Negro ancestors, as Pastor Fredericks preached. Ruth had lived through finding Mr. Wilcox's dead body and her friend Nettie's disappearance. She'd been taught all her life better days were ahead. She'd buried Stella Carter and her baby, so Ruth had to stay alive to tell their stories, staying steadfast in the pride of their race, even when others, like Mrs. Exner's daughter, were not. The Yuells were no quitters and Ruth prayed she wouldn't be the first.

CHAPTER FOURTEEN

Ruth and Ellie got back to campus in the late afternoon. A knot of apprehension hit Ruth's stomach. As she paid the cab driver, she saw Norma Reed. Ruth's dry eyes stung like fire because the tears of mingled joy and sadness wouldn't come. *Was she all cried out?*

"Ruth. I'm here." The tall, lithe young woman gathered Ruth into her embrace tipped off by Ellie that their college friend wasn't doing well.

Ruth gulped, trying to stay calm. She conjured up Ellie reading Mother Goose and other fairy tales to her summer charges, far away from her recent experience. *Best to think of happier times. Best to get over things and get on with life.*

"You want to talk?" Norma asked hesitantly. "More than family?" *Was she going to go on like this and cry at every simple question? What would everyone think? What was she going to do?*

"Go ahead and cry," Norma said.

"All I've done is cry," Ruth replied angrily as she tossed her sweater on the dorm bed. "It doesn't do any good."

Norma walked over, sat down, and grabbed Ruth's hand.

"It wasn't my family, exactly." Ruth faltered as the whole story tumbled out about Jace Prue's death, the false accusations, and her emptiness. "But *somehow*, I've got to get past being raped and the emptiness of my heart being broken by Devon."

As Ruth headed back toward the suitcases, Norma grabbed Ruth's shoulder and swung her around. Her words were awkward, coming out haltingly. "Life can be good. Sometimes, life is very bad. We love you. Always talk to us. We...we won't tell anyone. Believe us." Ruth fell to her knees and Norma embraced her until all her dry sobs ended.

Then Ellie lead Ruth to her bed and covered her. Ruth slept in her clothes.

၈ဝ

Ellie and Norma went out to the hall. "I've already told the girls at the apartment. I'm coming back here," Norma said. Ellie startled in pleased surprise. "I know I'm white and all, but Ruth is my friend and she's in trouble."

Ellie had no answer, just a profound sense of gratitude that Norma had come to help with Ruth. Norma's selfless act indicated things were all equal between true friends. Ruth had help, even from unexpected places. Ellie smiled a relaxed smile for the first time since she'd gotten off the train in St. Louis.

၈ဝ

For Ruth, campus life from that incident on slowly improved at a rate of one hour at a time, then one day at a time. Ruth congratulated herself for getting through things without crying and returning to her previous routine, existing on autopilot and instinct.

Life was not a game with simple instructions typed on box cardboard. Since the rape, Ruth felt as if pieces were missing and other pieces had been added. Rules and relationships changed. Ruth reflexively crumbled the letter pages from St. Louis, telling her to get on with things. The encouraging letter writers and advice givers didn't know and couldn't touch the heart of her sorrow. Beginning again required facing the pain with the time, energy, and patience stretching far over Ruth's mental horizons.

Memories of home and Devon alternately comforted her and plagued her. There were no letters from Devon or anyone else from the St. James family. Ruth cursed herself and tried not to be depressed when she got mail and looked for his handwriting.

Restoring a social life was also difficult. "Come. Please come," Norma would ask as Ruth tried to refuse invitations to go out with other dorm friends. "I won't go without you."

Ellie would put her hands on her hips to agree. "Me neither, Ruth. So you might as well put away your pout and get moving."

Ellie and Norma pestered her from love and concern, Ruth knew, but other people had their own agendas. Miss Osborn needed Ruth to succeed for the sake of her own career and the civil rights program at the university. "The incident is over now. You can't do anything about it and you can only make things difficult for yourself here." Ruth's palms were damp as she omitted the rape, talking about the beating and shooting. "I thought Jace Prue would kill me and my sister, Sylvie, so I reacted in self defense."

"Can't give you any extra time on your assignments, Ruth," Miss Osborn said after everything had been reviewed. She'd been patient enough, her matronly sigh indicated. "You look fine. Get your work done." Mrs. Osborn closed the file with a thwack. "And...keep your nose clean."

So those cold words were the end of mourning as far as the university was concerned; as icy as a water bucket thrown on a drunk. Ruth rushed back to the safety of Ellie and Norma; praying she'd be able to stay in school and not have to return to St Louis to face the ridicule of being sacked because of the scandal.

At least Ruth was still in school.

ⓒ⊕

ST. LOUIS – 1958

At Christmastime, Ruth went home, stayed close to the house, and playacted for everyone, including her family. She kept up her well-groomed appearance, answered questions, and was on time and cooperative with every Yule-time plan. Trying to look "fine," as Miss Osborn suggested; smiling through the phantom ache of her true, hidden sadness. Questioning eyes looked at her with relief, followed by relieved sighs. *That was good.*

Ruth only foundered when she was alone and at night and her memories intruded. She only lied once when she told Lady Dee she had a morning headache when a sleepless night left smudges under her puffy eyes.

ⓒ⊕

There were no contacts with the St. James family other than seeing them in church on Christmas Eve night. Ruth only once dared herself the luxury of craning her neck to see the back of Devon's head. There was no conversation, only stiff smiles with no eye contact, as the St. James family hurried from the church.

Their true, and complete, estrangement now was clear. *Thank God, Devon's letters are safe.* All mementos were banished from the Yuell home but sometimes, when Ellie and Norma were away at classes, Ruth would find the tattered letter box under her bed, pretend it was her freshman year, and that Devon still loved her.

Sometimes, Ruth could almost make herself believe it.

ⓒ⊕

In late May, 1959, when students were preparing to go home, Miss Osborn called Ruth to her office. The St. Louis police had called. "You are excused to leave early," the administrator said. "You've finished your tests and all but one of your assignments. Send it to me and I'll get it to the professor. Here are the train tickets for this afternoon at four p.m."

Ruth needed to return to St. Louis to identify a possible suspect in the Prue case. They wouldn't say much more. The suspect, with the presumption of innocence, deserved the right to the speediest process the law could render, the detectives told her father, and then Miss Osborn. Ruth was going home.

೦೦

Ruth arrived in St. Louis. Perhaps time did heal old wounds. Time was also an attitude for Ruth. It was *time* to: recover ground and meet skeptical people, even hostile people, head on. Ruth needed to rebut what they thought she did or caused on the night of Jace Prue's death. Convicting this suspect could provide a platform. Proving she was a victim, not a criminal.

Ruth and her parents returned to the same police station and the same interrogation room as before.

Reilly Ellis. He was the man who the police had in custody on other charges and who could have stopped Ruth from being raped. The police identified him as a small-time crook and fence of stolen goods. He'd come to Prue's room to get some jewelry. "Jace always was a mean weekend drunk when he got liquored up."

Ellis knocked out Leroy because he thought Leroy might be another fence Prue had called. Ellis grabbed the jewelry because Prue promised him and he wasn't taking any chances. Ellis heard the gun go off and, expecting the worst, he had fled into the night.

Prue was smart enough to know that if he took Alice's jewelry, she'd never turn him in. *All this pain and betrayal for a few pieces of jewelry?* The realization almost made Ruth physically ill.

There was a lineup. Fear, bile, and disgust came to Ruth's throat as she saw him. This Negro man with the mustache, wavy hair, big hands, and darting eyes was Prue's accomplice.

Reilly Ellis allowed her to be raped and his cowardice unleashed whispers, doubt, hate mail, and heinous calls about her and her family, interfering with their reputations and civil rights efforts, leaving Ruth to feel like an exile separated from her family, community, and ripped away from Devon St. James by the scandal. Ellis murderously sullied the life-long bedrock of the integrity of her father and mother with only his pitiful freedom to give in return. *Not nearly enough for the shipwreck of lives he allowed.*

❀

Ruth answered questions, told her story, and defended her actions in any number of encounters. If people looked at her with police eyes, she looked right back and held her ground. Unsettling at first, but Ruth swallowed her apprehension.

The stoic white faces of the police and the detectives asked her to describe the man who was there the night Prue was shot. Her rape wasn't added as charges against the man, because the police wrongfully suspected her complicity in the crime. Ellis made no attempt to stop Prue and didn't seem a bit remorseful, so Ruth wanted the charges amended to include the rape. Immediately. The authorities complied and began the paperwork. After living through many ugly, malice-filled, and gossip-mongered months, the proper charges were finally filed. Ruth became an innocent party for the first time since the shooting.

"Did I really manage all that?" Ruth asked her father after each session.

"You were wonderful," Dr. Yuell said with a hug.

❀

Ruth realized she was cleared now and testifying for the prosecution. Her mind reeled. She turned from murderess and accomplice, to innocent victim and witness.

There were still all the made-up minds and open wounds in the community. So many relationships had been affected or sacrificed. Some would heal. Some wouldn't. Ruth's bones felt picked clean and she'd lived on prayer and Yuell family grit for months. Optimism seemed like a new and alien emotion.

❀

Until the trial, Ruth worked with Meggie at a downtown department store pressing and hanging clothes.

"You OK?" Meggie asked repeatedly.

"Don't want to talk about it anymore. Or anyone." If Meggie was fishing to bring up the St. James family, Ruth cut her off. "Don't say his name because he's dead to me."

Meggie bit her lip. "Oh." Meggie knew Devon treated Ruth unforgivably. Not one word or one letter. But Meggie wanted to tell Ruth that Devon thought he had reasons. Even though it was painful, perhaps, Ruth should listen to what he had told Meggie. Meggie bit her lip and tried again. "But...Ruth...."

"Please, Meggie," Ruth warned raggedly, not looking up from her work. Ruth didn't want to reopen old wounds for anyone but the jury.

Ruth's tone tamped Meggie's resolve. Meggie would have to try again—at some other time.

◕◔

Hot summer-morning sunlight poured through the windows of the courtroom. Its rays sizzled off the walls and paneling, obscuring the judge's proscenium. Ruth could see little. She heard the judge's dignified, muffled baritone voice and the conversational voices of the attorneys; a sea of white faces except for her family, a few friends and the defendant.

Ruth still smarted from the authorities' earlier accusations and betrayal but she swallowed her distrust to obtain justice for herself and Leroy. Ruth's reputation might have been in as many tatters as the skirt she wore the night Prue died because of their mishandling the case, but now the police and state's attorneys forgot their complicity and became her advocates. Subsequent police work corroborated her entire story. Ruth was, suddenly, a friend of the court, like Cinderella fitting the glass slipper.

The police arrested Ellis trying to fence another black girl's jewelry after her date with a petty criminal. Ellis first confessed his part in the Prue incident, and then recanted his confession. He was only there *after* everything had happened to the Yuells, with the exception of knocking Leroy unconscious. Prue was already dead and no one was there, Ellis said.

Reilly Ellis looked very different in the daylight, like he was a good twin of the evil man who abandoned her to Prue. Some kind of special vampire, perhaps, who could withstand the sun's rays. This man sat there quietly. He could have been in a church listening to the service. *Did he only become a thief and coward at night?*

Ellis had a girlfriend. She was sitting in court in a too-short pink satin dress. If Mrs. Purdy would visit the courtroom, she'd call her a floozy. Ruth didn't know. *How could this woman stand to be near him?* The thought made Ruth's mouth dry as she craned her head to look for a path of escape whenever Ellis got up from his chair.

The man even smiled several times, worlds different from the time she saw Ellis in the glinting streetlight as Prue dragged her to the alley. Ruth took a deep breath into suddenly tight, sore-feeling lungs. Ruth wanted to make sure no one was fooled by this man sitting with such dignity in his chair.

The prosecution asked her tiny questions, building the story layer-upon-layer, brick-by-heavy-brick, trying to show the whole, painful landscape. She and the state's attorney traveled on a road of words through the senseless, shattering tale as Ruth tried to remain dry-eyed and polite. She remembered her promise to herself to remain calm, tell the story, and exclude Alice St. James. For the public record, it would now and always be Ruth Scott Yuell who pulled the trigger on the gun that killed Jace Prue. She hoped God would forgive her for wiping the gun clean of any vestige of Alice St. James, putting her own fingerprints on the black metal, and lying on the Bible.

Ruth pushed down panic and scalding shame as she recited everything in excruciating, exact detail, not wanting the jurors to miss one single, horrid fact in the retelling. Unbidden tears washed her cheeks, fell to her suit jacket, or slid under her blouse collar. As the last sounds of it hung in the air, the judge clapped his gravel and said everybody could go home for the evening.

Ruth sat in the scarred, wooden witness box for a few minutes waiting for the specters of the crime to disappear. It took all her courage to tell these strangers about the rape. The state's attorney skirted that issue and concentrated on the slaps, hits, and threats. Talking about those facts made her feel naked, even though she was fully clothed.

Ruth could lay her vow for justice to rest; just like she had laid the chain-link silver bracelet Devon had given her in the back darkness of her jewelry box. The necklace had been lost the night of the rape, never to be recovered. With the bracelet, Ruth carefully washed the blood from the links and polished the scraped, scarred edges, which had also fallen prey to Prue's attack. The bracelet could rest in peace in the box's red velvet lining. Someday when she was ready, it would find its way to a charity sale at church. Now, looking at the silver links in their neat row only made Ruth sad.

❧

"So help me God," Ruth whispered to herself on the second day as she sat down in the witness stand, just like she said when she swore on the Bible the previous day. Ruth vaguely remembered her civics teacher said the defense attorney protected the rights of the accused because the accused was presumed innocent until proven guilty. The defense attorney landed like a vulture trying to peck away at her story. The questions and the attorney's tone turned cold and doubting, the way the police talked and sounded right after the shooting.

The attorney for the accused thief asked Ruth about the rumors concerning her reputation, and then her recollections of the incident. So Ruth, in a voice more like her mother's than her own, proceeded to answer and rebut all the questions concerning the shooting and rape, herself, her brother and sister, her parents, the black community, and the so-called Chicago boyfriend story.

"Doesn't the defendant look very like other black men known to the court and to the black community?" the attorney inquired innocently.

"No, sir," Ruth answered back to him and all the gossipmongers, naysayers, critics, and doubting police. Ruth could hear her father saying, "Tell the truth and look in the eyes of whoever is speaking to you." The defense attorney looked down at his notes and asked silkily, "Please tell us about O'Neill Township." Ruth swallowed and looked at her parents. Dr. Yuell's brow furrowed and Lady Dee sat up straighter in her chair.

Ruth started at the beginning, so everyone knew she had done what was right and proper that day. "My dear friends, Eddie and Stella Carter, were expecting their first child. She was seven months pregnant. They'd asked my parents if my friend, Orlie Hanson, and I would go out on a last outing before Stella would stay at home until her baby was born. One of the tires blew. We were accosted by a deputy sheriff. Instead of listening to Mr. Carter's explanation about the tire trouble, the deputy attempted to arrest Mr. Carter and Mr. Hanson without any case or provocation. You probably saw that information in the official papers concerning the investigation." Ruth looked into the man's cold gray eyes. "Mr. Carter tried to explain the situation...and wanted to take care of his pregnant wife. The deputy initiated an unnecessary scuffle, the deputy's firearm discharged, and Mrs. Carter dove to the ground to avoid the bullet."

Ruth looked at the jury. Her eyes started to weep again but her voice remained strong. "Mrs. Carter hit her head. The deputy left with Mr. Carter and Mr. Hanson, abandoning me and my unconscious, pregnant friend without help in empty fields. A Negro farmer passing in a horse-drawn wagon took Mrs. Carter, who was still unconscious, to a midwife, who was the only medical help within miles. She and her stillborn baby are buried in the Baptist church cemetery on Harris Road. Subsequent investigations proved the truth of Mrs. Carter's and Mr. Carter's innocence and charges were filed against the sheriff's deputy." She wiped at her tears again. "But it was too late for Stella Carter and her dead baby girl." Ruth did not wipe her tears again before saying, "Is that all, sir?"

There were a dozen white men and women jurors to decide the killer's fate. Few black voters, so no black jurors were in the jury box. *Would they see this man in the cheap suit and black shoes trying to look innocent?* He had a girlfriend and an alibi. His girlfriend said they were together the whole evening and night. *Would they believe the thief and his girlfriend or her?*

〇〇

After two days and not much deliberation, Reilly Ellis was found guilty and within weeks, sentenced to forty years in prison for his various fresh offences and parole violations. His counsel filed appeals but they were denied and he was finally sent to state prison.

The man who raped her was dead. She wished Prue were alive so he could pay his debt on this earth. She'd have to settle for Ellis being in jail and Prue's never being allowed to touch her or anyone else in this life again. The rest of the truth could stay buried. Ruth was finished with it all.

✧✧

Ruth filled her remaining leisure hours of the summer working and talking about integrating schools in the Deep South. The trial, and the weight of the verdict, verified what the Yuells had been saying all along.

"Be gracious about your vindication, Ruth," Lady Dee suggested. "It is the Lord's way."

"Hate never got anybody anywhere," Dr. Yuell added. "We preach forgiveness and going forward. So it has to work for the individual...and that includes you."

Ruth bit her lip for a moment. "I'll try." But now Ruth knew from personal experience, just as Nettie said, lies could travel around the world before the truth even got up to get its boots on...and the taint of the lies stuck.

✧✧

During the summer of 1959, college students, including Ruth, were facing broader and broader audiences, talking about their experiences, hopes, and dreams for themselves and others. After two full academic years in Chicago, Ruth recounted only school experiences, good and bad, never referring to anything else.

Doug Wilbur, William Bessie, and Theodore Carvel spoke about their freshman year: How they had been treated, how much practice and training time had been given or denied because of their skin color, and the feelings of the white players on their teams. How they were tested, mauled, and bruised by the intentional dirty tricks and pranks of their white teammates.

Even though they had fine academic credentials, the basis for most of the boys' selection was athletic ability first and academic ability as a secondary consideration. "Take the easy classes, don't let it interfere with your playing time," they were told. A lot of the other white players took the easy courses, too. Their audiences couldn't believe that a student wouldn't go to college to get the best education offered to the student. "Believe it," each of the athletes replied.

Now they, too, felt like Ruth's laboratory experiment experience, skating on a thin veneer of tolerance and controlled in their mingling with the white students. Administrators had warned them away from being "too friendly" with the white female students. Several who had struck up friendships in their classes had been asked to see administrators. The sad implication was clear, Ruth knew first-hand.

"I'm thinking of taking some time off," Randall Bell said.

"Time off?" Ben Gallins asked. "What for?"

"I've gotten wind of some organized efforts for sit-ins at various locations in Southern states starting soon. I want to be a part of that, rather than sitting in classes being a 'show Negro' right now." The bluntness of his statement made a few of his peers gasp.

Lou Williams muscled himself to the front of the small group. "Aren't you scheduled to start baseball in the spring?"

"Yes," Randall replied. "I've talked to my parents and since I want to become the first Negro lawyer from my family rather than the next Jackie Robinson, they're backing me in thinking that breaking things down in Alabama, Mississippi, and all the other Southern states is just as important." Ruth thought she recalled Randall's family as two or three generations from slavery in a Louisiana cotton field. His grandfather or great-grandfather had run away around the time of the Civil War to fight for the Union army. "I've got the paper right here in my pocket with the address and all. They said they can put me up in someone's home down there to canvas all the area for future voting registration efforts."

"What are you going to do about school?" Ruth asked.

"Get back to it when I think I've done some good. My father talked about getting the itch to serve his country during the war. Guess this is my itch to help see things get done to break segregation without a uniform."

Ruth remembered her college history professor mentioned his uncle hearing about the plight of all the countries in Europe years before the United States entered World War II. He'd quit his job, kissed his family goodbye, and joined the Canadian Air Force to go over to Europe and fight. *Was this one of those benchmark times?* She grabbed Randall's sleeve. "Are you going to be able to get back to school?"

"No guarantees," Randall admitted honestly. "But I can't pass up this chance. I'll do anything to help."

◌◌

Ellie came to St. Louis again and she and Ruth got back to Chicago. Everyone came back to campus and recounted their summertime stories. Ruth shared what she could in edited form. As before, Ellie, Norma, and Miss Osborn were the only persons outside of St. Louis who knew varying amounts of the personal details. It seemed like the courtroom again as she answered questions from Miss Osborn, who wrote the information in papers sheathed in a neat manila folder. The woman's face seemed to be caught in a perpetual frown as she asked for some clarification with a few follow-up questions and kept writing.

Ruth wondered why she needed to know. "Is all this necessary?" she asked.

"Yes. All our scholarship students are monitored when incidences occur. Yours is a special program," Miss Osborn replied.

"What...what if the file couldn't be closed?" Ruth attempted.

"But it was," Miss Osborn responded coolly as she stood up.

Ruth rushed to her feet.

"And you won't have any more reason to be monitored again, will you, Miss Yuell?" the older woman said as she looked at Ruth. "Will you?"

Ruth didn't reply at first. "I'm thinking of accepting the opportunity of aiding the voting rights efforts being planned in the South."

Miss Osborn raised her head slowly and peered over her horn-rimmed half glasses. "You are going to...go to help care for a family member in the South?"

"No. No. I'd go to participate in voting rights and organizing protests," Ruth repeated hesitantly.

"Yes, I see. You're saying you're going down to the South to care for a family member," Miss Osborn said slowly, looking meaningfully into Ruth's eyes. "There is a university form we might use in this situation. This form must give the university a reason *they* will understand explaining *why* they should hold your space and scholarship while you are away." Miss Osborn put the form on the desk and repeated, "You were telling me you might be needed to take care of a sick relative in the South, this or next semester?"

Slowly, the trend of the conversation became apparent to Ruth. "I've got to go to take care of my relative down in the South?" Ruth tried not to smile.

"Yes, yes," Miss Osborn encouraged gravely. "So sorry to hear about that." She looked up at Ruth. "I'll also put the arrangement for your academic placement and scholarship in writing and give you a copy for your files, so there will be no one who can dispute that you *are* returning to this institution." A twinkle came to her eye. "If there are any more people in the dormitory with concerns, please tell them that medical problems are another good reason to ask for a leave of absence."

❦

Ruth and Ellie bumped into each other as they came through the door. They said simultaneously, "I've got to talk to you."

"OK," Ruth said. "You can tell me first."

Ellie took a deep breath. Then, she looked down at the floor. "I don't think I can stay here this semester. I want to go home to help with the sit-ins and organizing demonstrations in Birmingham."

Ruth looked at her dumbstruck. "Me, too!"

"What!" Ellie squeaked.

"Ever since we left St. Louis, I've felt things haven't been right. I keep thinking about what my friend, Randall, said about changing things down South," Ruth offered.

"I know. I know," Ellie said. "I didn't want to come back this year either. The churches are planning to move as soon as possible with voting registrations efforts and demonstrations and...marches." She grabbed Ruth's shoulders. "I want to leave right now!"

"I've already talked to Miss Osborn."

Ellie's eyes widened and her grip loosened.

"No. No," Ruth exclaimed, knowing Ellie thought the administrator might give them trouble. "She's with us in an 'underground' way." Ruth swallowed. "She...she's going to put down on the request for a leave of absence on the pretext I have to go down South to care of a sick relative." Her voice was loud with astonishment. "She's even going to give me a letter to *prove* I can get back in school when we're finished."

"What!" Ellie said, now pulling away.

"She said medical excuses were good ones to consider," Ruth laughed.

"Then we'll have to think of something to get me back home," Ellie said, now laughing too.

Ruth sobered after a minute. "What am I going to tell my parents?"

"Just what you told me, I guess." Ellie shrugged. "You're getting a signed statement saying you can come back to school. I think that should ease their minds a bit." Ruth moved to get change for the long-distance call on the hall pay phone. "Others have a lot less."

"You're right. You're right," Ruth replied. "We've been working on these issues for as long as I can remember. It's something I *have* to do."

"Let's pray on it and make the calls," Ellie said. "Then, I'll see Miss Osborn."

❦❦

It hadn't been an easy task to persuade her parents. They all knew these efforts were fraught with danger and uncertainty.

Leroy wanted to join their effort, too. "I'm glad you called because you've pushed me over the edge." He paused. "Even though I'm in my last year of graduate school, I've been thinking about it myself, but with everything that's gone on...."

Love for her brother rushed through Ruth. Leroy had gone through so much, too. Tears sprang to her eyes. Ellie became concerned but Ruth gave her a teary-eyed smile and motioned her away. "It's OK, Leroy. You did it for me."

"Well, it's time we took our activism on the road!" he exclaimed.

"I've got my leave of absence in writing to protect my slot here and my scholarship," Ruth added.

"Better get another copy of that and send it home." Leroy needed to convince his parents to acquiesce.

"Did I tell you we could all stay with Ellie's family?" Ruth asked. "And two aunts who will be happy to house and feed us while we're there."

"That helps a lot. Because I figure paying to get down there will tap just about every cent I've got saved outside of what I need when I get back to my studies." He sighed into the phone. "And not being able to work for pay...."

"It'll be worth it," Ruth replied.

"You know I'm not saying that!"

"I know," Ruth said. "I'm just nervous."

Even with the official papers, she and her brother were putting themselves behind in school and personal finances to go down to face dangerous and uncertain situations. The South was a tied-down place where unspeakable things routinely happened to people of their race, including personal and human rights injustice and unjust laws and codes.

"Good luck and Godspeed to us all," Leroy replied as the hung up the phone.

"You think you're going to leave me out of this thing?" Norma exclaimed. Norma's vehemence seemed as much a surprise as Ruth's parents' acquiescence to Ruth and Leroy leaving for Birmingham.

"You can't be serious!" Ellie exclaimed.

"You bet I am!" Norma's lips got anger-tight. "It's the right thing to fight for *and* the a story of a lifetime I'm not going to miss."

"What are you going to tell your parents?" Ellie questioned. "It's dangerous down there! We're going because we can't stay and do nothing."

"Same for me. Some white people see the injustice of it...and I hope you know by now that includes me!" Norma headed out the door. "Don't know yet, but I'll think of something to tell my folks. Think I'll tell them everything you've told me since we met."

☙❧

It took the entire fall and some of the spring semester, but they were accepted as desegregation volunteers down in Birmingham. The four of them sat at the Yuell kitchen table, getting ready to leave for Alabama by bus the following morning.

"Thelma's coming too, but it's difficult for her to get away from her clinical time," Leroy said. "She can join us for six weeks."

"How's Sylvie?" Ruth asked.

"I told her I was just stopping on a day off from school." Leroy shook his head. "Father's monitoring her in her new job at the hospital laundry. She's doing fine and going to be too busy to miss us."

"Have you read over everything we're supposed to do?" Ellie referred to the rites and customs she'd written down. Norma had organized, edited, and typed the information—like going to a foreign country. "Think it might be helpful."

"Police are trying to harass the volunteers by jailing them for things like jaywalking and loitering." Leroy looked at his sister, remembering the brutal police interrogations in St. Louis and the heartlessness of the O'Neill Township deputy sheriff. "They've got plenty of power trying to keep things status quo."

"Are we going into Dallas County, Alabama?" Ellie asked with a wispy breath.

"We might," Leroy replied, looking at the information. "Got a new sheriff in Selma, I think, or someone running for sheriff named Clark...if I remember his name. He's big and he's mean."

"Thought we were starting in the larger cities like Birmingham before going to the smaller cities like Selma?" Norma knew they were going against entrenched segregationists; they were some of the first outside people down there to start the canvassing.

"They can be rough," Leroy continued. He didn't need to say a thing. Everyone knew the authorities routinely used brutal force when they could get away with it. They had so far.

"So we've got to use the 'Colored' bathrooms," Ellie replied, pointing to herself and Ruth. "Don't give them any chance to send us packing."

"Be polite and take the taunts and abuse of the locals." Ruth remembered her training in St. Louis.

"Protect your head, neck, and eyes with your arms against any clubs or sticks," Norma added. "Use your purse or pocketbook as a shield if any dogs are involved."

"I'm taking several old ones for that reason," Ruth replied.

"Perhaps we're getting ahead of ourselves." Ellie tried to ease the tension in her chest. "We're slated as a canvassing group for voter registration, the exact what and when of the demonstrations haven't been outlined yet. We'll have the use of a truck at times but we need to be back at our temporary residences well before dark."

"I know about cross burnings and things happening in the night from the newspaper clippings I researched as my interest in civil rights grew," Norma said, her voice trailing off. "I've never been told I couldn't do anything when it came to public facilities, except not being able to drink hard liquor till I was twenty-one."

"Guess I'm the only one who's seen the torches and KKK," Ellie said, closing her eyes. "Once, my cousin Zack Beal and I were going down to the fishing hole to dangle our feet in the cool water when we saw them. On horseback and some in pickups with their lights turned off, heading toward the sharecropper farms near our own."

Norma scooted to the edge of her chair. "What did you do?"

"Ran till my throat was on fire," Ellie said. "Grandfather knew exactly who they were after. Family had fled that afternoon to the next county and then north to Cleveland, I think."

"Thank goodness they knew beforehand." Ruth shook her head. "Did the mob do anything?"

"Just burned a cross and strung a hangman's noose, because it was one of their members' property and he didn't want the house burned down. But if there had been somebody home...."

"We can't scare ourselves," Leroy said emphatically. "That's the tactic they've used for too long and we're trying to get people *everywhere* to see how wrong it is."

"I don't want to think of how many generations have suffered," Norma whispered.

"Once people know, we might be strengthened or disappointed," Ellie replied pragmatically.

"Hasn't Dr. King and other leaders said, 'We've come too far to go back'?" Ruth asked. "I know I have." Ruth didn't care if she had to go to jail. She was going to work for something good and make her life count!

"We're with you, Ruthie," Leroy said, trying to calm his sister.

"She's right, though, Leroy," Ellie replied. "She got a raw deal in St. Louis and O'Neill Township because I believe *everything* she said is true. So if she gets a little righteous about it, I'm just going to tell her to 'Preach on, sister!'"

❧❧

"It's hotter than Hades!" Leroy wiped his brow and the back of his neck. The temperature was over eighty degrees and the humidity was even higher. "Is summer always like this?"

"This is a cool day," Ellie mocked. At ten in the morning, the men's white shirts were plastered to their backs and women's arms were tired from fanning themselves with the leaflet packets or wood-handled cardboard fans. Caravanning down for safety's sake, they'd been assigned to canvas four miles from Ellie's home with three other groups; parking their vehicles and wagons in the church lot.

"We're getting more and more people involved." Ruth faced Leroy, shading her eyes from the sun.

"And more and more attention." Leroy looked over his sister's shoulder, seeing a shiny-clean black and white police cruiser with a lollipop red police light slowly headed in their direction. "Everyone over here."

Ellie, Norma, and Ruth knew they needed to stay close together now. The women quickened their steps.

The siren yelped. Four sets of eyes watched a head come through the front driver's seat window. They saw Deputy Sheriff Nance, known to them from a newspaper article, speaking about his hostile view of the "outside people" and "troublemakers" canvassing the residents. "What you people doing away from your porter and maid jobs in the middle of the week?" he said with a smirk. Two other unseen laughs identified three hostile people in the car.

The canvassing group stayed silent. They were not to engage in any verbal confrontations with anyone. "I said, 'What are you *porters and maids* doing away from work?' You're not from here!"

"We visit people in the neighborhood," Leroy said in a strong voice.

"More like making trouble, from what I hear." A faceless, unknown voice came from the car's interior.

The deputy swiveled his head and cocked his mouth, so the volume and meaning of his words would make an impression. "Mighty dangerous on these streets with farm equipment and all." He gave the group a cold stare. "Been warning people. Don't want to see anybody get hurt."

The deputy honed his gaze in on Norma and the camera hanging around her neck. "Wouldn't take you for a nigger-lover." He shook his head in mock sadness. "Noooooo, sir." He talked to the unseen voices. "Such a pretty girl. What's this country coming to?"

The group looked at him impassively. No one moved. A fat bee and several other bugs danced in the bright daylight as the sheriff's head retreated into the car and he slowly moved his beefy forearm to pull away from the curb.

"At least he didn't spit on us," Ellie said, remembering when she and Ruth had to clean spittle from their blouses when four white men in Bogart took offense at their canvassing. Leroy hadn't been able to shield them.

"Farm equipment," Norma said. "That's a new one."

"We've been warned," Leroy replied. "Norma, you're going to have to stay at the church and fold fliers for a few days."

The deputy had singled Norma out, which wasn't a good sign. "The next step might be jail for trespassing or loitering." Leroy quickened his pace. "We've got to report back." The larger group had tallied four black eyes, various cuts, and contusions; one white student had been sent home for medical treatment after getting a swollen wrist and mangled shoulder after talking back to some local white residents. Packets of leaflets were routinely snatched and torn up as white youths scuffled with the canvassers.

Fire and nooses were another signs of intimidation. Several suspicious fires smelling of fresh kerosene in a barn on one farm and a shed at another along with a few nooses thrown on lawns and gardens showed pressure was building. They'd heard of an unexploded bomb found on the porch of Dr. King's house a few weeks before.

"It's going to be worse when the protest marches start," Ellie noted as they started walking again. "But that might take some time yet. Don't want to risk it if the local people need more time to organize."

"Sure was a dust-up in February in North Carolina," Ruth agreed, thinking of the first well-publicized lunch counter sit-in.

"Going to use mostly people from the outside here so the local people don't get hurt?" Norma asked, her journalistic brain considering the options.

"We can talk, but not here," Leroy said. "The less the opposition knows, the better."

❦

"Norma has to go home, doesn't she?" Ruth asked as soon as she and Leroy were alone.

"Can't protect her," Leroy replied softly. "Can't even protect ourselves. We've been warned by a very unfriendly source. One thing they might hate more than uppity Negroes is white people who support their cause."

"Retribution would be harsh," Ellie said. "A maid heard about the incident in the police commissioner's office." Neither had heard her coming in.

"You've got good skills for a cat burglar," Leroy said, trying to lighten the mood.

"Thought as much," Ellie said, ignoring his comment. "It's going to be hard to tell her."

Norma walked in. "No need to say it. I've got to leave." Her face was grim.

"Yes," Leroy agreed in one swift word.

Ruth was more kind. "You know these dear people are going to take the wrath from both sides if anything should happen." She'd purposely left out the word "bad." "We've started to build momentum here. Some wire services and television interviews. Racist people are waiting to just clobber us, either by setting more restrictions on our activities at the best and to see lots of our blood at the worst."

"Don't like it when other white people take up our cause," Ellie added quietly.

"So, if I go do they win?" Tears came to Norma's eyes.

"We'd rather have a live friend to come back and fight next summer or another day." Leroy walked toward Norma to hug her. "You know I could be arrested for doing this if we were on the street."

"So I guess I'm an example of the 'cancerous whim of the majority'?" Norma wiped her eyes.

"Something like that. But we'll *invite* you to come back when support and protection gets stronger." Leroy crossed his arms. "Reverend Northup went to the general store to get you a bus ticket for this afternoon as soon as I told him."

"Out before sundown." Norma thought that's when the Klan did their worst.

"We want you to stay safe…and we know two other things," Ruth replied. "We're in this together and we want all of us to live."

Leroy steepled his hands over his nose and mouth as if to pray. "We're in this together."

◖◗

The number of protests based on their canvassing started slowly and built steadily in the year they spent in Alabama. Norma came back three months after she was forced to leave and the foursome stayed together. They all became seasoned veterans facing full-blast fire hoses, dogs, and had a few one-day jailhouse incarcerations. "Nothing like the forty to sixty days in jail for being a Freedom Rider, but I've caught up with you and your days in the poky, Leroy," Ellie teased.

Ruth shook her head. "I'm glad we've done all we can before we head back to college."

"You still trying to have Dr. King sign your church bulletin, Norma?" Leroy asked.

"I keep trying but someone said he had to leave," Norma shrugged. "He was already an hour late."

"He doesn't want to sign things because he doesn't want to be considered a celebrity," Ellie said with exasperation. "The only swelled heads here should be the ones we show the reporters getting bopped by the police." Ellie pressed her lips together. "A show-and-tell for all the people who need to know why we're here."

◖◗

They'd been working, protesting, and organizing for eighteen months. Ruth, Ellie, and Norma were sitting on the cots they'd used in a bedroom on her aunt's family farm. They'd been in two states and seen more fields, dirt roads, and Southern police then they could remember.

"We're going to have to go back to Chicago or risk losing everything." Ruth read the letter from the university. Chicago seemed universes away from the humid green fields and dirt roads they'd walked.

"I bet if we put all the walking we did in a straight line, it would stretch to the moon!" Ellie said. "We all had to get our shoes resoled. How many times?"

"I'm two classes away from my senior year, and the freelance work has been a once-in-a-lifetime boost for my journalism career," Norma noted.

"It's about that for us," Ruth said glumly. "Ellie and I keep missing our semester-long clinical requirements in nursing."

"They couldn't keep on holding our college places forever, I guess," Ellie replied, emphasizing the contribution of their seemingly staid college administrator. "Miss Osborn's managed to give us as much time as she could and we should be grateful."

"I'm grateful." Ruth tried to retain her sense of humor. "I've got the sleepless nights and tired feet to prove it."

"Just think what we can tell our grandchildren," Norma replied. "So much packed into a year and two summers!"

"Well, you can show them your notepads and the news clippings from your scrapbook," Ellie said. "We've just got memories of bumps and bruises."

"I've got pictures of you...and they were even in the national news service," Norma huffed without heat.

"Yeah, as I told you before, it showed my backside being deluged by that fire hose," Ellie sniffed, remembering the feeling of almost being drowned on dry land. "Also got you an intern job at the *Neighborhood Times*."

"Thank the Lord for that, but I didn't see the fire hose coming," Norma replied. "At least I kept the camera and film dry. You wanted to participate in the action and told me to take pictures." Norma looked at the clear plastic protecting the article and photograph. "Just put that plaid shirtwaist dress into storage and show it with the picture!"

"What people *do want* is our first-hand accounts from down here in Alabama... and Mississippi," Ruth said.

"Now that we 'Marines' have come and plowed the way, lots of people are getting involved," Norma groused.

"That's what we wanted all along...and what we prayed for, remember?" Ellie reminded her friend. "If we'd come down here with nothing to show for it, what would we say then?"

"All right...all right," Norma surrendered. "I didn't mean it that way, except it should have *happened* many, many decades sooner." She frowned. "Most people just sat on their couches and got convinced."

"Isn't that the way with most things, especially when doubt and hazards are involved?" Ruth asked.

"Doesn't make it right," Ellie said, "but it does go along with human nature."

"Taught me a lot of things and gave me back my backbone," Ruth said thankfully.

CHAPTER FIFTEEN

CHICAGO – 1961

Notoriety greeted Ruth, Ellie, and Norma on campus. Students at school and some of the administrators wanted their first-hand knowledge about the civil rights movement. Ruth used every opportunity to promote equality and justice and publicize how people could help.

For strength and comfort, Ruth fell back to rereading some of Devon's letters. Inexplicably, even though Devon bitterly disappointed her, the sentiments in his letters still brought her some comfort and renewal. He talked of honor and duty, which transcended their failed relationship. *Pain to purpose. Wasn't that healing?* Ruth tucked several of them in her purse and as she took to the podiums or stood up in class to talk about whatever the students, professors, and citizens wanted to know.

Along with the widespread publicity of being the first black female students to actively participate in the South, the vulgar phone calls on the dorm phone and hate mail soured some of the congratulations they received. Many were just ugly but others were sinister and threatening. Just like two years ago in St. Louis— more hate mail and hateful calls. *Would she ever be able to escape invectives? St Louis! Now here in Chicago? Why did they think it was so wrong for her to exercise her freedom?* Ruth wasn't going to sit quietly or give in!

Ellie was about to ask why Ruth was so quiet after a break from their speaking engagement at the Baptist church near the university.

"Don't you go getting too cocky, sister," Lucas said as he walked over to their table. Ben and Clara weren't far behind. All were dressed in dark clothes.

Ruth looked to see what he had snatched from his head. It was a beret. As Ruth recalled from her freshman year conversation, Lucas said great and lasting racial or social changes couldn't come through non-violence. She was back to tell him he was wrong.

"Hear you're being a bit too smug when you talk about everything," Lucas said cynically.

Trust Lucas to talk as if his words were a stop or yield sign in the roadway. Lucas's conversation always minimized progress to his harsh view of everything.

"You'll be fighting till your breath is gone and whitey will grab everything back as soon as he can."

Ben and Clara nodded their heads. "All I'm saying is we're going to have to take things back by force. That's all they understand," Lucas sneered. "You and your sister here with your proper dresses and gloves aren't going to get it done." He waved the beret over his head. "I'm black and I'm gonna say so!"

Ruth saw people were listening, looking, and then looking away. She got up to face him. *He'd come in here to provoke this!* "How dare you come in here and speak to me like this. This should have been in private!" Ruth's face blazed with amber flashing darts. "You're very wrong! You don't even know what has or what hasn't been accomplished!" Lucas's eyes were blazing but Ruth didn't care. "I've sacrificed two semesters of school and two summers to work for justice and equality for our race." She looked him up and down. "As far as I can see, you've stayed up here in Chicago, only to get a new set of clothes and a worse attitude." She sat down slowly. "Neither is becoming! Good day, sir."

Ruth pretended not to be affected, holding her head high. She'd been taught to ignore obstacles and go on. *She'd been taught that since she was a child.* No opposition inside or outside of her race was going to deter her now.

Ruth went back to the dorm and threw away the hate letters in the trash by the dorm mailbox and tried not to listen to the obscene calls. She smiled at the receptions and parties and ignored any hateful eyes and stares. This had turned into a war on two fronts: the white segregationists on one side and the people of her own race, who now advocated violence, on the other.

୧୨

EMERGENCY ROOM AT 6:00 P.M.
CHICAGO – 1967

Ruth stopped her narrative. Norma got up to stretch her back. She barely managed to miss the IV pole.

"Everything worked out fine for me...but you guys really were pistols down in Alabama, pardon the pun," Norma interjected. "You got me on that bus and let me worry if you all were OK for days!"

"You still thinking about that and not concentrating on the story?" Ruth gave an innocent tone.

"This is a part of the story where I'm prominently featured," Norma replied in a brisk, sarcastic retort.

"Touché," Ruth replied, a slight smile on her face.

"Just give me a second to flex my knuckles and we can start again." Norma stretched again and sat back down.

"Where were we?" Ruth asked.

"About the time Leroy started working for the NAACP," Norma said, looking at her notes.

CHICAGO – 1962

Ruth and Ellie spent their senior year spring break in Birmingham, Alabama, as the entire Yuell family celebrated Ruth and Ellie's last semester at college, Leroy's new position with the NAACP in Birmingham, and Thelma and Leroy's birthdays.

Ruth knew things were changing when she was able to sit anywhere she wanted on the bus, an unheard of luxury for Negroes just a few years before. However, one surly white bus driver stubbornly put his hand on Ruth's shoulder like a school traffic monitor and said, "You used to have to wait for the white people to get on."

"Excuse me, sir. Please remove your hand," Ruth began. "Let's see, Mr. Taylor?" she said looking at his pocket badge. "Will we have to see if your company's policy has changed by a call to your supervisor or the mayor's office?"

No more back of the bus for Ruth or anyone else. *Thank you, Lord, for Rosa Parks*, she prayed silently. Ruth just sashayed up the steps and sat down.

After putting away their suitcases when they got back to campus, Ruth and Ellie talked about their post-graduate plans.

"Would have loved to go to school in Alabama, just to be one of the first Negroes to be admitted to study there," Ellie noted. "But now I've got to earn a living." Some more black students are fighting in the courts to enroll down at the University of Alabama and other Southern all-white public universities as television, newspaper, and magazine reporters actively followed them around to note their progress. "If I could make better money, I'd be down there trying to help them myself." Though hard-won victories emerged for Ellie's friends and family, the family acreage still suffered. "I can make more money up here and send it down to them. If I work down there, we'll have nothing to pay off the debts."

Ruth and Ellie were going to work in the same hospital after they passed their licensure exams. "I've got a spot in pediatrics." Ruth felt relief that she had a position. Her acceptance letter was safe in her desk drawer.

Ellie handed Ruth an envelope. "They sent me a letter, too. I'll be working on the adult surgical floor," Ruth said, unfurling the paper. "We'll be getting the three-to-eleven shift, if we're lucky, or the night shift from eleven to seven. Right?"

"Only one weekend a month off," Ellie replied. Sick people needed care twenty-four hours a day. The Director of Nurses bluntly told them they were the new hires and not to expect more. "We'll have to work a while before any day shifts open up."

"Norma's got a place at the paper," Ruth reflected. The articles Norma sent back to the local newspapers when they'd been working on the civil rights activities had gotten her several job offers. "Her hours will be as crazy as ours but at least she'll be near her new boyfriend, Elliot."

❦

Ruth, Ellie and Norma graduated with the Class of 1962! Ruth decided to go to graduate school to study for her master's degree. She'd already taken some preliminary classes with the extra time she had from her former goal of trying to graduate in three years—one blessing from a dark time. Ellie was right about the higher salary helping to pay for things. Ruth figured she could pay her living expenses and her graduate degree fees if she was very careful with her money. She'd done harder things and survived. As a bonus, she, Ellie, and Norma found a place to stay together. Ruth relished all three prospects of study, work, and a new residence as she packed her things on the last week of classes.

❦

"Right proud of you three. Wanted to tell you, *again,* before you go," Mr. Dell said as he and his wife delivered their storage trunks from the basement.

"Yes. Said lots of prayers for you at church...and looked for you in all the newsreels and television news casts." Mrs. Dell swatted the air in emphasis. "Brought you some cookies so you won't be hungry on the road."

"You've got a place in our hearts and in our home and at our table...anytime, young ladies." Mr. Dell brought them each into the embrace of his long, bony arms. "Any old time."

Graduation was exciting. Her family, except Leroy, who couldn't leave his new responsibilities, stayed at a hotel that welcomed both white and black people equally. "Don't know if I'll ever get used to this new cultural tag of being black instead of Negro," Dr. Yuell whispered. "But I guess the old terms have too much baggage for the younger people."

"Don't know about that, father. Seems to me it's not just the name, it's the anger the other Negro groups carry," Thelma replied.

"I know what you mean," Ruth replied. "Every time I see my old acquaintances, Lucas, Clara, and Ben, they sound more strident. They're called by African names now." Although Ben never said much, he was now wearing long Caribbean dreadlocks that overwhelmed his head.

"Call me black, too," Sylvie said, wanting to enter the conversation.

"These kinds of rifts are splitting the emphasis off of things which have worked," Dr. Yuell said with a sigh.

"Afros, tribal cloths, and telling about the tribes are nothing new," Lady Dee noted.

"Yes. I want an Afro, too," Sylvie insisted.

"It won't be easy with your fine hair, dear," Lady Dee replied.

"Perhaps we can manage one of the close-to-the-head cuts for you, Sylvie," Ruth said. "They do them now down at the beauty salon."

"But it's exciting and new to the media and the younger people," Thelma said. "Seems like they're a bit like sheep."

"You'd be the one to use an animal example," Ruth noted. "You'll be graduating next!"

"It has been a long haul," Thelma replied. "So many years and I'll finally be able to be the vet I've dreamed of being."

"What are you going to do?" Ruth asked.

"Working with a white veterinarian on the other side of St. Louis who's mentoring me," Thelma replied. "There's lots of new homes there."

"I like our home," Sylvie said with a big smile.

"Let's make a toast to home." Ruth raised her glass.

"Let our second toast be to the graduates!" Dr. Yuell announced.

"Graduates," Sylvie repeated.

◑◐

The Yuells' drive back to St. Louis included a side trip to Memphis to visit some of Dr. Yuell's extended family. Remembering the times of segregation and the restrictions they'd endured, there was less need to plan driving trips so carefully anymore, to use the bushes for restrooms, carry the Mason jars with soap and water, or carry several entire meals to feed their family because the white establishments refused to serve them. They enjoyed long-denied rights now.

Ruth was able to go to some movie houses and sit on the main floor. Still, some whites taunted in drawn out nasal hatefulness, "Here comes the Nigras!" Ruth ignored them. She was their equal in every respect. Ruth knew it down to her bones. The Yuells also ate in a few restaurants where the colored sections had been removed and went to the restrooms—not bothering to look for the colored sign. These discoveries were almost as delectable as eating Lady Dee's homemade sweet potato pie! Generations had prayed this would happen and it was happening in Ruth's lifetime.

"We're home!" Sylvie squealed with excitement as they pulled into the driveway. "I have lots to tell."

◑◐

They'd just started the first load of laundry from the trip when Lady Dee asked Ruth to sit down. "I've got a cup of tea for us." From the look on her mother's face, Ruth knew this wasn't going to be good news. "Do you remember the time when Meggie went to care for her aunt in Virginia?" Ruth nodded her head. *Was something wrong with Meggie?*

"She didn't want to leave you after the shooting and all," Lady Dee recalled.

"She promised her family, right?" Ruth tried to fill in the blanks of the conversation.

"Devon was in Washington, DC, at the time," Lady Dee said haltingly. Ruth's face stiffened in wariness at the mention of his name. "She came over to see us a few days before we left for your graduation."

Ruth couldn't figure out what Lady Dee was saying. Meggie and she corresponded the whole time she'd been in college and seen each other when Ruth returned home for vacations and the few days before and after Ruth's time in Alabama. "What?"

Lady Dee closed her eyes and asked God to help her with what she had to say. She looked into her daughter's eyes. "Meggie and Devon are getting married at Christmas."

The force of the meaning lifted Ruth from her chair. Her leg caught the table as she rose, jolting the cups and saucers.

"Meggie and Devon?" Ruth whispered with horrified eyes, her hand cupping her throat. The strength went out of her legs and she plopped back down on the chair, rattling the china once more. "Meggie?"

Lady Dee nodded her head, knowing this was hurting her daughter profoundly. But she needed to tell her before someone else did and Ruth needed time to gain a public face for this. Lady Dee owed her daughter that much, even as her own heart was breaking at having to tell Ruth.

Ruth didn't know what hurt more. Knowing Devon turned to her best childhood friend or that her childhood friend kept her in the dark about all this. "How?"

Lady Dee shuttered. This fresh betrayal brought back her remembrances of Ruth's monosyllabic utterances after the rape and shooting, when Devon deserted her daughter the first time. She hated this flat-as-a-pancake look on her daughter's face. How many sleepless nights had Lady Dee spent looking at the ceiling while praying about the rape and Ruth's snub by the St. James family? Now Devon, a member of the same St. James family, betrayed Ruth again...and so had her best childhood friend. *How could Devon be so heartless and Meggie be so weak?*

Life and love was so unfair sometimes. Tear-rivers flowed down Ruth's young cheeks. Again. Lady Dee wanted to fold her daughter in her arms like she'd done when Ruth skinned her knee or bumped herself. But Ruth's posture was stiffly unapproachable.

Her daughter might bolt or shatter, like her collection of glass figurines in the dining room cabinet. Lady Dee just sat there helplessly, waiting for Ruth to surface again like a breeching whale Lady Dee had seen in a travelogue somewhere. Her daughter couldn't sit here in her grief forever. Lady Dee was glad she'd planned this more trafficked spot. Ruth's room would have been too den-like a place to break the news.

Lady Dee remembered pacing a groove in the downstairs hall, looking up to Ruth's bedroom door, waiting for her daughter to come down when she'd been getting over the rape and shooting. This was another shock, but Lady Dee prayed it wouldn't wound Ruth in the same chasm-deep way.

The time seemed like hours for both women. "How?" Ruth asked again.

"Before I tell you, I've got to say, this has been a burden on your father and me." Lady Dee bit at the inside of her lip, hoping she could hide some of the bitterness, pain, and distaste she felt. "We are so proud of you and your accomplishments in regards to your diploma and your work in Alabama." Lady Dee grabbed the dainty handle of the gone-cold teacup to settle her dry throat. "We didn't want to shadow your graduation with such news."

Ruth nodded with understanding. Her eyes told her mother she needed to hear the rest.

"Meggie came over here like a scared doe, not knowing what to do, yet knowing what she'd done," Lady Dee reported. "I asked her for every detail, because if I were you, I would want to know every single thing about the business, so I could get it behind me."

Another tear fell. "Said it all started when Devon came to pour his heart out about Jace Prue at Christmastime after the shooting. The darned young fool had almost been choked with jealousy when Prue intimated he and you were involved in some way. Devon stayed away from you because of it."

Ruth's tears flowed faster. "I told Devon. Prue was talking nonsense and I was committed to him completely," she cried. "I never had anything to do with that man!"

"I know. I know, darling, but there's no accounting for men when they get headstrong," Lady Dee replied. "Devon couldn't see the truth from his bullheadedness." Lady Dee waved her hand. "Devon cornered Prue in his room in the back of the diner."

Ruth's eyes flew open and she rose up from her chair like she was going to run. "He never said a word to me!" Lady Dee grabbed her hand.

"Guess he never told anybody." Lady Dee tugged at her daughter, coaxing her to sit down again. "Prue alternately denied and reaffirmed Devon's accusations, whipping Devon up. Probably like a fat cat with a mouse by the tail."

"So Prue baited him and Devon believed it," Ruth said flatly. "That's why things were never the same." Ruth fisted her mouth as she sobbed out, "Things were never the same!"

Lady Dee wondered how many hours Ruth wasted worrying about Devon St. James. Lady Dee wasn't prone to violence of any kind but her hands itched for the broomstick to hit that fool boy's bottom till he couldn't sit down. She wanted to throttle Eleanor Blaine, too. Eleanor's forked tongue continually wagged in Regine St. James's ear about the business; taking advantage of the ill, distraught woman.

"Then, the shooting happened and Devon was working in Washington." Lady Dee didn't want to say she'd heard rumors Devon was told to stay away from St. Louis *because* of his involvement with Ruth.

"Devon came to Meggie to find out what had happened to Jace Prue," Lady Dee said.

"Not to me." The words came out like ice.

"I don't know what to tell you, dear one," Lady Dee said softly. "He was caught."

"Caught?" Ruth said, astounded.

"He found out, from Meggie's lips, how wrong he was the whole time. So much time had passed...."

Bitterness flared on Ruth's face and in her eyes. "So what are you...or...or... Meggie trying to say?"

"I don't know what really happened," Lady Dee said. "But with the wisdom of years, I think when Devon heard what Meggie had to say, he was caught in the guilt of abandoning you twice, which snared him even more. Shame from believing *and* doing the wrong thing is a terrible load. Guess Devon couldn't get over it all and...and he latched onto the messenger." She looked at her daughter. "Men's pride can be a twisted thing."

Ruth got up from the chair and started pacing between the table and the white porcelain kitchen stove. "I was the one who waited and agonized for months and months about him. I was the one who was beaten up and raped. Leroy and I were the ones *suffering the awful things that happened that night*. I poured my heart out to him in letters for two years!" Ruth fumed as she wiped tears away with the back of her hand. "All he could think about was himself?"

Lady Dee just let Ruth pace it off. There was no going back. Love had died and another love had come.

After a few more minutes, Ruth stopped to look out the window. "What *else* did Meggie tell you?"

Lady Dee thought about the second half of the ill-fated couple. "Nothing about either family."

Ruth took a scared intake of breath. Only she herself knew about Alice. "Nothing about *either* family. Even less about me." So the occupants in the first triangle were a jealous young man, who couldn't comfort the girl he *said* he loved, a dead rapist, and Ruth. In the second triangle, Devon ran to her best friend, Meggie, who defended Ruth, they fell in love and left Ruth alone and facing the humiliation as the jilted girlfriend. "And this turned to love?"

Ruth thought about how she and Devon had become close talking about civil rights and making strides for equality. With Meggie and Devon, their love bloomed over refurbishing his estimation of Ruth's character—what an ironic, bitter pill.

Lady Dee felt she needed to finish this mess. "As I said, they're getting married at Christmas."

"You're sure," Ruth said weakly, as she stood to look out the window, pulling her arms tightly around her body. "You're sure?"

Lady Dee nodded firmly both times. There was no doubt. Eleanor had spent so much time talking about it her voice must be sore. "Yes. Meggie told me herself. It's all over the neighborhood."

What else was there to do? If Ruth told the truth when Jace Prue died, Alice and her family would have been swept into the scandal perhaps started by Alice's kind offer to drive Sylvie to work.

And now, what about now? If Ruth chose to spread the true story, Mrs. Blaine would be fighting mad for her dear Meggie and her new fiancé. Ruth would be accused of being spiteful because her former boyfriend was marrying her best friend. Mrs. Blaine would ask why a secret was no longer a secret. Ruth had to admit her reasons would be sinister and she'd be just as bad Eleanor Blaine.

The last strands of an invisible rope broke in Ruth's heart. She felt a physical pain as she slumped into her mother's arms. Ruth's grieving deadweight pulled both women to the floor. But this grief was much, much bigger than the hurt inflicted by Devon. Lady Dee prayed that someday her daughter would be whole again.

Ruth would tell her parents she was leaving for Chicago in the morning.

ᏃᏃ

EMERGENCY ROOM AT 6:15 P.M.
CHICAGO – 1967

Norma offered Ruth some water, pulling the thin paper from the bendable straw and guiding it to her friend's lips. "Are you sure you want to keep going?"

"Nobody else is here yet," Ruth said, with a calmer voice than when she began talking about Devon and Meggie. "I'm satisfied so far and if you can get the rest down while I'm here, I'll be grateful."

"Only if you're feeling strong enough," Norma replied, indicating to her friend her willingness to continue.

The rape, Devon's betrayal, and his marriage to Meggie had each taken Ruth months and months to consider and process. This time she'd thrown herself into work and her graduate studies. "I want to start in again about three years or so later...."

ᏃᏃ

CHICAGO – 1965

Three years after the dust-up about Meggie and Devon, Ruth felt better. This was at a watershed time of looking at her career and her life. "Three years gone?" Ruth said out loud, but there was no one in the apartment. Ruth felt she needed this opportunity to quietly recall the three years she'd spent on her own in Chicago before she plotted her future. Ruth looked first at the pictures of all her friends. Almost everyone seemed scattered with the wind except for Norma and Ellie.

Dear Norma was half of a correspondent team with her now-fiancé, Elliot. Ruth scoured her friend's letters plus articles in magazines, papers, and television news interviews to discover the couple's whereabouts. Ellie was in a serious relationship with a black doctor named Jack Weaver. She, Ellie, and Norma still shared an apartment and expenses, but Ruth didn't know how much longer that would last.

The only one of Ruth's original Chicago college group left in town was Thomas Wills. Ruth dated him on and off these past three years as he aspired to become the first black partner in a prestigious local law firm. Nothing serious developed with him but a nice change from Ruth's nose-to-the-grindstone schedule of graduate school and full-time work.

There were other changes, too. The civil rights movement, once a strong crystal blue wave of change firmly based on Christian principles of non-violence had been out-shouted and splintered into more moments and voices then Ruth could count. Some were armed and militant—fighting off all comers, including the police, the FBI, and the courts. Ruth remembered Lucas, Ben, and Clara with regret. Lucas was dead, Ben was in prison, and Clara fled from outstanding warrants for her arrest. A few others, on the fringe of Ruth's acquaintance, talked of being black and proud, following revolutionaries, joining the African separatist movement, or said crazy things, like wanting to "fight to the death."

Ruth winced when one young man had the audacity to call her an Uncle Tom because she hadn't taken to the streets to fight in dealing with inequality. Even though Ruth told him about the danger she faced in the Southern protests and the change birthed from these strategies, he retorted, "Too slow, too much compromise."

What would history say?

❦

The phone rang. "Ruth, you found a boyfriend yet?" Thomas asked. "I'd miss you if you did."

"No, Thomas," Ruth said with a sarcastic edge. Up to that point, relationships were low on Ruth's list of priorities. *Would she ever have time?* "Not yet."

"Can we start this conversation over again," Thomas offered. "I'm just saying, I miss you when you're so busy." He held tight to the phone. "I'm sorry I'm not always here for...you."

Thomas wanted to be a law partner with the same fervor she expressed toward her master's degree and her civil rights efforts. A little time away from theses activities seemed warranted. Thomas could be charming and he was an intelligent and able conversationalist. Ruth enjoyed his company when she had time in her schedule. Impulsively, Ruth said, "I've got some time now. Would you like to get some coffee?"

☙❧

Ruth lifted the coffee mug to her mouth. "Thomas...I don't know how much time I'm going to have before I have to go down to St. Louis. Lady Dee said my father is overworked and might be ill. I need to see him." Ruth didn't feel like confiding what her siblings and her mother wrote concerning her father's health. "Leroy's coming, too."

"St. Louis?" Thomas asked. "I was hoping I could take you to an important dinner next week."

Ruth's look turned sour. Thomas must have seen it, because his tone became conciliatory.

"You've caught me...and I'm acting badly. I want to enjoy this time with you. I can't help but think we're good together."

"Thomas. I've got my father to consider now," Ruth repeated. "I've got extra weekend work in order to be able to get away." She shifted in her chair. "I'm also thinking of devoting more time to rights initiatives here. They need all the hands we can get." She swirled her coffee in the brown mug cupped in her hands, hoping Thomas's attitude had softened. "Besides helping sick children, I've never felt more alive than when I've helped getting things organized here."

"I understand. I understand. Your efforts take your time and please call me when you get home. I want to see you again...to try to see you more often...I guess." Thomas's words dwindled away.

"It's always good to see you," Ruth replied. "I'll call you when I can. That's all I can promise."

Thomas looked like he wanted to say more but thought better of it and grabbed for his coffee mug instead, taking a quick gulp. They walked to the parking lot in silence and parted at the L station.

As she folded the clothes for the trip, Ruth considered what she was going to do with her spare time. She'd considered joining seminars and activist groups putting pressure on ending the remaining overt practices of denying blacks their rights in the South. The movement's efforts were shifting to consider northern inequality problems as well. There were demonstrations, marches, placard-carrying, mailings, and telephone campaigns where Ruth could work and walk the protest lines.

Dr. Martin Luther King, Jr., had come to Chicago several times. Ruth remembered her first march on Chicago pavement. Her group of marchers was headed by university and hospital faculty. Ruth could see his and the other dignitaries' bobbing heads in their long procession. She'd tell her father and Lady Dee about reawakening her protest skills and seeing Dr. King.

Father had been so right. Long before any of this began, her father had said that Dr. King was "a fine young man." Now she had to think of her father.

Lady Dee's letter weighed heavily on Ruth. Lady Dee's hesitant voice on the phone when Ruth called didn't help. "Even Dr. Means says your father really needs to rest a bit." You, Thelma, and Leroy need to be here to evaluate the situation."

❧

ST. LOUIS – 1962

"I don't argue with him to slow down anymore. It's just a waste of good breath," Lady Dee said with exasperation as she took Ruth up the stairs. "But I do shed more than a few frustrated tears."

"Such talk only makes him angry and he won't change either his schedule or his attitude," Thelma agreed. "Don't think we haven't had many heated discussions!"

Nothing worked. Sylvie only got exasperated, too, and started fretting, "Father tired." A lone tear came down her cheek.

During her stay, Ruth and Dr. Yuell talked of the problems they'd both seen and did their best to help. "The new generations coming here don't have the values and mores which got us through being poor and onto a better life. It's long and hard work helping them to understand what needs to be done to protect their freedom and equality."

Both in Chicago and St. Louis, there had been several booms and busts in the economy. More and more of Ruth and Dr. Yuell's black clients had diminishing interest in their Southern black culture or church-based morality. Fewer experienced the strengths engendered by the family togetherness and moral ethics. Their professional time was frequently spent trying to patch people and families together within the negative forces of broken promises, lives, and homes. Many of Ruth's clients were housed in high-rise apartments, more like a sardine's life than the grassy, fresh-air time of her youth.

Finding work for people plagued both Dr. Yuell and Ruth. "Work for an illiterate and unskilled labor force that pays a living wage is gone," Dr. Yuell said. "Can't support a family."

A growing number of their clients were parented by welfare recipients who had no tools to escape their situation. Other parents were hopelessly addicted to drugs, liquor, and aimlessness caused by the vicious cycle of their poverty. Some families were open to the help and their fellow workers could steer them toward;

others saw health professionals only as instruments of the system they needed to scam as a conduit for their welfare checks. In sizing up health care workers, the latter group knew all the right answers in order to get the highest level of benefits. Both Dr. Yuell and Ruth shook her head in dismay, praying to get everyone out of the cycle of poverty.

The welfare laws didn't help. Women got greater benefits if authorities found no husband or man involved in their lives. This practice encouraged both men and women to remain unmarried and rewarded unwed pregnancies.

Ruth's very first hospital case, after her orientation session, was an eighteen-year-old mother and her three sick children without food or electricity and a disconnected telephone service. The woman looked to Ruth for answers in what was supposed to be a hospital visit for the one hospitalized child. Ruth took detailed notes and handed them over to the social worker with a short prayer.

What a tangled web! Life situations changed. People's strengths and support systems were built and crumbled. They fought poverty and addictions, had weddings, babies, divorces, and deaths in a seemingly endless upstream swim.

Ruth spent as much time as she could with each client family but sometimes she felt like she was only a disinterested visitor in their eyes. It was exhausting, like trying to slow down runaway horses, with families just trying to hang on as Ruth sped alongside their lives, trying to help the children regain their health by giving patient care and dropping off papers and instructions like a Wells Fargo rider.

Dr. Yuell and Ruth knew it didn't take long for people's financial and other resources to dwindle. Initiative died in the eyes of some of her client families who didn't have the skills required to get jobs. "Many lives are still in, or only an eyelash above, poverty," Dr. Yuell declared. "You *know* why I need to work so hard. I won't stop till I drop."

Ruth considered her father's words and his unswerving devotion to his work. "You go on back and try to do the same where you're working."

ᏃᏐ

With several days left in her visit, Ruth spent many hours staring at her room's ceiling, still wondering what to do—for her father and for herself. When she rolled over for what seemed to be the hundredth time, she noticed a dim light coming from underneath the threshold. *Who was up at this hour?* Ruth turned on her right side to take a look at the clock. Three a.m. Ruth twisted to tiptoe-find her slippers while grabbing her chenille robe, wiping gritty fatigue from her eyes as she walked down the stairs.

Ruth found the still body of her father sitting in his easy chair. His head was tipped back against the pineapple-patterned white doily covering the softly-rounded overstuffed chair back. Her father's reading glasses rested on the neatly folded evening newspaper sitting unopened on his lap. Ruth felt for a carotid pulse in his neck. There was none. She quickly turned the strong single-bulb reading light behind the chair to check his eyes. He had been dead for some time. His hands were cold and there was no radial pulse. Ruth wondered if she should pull him from the chair. Ruth checked everything again and said, "Hope you'll save us some places in heaven."

Ruth knocked on Leroy's door and he jumped to get to the living room. He touched his father and looked at Ruth with bleak eyes. "There isn't any chance to get him to hospital? He's been gone too long?"

She nodded her head. Both started crying. "We'd better get Lady Dee and call Thelma and Dr. Means."

"Then we'll wake Sylvie and start making the other calls," Leroy replied numbly.

Ruth put her arms around her brother's neck. "I'm just glad we were home."

They'd been near their father but didn't get to say goodbye. Ruth knew her father would understand.

❦

Her father, in his early sixties, was still a young man by the standard of the age of his peers but he was worn out by his work and his activism.

Nothing was going to be the same, Ruth mused.

Lady Dee walked with elegant posture on Leroy's arm as they followed the casket through the Gothic doors of their church. "He was able to take care of his patients to his last day," was all Lady Dee kept saying as people sought her out again and again. This would be his last trip within these walls, Ruth thought sadly, as the church bells mourned his leaving. Ruth looked around at the churchscape. She solemnly walked behind his casket as Dr. Edgar Williams Yuell made his final exit.

Ruth had no more tears left as she rode from the cemetery to the house for the reception. When she'd talked to Thomas about going to see her father, she'd expected to only be gone a few days. *Why wasn't there more time?*

Ruth checked her purse as she got out of the sedan to make sure she had everything she needed. Her thoughts scattered. She'd been so sad but she'd been organized, making all the necessary funeral and burial arrangements for her father with Leroy and Thelma, urging Lady Dee to rest.

"You must be so tired, Ruth," Lady Dee said. Her mother was a fresh widow, just losing her soul mate, and she was worried about her daughter. Lady Dee must have been expecting this for a long time, Ruth sensed.

"I'm worried about *you*," Ruth said truthfully.

Leroy sidetracked their conversation. "Everything ready?" he asked.

"Let me see," Ruth looked at her mother to assess the public rooms in their family home. "All the church ladies are here to help and the tables and chairs look well-placed."

Her father must have been watching down on them, and, just as in life, he wanted them to reflect on the good times they'd all shared. Ruth was glad the greeting from the neighborhood was sweet, unmarred by any past unpleasantries. People came from everywhere to share their memories of Dr. Yuell. In those tear-shining hours, fond memories, stories, and reminiscences all came rolling out in hour-after-hour conversations at the wake and the funeral. Some they knew and others they didn't, bringing back the husband and father they had lost. All so sad and sweet all at the same time, like when Grandmother Addison would give the Yuell children a half-spoon of honey before and after the cod liver oil medicine when they were younger. "Makes it go down better."

☙❧

Ruth rushed back to Chicago with an aching heart, needing to review her departmental budget and make plans for her unit. She'd already used up all her vacation days and gotten two leave-of-absence extensions.

"Sorry, Miss Yuell. I know it's only your third day back but we're short-staffed with a flu bug going around and you're going to have to take a shift on the floor," Mrs. Reginald informed.

"I'll do it gladly but I'll still have to go back to the pediatric floor because the new playroom opens in several weeks." She looked at her floor assignment.

"Sorry. Perhaps if there's some time after lunch but right now I need everyone for patient care assignments," the personnel director said. "As you can see, you've got Medical—3C."

☙❧

Ruth hustled to the door of the last patient room under her supervision. A new case, Ruth saw, on her clipboard notes.

Ruth checked the name, knocked on the door, and heard a faint reply. The room was dark with only the light from the window illuminating the patient's bed. Ruth rifled through her pocket for a pen and said, "I'm Miss Yuell, your charge nurse. I'm sorry I've been running behind this morning. Please excuse my tardiness, Mrs....Miss?"

"It's Miss, Ruth...and I'd forgive you anything."

Ruth was shaken when this frail patient knew her name. She looked from the lady's face and then back to the nurse's notes. "I'm...I'm sorry," was all she could sputter. *A family member of one of her pediatric patients?* The lady gave a wan smile.

"You won't find it there, or in my face, even. Seems like it's been forever, Nee-Nee." Huge tears started to fall down her gaunt cheeks.

The clipboard fell from Ruth's hands. Ruth half-fell and half-knelt. "Nettie. Nettie, is it really you?"

Ruth pushed the button on the speaker. "I'm going to be delayed in this patient room." Thank God there are other nurses, Ruth thought, because she wasn't going to let Nettie go.

As Ruth touched her arms, there were hard bumps under the skin and when she went to hug her old friend, Nettie's waist was bloated, straining the thin fabric of the hospital gown. There were other changes. Bad ones. Ruth didn't care. She was going to hold her friend, Nettie.

After a few minutes of rocking and sobbing, Nettie pushed Ruth's arms away. "This stomach of mine. I'm not pregnant, just sick." Nettie used the time as her joking settled in the air to swipe tears from her eyes and point to an even darker corner of the room. "There's a chair over there. Bring it over closer. I want to see you, too."

Ruth twisted to her left for the light pull chain. "Let me get the light, so I can see you better...and then I'll get the chair." Ruth's eyes readjusted to the bright bulb's glare. Nettie looked years older than her real age, like she was her own mother rather than herself. Nettie was a junkie.

"Looking bad?" Nettie said baldly as Ruth surveyed her closely.

"You've been sick," Ruth replied simply. Her sad inventory mounted. Ruth could hear Lady Dee's voice in her mind saying, "Mostly scraggly skin and bones."

"Real sick," Nettie stated flatly, "but you can see it as well as me. Can't you?"

"What happened?" Ruth overrode her usual good manners, wanting to know how Nettie had come to this state.

Nettie wanted to talk about when she left. "Everybody who could care for me and Sylvie was gone. Like a tornado, ruining everything. You understand?" Nettie's eyes grew beady and hot. "Grandma...then Grandpa," she began with a painful catch in her voice. "All gone in a summer." Ruth sat there holding her hand. "Hid the pills and just went to the barn and cried and cried. Albert was the only one to go to. He'd play his horn and I'd cry at the sad sweetness of the notes. He was feeling sad, too. Showed me the bruises his daddy had whipped on him."

Ruth readjusted her arm and said, "Go on."

Nettie seemed to think a minute and then continued, "His daddy said Albert's music was all foolishness while he beat him and broke all his records. Every one! Made Albert angry and I came up with the crazy plan to get the school trumpet and run away up north so he could play his music and I could get away. Just get away from all the dying and the pain."

"We looked for you for months," Ruth said softly, more as a comfort rather than a curse. "Didn't a year go by, including now, when the folks who move away don't write at Christmas and ask if we've heard anything about you. Lady Dee will be so happy I've found you."

"Don't tell anyone about me," Nettie said angrily, giving Ruth a glimmer of Nettie's feistiness. "Don't want anyone to know I've landed in this pot. Understand?"

"Let's keep it till later." She smiled reassuringly and ran her hand over Nettie's cold arm. "You need another blanket?"

Ruth came back with several blankets, spreading them over her friend.

"It's a cold place up here. You know I've never been warm here. Not even in the summer much." The sad, sick woman looked at her surroundings. "We got up here in three days hitching and all. Don't remember exactly. Just know I took the savings from beneath the floorboards. Didn't steal that, you know. No use leaving it to rot or for strangers. Right?" she asked Ruth. "Only took the trumpet."

Ruth nodded her head and Nettie continued with a regretful tone. "But I *did* steal the trumpet. It's all I've got left from it all." Ruth startled to think anything of value belonging to Nettie still existed. It must have cost her dearly not to sell it. Junkies sold anything for a fix.

"Don't know whether it was guilt or just wanting to hold on to one last thing. One single thing," Nettie stated. "I'd get the old Baptist preacher down the street to lock it up for me, when I was tempted to sell it. Told him it was a family heirloom," Nettie laughed mirthlessly. "Tried to stop using a million times. I still got some brains, if not much else. Trumpet's in the closet under the blanket," she motioned. "Go get it."

Ruth knelt by the linoleum until her hand bumped into the suitcase-like box. Finding it, she gently pulled the instrument case to her and grasped the brown leather handle worn through to the metal.

"Where do you want it?" Ruth asked.

"Just put it next to me, here," Nettie patted to the side of the bed by the door. "I can pat it and still talk to you." Nettie closed her eyes. "Albert's dead. About five or six years ago now, I think."

"How?" was all Ruth could ask.

"We were really stupid," Nettie began. "Albert was getting some gigs around town. I was working at the kitchen of the corner restaurant. Cook would slip me some food and I'd take leftovers to Albert so we weren't starving. Then, after the restaurant was closed, I'd go to where I thought Albert was playing. Some nights the owner there would pay me extra to wash the floors and the waitresses would give me some of their tips to do their chores so they could get home. All the musicians would still be there. Even if it was mighty late, it didn't matter. They'd just keep playing for themselves. Lived to play, if you know what I mean."

Ruth knew all too well about people's passions.

"One night I got over to the club late after closing. Knew Albert would still be there over a drink or a cigarette. Still playing, trying to work out the music or experiment with some new sounds. The lights were still on, the back door was still open and three or four men were just sprawled there like they were dead. Like to scare me silly. I rushed over to Albert. His head propped against the wall and I started to look for where he was hurt or bleeding. He started giggling and mumbling."

"'Stop shaking me.' Albert laughed as if he'd said the funniest thing in the world. I thought he was drunk. Wish he'd only had been drinking," Nettie sighed. "Didn't know nothing then. Saw the roll-your-own cigarettes, I remember, but nothing else. Rolling reefer and sticking stuff into their store-bought cigarettes." Nettie shrugged. "Albert said everybody was doing it. 'Made the music better,' he said."

"What's the report say?" she asked, suddenly interested in the papers in Ruth's lap. "Say any different than what they told me at the hospital the last time?"

"What do you think it says?" Ruth inquired softly.

"The nice doctor at the other hospital told me some dates. Best I can tell, I won't see Christmas," Nettie stated matter-a-factly. "But I do know one thing. There is a God. Prayed I'd get the trumpet back to the school in St. Louis so I could rest in peace. The Lord brought you back to help me."

An unbidden tear started its solitary road down Ruth's cheek.

"I'm not dead yet, Nee-Nee. Now stop your crying or I'll start again, too. No time for that."

Ruth nodded and scuffed the moisture away with an angry hand and sniffed a bit.

Nettie picked up the thread of her story. "Albert started using needles. Reefer and doctored cigarettes just made me cough and feel sick to my stomach. Should've stopped right there but my cursed curiosity got to me and I loved him so much, you know." Nettie lifted one eyebrow. "Albert shot me up. It was a Friday night, I remember. It was cold and rainy out. I'd been pestering him for weeks to let me see how it was. How it felt. How come all he wanted in the world was his trumpet and the drugs? Really only wanted me when he needed money.

"I watched the flame bubble the powder into liquid and smelled the hot metal. Albert wound my arm tight. I closed my eyes 'cause I was scared and heard his voice say, 'You're going to feel good, Nettie.' Didn't even feel the needle. My arm and then my whole body started to get warm and felt like it was swaying in a warm summer breeze. A dry, puffy mist caressed me. I was floating and still sitting still. I felt fine, I started laughing. I opened my eyes and saw a creamy-white light glowing from my skin reflecting rainbow colors onto the mist around me. It was so beautiful I just stared at it for a while. I raised one arm, then the other, and then my legs, floating effortlessly in warm, breezy fog. I felt like dancing, like the white lady who danced with the ostrich feather fans you and I saw in the newsreel at the movie show." Nettie lifted her skeletal arms as if reliving the moment.

"A clear crystal ball, bigger than the size they have at the beach, floated toward me. I played and danced with it, watching it float and bounce off my arms. I just wanted to keep dancing and dancing, but the ball disappeared and the glow left my skin. I slept after that, I think. After that, all I wanted to do was feel like that again. Never was as good as the first few times. Worse. The high never lasted long, and the rest of the time, I spent scrambling for money to get more and listening to Albert's desperate rages for more drugs for him, too. I only wanted to keep the cramps and shakes away when I went too long between...that was pure hell. Yes sir, things fell apart with us both being junkies."

The medical chart said it all. *Once a waitress and cook's helper.... Five arrests for drugs and prostitution.* The story was all too familiar.

"I had to have more and more," Nettie observed. "Albert left me about a year after that. We cared about the drugs and not each other. Even lost the trumpet with him. But I got it back," Nettie said with a satisfied smile. "He needed money, so I told him I'd give it to him if he gave me the horn. Knew then...he was far gone," she swallowed and her eyes filled with tears. "Heard he died. Don't know where."

"And you? What about you?" Ruth asked. *Nettie has been alone for far too long.*

"What about me? Trouble with the drugs. Trouble with the law. Got sick from the dirty needles, the doctors said. Waiting to die, I guess," Nettie started to look at the wall.

"You're coming home with me," Ruth said firmly, throwing caution to the wind. "You got much to carry?"

"Few clothes, medicine from the hospital, and the trumpet. That's all, I think." After a pause, she inquired, "You sure?"

"Yes," Ruth said. *All these years you could have been safer and healthier and happy. In St. Louis. Anywhere but here.* "Very sure. I don't have a car." Ruth thought for a minute. "Have to make some calls. When I get off this shift, we'll have to take the subway. Your clothes here?"

"Couple worn-out dresses. Not much else," Nettie replied. "Plus my nightgown and the horn. That's all."

"We'll use my comb. Shoes?" Ruth asked.

"Only one pair of brown ones," Nettie replied.

Ruth started the hot water in the sink. "We'll get you a bed bath and a long nap after lunch."

Getting Nettie bathed was like bathing a pregnant rag doll but finally it was done. "Gotta rest, Nee-Nee," Nettie said. "Thought for sure you were married by now." No wedding ring on Ruth's left hand.

"No. No," Ruth stated firmly. "Long story," she said as she covered Nettie. "You rest now. We'll talk later."

My poor Nettie.

◖◗

It took about an hour to get a hold of Ellie and Norma and get things set. Ruth put Nettie's threadbare clothes, the medicine, and Nettie's discharge papers in the trumpet case. "Time to go."

Nettie came awake roughly, not knowing where she was. "Oh. Ruth. Thought I was dreaming but it really was you. You're a nurse, right?"

"Right. Got to get up to get to my apartment," Ruth related. "You've been discharged."

"OK. Hoist me up. You've still got a chance to back out," Nettie replied. "Oh, this hurts so much. Kinda funny. Can have a bit of pain medication now that I'm dying and don't even crave getting high."

Another nursing supervisor, Miss Simons, stopped them at the elevator on the bottom floor. "Shouldn't she be in an ambulance?"

"No ambulance," Nettie said, rallying.

"No. That's not necessary. Our transportation is nearby," Ruth replied hastily. "Thanks for your concern."

The block to the subway seemed more like ten miles as Ruth mostly carried Nettie to the ticket counter. "You sit here." Ruth looked into Nettie's tired, sweaty face as she led Nettie to a bench. "Watch the trumpet." A cab from the hospital would have cost Ruth her food budget for a week, but perhaps she had overestimated Nettie's energy. Ruth was relieved when Nettie's ashen skin with a yellow tinge became more like light chocolate as her breathing became deeper and more even.

"You get the tickets and I'll watch the stuff," Nettie said with a breathy smile. "Go on now."

Nettie dozed on the ride to the closest stop to the apartment. Ruth encouraged Nettie to continue her steps as they walked the block to the apartment house.

"Only stumbled a few times, Ruth," Nettie laughed as they both fell on Ruth's bed.

"Feel like I've run a marathon," Ruth breathed as she got Nettie into one of her own nightgowns, throwing Nettie's dress into the sink for soaking. "Tomorrow, we'll wash your hair and start trying to get some meat on those bones."

"Don't kid yourself, Nee-Nee. You won't be able to do that. No time left, hardly."

Ruth's heart constricted but without tears this time. "Hope we have some time to talk," was all she said. "I've got tomorrow evening off. Bet you'll feel better with your hair washed."

"Sounds good on both counts," Nettie replied as she closed her eyes to sleep. "Sounds good." Her lips started moving again. "Can't talk about Sylvie yet."

My poor Nettie.

ഐ

"She looks really ill," Norma emphasized the word "ill" with an ominous edge to it.

"As I said before," Ruth didn't want to say the words. "She's dying."

The words didn't register. "You say she's a bit older than us? That's scary," Norma replied with child-like candor.

"It scares me, too," Ruth replied.

"Can she eat with us? Do anything?" Ellie asked.

Ruth shook her head. "The doctors say she needs rest and to be kept comfortable. Food and anything she wants to drink, if she wants it. That's all she needs. I'll be sleeping on the couch for a time." Ruth didn't want to think what that meant.

"Just tell us what to do. Do you want us to stay with you? Do some cooking? What?" Ellie questioned.

Ruth also reconsidered Nettie's request to keep her presence a secret, but called Lady Dee and told her she'd found Nettie and the lost trumpet and that her childhood friend was dying. "Please don't say anything to anyone else. Nettie's so sorry to have things end like this."

"You know I'm here if you need help," Lady Dee offered.

"I know, Lady Dee. I know." Ruth promised to write her a long letter to explain. "I just need to know we can take care of the trumpet."

"Tell her we'll take care of it, honey. Don't bother her with the details now," Lady Dee comforted. "You need money for the funeral?"

"No...maybe," Ruth waffled. "I'm planning something simple." Ruth didn't want to burden her mother.

"I understand, Ruthie," Lady Dee replied. "Just be as kind as you always are."

❧

When time allowed and Nettie felt stronger, she and Ruth talked of the past and the present. The time in-between seemed too painful to touch for both of them. "I'm not ready to talk about Sylvie," Nettie said. "I'll tell you when I am."

Ruth respected her friend's wishes but she felt Nettie needed to know Sylvie was doing well.

Soon the fluid in Nettie's lungs became too great. She would pant and wheeze as her once-healthy lungs were drowning.

It was a cloudy Saturday about five a.m. "I want to tell you about Sylvie," Ruth said. "You won't be disappointed."

"Is she OK?" Nettie whispered, looking unsure.

"She's fine," Ruth reassured. "She lives with a loving family. She's been working in sheltered circumstances as a dishwasher in a restaurant, and now she's working in a hospital laundry. She's just as happy and gentle as she always was." Ruth couldn't bear to say Sylvie had lived with them since Nettie and Sylvie's grandparents died, just as Nettie would have if she and Albert hadn't bolted for Chicago. There was no need for any more pain. "She still has her 'Three Pigs' book."

Nettie smiled and coughed. "Good to know she's fine." Nettie squirmed a bit. "Time to go to the hospital," she whispered. "You've done all you can here. Wait till it's closer to regular morning."

"You sure?" Ruth whispered back.

"Know my own mind, Ruth," Nettie countered weakly. "Please."

Ruth nervously straightened Nettie's blankets. Even on this warm, humid morning, Nettie was so cold to the touch.

"Saw Albert last night and talked to Grandma and Grandpa Wilcox," Nettie said, looking at Ruth's face. "It's a good sign, I think." Ruth kneeled at the side of the bed and waited. "He's looking like his old self," her friend puffed. "God's got him another trumpet. So shiny gold it almost shines like diamonds. There's bright sun shining everywhere and warm like a Missouri summer morning. I felt warm. It's time for me to go."

At seven a.m., Norma and Ellie helped Nettie into the back seat of Norma's car in a new fluffy pink chenille bathrobe and slippers. Nettie sat on one side and Ruth sat on the other. Ellie said her goodbye. "I've got to work. Can't get a replacement." She looked at Ruth. "I'll come to the floor when I can."

"We understand." Norma rolled up the window and left Ellie and her worried face at the curbside.

⚭

The crowd at the hospital was blessedly light and Nettie was put on a gurney. There was a nurse and intern looking at her papers. "Need my slippers. My feet are cold," Nettie panted. "Can I have something for my pain, doc? Those pot-holes in the street hurt my belly on the ride over here. They're almost as deep as the road ruts back home."

The nurse looked at the intern. "I'll ask," was all he said as he looked from Ruth to the nurse and fled.

Nettie only spoke one more time in a soft whisper. "I see Albert."

Nettie slipped away about noon. *Time again for tears.*

⚭

Ellie and Norma packed Nettie's meager possessions at the boarding house as Ruth made plans for a small funeral. Reverend Holbrook, who had guarded the trumpet, was willing to do the service on Monday afternoon. Norma and Ellie would be coming. Nettie's social worker would be there, too.

On Monday, they sat in the small square chapel room at the funeral home. Ellie, Norma, and Ruth sat on the first row on the right. Pastor Holbrook and Nettie's social worker sat on the left. The shellac-shiny pine coffin sat between the altar rails. Ruth couldn't afford any flowers for the top of Nettie's casket so she'd brought Mother Addison's handmade quilt to drape it. The county would help pay for the burial plot. Norma and Ellie gave Ruth some money. There wouldn't be any reception after the burial, just a trip back to the apartment for a late lunch.

As Pastor Holbrook got up to give the eulogy, they turned to see someone coming through the door. It was Thomas. He sat down quickly behind the three of them.

"I called you yesterday and Norma filled me in...." He let the words trail off. "I'm sorry."

Ruth smiled weakly and turned around, nodding for Pastor Holbrook to begin his very calm and comforting eulogy. Ruth got up and said a few words about her exuberant childhood friend. Then, they followed the hearse to the cemetery in Norma's car. Pastor Holbrook had graciously taken care of the arrangements for the internment.

Ruth, Norma, Ellie, and Thomas came back to the apartment. No one felt like eating. Ruth baked Nettie's favorite pound cake and put it out on the crystal serving tray, a little like the funeral receptions she remembered from home.

"Thanks for being so understanding," Ruth started. "I know dealing with this was a challenge."

"We only wanted to help," Norma began. "We're glad we did, for your sake."

Ellie got up. "That's right, Ruth. We just wanted to help." She looked at her watch. "But if I don't get back to work...will you drive with me, Norma?" Ellie asked as she started for her purse. "You'll be OK without us?"

Ruth looked at Thomas and automatically said, "We'll be fine." She let them out the door as Thomas helped himself to more cake.

They ate a bit of the cake and drank coffee, mostly in silence. He put the plate down and started to knead his hands nervously. "Do you want me to leave?"

"No. You don't have to leave. I wanted to thank you for coming," Ruth said.

"I...I wanted to apologize. I felt we left each other on an uncertain note the last time we were together," he began. "I've wanted to call many times. The last time we spoke was when you were going to St. Louis. I was having a bad time with several cases. I didn't express myself very well when we parted the last time we saw each other."

"No," was all Ruth said as she escorted Thomas to the door.

CHAPTER SIXTEEN

The nursing director called to schedule a meeting the next afternoon. Ruth reviewed her files and noted how many reports needed catch-up work, heaving a sigh of relief as she saw that there were really only two that were overdue and neither involved any information regarding clients and families who were in the most jeopardy. "Thank you, Lord!" Ruth praised as she looked over the list again.

At one p.m. sharp, Ruth knocked on Mrs. Reginald's office door. "Come in," she invited.

There were three people in the office: Mrs. Reginald; her assistant, Mrs. Diambros; and Mrs. Simons. "Sit down, Miss Yuell," Mrs. Reginald ordered in a cool tone. "We would like to speak to you about a very serious matter. It has to do with Mrs. Fowler." She tapped her pen on a pad. "In my opinion, you've behaved in a most unprofessional manner!"

"Excuse me!" Ruth exclaimed.

"Did you or did you not take Mrs. Fowler from the hospital after her discharge?" Mrs. Diambros shot out. Mrs. Simons, who was sitting right there, had seen her leave with Nettie.

"Yes."

"Did you or did you not install her in your own apartment, pay her expenses while she was there, escort her back to the hospital, and pay for her burial expenses?" Mrs. Reginald asked.

"Yes to all those questions?" Ruth replied.

"Beyond this shocking behavior, are you going to ask the social services department or the county to compensate you for your expenses?" Mrs. Diambros concluded with a sanctimonious smirk.

Ruth never realized how hateful this woman was and couldn't fathom why she was angry. Steadying herself, Ruth took a deep breath. "May I refer to the paperwork?" Mrs. Diambros nodded her agreement and Mrs. Reginald reluctantly released the chart, handing it to Ruth.

"I just wanted to recall the dates for you," Ruth began. "On Wednesday, the ninth, Mrs. Fowler was assigned to me on 3C. I discovered she was a girlhood friend from Missouri. As you can see from the information on the folder, Mrs. Fowler had no known relatives or friends, no food, clothes, or transportation, and a terminal diagnosis of imminent liver failure. I was an available friend. I called her social worker with this information."

"Miss Yuell called the social worker *after* she had installed Mrs. Fowler in her apartment," Mrs. Reginald interrupted and looked at the other women.

"No. No. The social worker was unavailable when I made my first call to her. See my notations. The doctor had written the discharge order and the floor needed the bed." Ruth flipped through her notes. "With her doctor's permission, I helped Mrs. Fowler to my apartment *after* my work day was over and on my own time. Her condition was most serious. She died a little less then eight days later. As you all can see, I worked every day per my job description for the entire shift even though it was the first week back after my father's untimely death." Ruth sat back, her temper seething.

"I see," Mrs. Reginald said, but it didn't appear to Ruth that she did.

"And the expenses?" Mrs. Diambros asked.

"I never asked, nor would I ever ask, for any compensation for Mrs. Fowler's expenses. The burial plot was provided as is the policy of the county," Ruth said. "No more, no less."

"Do you think this behavior is in the best interest of our hospital?" Mrs. Simons asked coldly.

"I don't believe I've broken any policies. I kept Mrs. Reginald informed of my decisions as you can see on my notations here and here," Ruth said as she pointed to the dates and her handwritten notes. "Mrs. Fowler was a dying, penniless girlhood friend. What would you do in my place?" Ruth said as she got up from her chair in queenly displeasure. "Inform me if this incident will appear in my personnel folder. I have to catch up on my reports since my father's death. Please excuse me?" She took a few steps away and said, "I'm sure you'll all be coming to the new play room dedication." She bit her lip and concluded. "Highlighting the care and compassion I *thought* were hallmarks of our work here."

∞

As Ruth made her way home, she seethed about this petty inquisition concerning Nettie, but she wouldn't run away from her job. Could she continue working under such vindictive supervisors who dishonorably twisted Ruth's relationship and her intentions concerning Nettie? Ruth wished she could call Lady Dee or her siblings, but they were still grieving. Talking to Ellie might affect her friend's view of the hospital, which wasn't good, so she decided to talk to Norma first and get her opinion.

Ruth discovered Thomas sitting on the floor in front of the door. When he saw her, Thomas got to his feet, dusted his suit coat and picked up a bouquet of roses and red box of chocolates with nuts embossed from Ruth's favorite candy shop.

"I'd hoped Ellie or Norma would get here first so that I could leave these for you. They said they were going to be with you tonight," he said. "I'm so sorry about your friend and your father. I've been thinking," Thomas uttered haltingly as he raised his arms with the gifts. "These are for you."

Ruth opened the door and offered, "Would you like some coffee? I'll cook. I don't feel much like talking...but your gifts are beautiful."

"I understand. I just wanted to say I was sorry. And...and...there's more," he began nervously. "I've been offered a promotion as well."

"Congratulations!" Ruth said enthusiastically. Ruth hugged him. He bent his head and kissed her with a feather-light touch. Then he looked in her eyes and spoke softly. "I hoped I'd be able to wait. To give you more time. But I'm afraid I have to break my promise. Ruth, will you marry me?"

Ruth was speechless and numb from this new shock, albeit an honored one. She hadn't expected these words at all. Her emotions had rioted in grief for weeks, and now, with the unjust bushwhacking from Mrs. Reginald and the other two women. Ruth shook her head to clear it. "I've got to sit down."

"I know there's been so much happening. I didn't expect an answer tonight." Thomas came over and knelt before her. "All I ask is that you think about it. You will think about it, won't you?"

"Yes. Yes, of course. I'll think about it," Ruth replied, still reeling from his proposal. "But I'm so overwhelmed with...everything." She wasn't being very coherent.

"At least you didn't turn me down." Thomas seemed in a jovial mood. "I'd like to pick you up tomorrow night. Go to the movies. Dinner. You name it. The occasion is celebrating my promotion. OK?" He paused and added, "Why not bring Ellie and Norma and their gentlemen friends along. We can have a little party."

"I'll ask them and let you know." Ruth lost all her conversational skills.

"Well. Goodnight, then." Thomas came over, kissed her hand, and let himself out the door.

Time passed before Ruth realized he hadn't stayed for dinner.

Ellie and Norma kept interrupting Ruth's meal preparations with questions about Thomas and his proposal. For some unknown reason, she'd unintentionally blurted everything out almost before they got through the door.

The dating scene seemed like "slim pickings," as Lady Dee would say after the rape. Former male classmates from graduate school hinted about marriage, saying things like, "Be my wife and keep my house, but you don't need to keep nursing. You can teach Sunday school after our children are older." Then, there were the others who asked, "How much you making now, Ruth? Are you expecting any raises? That sure would be good bringing in two paychecks, wouldn't it?"

"Truth is," Ellie admitted, "I went right after Jack because he's such a wonderful guy. As far as work goes, I've had more times than I want to name where doctors have acted like pigs, alternately trying to grope me or brush up against me as often as they could. It's a mess! Do you get my drift?"

Ruth's lips thinned and she nodded. She'd had her incidents, too.

"Well, others do what Sally's sister chose to do in a different course," Norma retorted. "Her sister, who works in Ellie's unit, says the girl slept with her boss."

Ellie screwed up her face. "She's a single mother. Divorced a bum last September. She needed to keep her job for the rent, car payment, and health insurance. For her child, you know. Think her little girl's got asthma or something."

"Guess you're right," Norma paused, "but it doesn't make it any better."

"But we're not talking about them, we're talking about Thomas. Someone else will take him, if you don't want him," Ellie joked.

Norma had done interviews with women active in colleges and universities as well as those trying to break into management at her newspaper, in industry, television, film, and the arts. "There are other options now," Norma said, getting serious. "Things *are* changing...slowly. Women don't *have* to marry."

"As in civil rights issues, women can fight for their rights, too," Norma espoused. "Women can be happy in their single status and if marriage comes along it better be with the right person at the right time."

Which choice would she make for herself?

∞

Ruth didn't have any answers. She planned to lay everything out for Thomas when they met the next evening.

The phone rang. "Ruth. It's Thomas. I'm so sorry to have to break our date. I've been getting these headaches. They call them migraines, right? Got to lie down. We'll reschedule later. OK?" Click.

Thomas was ill. That threw Ruth for another loop. *Did he need medicine?*
Help? Chicken soup? "I need to go over to Thomas's apartment," Ruth said to
Ellie.

"You have to go to Thomas's apartment?" Ellie teased in a slow tone.

"He called and canceled our date. He said he's ill with a headache and he
sounds really shaky," Ruth replied defensively. "I'm just concerned."

"Sure. Sure. Did he ask for your help?" Ellie wiped the lid of the frying pan.

"Well, no. But he sounded so ill," Ruth advised her. "Listen, even if he hadn't
just proposed, I'd be concerned. I'm going to check on him."

⚭

Ruth took the short cab to his apartment. She had to buzz him from his mailbox button in the drafty hallway of the building several times before Thomas's
irritated voice answered. "Yes," was all he said.

"Thomas, it's me, Ruth."

"Oh. Oh. Come up," he rasped as the answering buzz let her open the locked
apartment entrance.

Ruth skidded on the linoleum in the tiny foyer, hitting the wall with her
forearm and feeling the pain in her twisted ankle. She took the elevator to his floor
wondering all the way if she had made the right choice.

"I'll be there in a minute," he called. Thomas stumbled away from the door
after he turned the lock. "I'm getting some ice bags on my head," bumbling his
way to the couch with mostly closed eyes. "Would you do that for me?"

Ruth crushed some cubes in a towel from the silver metal tray. Thomas
put his hands over his ears. "That sound is so loud," he cried. "Makes my head
pound."

Ruth slowly placed one ice bag on his brow. "That's good," he whispered.
Some of his facial muscles relaxed.

"Now, put the other on the back of your neck," she whispered.

"I've got a doctor's appointment late tomorrow afternoon. Will you come
with me? I need your company and professional advice." Thomas kept his eyes
shut.

"What time?" Ruth answered, without thinking.

"Look at the slip on the table," he replied, trying not to move very much. The
appointment slip said his appointment was for four-thirty in the afternoon, not
far from the hospital.

Ruth thought for a moment, "Can I meet you there? I can't miss any more
work."

"Yes," he said softly. "Yes."

"Yes," Ruth took a misstep and hissed at the pain in her elbow and ankle, trying to keep from disturbing Thomas.

"I'll put the ice cubes for you to use in a bowl in the freezer, refill the ice trays, and call a cab," Ruth said, limping a bit. "You'll be OK?"

"Yes. Thanks. Can't get up now," was all he said, so Ruth left for the street noiselessly after completing those chores, wishing she had some aspirin for her ankle pain.

ᴑᴑ

After a hectic workday, as her spirit and bruises still smarted, Ruth breathed a sigh of relief. Mrs. Reginald wasn't anywhere to be found and the pediatric unit was full. After consulting the address she'd written down before leaving Thomas's apartment the previous night, Ruth reminded herself she needed to rest her leg that evening.

"Has Mr. Wills arrived for his appointment?" Ruth inquired.

"Why, yes, Mrs. Wills. He said you would be here shortly," the short, white-uniform-and-capped woman smiled as she went to the inner office door to open it. "Your husband is in here." The receptionist closed the frosted window partition so quickly that Ruth was unable to correct her error.

"Hi, Ruth. Thanks so much for coming. Sorry I wasn't very good company last night." Thomas led Ruth to the only other chair sitting before the massive mahogany desk. Ruth was glad to see Thomas was moving without pain, not trying to hold all his muscles stiff and still as he had the previous night. She looked from him to the precise arrangement of medical certificates on the wall that read of Morehead College, Emory University, and Northwestern.

A tall, rail-thin doctor entered the room quietly, leafing through the chart as he went behind the desk. He extended his hand to both of them. "Mr. and Mrs. Wills, so nice to meet both of you," he began. "Mr. Wills, from your examination here last week, your symptoms are all common and treatable."

Ruth felt embarrassed. Being paired with Thomas in marriage while she was still trying to decide what to do. *Did Thomas see her discomfort?*

"I'm prescribing some strong medicine for your episodes. Try to take this *only* when you know you're going to be home for an extended period of time. No driving and no more than two doses of these in any twelve-hour period, Mrs. Wills." The doctor turned, handed Ruth a bottle from the desktop, and pinned her with a direct gaze. "Keep the medication in your care. Sometimes the patient is still in pain and groggy from the medication and mistakenly overdoses, forgetting they've already medicated themselves. Can I trust you to do this?"

Before Ruth could say anything, the uniformed nurse opened the door and said in a clear, no-nonsense tone, "Urgent call, line two, doctor." Thomas got up quickly and ushered Ruth out of the office as the doctor raised the receiver and nodded a smiling goodbye.

Within a few steps, they were out of the office and on the street. "Glad the appointment's over," Thomas said.

"The doctor...and nurse thought we were married," Ruth began as she walked with a bit of a limp from the previous night's mishap.

"Sorry about the mistake," Thomas replied with increasing good humor. "I was proud when he called you my wife. It's not so bad, being called Mrs. Wills, at least a few times, is it?"

"No. An honest mistake," Ruth admitted. "But I'm more concerned about the medication." She still had the bottle in her hand. "This requires close monitoring. Would the doctor have prescribed this, if he knew we weren't married?" Ruth frowned as she looked at the name of the drug. "You'll need someone to be there so you don't overdose."

"Guess you're right," Thomas agreed. "I don't know what else to do. These headaches are bad when they come and I can't let these headaches affect my work."

"Isn't there anyone else?" Ruth asked. She saw the hurt and sadness come to his eyes.

"Well...let me think," he said slowly. The heavy silence unnerved her as the sounds of their steps seemed harsh and magnified. "You'd better give me the medicine." He extended his hand for the bottle and put it in his coat pocket. "Would you like some dinner?"

Ruth thought for a moment and nodded her head.

They ate and had a lovely evening. Ruth was feeling good the mood had lightened. "Let's not talk anymore about the doctor, headaches, or pills the rest of the evening," Thomas requested.

At the door, Thomas gave her a chaste kiss and left.

"Well?" was Ellie's greeting.

"Well, what?" Ruth replied, not wanting to play into their speculation. "We went to the doctor and got something to eat."

"Did you accept his proposal or not?" they asked in unison.

Ruth was shocked. "I already told you, both...Thomas and...I need time."

Ellie pressed the subject. "Well, we thought since you went to the doctor with him and all...and you went out to dinner, it seemed you were leaning in his favor."

"I had to eat dinner, didn't I? As for thinking about his proposal...." Ruth's ankle began to throb painfully, even in her nursing shoes. "I've got to get out of these shoes before I hurt this ankle more than before. If you'll excuse me.

Goodnight." Ruth went to her room too tired to parry any more of their questions. She needed time and she was going to take it.

◶◵

The next evening, Ruth was cleaning up the dinner dishes. Ellie sat, paying monthly bills, and Norma and Elliot were at a movie. Ruth was glad for the quiet time. The phone rang and Ruth answered it. "Hello?"

"Ruth. It's Thomas," he said in the slurred voice of someone who's had too much to drink. "About the medicine. How much did the doctor say to take?"

"Thomas. Have you been drinking?" Ruth asked in a worried voice.

"No. Got a headache this afternoon. I think it was this afternoon and I just called...." Thomas's voice trailed off and did not continue.

"You called," Ruth prompted him, "about the medicine?"

"Medicine? I can't remember?" His voice went from slurring to decisive. "My head really hurts. I have medicine."

"Have you taken any?" Ruth voice began rising worriedly. *Why else would he sound unable to follow her simple questions?* "Is anyone else with you? Did you ask anyone to stay with you?"

"My head hurts." Thomas's voice became softer.

Ruth yelled into the receiver. "I'll be right over. Don't take any medication. Don't think about the medication. I'll be right over. Please, Thomas," Ruth said with tears forming in her eyes. "Don't take anything, sweetheart. I'll be right over." Ruth grabbed her purse as she ran past Ellie. "If I don't call you back in thirty minutes, call for help and tell them to go to Thomas's address." Ruth ran down the front steps to feel heavy raindrops pelting her skin as she ran for a taxi. A cab pulled to the curb at her frenzied waving. She jumped in and told the cabbie to hurry to Thomas's address for a medical emergency. The five-minute ride seemed to take an eternity as she sat praying Thomas hadn't overdosed.

Ruth thanked the Lord she had some money to pay the fare. A smaller problem compared to Thomas's possible overdose and the doctor's orders that she, "Mrs. Wills," was responsible to monitor his medication. *What was she going to do?*

The security door was propped open with a cardboard box from another tenant moving in on the first floor as Ruth dodged scattered boxes and debris. The elevator doors opened and she almost bumped into two men coming out. Ruth mumbled embarrassed apologies and watched the red numbers, which moved with snail's-pace slowness. She ran to Thomas's door, which was ajar. Thomas was slumped on the table with white pills strewn over the tabletop from the overturned bottle.

"Thomas? Thomas?" Ruth cried as she shook him.

"Ruth. Ruth? What you doing here?" Thomas asked in the same drunken slur. *At least he was talking and breathing.*

"Did you take any more pills?" Ruth asked.

"Pills?" he replied, befuddled.

"Get up," she commanded. "I'll help you get up. It's time for bed." Ruth threw his arm over her shoulder and rose up slightly to give his fogged brain some idea of what she wanted to do. He tried to help and somehow, they wove their way to his bedroom, like a drunken pair of pinballs as Ruth tried to keep their balance and momentum toward the bed. Thomas landed at a steep angle, mostly on the mattress.

"I've got to call Ellie," was all Ruth could wheeze as she headed for the door. Thomas's ponderous weaving gait and dead-weight fall on the mattress indicated he probably wouldn't move. Ruth wanted to count the pills and access the situation before calling for more help.

"Ellie, it's me. Don't call the rescue squad. I'll get home when I can," Ruth said breathlessly and hung up.

Thomas had only taken two pills.

☙❧

Ruth was so scared when Thomas overdosed, she realized he meant a great deal to her.

Thomas was embarrassed when he woke up early and found her sleeping in a chair in the living room. As he softly grazed her cheek with his fingers, she opened her eyes to his questioning look. His milky brown skin was blue-tinged under his eyes and his lips were a good deal paler than his normal complexion.

"How's your head?" Ruth covered her yawn with her fingers.

"You've been sleeping in the chair?" he asked. "How long?"

Ruth stood up and told him the whole story.

Thomas laced his hands on either side of her head and kissed her. Before she knew it, she was drawn into his arms. His warm body felt good against the knots and kinks in her frame, she thought, as she fuzzily identified he wasn't in his clothes. He was in his bathrobe.

Ruth's proper-daughter mind woke up and she jumped from his embrace. "You don't have any clothes on. You had clothes on last night when I put you in bed."

"I didn't *know* you were here last night. All I knew was I fell asleep in my clothes, got up, and went to the shower," he explained. "Thought I was dreaming."

"We've got to find some way to monitor your medication. I counted the tablets and called the doctor to ask how many he gave you. I'll leave two with you when I go. I'm not spending another night in this chair." Ruth turned to look at herself in the hallway mirror. Ruth's blouse and skirt were badly mussed. The cold rain and chair-sleeping left a chaotic pattern of irregular creases and wrinkles everywhere. She frowned, but Thomas placed his warm hands on her shoulders.

"I think you look beautiful," he said as he hugged her and kissed her ear. She turned to look in his face. His eyes were clear now. Ruth sighed in relief. Thomas took her stare as an invitation to kiss her again.

"I've got to go," Ruth whispered as her warm breath touched his lips. "Let me give you the pills." Thomas released her slowly. He watched her as she set the two tablets on the table and snapped her purse latch on the others, guarded in her handbag.

"I'm sorry this all happened but I'm not sorry you're here," he admitted. "Are you?"

"No." Ruth had done some serious thinking. "No," she replied honestly.

ღ

Ruth accepted Thomas's proposal after a few months of them seeing each other almost every night as they fought his headaches and wrestled with her concerns about their relationship. "I've got to call Lady Dee."

"Yes. I've got to ask her permission. Or do you think I should ask Leroy first?" Thomas asked.

"I think you should ask Lady Dee," Ruth replied, "but Leroy should be notified as soon as possible, too. I know it's what my father would have wanted in his stead." She'd called Lady Dee almost every other day since her father's death. Recently, mother and daughter had talked about her friendship with Thomas deepening into love but when Ruth got on the phone this time, she was nervous. "Mother," Ruth's voice faltered as she started to say hello.

"That you, Ruthie?" Lady Dee said with a light voice and a tinge of concern. Ruth almost never called her "mother."

"I'm fine. I'm fine," Ruth said, still a little breathless. "It's Thomas and me. I'm accepting his proposal."

"I see," Lady Dee replied.

"Thomas wants a time to call and ask you for my hand in marriage," she informed. "Wants to ask Leroy, too."

"That so?" Lady Dee replied, giving her daughter and her betrothed points for asking for permission. "You make good decisions, but think carefully. Think carefully."

"That's all I have been thinking about. I'm wondering if our love will last. All those things," Ruth said hopelessly as she stopped talking and bit her lip. "I think what we have is right. But I want a marriage like you had."

"Everyone does who thinks they are in love," Lady Dee said practically. "I was blessed. I'm just telling you to be very sure."

"I know we've talked all about it," Ruth stated, trying to be optimistic.

"Lord knows marriage would be a right and fine thing, Ruth. Just hope you're thinking of a presentable engagement time." Now it was Lady Dee's turn to sound tentative. "I told Thelma I thought things were changing with you and Thomas. She thinks everything is happening too fast. It's got her all riled up. Says she won't come to the wedding or send a gift, honey, if you don't take time to consider everything about this life-long commitment. There's no use sugar-coating it. She won't approve unless you give it more time."

"Thelma?" Ruth looked at the phone receiver, as if she'd been slapped. "Thomas and I have known each other for years!"

∞

Thomas came over to the apartment after Ruth told him about the conversation with Lady Dee. "Let's call her again and see if we can get this straightened out."

Ruth called Lady Dee again.

Thomas took the phone. "If this isn't the right time, Mrs. Yuell, we can call back."

Ruth heard Lady Dee give a deep sigh and ask about her daughter. "Ruth seems a little shaken, Mrs. Yuell. Should I call back later?"

"No, son. Just had to tell Ruth her sister wants you two to take your time about this commitment. It is Ruth's decision and I give her my blessing. Ruth's father would be happy for her, too, if he were still alive."

"Thanks. Thanks," was all Thomas said. "I'll get back to Ruth. I'll have her call you tomorrow." He hung up the phone.

Ruth sat there, too numb to move.

Thomas got her attention by grabbing her fingertips and lifting her hands. "Let's go over to the couch."

Ruth compiled, getting up like a robot as Thomas sat down and pulled her down next to him. "Let's start planning the wedding...and for our future. Then I'll call Leroy." He smiled and rubbed her arm. "We can keep it small if you like. I love you." He gave her a quick hug and a kiss on her temple. "All weddings are nice."

∞

Ruth's estrangement from St. Louis deepened. Thelma's rejection stirred up all the awful pain from the past. Ruth couldn't go over that fetid ground again. Ruth believed, in time, situations and hearts would change to embrace their relationship—even Thelma's stubborn one.

Ruth wasn't burning a bridge but making a statement with her marriage to Thomas. Ruth didn't have to explain Thomas or their relationship to *anybody*. The comfort of being loved and needed after so long and so painful a time was wonderful. Thomas knew about Madison Township and the story she related to everyone about Jace Prue's death. *She and Thomas accepted each other for what they were and they still loved each other.*

When Ruth announced their engagement, other people expressed their concerns, reminding Ruth of the gossip and betrayal she had experienced in St. Louis after the rape and shooting. When people noted, "Why is he always leaving or cutting evenings short when we disagree with his point of view?" or, "Why does he always make you spend time with his friends and not your friends?" Ruth felt torn between her loyalty to her fiancé and these comments and questions about his reserved nature, his hermit-like dedication to his work, and his headaches.

Ruth went over it and over the pros and cons, carefully examining each part of every argument for and against the marriage. She and Thomas thought they had answers to rebut all arguments. First and foremost, they had a good long-term friendship that turned to love as a foundation for their marriage. They had weathered the challenges and strains of their differences and grown closer. After all, they were older now and had bypassed the blush of romantic love to consider a deeper, more lasting bond. Besides, Thomas's doctor had ordered rest and avoiding crowds and stress to prevent Thomas's debilitating headaches, so Ruth attributed many of Thomas's current quirks to his health issues.

Thomas and she persevered. They made plans. "Listen, Ruth. I'll be spending extra time at work to get some time off for the honeymoon." Thomas looked at his schedule. "Had to take a bit of time off when the headaches began and I've got to make it up."

"As a matter of fact, I was looking at my vacation days and I'm going to have to do the same," Ruth replied. The time taken for her father's funeral had left Ruth without any paid time off. "I've been thinking of taking on some private duty shifts in order to tide us over for the salary I'll be losing when we go on our honeymoon."

"I'd love to say I could freight the whole bill, but I can't right now," Thomas said. "Paying for my mother's care has been a drain." Ruth's expression became sympathetic. Thomas had talked about his mother in the Bronx. He paid all her nursing home expenses.

"I can't wait to meet her. She's so lovely to talk to," Ruth replied. "Remember, you still have to give me her address for her invitation."

"Yes, Yes, I will," Thomas said, sweeping Ruth into his arms. "I don't want to talk. I just need a kiss."

Ruth smiled and put her arms around his neck. They had time for *all* the addresses later.

๛

The excitement and planning of their marriage ceremony and the reception erased the fatigue of the extra private duty shifts. With Thomas so immersed in his work at the law firm, Ruth was only able to talk to him on the phone. So Ruth took over the wedding preparations with what little extra time she had.

They selected their honeymoon dates. "That time's OK for me, Ruth, but I've got to go," Thomas said. Ruth put down the receiver, thinking this was a lonely way to plan a wedding but knowing Thomas's work and her own circumstances prevented them from seeing each other.

Ellie and Norma were kind enough to get up for a crack-of-dawn meeting in the hospital cafeteria to go over the wedding plans. Since Thomas's mother was ill and unable to come to the wedding, Ellie and Norma would "host" the rehearsal dinner while the three of them would also cater the wedding reception. They decided to make filet mignon for the rehearsal dinner and chose canapés and other finger foods for the wedding reception. "You could do this for a living," Norma laughed. "Best cook I know."

"Yes, I could," Ruth agreed, looking up from her shopping list. "Can't tell you how many receptions and parties I worked on in St. Louis." The phone rang and Ruth reached over the myriad of papers.

"It's Gail from the registry," the no-nonsense voice informed. "Your extra shift this evening is cancelled and I don't have anything to replace it. Do you still want to remain on-call?"

"Thanks, Gail, but no," Ruth said. "Put me down for anything tomorrow since it's my day off at the hospital." With all the talk about food, Ruth wanted to see Thomas and prepare a nice home-cooked dinner for the two of them.

"So you're going over to see Thomas instead?" Ellie guessed.

"Think I'll surprise him with a nice home-cooked meal tonight."

๛

On her breaks during a busy day in pediatrics, Ruth planned their special meal. She consulted the grocery ads, stopping by the two stores to select the meat and produce. Ruth remembered the first time she'd looked in his refrigerator there had only been a brown bag with some weeks-old, half-eaten stale sandwich and a few bottles of beer. "I don't even know how to boil water." Thomas gave an unconcerned shrug. Since they'd become engaged, Ruth had supplied Thomas's bare kitchen with tag sale pots and dinnerware as well as spices and condiments for their meals together.

Ruth juggled several parcels—a bit more weight than she'd anticipated carrying. The greens looked so good at the one market, Ruth thought she could make them and pack up the leftovers for Thomas to eat later. She put down the heaviest of the three bags when she got out of the elevator by the door and shifted the weight of the other two in order to get her key, hoping she hadn't squeezed the other bags too tightly as she pushed the door open. She lifted her head to see Thomas's keys and glasses on the table. Ruth's brows lifted because Thomas told her he'd be working till seven. She wondered if he had come down with a headache and been forced to come home. Concern lanced through her as her steps quickened. The bedroom door was half open. "Thomas?"

The couple in the bed didn't hear her. A man's slender back and muscular buttocks were on top of a woman. Ruth saw her loam ear and nappy hair as well as a pale palm and clenched long red nails under the tangle of sheets. "Thomas?" Ruth whispered as the meaning of the scene crashed upon her. She took a step back.

The unknown woman wriggled from beneath Thomas and called with a smirk. "So you've found us?"

Thomas seemed busy pulling the sheet around him and trying to get up, leaving his partner in full nudity.

"Cover yourself, Estelle."

"You've got the sheet," the woman replied, still smiling, as she got up to retrieve her underclothes and grabbed for a pack of cigarettes on the bedside table. She lit one with a smoker's precision and sat down with one leg under her on the bed. Her red bra and panties sat in a pile at her side. Estelle saw Ruth's eyes focus on the underwear. She took a short drag on the cigarette. "He likes red underwear."

"Shut up, Estelle," was all she heard from Thomas's familiar voice.

Ruth turned for the door.

"I can explain," Thomas said, trying to keep the voluminous sheet around his middle.

Ruth grabbed for the grocery bags. The front door was still open in her flight to the bedroom door to see if Thomas had been stricken by a headache. She calmly picked up the things in the reverse order where she had left them and headed for the door.

Thomas called again to her back, not wanting to be seen on the landing without clothes. Another muffled "I can explain!" came as she went to through the apartment entrance doors.

Ruth looked at the street with shocked comprehension. *The bags were getting heavy.* Since she was no longer going to marry Thomas, she could take a cab and put the rest of the money she'd set aside in a wedding account into her savings. She could afford the cab and the meal she was going to cook for herself, Ellie, and Norma.

☙❧

"What are you going to do?" Ellie said, getting up her courage to ask Ruth as they ate the chocolate cake Ruth had baked. She feared her friend was too calm after the debacle of finding her fiancé in bed with another woman.

Ruth took a sip of coffee and considered Ellie's question. "First I'm going to have chocolate cake." She considered her options. "Then, I'm going to praise God I found out Thomas's true colors before I married him." He'd called several times while Ruth was cooking dinner.

Both Ellie and Norma had intercepted the calls and talked to him quite bluntly. "You'd better not show your two-timing, balls-in-a-bed-with-another-woman face around this apartment or I'll skin you alive...and you know this Alabama girl can do it!"

Norma had been more concise. "Don't come ever again or I'll let Ellie at you. Twice!"

Ellie stirred her coffee nervously. "We've given you some time, so what are you going to do?"

"I've got a plan," was all Ruth said, not making eye contact. "I'm working on a plan."

☙❧

Ruth spent most of the night composing a letter to tell people in high mannerly tones to change their schedules because the Yuell-Wills nuptials had been cancelled. She'd fill out the envelopes that evening after a leftovers supper from last night's dinner. Ellie took Thomas's apology bouquet of roses to give to the nursing home next to the hospital and stopped at the bakery to cancel the cake and rolls. Norma cancelled the meat market and grocery orders.

Ruth needed two more things: the phone book and her key to Thomas's apartment. She paged through the directory looking for a moving company. "That's right," Ruth said. "I'm the future Mrs. Wills and I'd like to make a delivery to my husband's office."

Before leaving the apartment she tucked a large black permanent marker, some tape, and a load of brown paper bags in a satchel by her purse.

Ruth took a cab to the apartment. She checked her watch. The movers were expected there in about an hour. She needed to get busy.

◒◓

The message had been written and the parcel swathed in the taped and interlocked brown bag cover. Ruth took out her handkerchief, blotting the sheen of sweat from her brow. "Lady Dee wouldn't be pleased if I got too warm," she said to herself. The buzzer sounded, telling Ruth the movers were there. "Do you have the appropriate box?"

"Yeah, lady," was the reply. "We've got it."

"Good. Good," Ruth said. "I'll let you in."

Packing the box took about five minutes. "We'll get this into the truck and then you can pay us." Ruth heard the bang of the moving truck door slamming down in place.

Ruth paid the two men a $100 tip in crisp twenties and promised a $200 bonus if they got past the receptionist and carried the big box to the exact door number she gave them. "Be sure to take the brown paper off in the hall as I've instructed."

The thickly built man in the blue mover's jumpsuit said, "I'll stay there all day for that kind of money."

Back at her apartment, Ruth had torn a second and third $100 bill each in half. "Half now and the other half at the *delivery address* on this card when you're through." She made sure she had the same sides of the two bills. They'd have to follow her instructions before they could piece these with the other halves. "Someone will be there with the rest of your bonus."

The shorter man of the team took his pre-offered half. He shrugged. "Sounds funny, but it ain't illegal."

"Of course not," Ruth replied. "I just have to make another phone call, if you'll excuse me." She heard the truck ignition rev and leave.

"Are you at the building, Elliot?" Ruth asked. "Do you have the envelope?"

"I'm just about to go to the tenth floor," he said. "Think I can stall for about ten minutes and tell them the reporter is running a bit late."

"Good," Ruth replied. "Just make sure the men take the box to number 242."

"Number 242," Elliot replied.

"I owe you a dinner," Ruth replied.

"If this is going to go like I think it will," Elliot said drolly, "I think the entertainment value should suffice."

"One can only hope," Ruth said as she hung up the phone. She looked at her watch. She looked around the apartment to make sure it was as if she had never been there. Everything was the same except for the item on the moving truck. Ruth locked the door, wiped the key with her handkerchief, and gave it a good shove under the door. She wouldn't need it anymore.

∾

The moving men were right on time, Elliot thought. He'd be able to get back from his early lunch break without anyone at the newspaper knowing he was gone. Norma would reschedule it with the law firm when Elliot called and said the delivery was over.

The movers came to the desk and were polite but very insistent about the long rectangular box and needing to put it by the "242" hall.

"Are you sure?" the receptionist asked.

"Listen, ma'am," the burly one said. "You don't want us leaving and have to pay us again to come back if no one is properly dressed for this work or strong enough to get this thing out of your way. Fire hazard."

"Seen it too many times before. That's why we're telling you," the other mover said. "You want to get things as close to the right door as possible."

The receptionist looked skeptical and called a number to make sure what the men said was true. The answer must have been in the affirmative because she motioned for the movers to go in. At the time she looked down for the phone call, Elliot got up and shadowed the men while standing in front of the large rectangular box. "Make a left after the first set of cubicles and it's the third door on the right. I've got the other envelope."

"Got it," the burly man said while simultaneously reaching for the box. "Ready, Ed?"

One whipped out his penknife and took off the box and the brown paper as Elliot got his camera to immortalize the message scrolled neatly in large block letters on Thomas's blue quilted mattress: **The Yuell and Wills engagement and wedding have been cancelled.**

A crowd started forming after the first of the secretaries let out a loud croaking laugh as she read the message. Elliot was only able to get one picture in the confined space as Thomas was called by his colleagues to look at the message. The movers made another $100 when a startled and infuriated Mr. Wills asked them to take the offending bedding to the dump! They took their time re-taping the box they'd sliced in several pieces, making sure they worked slowly so everyone could get a good look at the mattress as the client with the other two $100 bill halves had requested.

Elliot slipped them the envelope with the other halves of the bills inside.

This story was going to last them for years, they thought.

Ꙭ

Thomas yelled for a long time at the front door. Ruth was glad Norma and Ellie were there. He threatened many things and Ruth let him get his anger out. Enough was enough, though, when the curse words were well outpacing the King's English. "Mr. Mathers in 307 is my attorney now, Thomas. Would you like me to talk to him?" Ruth had retained another lawyer in Thomas's firm and sent the retainer by messenger before the delivery of the mattress.

Thomas sputtered a bit, still pounding on the apartment buzzer deck.

"If I think you're acting improperly, I'll tell him everything."

Thomas shouted a few more epithets and left.

The phone rang. "I'll get it," Ellie offered. She listened, quirked her brow, and said, "It's the other woman."

Ruth's lips thinned. She took a deep breath and took the receiver.

"The mattress was a nice touch," Estelle began. "You've got more spunk than I gave you credit for."

"You can have him now," Ruth replied.

"Have to tell you a few things before I can take him with clean hands," Estelle said.

"Such as," Ruth retorted, trying to sound bored. "Clean" wasn't the adjective Ruth would use to describe Thomas Wills now.

"There was no mother. She died years ago in Mississippi but Thomas wanted a more respectable past," Estelle reported. "It was me on phone with Thomas dialing the number to my apartment."

Ruth winced at that. She'd been too naive. "And the other?"

"We've been together for years," Estelle stated dispassionately. "He thought he needed someone more sedate."

"If the definition of sedate includes someone who knows who they are, has integrity, and is truthful, than I'm guilty of being sedate. If it means someone who would have cooked and cleaned for him, saved with him, bore his children, and held his aging head, then for *those* attributes, *for the first time in my life*, I'm guilty as charged! Please thank Mr. Wills for showing me he wasn't a black warrior, never would be...and for being so careless!"

As Ruth hung up the phone, she thought she heard Estelle say, "Ouch!"

Ruth held her head high as the information of her broken engagement circulated through the hospital. At least it had been too soon for the wedding gifts to start coming to the apartment. She and Thomas were scheduled to put their selections in registries a few days after the scene in his bedroom—a spared humiliation by a few days.

Ruth was strong. Revenge was sweet, but lonely. She'd been such a fool to get involved with Thomas in the first place. Love and marriage could be for other people for a while. A long while. Norma and Elliot would be spending their honeymoon writing about and photographing several locales around the world. Ellie and Jack planned on going to Niagara Falls. Ruth had been looking at brides' magazines and dreaming about a cruise before her snake of a fiancé showed what a louse he was—causing her to mix her metaphors in her fury! She'd be spending her free time finding another apartment.

CHAPTER SEVENTEEN

Six months later, Ruth still hadn't been able to keep her promise to rest. Both Ellie and Norma were now happily married and Ruth thought she now might have time to herself. She'd used her Saturday off to get "out of boxes" in her new apartment, but on Sunday she'd been on the phone to St. Louis when another family time bomb exploded.

On Monday, Ruth had finished her shift and fixed three chicken casseroles, now cooking in one of the hospital cafeteria ovens. "I think twenty more minutes should do it," Ruth called. She had *promised*, and even though her head was in turmoil from her all-Sunday-long conversation with Thelma, Ruth couldn't break her word. The show had to go on, so to speak. One of her head nurse friends, Hildie Katz, had asked Ruth to make the entree for the baby shower lunch for a nurse who was expecting in a few weeks. Ruth shook her head and let out a deep sigh. She was now cooking for people she didn't even know.

"That sounds serious," Evie Sikes, the head of the hospital cafeteria observed.

Mrs. Sikes didn't know the half of it. First, Thelma scared Ruth by telling her Dr. Means had ordered Lady Dee to rest because her blood pressure and heart rate had been erratic recently. Before Ruth could express her concerns, Thelma steam-rolled the conversation into talking about the stress of caring for Sylvie.

"I guess," Ruth said, half-heartedly. "Cooking takes my mind off of things, Mrs. Sikes." Ruth had talked to Evie many times over the years. Evie had the reputation of being a loving, good listener and a stickler against gossip. But Ruth also talked to her about Sylvie because Evie had a nineteen-year-old grandson who had the same learning challenges. Ruth's new revelations would be safe with the friend she now called by her first name when they weren't working at the hospital.

Were cooking these casseroles in the hospital kitchen God's way of telling Ruth she needed someone to talk to about her lonely situation?

"Things can have a dragging effect, I'll say," Evie replied. "Since you've got twenty minutes to spare, why don't you sit down and have a hot cup of coffee."

Evie was always dishing out good food and the best peach cobbler Ruth tasted this side of St. Louis. To keep her figure, Ruth could indulge in only an occasion treat. Evie's cheerful attitude shining from her round face and buxom, strong body fueled her progress from the assistant cook position to the head of the cafeteria in her tenure at the hospital. But Evie hadn't had an easy time. She was a widow who talked about having two grown children. Ruth couldn't quite remember. Her own concerns were heavy on her mind like a weighed cord pulling her down.

Ruth's family wanted her to take Sylvie. At least until Lady Dee was feeling better. *Till she was feeling better? Did they know taking Sylvie could cost Ruth her hard-won job as a nursing supervisor? How could she take that much time off to care for her?* There were several reasons to talk to Mrs. Sikes.

Evie saw Ruth's thoughtful scowl and the creases in her forehead, knowing Ruth needed to get things off her mind. "I cook here because I can't cook small." Evie swatted her hand in the air. "When I get started, I usually have enough left-overs to feed my kids, the widow Emory and half the neighborhood." Ruth smiled wanly and looked at the oven doors.

"That's why I make this space and the ovens available for the people who want to have parties here. Know other people are itching to get some cooking done, too." Evie considered her next words carefully because Ruth's frown remained in place. "You need to talk about what's bothering you?"

Ruth looked around. *Was it that obvious?*

Evie thought Ruth needed some reassurance. "No one's going to be here for dinner till three p.m." She pointed to the sign. "The floor's still wet by the door and people who want sandwiches and coffee are way off." Most of the dining area remained cordoned off for cleaning and sweeping after the breakfast and lunch crowds.

"Since the food is so good, I think you should try white linens and candlelight to get a bigger crowd." Ruth chuckled, trying to shake off her bad humor. *Did the effort seem hollow?*

"Laughter doesn't always hide things," Evie replied, wanting Ruth to get things off her chest. Evie knew what it was like to lose your love.

"I know," Ruth admitted. "It's just I haven't been able to take it all in yet. Too many things have been happening."

Evie nodded and her eyebrows rose expectantly. If Ruth was going to say anything, she needed to sit back and let the girl do it. Several minutes disappeared in silence.

"My sister, Thelma, called to tell me she's getting married," Ruth began. "It's a double wedding with my mother who's marrying a long-time family friend."

A few more moments of silence. Evie nodded again. "To a man who I esteem greatly...Dr. Means...but I *detest* Mrs. Blaine and one of his nieces...and there's been a *severe* strain with the other one."

"That been so for a while?" Evie asked.

"Ever since Mrs. Blaine and Calli Winston, the disliked women in question, stepped into the picture when they came to St. Louis in our school years," Ruth replied glumly. "Even though my father and Dr. Means were long-time partners in practice and the finest of friends, his relatives, Mrs. Blaine and Calli, were always gossiping against my family."

"Are you planning on moving back there?" Evie asked. Getting a perspective might be just what Ruth needed. She'd never spoken to Evie about specifics.

"No. No," Ruth replied. "It's about Sylvie." Ruth bit her lip. "My sister, Thelma, says Sylvie's care is affecting my mother's health...and with her impending remarriage...." Ruth sighed. "Thelma says I need to take Sylvie for a while." Ruth thought a moment. "Leroy travels for the NAACP and is single and Thelma and her fiancé are veterinarians. They're saving to buy a practice in Atlanta. Thelma shares a studio apartment with another aspiring female vet and her fiancé lives in a converted tack room behind a horse farm now." Ruth's eyes misted. "Sylvie's never lived with anyone...except family." *Now wasn't the time to open up the story of Sylvie and the Wilcox family.*

Evie got the picture of Thelma and her beau living in a tack room...and a long-term guest with special needs. A traveling brother couldn't be a stable environment for Sylvie either, so everything pointed to Ruth, the single nurse sister. "This seems like a big change for you." From the sound of this girl's dear voice, Evie knew Ruth had already made her decision, no matter the personal inconvenience. Sylvie was a lucky sister.

"They'll manage until I get home for the weddings."

Evie looked up to see something else flicker in Ruth's eyes. *Fear? Regret?* "Is there something else?" she ventured softly.

Ruth didn't want to mention anything about the Jace Prue mess, so she brought up her most recent concern. "I've just moved into a smaller apartment and now I'm going to have to get a bigger one...," she said, and the rest tumbled out, "...and face the man who I thought loved me, and then married Calli's sister, my former best friend, Meggie, who's his wife...at this wedding."

This was a tangled mess! Evie tried to maintain her impassive expression. *Ruth's best friend had married the man Ruth had once loved?*

"I can't very well sneak into town, take Sylvie away and not attend the ceremony." Ruth's eyes clouded.

"How long do you have before this all happens?" Evie asked.

"Three months. Perhaps a few weeks more," Ruth replied glumly, thinking she might run into a dead end trying to find someone or some program to help her with Sylvie while Ruth kept working.

"Short time in this circumstance," Evie replied.

"My sister, Sylvie, has worked well as a dishwasher in a restaurant and in laundry at a local hospital in St. Louis." Ruth swallowed, hoping to get some positive response. *You won't know until you ask.* "I was wondering if you might consider letting Sylvie come to work here in the cafeteria?"

"Worked in a restaurant, you say?" Evie asked.

"Yes, for several years when I was working there...and some time after when I was in college," Ruth replied, trying not to think of anything else beyond work. Ruth never talked about it. Her throat suddenly seemed tight and dry.

"I'll be sure to pray on it, as well as look around the neighborhood for another place for the two of you," Evie said, a light coming to her eyes. "There's sure to be an answer coming soon." Evie put her hand to her chin. "The Lord works in mysterious ways."

☙❧

"Mama, why were you so fired up for me to come over this evening?" Beryl Sikes, Evie's older son, asked in confusion. "I was just here yesterday." A wary thought entered his mind and his frown deepened. "Are you not feeling up to par and you didn't want to tell me over the phone?" Concern creased the brow of the six-foot man, built like a professional wrestler or football player. "You're always working too hard."

"Now, now, Beryl," his mother began, thankful for his caring. "It's not about me. It's about you."

The man's brows shot up high on his fully bald head. His dark amber eyes looked confused. "Me?"

Evie didn't waste any time getting to the point. Her son liked plain-speaking. "You know we've been meeting roadblocks in trying to get our shelter home started."

Beryl knew very well the family's goal of starting a sheltered home and workshop with his nephew, Ralph, as one of the center's occupants. Everything sat stymied by red tape and problems. He'd been railing about it at this very kitchen table last night, over a plate of smothered chicken and greens. Beryl let out an exasperated sigh. Ralph was eighteen, almost nineteen, now. Beryl's younger brother by a year, Pete, had been alone since his wife had left under the strain of Ralph's care seventeen years ago. With many hospitalizations and surgeries, the sweet boy, now almost a man, was doing well. He looked the spitting image of his father, healthy and strong, but Ralph would never have the mental capacity to go along with his size. The experts they trusted said Ralph would always be a third grader in his heart and his mind. But the heart and mind of a child was a fine thing and the Sikes family wanted to nourish and cherish Ralph in every way possible.

The "almost a man" part about Ralph's situation was giving the Sikeses problems. Ralph needed twenty-four-hour supervision. Ralph's schooling could continue for another year or so, but then he would be summarily released from the program, which monitored him for daytime hours. Pete and Beryl owned a metal salvage and welding shop. The business needed Beryl and his brother's full-time availability and attention. Financially, when they considered the family business and looked at the numbers, Evie was the most obvious choice. Even though Evie liked her job at the hospital and she'd be penalized for her early retirement, Evie was slated to leave the hospital to care for Ralph.

Both Evie and her sons knew other families being penalized in similar situations. They'd looked into every possible alternative with no luck or answers to their dilemma. They'd finally come up with a plan by scouring the local organizations and foundations to see what they could do to set up their own sheltered workshop or home. They'd found the resources but *not* the full-time, qualified administrative and medical team member necessary to get them to the next step.

"I've been talking to Ruth Yuell down at the hospital," his mother started. "She's about to be in the same boat."

୧୨

Ruth picked up the phone in her small office off the pediatric wing. "Ruth Yuell."

"Ruth. It's Evie Sikes." Ruth heard the rushing breath of her friend who ran the cafeteria.

"Need my recipe for chicken casseroles?" Ruth quipped. She was grateful for the time Evie had spent with her concerning her problems.

"That would be fine. It's a good one," Evie replied. "But the reason I called was my son might have an answer to your concerns about Sylvie."

"Sylvie?" Ruth asked.

"Yes," Evie replied. "He's got an idea for her employment and helping out with the situation." Evie hoped the Lord wouldn't think glossing over everything would be considered a sin. She'd have to ask the Reverend Edgars on Sunday. She wasn't sure of the answer. "Can you come over at six tomorrow?"

"I think my calendar is free," Ruth said, thinking out loud. "I guess I can stay and do paperwork and come over about then." She looked at the blank space after four p.m. "You say this is about Sylvie?"

Evie didn't want to go into it before Beryl had a chance to speak to Ruth. So she rushed on. "Our address is...," Evie spoke quickly, giving Ruth her address and home phone number, while all the time praying the other woman wouldn't have time to change her mind. "We'll see you tomorrow at six." Evie hung up before even saying goodbye. She knew rushing through the message wasn't the *only thing* she'd need to apologize for when Ruth heard everything she and her son had to say.

ତ୨ତ୨

Beryl's scalp was sweating and he'd written down everything on large white-lined index cards, as he had in his debate classes in both high school and college, so he'd remember what to say and in the most persuasive order. He'd been nervous before, but never like this.

ତ୨ତ୨

Ruth showed up promptly for dinner with Evie and her son. Ruth recalled Evie mentioning the street and the unique scalloped wood shingle accents. "The first owner was from the East and wanted to have some reminder." Evie took another sip of coffee. "Pete went down to the historical society or some place to find out."

When Ruth was on her way to a nursing conference, her taxi had gone down the street because of a detour and she'd seen the large home on a corner lot. Ruth tried to remember Evie's comments. "Previous owner built a workshop building behind the house. Think he worked on clocks or something."

Ruth heard footsteps at the door and pinned a smile on her face. Her smile wobbled a bit. Instead of Evie, a large scowling man filled the doorway. "Is this the Sikes residence?" she said weakly, thinking she'd made a mistake. This man didn't seem to want any visitor at his door.

"Sorry, Miss Yuell," the bald man said, letting Ruth through the door and extending his hand. "I'm Beryl Sikes, Evie's son." He looked into Ruth's eyes and lost his train of thought.

His voice was a whiskey bass, Ruth thought, reminding her of preachers and orators.

"Yes, I'm Ruth Yuell," she replied. Her hand was still captured in the man's large hand. *Was he staring at her?* His amber eyes never left her face. Ruth was the first to look away. "Family pictures?" she asked, moving away from the door and looking at the wall to see if she could find Evie as she retrieved her hand.

"Mother is in the kitchen, but I'm sure she'll be out soon, now that she hears voices," Beryl replied. "Those are pictures of the Sikes and Endicott families." Beryl decided he'd take Miss Yuell's lead and fall back on the pictures as a means of discussion or getting her interested in some other topic if their conversation went badly. "Won't you sit down?"

Ruth followed the sweep of his hand to see a large old-fashioned parlor and columned dining room reminiscent of the St. James home. Her face puckered a bit at the memory.

Beryl saw the frown on this woman's face. Miss Yuell's smile had vanished. *This wasn't going well.*

Ruth rallied and looked at the man. Beryl Sikes, she remembered. She forced a smile as she sat on the opposite side of the opposing couches situated in front of the large fireplace. It was a long way from the foyer. *Did she need an escape plan?* After all, Evie had said her son was part of the discussion concerning Sylvie. Ruth tried to calm herself.

Evie bustled into the room, carrying a canapé tray. "Beryl, did you ask Ruth what she wanted to drink?" Evie looked into her son's cloudy eyes. *Not good*, she thought. "What would you like?"

"Water, for now," Ruth replied.

"I'll get your glass." Beryl put his hand on the arm of the chair to get up, "And a beer for myself." He'd almost forgotten his manners and quickly added, "Something for you, mother?"

"Nonsense," Evie said, forestalling her son by a clasp on his arm. "I'll get things while I check the roast." She turned slightly, looking meaningfully in her son's eyes. "I'll be back with the drink tray."

Beryl's expression remained stony, even though his words were polite. *Could he really help her with Sylvie? Perhaps, this had all been a mistake.*

Beryl took a deep-chested breath. "My brother, Pete, and his son, Ralph, are at the ballgame." He stopped to collect his thoughts. "Ralph is a sports fan, no matter the sport or the season."

Ruth thought she might introduce the subject of Sylvie. Her nervous hands formed a polite ball in her lap. "My sister, Sylvie, is coming to live with me."

Beryl turned his neck to see if his mother was bringing the drinks before replying. *Blast*, he thought. *What was taking so much time?* "My mother said she needed special assistance as well."

Introducing Sylvie's name stomped on any effort for continuing light conversation before dinner. "Yes." Ruth tried to keep her tone even and her concern off her face. She wanted to hug the information close to her. Having Sylvie here was going to be a big change. "My sister needs monitoring. She's worked well in sheltered situations: a small restaurant doing the dishes and in several duties in a hospital laundry at the present time."

Beryl noted that the golden highlights in the woman's eyes dimmed a bit. "Was there some reason you're sister changed from the restaurant to the laundry?" he asked, knowing his nephew Ralph was scared of the blue flame of the welding torches. He would never be able to work in the hazardous environment of the metal shop.

Ruth sat up a bit straighter. "The reason?" Illogical thoughts entered Ruth's mind as small bolts of fear sheared from her stomach to her fingertips. *Did this man somehow know about her past? Was he going to say something?*

Evie heard the change in Ruth's voice. She closed her eyes for a second, berating herself for the decision to let Beryl handle things. Evie immediately headed back to the living room. "I've got your water here, Ruth. I was telling Beryl about the changes in the pediatric ward during your tenure," Evie began as she turned to give her son a hidden frosty look. "I love the murals on the wall. What did you say the name of the artist was?"

After a few minutes of leading the conversation to safer topics, Evie led them to the dining table, through prayers and dinner, keeping the conversation on areas of more impersonal, yet insightful, information about Ruth's life and interests, her other family members, and local friends from the hospital.

Every time Beryl opened his mouth, his mother's brow lifted slightly, alerting him about his words and tone. Dually warned, Beryl tried to keep up with the conversation, mentioning the family business and anecdotes since he'd made such a hash of things at the beginning of the evening.

"This was lovely, Evie, and a great dinner," Ruth complemented as she shifted her weight to leave her seat. "Can I help you clear?"

"No, child," Evie replied. "It's Beryl's job to do that when company comes."

It was all Beryl could do to keep his eyebrows from flying up on his skull. His mother infrequently trusted his big-as-ham hands in touching her good china. "That's ri...that's right," Beryl stammered with more feeling the second time as he got the drift of his mother's bent. "You sit right there. As our guest. We'll get the dishes."

The man's tone was commanding and deeply resonant. Ruth looked up with a questioning face to see Evie smile in agreement. Ruth frowned a bit but eased back in her chair and stayed put. Her feeling of ease evaporated as she watched her hostess make more trips than necessary to what Ruth knew must be the kitchen with Evie's son nervously carrying only a few plates.

In the kitchen, both mother and son were gritting their teeth, both hoping the good china stayed unscathed by this maneuver.

"Now, we'll bring things up over dessert with the first cup of coffee," Evie said, pouring from a china pot. "You let me speak about things over the red velvet cake and we'll pray she'll listen." The hostess shot up one-word arrow prayers to the Lord as she finished pouring and carried the dessert tray to the buffet next to the table.

After a few bites and willing her nerves to calm, Evie started in again. "When I spoke to you about our conversation in the cafeteria, I wanted you to hear more about our efforts to make a sheltered environment for people with needs like Ralph and Sylvie in the community." Evie put her cup square in the saucer. "My grandson Ralph will soon be released from the last of the county's programs for handicapped children and has shown he has aptitudes to work in a safe environ-ment." Her lips thinned. "But it will take time to see how many hours and how often he can work. There's nothing else available other than our own personal supervision."

"With help from grants and other interested people, we were hoping to expand this program into the community to help other families like ours who have reached the end of helping resources," Beryl said, thankful that he'd found his voice and reason again. This program and the rest of what they planned were important to his family. "Are you interested?"

"You're planning to start with Ralph and Sylvie and expand to include other needy adults?" Ruth asked.

"In part," Evie replied, seeing the interest in Ruth's eyes. "We personally know of another half dozen who are going to be without work or supervision within the next few months...and they're feeling as helpless as we are." Evie took a deep breath. "So that's one reason we need to get up and going."

"Our plan is to provide transportation and sheltered work in businesses which will see the benefit of employing people with challenges like Sylvie and Ralph." Beryl twisted a bit in his chair but his eyes never left Ruth's face. "Prospective employers can't always provide steady part-time or full-time jobs. These dear people need supervision but their parents, guardians, and caretakers need to con-tinue their jobs or have the opportunity to have a full time job themselves without having to worry about their loved ones." He wondered if it was right to mention the other reasons so baldly, but vowed he just had to plow ahead. "Some of these people haven't had a day off or a vacation. Not to mention when caregivers require hospital care or surgery. So we're trying to assist with these temporary live-in needs, too."

"So there would be a liaison person to monitor clients like Sylvie and Ralph, provide transportation and supervision in concert with their families' working schedules, and some vacation and emergency housing?" Ruth replied, hoping she understood the Sikeses' innovative concept.

Beryl couldn't have said it better himself—a dream, so close and yet so far away, for families like the Sikeses and Miss Yuell's.

"Well, if I can finish getting permission from the hospital administration, Sylvie will be working under me," Evie noted, not wanting to pressure Ruth in any way with the rest of the plan.

"That's wonderful!" Ruth exclaimed, leaning closer to Evie to hear her words. One of her biggest worries involved a routine so Sylvie remained safe and occupied during Ruth's work hours and some of the errands needed to run a household.

"Now, let's not get ahead of ourselves," Beryl said with what seemed like a scratchy voice. "There are other things to consider before we can make any promises."

"Oh." Blood rushed to her face in mortification. This plan had sounded so hopeful.

"Now, Beryl," his mother said swiftly. "I'm keeping my word on getting a job for Sylvie, even if the other parts of the plan fall through."

"I know. I know," Beryl said, sounding repentant. "It's just, I thought we should lay *everything* out before we talk about individual jobs."

Evie puckered at this. She wanted to give Ruth some good news before hitting her with the rest. Ruth needed some positive things to hang onto before Beryl plopped the rest of the information in the basket.

Ruth looked at each of them in turn, not knowing whether to be hopeful or not. The single bite of red velvet cake she eaten churned in a knot in her stomach. "Go on."

"I'll let Beryl tell you the rest, child." Evie put her napkin next to her dessert plate. "Don't jump to conclusions on anything." She patted Ruth's shoulder. "Take some good time before making up your mind."

Ruth nodded, wondering what more she needed to consider. It seemed as if she'd understood the Sikeses' program.

"Promise me, you'll let us talk about this again, after tonight, before you give an answer," Evie said and left quickly for the kitchen before Ruth had a chance to reply.

Ruth looked at Evie's son. He looked grim.

Now Ruth didn't know what to think. She wanted to leave and yet this was the best hope so far she'd had in getting employment for Sylvie. Evie had said, and her bear of a son had concurred, that Sylvie's possible job at the hospital would not be in jeopardy if Ruth didn't agree with the rest of the information he was about to tell her. Ruth sighed and stayed put, looking straight into Beryl's citron and loam gaze.

❦

Beryl thought his scalp must be sweating again but he didn't want to betray his nervousness. He swallowed some water and wiped his lips with his mother's lace-edged linen napkin. "There are certain restrictions concerning the grants for our plans," Beryl began. "We're planning to accept both men and women in our program. But we don't have any required medical personnel involved as yet."

Was that all? Ruth allowed the knot in her stomach to ease. "Will my involvement help those issues?" Ruth's hand went to the discomfort in her stomach. "How much time will it require?"

"Yes, your baccalaureate and master's degrees will definitely help one of the paperwork gaps in their requests," Beryl replied.

Ruth might have smiled but the man seemed neither pleased nor relieved. "There's more?"

"A whole lot more," Beryl replied. He wished he'd had a towel to wipe his head or an easier way to say the rest. "My brother and I are both single men. He's divorced with no woman to marry with Ralph and all and I've been too busy concentrating on business and taking up my part for the family as well." Beryl's throat dried up but he continued doggedly. "With our wanting to help clients of both sexes on a twenty-four-hour basis, at times, someone needs to marry to carry this off."

Ruth sat there for a moment, letting the words circle in her mind. Her sable eyes sparked when the true meaning of his words struck home. "You mean you... you and...or...me?" Ruth squeaked, lifting her hand to gesture back and forth between herself and Evie's son to stabilize the thought.

"Yes," Beryl's trench-deep bass voice replied, staring at Ruth like a statute. He held his breath and barely blinked because he thought Ruth might bolt if he moved.

Ruth didn't know whether to begin by saying, "Let me get this straight," or, "You've got to be kidding." Manners won out and she said, "Let me get this straight." She tilted her head in anger and concentration. "You're telling me I'm the candidate for marriage. Out of the blue, mind you. Because...the grant requires a married couple in order for you to get money."

"That's correct," Beryl said, still not flinching. "We've considered funding this personally but the amount of capital and the risks might take our family business under." Best let the adversary see a show of strength, his old football coach said, and this was an adversarial situation, if the flinty sparks from Miss Yuell's eyes were any indication. "We're trying to help a lot of people. Overnight lodging would come into the picture a good deal...and a stable married couple leading the application would almost certainly enhance our chances."

In this day and age, Ruth fumed inwardly. *They were in the 1960s after all, not the Middle Ages!*

"It's the only way this go-round," Beryl said. "I give you my solemn word. I've checked things from every angle. Two other grant packages are considered to be ahead of ours just because of this issue. We might not even be considered for a final decision with no married couple in our application." He bit the inside of his lip. "Please check into every aspect of their concerns in their written comments and see for yourself. I've got the information here."

Ruth saw the papers but wanted to study this man's face, which verified the grim truth of the matter.

Evie came through the door from her position of eavesdropping from the kitchen. "I was going to ask Harvey Benson to marry me, but we'd be too old according to several of the grants' stipulations." Evie didn't apologize for listening. She hoped the good Lord and Ruth forgave them for involving her in their family's dream.

"Are you sure?" Ruth repeated the crux of the unassailable truth. She was going to look at all the paperwork and make all the necessary calls to verify things—if she even decided to *consider* this outlandish idea. Ruth felt too flummoxed. "The other parties interested in heading up the other grants have the proper personal credentials and licenses?" Ruth didn't want to mention the word—marriage.

"Here are all the names, phone numbers, and addresses of everyone and you can decide for yourself," Beryl replied.

Evie tried another tack. "You can leave now, Beryl." She tilted her head and gave her forbidding one-eyed stare. For years and years, since her two boys were knee-high to a tadpole, everyone in the Sikes household knew this look meant she would broach no argument.

Beryl cleared his throat like he was going to say more, thought better of it, and left without another word. *He really needed a beer.* He'd walk down to the corner tavern and let the ladies talk.

Ruth was going to say something herself but Evie cut her off. "I know it's not polite to interrupt guests, but this is all too important." She sat down in her chair next to Ruth and the words kept pouring out. "It's not only the paperwork and the grant money, Ruth. I was thinking of you."

Now Ruth was truly astounded. *Thinking of her? What on earth was Evie talking about?*

Evie got a lavender-printed handkerchief from her pocket and sniffed. She knew she needed to be as blunt as her son now. "Isn't it clear to you? When you look at the situation dispassionately, your sister and brother have dumped Sylvie on you because they want to get on with their own lives—in their own way?"

Ruth's eyes got wider. There was a big intake of breath. "What do you know about my life?" she spat indigently. *Sylvie was so dear. As for her siblings, how dare someone talk about them that way?*

Evie's voice rose. "I know what it's like to get everything foisted upon me because I'm a strong and resourceful woman." There was no time to stop and be prissy about things. "We're here alone now, so we can talk woman-to-woman." Her right arm swept across the room. "My auntie took a look at my situation and went out hunting for a man for me. An arranged marriage, right and tight." Evie got up from the chair and reached for a gold-framed picture. "That's my late husband, Clyde Delbert Sikes. Bless his soul." She wiped the picture lovingly with her hankie. "We would have been wed twenty-seven years when he passed from a stroke." A lone tear fell from her eyes unheeded. "Would have liked to have a hundred more but there's no changing death or taxes." She looked into Ruth's questioning eyes. "Thought you might like to have some help caring for Sylvie, and have a good man in your life, like my honey bear."

The endearment softened Ruth's attitude a bit. "I don't know," was all Ruth would say, not wanting to be pushed into anything or give Evie false hope. Ruth still smarted from the attack on her family.

"A good man," Evie persisted. "Then, there's your upcoming trip to the wedding and facing all those folk who thought you should have been married with babies long ago." Evie shook her head. "Don't care what they say about this new-fangled liberation stuff. Some women are born nurturers and you're one."

Ruth felt uncomfortable again. This situation and the specter of her mother and Thelma's double wedding rose in her mind. An unbidden thought popped into her head. *Wouldn't it be nice to be able to thwart the gossips for a change?* Ruth covered well. "My mother and my sister are getting married. They should be the center of attention."

"Attention can be ringed on three as well as two without too much problem," Evie replied dryly. *Keep talking about Beryl.* "Beryl's a man with a spotless reputation, an education, and a profitable business as far as bringing money in is concerned."

Manners wouldn't allow Ruth to argue against a mother's characterizations of her own son. But she could ask a question. "Why is Beryl the volunteer instead of Pete?" There must have been a lot of discussion concerning this question, Ruth thought, because Evie was clear-eyed and direct with her answer. She'd already said she and her beau Harvey Benson were too old.

"Beryl's the most qualified applicant with his business degree and I thought you'd both have the best matched temperaments to share your lives together," Evie replied honestly. "Brought out a good meal, got the particulars of this grant problem set out, and I prayed to let the good Lord take it from there." Evie thought her answer settled the conversation but Ruth had another question.

"Why me?" Ruth asked, folding her arms.

Evie shrugged. "Good woman, with a good head on your shoulders and the right credentials, you're getting Sylvie...and we're all running out of time." The older woman didn't pull any punches even when the stakes were high. Ruth started to get up. Evie knew she had said all she could say. As she went to get Ruth's sweater and purse from the hall closet and led her to the door, she repeated. "Remember, your promise. We'll talk again before you give us a final answer." As Ruth stepped out onto the porch, Evie added, "There's a bit of time for courting to decide. Either way, Sylvie *can* come work for me. I won't stop Sylvie's job, no matter what."

❀❀

Ruth thought and dreamed of little else that night and the following day. She tossed and dozed, thinking of Sylvie, Lady Dee, Thelma, the Sikeses and unknown needy families looking for help. Good thing Ruth could compartmentalize things well or she would have been a wreck the entire workday. "Have me talking to myself more than I already do," Ruth said to the empty air, as she walked home in the late afternoon. Ruth yanked on her sweater as it fell from her shoulder.

Her steps faltered as she spied a large man waiting at the banister of her apartment entrance. Ruth squinted. Beryl Sikes! Ruth almost turned and headed in the opposite direction. Then, she saw the white bouquet that looked like roses. Something was spinning like a basketball on what seemed like the tips of the man's fingers, which looked like a rectangular box resembling something candy would come in. He must have been sitting there for a long time. *The man must detest idleness!*

❀❀

Ruth was right. Beryl had been sitting there for an hour, pacing and squirming, berating himself about how badly he had handled things the previous evening. He'd been lumpy-fisted in both his manners and his presentation of the facts. Hadn't even been able to guess when she'd be home after her shift at the hospital.

Beryl had to hand it to Ruth Yuell. He would have lost patience with the whole dinner debacle if he'd been presented with the same information. He could see himself leaving the table and not looking back. Her behavior was a big plus in his estimation. Beryl ran his hand over his chin as he balanced the candy in his other hand. Miss Ruth Yuell.

She was articulate and never simpered like most of the other women his mother and the rest of the church ladies had thrown his way. Right pretty on the eyes as well, he had to admit. He'd love to see sparks fly from her sable eyes, for reasons other than anger. But that was something he couldn't tell his pastor.

❦

Beryl was caught in his sensual musings and box-twirling as Ruth came to his side.

"You're going to bore a whole in the box or squash the candy," Ruth observed.

Beryl's stomach jumped but he stayed calm as he put down the candy box and pulled on his ear lobe as he rose slowly. "Thought we might start over again," was all he said. "Candy and flowers to ask for forgiveness." He turned and handed the candy box to Ruth. "No talk about the grant or family pressures." Then he gave her the bouquet. "Perhaps dinner?"

Ruth dipped her face into the white roses, savoring the fragrance and thinking of her response. "Something quick, I've got the new budgets and the fiscal year-end report." She stopped to hold out the flowers. "The candy can sit on the table in the apartment but these roses need water and a vase."

Beryl just felt glad Ruth didn't throw the candy and flowers in his face. He knew from his mother's recent conversation that she, too, spent extra time with the same budget efforts for the hospital cafeteria. "I'll wait here on the step while you get ready."

Ruth noted the knife-sharp pleat in his long sleeve plaid shirt. "A casual place?"

"Got just the thing in mind," Beryl replied, his smile becoming more relaxed.

Ruth smirked, not wanting this man to think anything more than that he was apologizing for the ambush last evening. But she couldn't help to think that Beryl Sikes had a handsome smile.

❦

They talked about everything without mentioning the grant or their relatives' needs. But Ralph and Sylvie were not excluded from the conversation because of their dear places in the lives of the two people sitting on either side of the table for two in the back of Puccini's Italian Restaurant.

"Did Beryl tell you he made all the ornamental iron work, inside and out, for this place?" Angelo Puccini stated with pride as he scanned his family restaurant. "Theresa, my daughter, said we had to spruce up the place a bit and Beryl had all the right ideas when it came to the metal." Angelo stopped for a moment before adding. "He's a good man."

After a somewhat embarrassed look at Ruth, Beryl wiped one side of his mouth with his napkin. "I'll have to talk to you if I need a new marketing plan, Angelo, but Miss Yuell isn't here to hear about the family business." He wiped his mouth, changing the subject. "The cannoli was excellent."

Ruth looked at her watch. She'd said she needed a quick bite and three hours had evaporated. Now it was her turn to be embarrassed. "I've got to get going. I've already taken up enough of your time."

"My goodness. Angelo. The bill, please." Time had gone by quickly. Beryl hoped things were smoothed over. This apology dinner seemed sweet like sugar instead of sour grapes. Beryl had enjoyed himself, he thought with a smile. "Gotta get you back home."

His hand became gentle as he put his fingertips to Ruth's back, involuntarily guiding her to the front of the dim candle-lit restaurant. They walked in relaxed silence to Ruth's apartment building. "I won't ask to come up to your place but I need to know one thing."

Before Ruth could ask him what he was wondering, Beryl dipped his head and captured her body in his grasp as he kissed her with speed and caressing force. Her gasp was swallowed in his mouth. He let her go quickly as he had grabbed her, making sure her feet were squarely on the ground. Beryl turned without looking back. "Honey, Miss Yuell. Pure honey."

❧

Tonight was no better than the last, Ruth knew, from the tossing and pillow punching she did in the dark. Yes, much worse, it seemed to Ruth as she looked at her morning-weary face in the mirror. Last night had been an enjoyable evening but this man and his mother were asking Ruth to commit to a lifetime with him—a covenant relationship before the church and their communities, families, and friends. Since talking about the grant and its concept were out-of-bounds topics last night, Ruth didn't even know the timetable involved in the decision.

Think about the man, instead of the grant and those needy families, Ruth fumed inwardly, trying to find the cosmetic concealer lost somewhere in her makeup drawer. *He wasn't a charity. She'd be legally locked to him for life. He was a good conversationalist.* Rattle, rattle. *He had at least one other family who esteemed him, called the Puccinis.* Rattle, rattle. *He owned a business, which must be solvent since his assets would have had to be checked out by the grant authorities.* Hadn't Evie mentioned it as profitable? Rattle, rattle. *And such soft lips for such a big man!* Ruth startled at that, looked in the mirror, and slammed the vanity drawer. "Oh. Men!" Ruth shouted between her gritted teeth, giving up her search and instead storming to the kitchen for the ice tray. *Would she have time to use some ice or a cool cloth on her eyes to relieve the puffiness?*

❦

Ruth decided to take her late coffee break in her office. She wasn't going to go to the cafeteria and be bombarded by Evie! *Perhaps putting everything on paper would help her through this.* Ruth gritted her teeth against the afternoon-bitter coffee. Writing things down helped when she was thinking through other situations. In fifteen minutes, she had a page of written information. As she looked at the columns, most of what she knew was scant because knowing took time. There were a few more impressions based on two days of interactions but the things she *really* knew seemed to be about Evie Sikes and not her older son. They'd spent and hour and a half the night before last and three hours last night. The phone rang, almost making her tip over her now tepid coffee cup. Ruth heard Beryl's bass-warm voice on the other end.

"Will you see me tonight again?" he asked.

"Why?" was all she replied as she heard Beryl sigh.

"We need more time together to see if I'm any kind of fit for you," was his succinct reply.

"What about you?" she whispered as her heart sped up, not knowing if she really wanted to hear the answer.

"I'm committed to you," was his equally short reply.

"Five o'clock at my house," Ruth replied like she was saying a line from a transportation schedule. "Take me someplace different," she added. "Mr. Puccini is *your* cheerleader."

"I understand," was Beryl's reply.

Ruth hung up the phone. She didn't understand. Life had taught her about danger and betrayal.

How could he be so sure when she was so undecided?

Ruth looked down at the paper. She'd written her first name on one side of the line and the last name "Sikes" on the line a few inches after it. Ruth balled up the paper and threw it in the garbage. "I've got to get back to work."

❦

"Ellie, I've got to talk to you," Ruth said into the receiver, wishing she'd decided to confide in her friend long before now.

Ellie was concerned at the tone of her friend's voice. "Is anything wrong, Ruth?"

"Yes. No," Ruth said hesitantly as the scales in her mind weighed her predicament. "Thelma has asked me to take Sylvie," she began. This was the place to start.

"Oh?" Ellie said, thinking she needed more information before jumping in.

"And I've met a man."

"Oh!" Ellie repeated happily, thinking her friend deserved happiness as she scanned the home she and her husband, Jack, had purchased. Soon baby and toy litter would be scattered about, she hoped, thinking she couldn't have been happier! "Go on," Ellie encouraged, knowing she were more curious about the man in question but not wanting to get Ruth sidetracked.

"He's made me a proposition." Ruth wondered if she was explaining this part of the situation properly.

"Proposition?" Ellie said more darkly, remembering Mr. Thomas Wills. "What kind of proposition?"

Ruth bit her lip. She needed to be clinical about this and not bring up Evie Sikes's name too soon. "He's got a nephew, much younger than Sylvie. His mother, who I know very well, and his brother, who I haven't even seen, are putting in a grant to help needy people, like Sylvie and Ralph, the nephew, to have care and sheltered work during the day so their relatives and people who take care of them have time to work themselves."

"OK," Ellie said tentatively.

"He also needs a wife to get the grant," Ruth said, letting silence hang in the connection.

"And...and...it means you?" Ellie asked, as she considered the facts and tried to finish the puzzle.

"Yes." Ruth's tone wasn't enthusiastic to even her own ears. She wondered what Ellie was thinking.

"Do you care for him, Ruthie?" Ellie asked. "At all?"

Ruth squirmed in her chair. She'd wanted to talk about the business side of things first before talking about the matter of love. But to be truthful, Ruth's own mind fell back to the issue of love whenever she thought about the situation. Ruth answered with a question of her own. "Does it count as a good thing if when he kissed me I felt the breath go out of me and there was a feeling in the pit of my stomach like I was falling?" Ellie stayed silent. "Is this promising or am I just a love-starved old maid?"

Ellie laughed at that. She retreated to think about the whole picture. "You've got a love situation and a business situation all tangled up."

"I guess," Ruth replied sheepishly.

"OK. Let's see. If Sylvie wasn't in the picture, would you still see this guy?" Ellie asked, letting the part about the kiss hang for a moment as she tried to consider Ruth's whole dilemma.

The question put Ruth back a bit. She'd been so focused on the *whole* situation and not the relationship aspect. "I hadn't given that scenario any thought."

Ellie let Ruth's words hang for a minute. "Perhaps that's been part of the problem." Ellie loved this woman like a blood sister, maybe even more, since there was no sibling rivalry involved. In her estimation, this brave, healing soul needed someone to love like she loved her husband Jack. Nothing less. "Go and think about it a bit." Ellie pursed her lips. "Call me tomorrow. I'll get back to you as soon as I can if I'm not here." Ellie hoped her love and earnestness came through the line. "I'd tell you to call Norma. But she and Elliot are in Turkey, I think."

"Yeah, I know. Love you too. Thanks, El," Ruth replied as she hung up the phone. Maybe she needed to be somewhere far away on a camel.

❧

Beryl was dead tired. Two nights without sleep and pacing the floors like a man with a fretting baby. Then, there was all the specialty ironwork to get done during the day. Beryl was beyond thankful they were getting new business and repeat customers from their business expansion. Yet, having so many things weighing on him and the uncertainty of the grant made his shoulders sag. No rest for the weary. He'd have to get busy and do whatever Ruth wanted him to do. She was a fine woman and the lynchpin in his family's shelter program. Getting her to come over to their side was vital. Beryl hoped he could give her the answers and the romance she deserved. He felt he might be a bit short in both areas as well as time. The information he'd gotten this afternoon hadn't helped. His throat was dry as he'd pulled his truck to the curb and stood next to Ruth's buzzer box. He knew he had pressed it when he heard her now-familiar musical voice say, "I'll let you in," in bell-bright tones.

He trudged up the stairs. They exchanged helloes and Beryl had decided long before coming this early evening, not to touch her again. He'd followed a silly irresistible urge the previous night. He wasn't that kind of a man. Miss Ruth needed to know she could count on him to keep himself steady—in any, and all, circumstances.

"Can I ask you to share the coffee I smell?" he asked politely. "I'm feeling a bit tired."

"I was about to offer you a cup," Ruth replied with a muffled voice from the kitchen. This situation seemed well beyond conventional courting behavior. "Feel a bit bushed myself."

Ruth came in with a tray of two steaming mugs. "No cookies," she said sternly, handing one into Beryl's beefy hand. She wanted to indicate she wasn't being stingy in her hospitality, but they were going out to dinner. "I could have made some savories."

"Don't bother," Beryl said, stifling a yawn. "A few sips and a sit on the couch should fix me up." Her couch was sure comfy, he thought, burrowing into the seat. He'd have to ask her about it.

Ruth watched Beryl. She made her coffee medical-strong, she knew. She said on the opposite edge of the couch as she rested her head on her hand. She hoped he like it.

◕◔

Ruth woke up with a start. She'd been dreaming of her father. They'd been having a pleasant conversation on the porch swing as a warm breeze caressed her face. He was saying how proud of her he was. Ruth was so glad her father was happy and she was with him. Tears came to her eyes. It was dark except for the light she had inadvertently left in the bathroom. She'd located the under-eye concealer in the back of the drawer after getting home and just gotten it on before Beryl had buzzed to come up. Thank goodness she remembered she was in her apartment or she would have been disoriented and afraid. *What was the matter with her?* Ruth rubbed the back of her neck as her fuzzy thoughts cleared. Instead of fear, her body felt lazy, pleasant bursts of electrical currents traveling throughout her body from her left hand. She looked over into the shadows to see a sound-asleep Beryl Sikes and her hand imprisoned in his burly grasp. Ruth detected the soft rumble of snoring. She closed her eyes again to enjoy the feeling for a second more. Her mouth dried, and she blushed, wondering if she could free herself without waking him.

Her stomach growled. Dinner, and covering Beryl Sikes, were the next tasks at hand.

◕◔

He must have fallen asleep, Beryl thought, as he scrubbed his face with his hand. Neither his mother or his brother and nephew were home yet. He'd had this dream and he usually didn't remember anything of his times in slumber. There was this lovely slim woman in his bed underneath him, which was strange because he had never brought another woman into bed under his mother's roof. The vixen in his dream tantalized him. He had his hand at the small of her back. He felt her ribs move against him. Beryl was trying to see her face and the sable brown love-drunk eyes of Ruth Yuell assailed him. He kicked the coffee table and found his arms trapped in a blanket. Bright light flew into his eyes, blinding him.

"Are you OK?" Ruth heard the commotion and came running. "I was just fixing us some dinner." She put the mixing spoon down. "You fell asleep." She wasn't about to share the rest.

"I'm fine. Fine," Beryl said, trying to rally himself from his dream and appear as rational as he could. "What are you making?" He tried to grasp anything from the threads of disjointed words he'd heard.

"I've got some pork chops and some green beans." Ruth looked at Beryl's face. He still had a glazed look. Nothing was registering or pleasing him, it seemed. "Will scramble some eggs when I get back to it." She'd left the whisking in the forgotten bowl when she'd heard the loud, blunt noises in her living room. Perhaps he was a deep sleeper and didn't wake up well. "Do you need some more time?"

"Waking up in strange places," Beryl replied lamely. "Pork chops and eggs are good."

⦚

Beryl talked conversationally during the meal through Ruth's barrage of questions—fielding all of her probing and information-gathering inquiries as honestly as he could. *She deserved it.* Ruth was, after all, the sacrificial lamb to his family's concept, even thought her sister, Sylvie, would benefit. He stirred his black after-dinner coffee wondering if there was anything else he could add to each query to give her everything she needed to feel comfortable. It was a laughingly short timeframe.

He'd better let her know. "Miss Ruthie, I'll answer everything and anything you have to ask, but something's come up." This wasn't going to be easy. "The grant people want to see you and me day after tomorrow."

"See me?" Ruth's coffee cup rattled to the saucer.

"I've been able to tell them we're engaged to be married, allowing you to call and ask questions about the grant. I've gotten all the time I can, telling them they're interfering with the final days of our wedding preparations," Beryl stated and looked straight into her eyes. "I'm sorry I told the lie, but I didn't know what-and-if was going to happen with...us." He wanted to give her an out to shield her from embarrassment. A broken engagement seemed like the best tack to save Ruth, if she decided against the plan.

Ruth tried to concentrate on Beryl's words but the specter of the meeting with the grant authorities scared her. This official meeting was coming too fast, rushing her. "Can't it be postponed?"

Beryl shook his head. "It's our turn...or we lose out," he said. "I didn't know anything about it till the call this morning." He put the cup down and stared at it. "I really tried my best for more time."

Ruth looked at the man sitting next to her. She could feel the regret and defeat in him somehow. "I'll go," she said, not guarding her words. She wanted his pain to stop. "I'll go."

Beryl turned and grabbed her hand.

The same one he'd had in his firm grasp when they were sleeping on the couch, Ruth thought.

"You will," Beryl said in wonder. "You will?"

"I'll go as your fiancée," Ruth said. "But when...when did you tell them we were marrying?"

"Three days after the grant is decided," Beryl replied. "That will give you some time...." His words stopped and he looked away. More grace time for her to back out.

If I decide to, enough time for me to let you go. Ruth couldn't bring herself to say the words. There was a sting of loss traveling over her heart.

Beryl rallied because Ruth had promised to come to the meeting. "It wouldn't do for a man's fiancée not to have a token of her future husband's affection." Beryl fished into his pocket.

To Ruth's surprise, Beryl pushed his kitchen chair away and kneeled on the well-used speckled linoleum. Thoughts rioted in her mind, not the least of which concerned washing the kitchen floor the day before and knowing it was clean.

"A man would come to give this ring as a sign," Beryl said, putting the yellow-gold band with the single diamond on Ruth's finger. "He'd say this was all he had right now but as they grew together, he hoped there would be more riches in their future." Beryl got up, grabbed Ruth by the waist. "He'd kiss her and tell her he'd love her and protect her forever on this earth."

Before Ruth knew it she was lifted to her feet, trapped in a warm embrace and a gentle probing kiss. Her lips danced with Beryl's changing caress. *Yes. Honey*, she thought, as her arms twined around his neck. At least that question was answered. Her legs were losing strength. She sagged against him. "When do we go?"

Beryl said from a place that seemed far away to Ruth, even though he was holding her. "Day after tomorrow. Three p.m."

The sound of his voice became stronger. Although she wanted to look in the amber depths of his eyes again in silence and feel his heart beating, she had to tell him something. Two things. "I'll cook smothered chicken after the meeting and I can't wear an engagement ring to my workplace because a proper lady, who hasn't had enough time to consider things, shouldn't wear a ring or tell anyone."

"Fair enough," Beryl said. He kissed Ruth on the forehead and walked to the couch to get his jacket. He knew he had to leave or risk losing his credit as a gentleman in his almost-betrothed's eyes.

❧

"OK. OK. There's chemistry and romance, but what if things don't go through," Ruth said to Ellie, blowing at the wispy bangs on her forehead. It had been another hard day at work. One nurse was ill and another was on vacation. Over the phone was no way to get advice.

"I'm no clairvoyant, Ruth," Ellie said. "But this man seems to be thinking of you, even when he's under pressure." Ellie wanted to give Ruth her best advice, but she didn't want to tip the scales one way or another, so Ellie shut up after her observation.

"It's too soon," Ruth said stubbornly. How could she let herself get embroiled in such a decision as marriage based on meeting a man three times! An errant thought intruded. *Hadn't Lady Dee said she knew the moment she met her father? Oh, great!* Ruth scolded and blurted, "He doesn't know about me."

Ellie had wondered if some of Ruth's fears also stemmed from her past. "You mean Devon and that Prue character?"

"Don't forget Thomas," Ruth said unnecessarily as if Ellie could forget the jerk. The only thing making the memory of Thomas bearable for Ellie remained Ruth's kiss-off with the mattress episode.

"You're *not* supposed to run your life with those three albatrosses around your neck," Ellie cried. "In this case, past *does not* dictate the future...with Mr. Sikes or any other man, for that matter. Cut 'em loose!"

"I'm going to tell him the whole truth," Ruth said steadfastly.

"When?" Ellie knew this could affect everything, but it was better to know Mr. Beryl Sikes could be thrown in the pot of the rest of the losers if he couldn't recognize all of Ruth's fine attributes. Ellie's heart clenched knowing she'd be there picking up the pieces if her dearest friend experienced another heart-mangling.

"After the meeting," Ruth replied, "or I might not have the strength."

"We can talk after," Ellie said, trying to sound nonchalant. She'd have to look through the house to find Norma's number. Even if that girl was in the middle of the desert, Ellie vowed to find her. This was too important!

CHAPTER EIGHTEEN

The meeting had gone well. They hadn't asked Ruth if she knew Beryl's favorite color or what his favorite foods were. Ruth didn't know what they were going to ask. Their cover story indicated Ruth had known the Sikes family for over five years, which was true. They'd asked about Ruth's training, her academic credentials, and Sylvie. Ruth spent most of her time in the interview telling the panel about her sister and her work as a pediatric nurse.

"And you interrupted your final wedding planning to come here?" the woman in the tweed suit said as she took her reading glasses from her nose. *Was her look skeptical?*

"We...we were going to put our names in several more bridal registries," Ruth replied. "We haven't done enough according to my future mother-in-law," trying to parry the question.

"And your family lives in St. Louis?" the kindly man with the close-shaven white beard asked. An inch or two more on his whiskers and he could play Santa. She went on by rote, telling them about her mother, deceased father, and what her siblings were doing.

"Your sister, Sylvie, is coming to live with you?" This man sat in the middle of the dais, and at the beginning had introduced her and Beryl to the panel members.

Ruth put her ice-cold hand in Beryl's. "Yes. My mother's health needs strengthening and my sister and brother are unable to give Sylvie the care and attention Beryl and I can give her at this time." Ruth sighed as the gentleman seemed satisfied. Ruth looked over to Beryl, who smiled at her reassuringly. He squeezed her hand and she felt the pressure of his engagement ring. *There was going to be an inquisition tonight. Would it be like this one?*

❧

"I don't like it, mother," Beryl remembered saying as he cinched his tie to go over to Ruth's apartment. He wanted to dress more formally to show her his gratitude for how wonderful she'd been at the meeting. Another bouquet of white roses headed her way from the florist. "The light just went out of her eyes at the last question."

"It could have been relief, Beryl." Evie didn't want to take away any of her son's optimism. He'd followed this path to care for the grant and toward marriage faithfully and deserved some good feelings for as long as possible, no matter what the outcome. "Didn't they as good as tell you...you had the grant money?"

"Yes. They asked me to set up an account at the bank," Beryl said, straightening the tie silk. "The information marks it as an acceptance step."

"Well, then, the two of you need to celebrate," Evie said with finality. "Buy some champagne. Now go on and get."

❧

With everything she had to say, Ruth was surprised she concentrated as well as she did on the dinner preparations. She'd cut the roses down and put them in some cordial glasses she'd gotten at a rummage sale at church. They were pressed glass and not crystal, but they looked genuine with the creamy white flowers within their water baths.

Ruth turned the oven down to its lowest setting, not wanting the dinner to dry out. The set of baking dishes and covers were ready for service as the buzzer rang. Ruth gulped against a dry throat. *Where would she begin, she wondered, as she twirled the diamond and gold ring on her finger?* She looked at the ring once more in the kitchen light. This might be the last few hours it would be hers. Beryl would probably want it back.

❧

"Thanks for cooking again, Ruthie." Beryl smiled and patted his stomach. "We should have celebrated in a restaurant with wine and music." He tried to sound relaxed. "Do you dance?" He tried to pour more champagne in their glasses. He frowned when Ruth shook her head. Her mood seemed like an ending rather than a beginning, which worried him.

Ruth refused more champagne because she needed a clear mind to focus on everything she needed to tell him. "Even though we were strict Baptists, we learned a few cotillion dances, and in college physical education they made us learn some basic dances." Ruth smiled at the memory. "Nothing fancy, but passable."

Beryl was going to say something about them going to a dance club, but he caught himself. He twirled the small bottle on the tabletop instead and watched the label whirl in the light.

"There's something I have to tell you," Ruth blurted.

Beryl's stomach fell. All the bubbles in this evening were going to pop dead away. He looked at Ruth grimly.

"I'm not the woman you think I am," Ruth began.

Beryl's mouth flew open.

"It all started on an innocent picnic...," Ruth began. She continued the saga through, and including, the picnic and Stella and Devon. Then Jace Prue's death, including Alice's part in the incident. Ruth wasn't feeling so badly when she got to the part about Thomas Wills because somehow Beryl was no longer sitting on the other side of the table. He was sitting next to her and holding her hand. She remembered him stroking her cheek once or twice, she thought, too intent on telling the whole story and not wanting to be distracted by looking in his eyes. Ruth thought she couldn't have borne seeing disgust in Beryl's gaze. If she did, she might cry.

Ruth felt like she'd been running a long way and was panting for breath. "There's nothing else to say."

"One more thing," Beryl whispered, tipping up Ruth's chin. "Say, 'I'll let these things go.'" He kissed one edge of her mouth and then the other.

"You don't understand," Ruth replied as she shivered. *Was she going to have to go over the whole thing again? Was Beryl deaf?*

"Let it go," he whispered again. "Say it." He nibbled kisses over her lip.

Ruth's neck became boneless, falling back into Beryl's hand. "I...I let them go," she whispered.

Beryl swept her up in his arms and carried her to the couch. "Not another word from you," he instructed with loving eyes. "Not one more sweet word, Ruthie mine." Ruth closed her eyes and only heard his footfalls and the touch of her settling into his lap as he whispered another command. "Rest."

ᎯᎯ

Ruth didn't know how long she was there. His fingers were so light on her temples. *How could such big hands be so gentle?*

After a time, Beryl kissed her forehead and said, "Wasn't that a sweet potato pie I saw in the refrigerator when you asked me to get the butter?"

Ruth almost snorted at the abrupt change in conversation and mood. It felt like falling off the parachute ride at the fair. First, you were looking at all the pretty scenery and faces below you and when you reached the top there was the click and the parachute expanded, throwing you with billowing ease back to earth.

"I need something first," Beryl said as he shifted a bit.

Ruth turned her head, not knowing what he wanted until his lips came down on hers. *He wanted another kiss?* She gave it willingly. *He'd heard everything and still wanted her kisses.* Ruth still had his ring. *Where was she?* Oh, she remembered. She was with Beryl. Ruth felt like a parachute floating to the ground on a warm breeze.

The wedding ceremony took shape in just a few days. It would be an elopement of sorts since no one from her side of the family knew. Everyone in St. Louis was planning Lady Dee and Thelma's double wedding. Ruth didn't want to steal their thunder. *But she could have her own.*

Ruth started wearing the engagement ring the morning after the grant victory. She smiled like a teenager when people openly admired the rolled yellow-gold band and handsome white sparkling diamond. Ruth kept to the line about knowing the Sikes family for many years and she and Beryl wanting to be settled before Sylvie came to live with them. Evie did the same. Ruth was known as a friendly but private person, so most people never questioned the turn of events.

"Remember, tonight's the family dinner," Evie said. "Need to let everyone congratulate you."

Ruth knew it was more than that. She hadn't even met Pete and Ralph.

"Just remember I'm the handsome one," Beryl whispered as he brushed his cheek on her temple.

◌◌

The evening went well. As Ruth looked at the family albums, it was easy to see Beryl inherited his muscular stocky build from the paternal side of the Sikes family and Pete was more like Evie's Endicott side. Ruth looked at Ralph and smiled. The young man was a mix of both families; a muscular chest but slimmer body. His face was rounder and flattened a bit, hinting at his disability. His manner, vocabulary, and voice inflections indicated he was more a child than a man. "I stay away from the fire," Ralph said when she remarked about a posed shot of Pete, Ralph, and Beryl in front of the newly-renovated building housing their salvage and welding business.

"It was an old brewery teetering on being torn down," Beryl said. "We even renovated the old water tower on top to keep the authentic look of the place."

"He's got a love of old things," Pete said simply.

"I'd like to see it," Ruth said. Welcoming all the information she could glean about her future husband.

"When the weather's nice we play catch out in the work yard," Ralph said excitedly. "Uncle Beryl will teach me how to do a curveball!"

"That sounds like fun," Ruth enthused.

"Uncle Beryl likes to throw to me." Ralph smiled back. "You going to live with us now?" His look changed a bit. "You could sleep in my room, if you need it."

Pete looked embarrassed. "He's never known many married couples and the arrangements of where you sleep. So we've been trying to help him understand."

"Uncle Beryl is a good man and I think we'll let him decide," Ruth said simply. "Married men and women usually do things together." Ruth shoved the thought from her mind. *What were they going to do?*

ꙮ

"Heard you talking to Ralph about the sleeping arrangements," Beryl remarked as they were wiping the dishes. "Asked them to leave us alone, so we could talk." Beryl put the last of it away on the high shelves in the cupboard. He wanted to get this sorted out before the wedding. "It's not an easy subject after so short a time."

Ruth could only nod. Beryl hadn't said anything she could object to...yet. Ruth held her breath.

"A man forced himself on you. Years ago, but it's got to leave a mark," Beryl said. "Touched you with rough hands and violence." He looked over to her, turned off the sink light and led her over to the kitchen table. They sat down.

Ruth could see he was struggling for words. "Go on," she said as she touched his hand.

"I want this marriage to be of our like minds and bodies. In every way," he began. "But there's time."

"I want that, too," Ruth whispered. "I've...I've never been with another man. Before or since."

Beryl stared at Ruth. "Don't know where to go from here, except I promise from this day forward not to touch another woman but you, all the rest of my born days."

Ruth was touched by his fidelity pronouncement.

"Know I should have waited and I'm not proud of it now. You're such a *fine* woman." The right side of Beryl's mouth quirked a bit. "I've got scarred worker's hands."

Without thinking, Ruth put her one hand on his and pulled it next to her face and put her other hand on his forearm resting on the table. "What should we do?" she asked, tears coming to her eyes.

Beryl shrugged. "Just take it slow, I guess." He thought a minute. "But we need to start and stay in the same bed with one another after our wedding day. That's what I think." His hand left her face.

"The bed?" Ruth asked.

"We'll go slow. Not even think of doing things before you're ready," Beryl said with conviction. "Best to talk everything out and be with each other in bed every night. We got to try."

"So we'll get used to each other," Ruth ventured, not really knowing what to say. They'd only known each other a few weeks. There was so much baggage from the past.

"In life and in love," Beryl promised.

⚚

Ruth wore a white brocade suit with a satin finish and short generous blusher veil sprinkled with seed pearls around the crown of her head. The white gossamer brushed below her chin. *If she and Beryl had any daughters, she could use this as part of a longer veil.*

"You look beautiful," Norma said with bright tears in her eyes.

"You're the last of us to marry," Ellie agreed. "The most beautiful."

"If we don't stop we'll muss our makeup," Ruth said, reining in her rioting emotions, so happy her two closest friends were here to bless her and Beryl's wedding.

Evie knocked softly on the door and turned the handle. "You sweet ladies ready?"

The house was decorated beautifully and in such a short time. Evie placed to-the-floor white tablecloths on all the tables in the house. Bowls and vases were packed with every kind of white flower, perfuming the public rooms downstairs. Ruth smirked to think if she had any kind of allergy, she'd be sneezing through her wedding vows.

"Hope we did right by you," Evie said. "Everyone is here, including everyone we've both invited from the hospital."

"It's *very* beautiful," Ruth replied, trying to commend her friend and future mother-in-law. Deciding on having the ceremony in Beryl's home seemed the best way to celebrate this beginning. Honoring a home well-made, before, now, and in the future.

Ruth had been up most of the night considering if marrying Beryl was the right thing. She turned it over and over in her mind. In this day and age, the common method of cementing relationships before marriage revolved around romantic love. But with two well-intentioned attempts at romance breaking her heart each time, her more arranged situation with Beryl seemed a wiser and steadier alternative. Beryl tried to indicate at every public gathering theirs was a love match. *Would pretense become fact after the ceremony?*

Three things were in her favor. Beryl and she shared a common interest in helping their relatives and others in their non-profit venture. Secondly, Ruth knew he showed profound love and respect for his mother and family, which indicated his character, and Ruth was confident Beryl would never taint Evie's friendship with Ruth with a lie. Then, there was Beryl's declaration of lasting love: to never touch another woman.

Ruth found herself at the top of the stairs. Pete gently touched her arm. Ruth looked into his kind, questioning eyes. Ruth smiled and felt a floating feeling invade her body as if she was infused with champagne. They walked sedately. At the bottom of the stairs was a small aisle between the five rows of white and gilt chairs festooned with white daisies, mums, and fat satin bows. Large round tables for the after-ceremony celebration in the garden graced what seemed to be every other space. Ruth waited as two of Beryl's friends rolled the white runner down the polished wood floor, from the pastor's and Beryl's feet. Lady Dee would have been proud of her daughter's composure.

Ruth looked into Beryl's eyes. He gave a relaxed and confident smile, seeming to draw her toward him. He lifted his forearm, wrist, and hand to beckon her. Ruth's eyes glinted merrily as his simple gesture eased the last of her nerves. She looked at everyone, smiled, and walked slowly to Beryl to the sound of the "Wedding March" played on the family piano. Beryl, in turn, reached for her free hand and tucked it in the crook of his arm when she reached him. Then, Ruth heard the pastor intone, "Dearly Beloved...."

෴

Three days after her wedding, Ruth said a short prayer of thanks for several things. Ruth's nervousness about going to St. Louis and her anxiety about her mother's and sister's weddings were gone. Her feelings for Beryl were a third blessing. In such a short period of time, she'd come to love this man.

Beryl's friends and family quickly gave Ruth revelatory confirmation she'd made the right decision. He'd told her nothing of his community and social standing. Ruth esteemed him even more for not touting himself. He wanted her to know him as a man first.

"Wanted him to run for alderman but he's devoted to Ralphie, Pete, and his mother," Mrs. Ells, the corner green grocer, gushed.

"That's the truth." Wilma Pratt's big purple hat bobbed in agreement. "All we can get him to do to put himself forward is marching in the Labor Day parade!" As if having a wonderful idea, she added, "Perhaps you can persuade him to make a run." Ruth tactfully excused herself from the conversation. She needed to live with Beryl and get to know him better before suggesting *anything*. They were newlyweds! Soon to be a new family, bringing Sylvie from St. Louis and getting her acclimated to Chicago and integrated into the new grant project. There didn't seem time for any other additions or options within their new life.

She and Beryl had called to inform her family, still keeping up the pretense of a long informal relationship, igniting into love. Ruth was so glad fiction was evolving into fact. Being Beryl's wife seemed so natural now, as if she'd known him all her life and loved him for years, rather than a handful of weeks.

When Leroy and Thelma pointed to the fact Ruth had never mentioned Beryl to them, Beryl smoothly replied in his phone answer, "Your sister's a private person and the announcement of your double wedding kicked me in the trousers enough to know I wanted the same with Ruth. Immediately. Ruth did me the honor of becoming my bride."

"Beryl is a lovely and persuasive man," Ruth interrupted, looking at him with love in her eyes. She wanted to take some of the heat off of her new husband. He'd already been so thoughtful and kind to her. He left the phone and raised her hand to kiss her knuckles. Ruth almost didn't hear her brother's next question. They'd find out soon enough what a dear man he was, she thought, not wanting to talk anymore. She wanted to be with Beryl. "Enough. Enough," Ruth said. "We'll answer all your questions when we get down there. I know you've got a million things to do." Ruth had only one thing on her mind as she put down the receiver. Beryl led her through the threshold of their bedroom.

੭੭

A while later, Beryl stroked Ruth's cheek. He wanted to take the worry crease from between his wife's brows. "We've got to develop a strategy, you know," he began as he turned on the bedside lamp.

"I know," was all Ruth said as she turned away with a sigh. "I'm just sorry I got you all mixed up in this."

"My dear young lady," Beryl began with a bit of a wry smile. "I thought my mother and I got you mixed up in this." He was so grateful Ruth was in his life... and his bed. "You have to let me stand beside you with these issues."

"What do you mean?" Ruth asked. She'd shouldered everything for so long. *What did Beryl mean?*

"Now don't go getting your dander up." Beryl wanted to make it clear he just wanted to help, not take things over. "A new voice and perspective might help a bit." He wanted to be gentle but he also wanted to protect her, more fiercely it seemed every day.

In Beryl's mind, the truth had to come out to "free" his wife. Else she'd be dragging these secrets for only the Lord knew how much longer.

The memories came back, making Ruth feel uneasy. She turned toward the wall so Beryl wouldn't see her discomfort.

"Let me talk to Devon," Beryl started.

Ruth rolled back to face her husband with a look of fear and incredulity in her eyes. "Devon?"

"I won't shame you," Beryl replied softly. "You've been carrying this all too long."

Now Ruth was flustered. "I...I *never* thought that." She hoped her tone told him she was sincere in her trust.

"Don't you think it's time?" Beryl persisted.

All Ruth could do was nod her head in reaction to his honesty, choking back tears.

"Let me kiss it away," Beryl said as his full lips devoured one salty rivulet and then licked the trail back to his wife's lashes. "Silence is as deadly as carrying the load about the *real* truth." As she molded herself to his caress, he repeated, "I won't shame you."

Beryl looked down at his wife relaxed in slumber. He had other things to do for his wife while they were down in St. Louis. His second task was to put the meddling Eleanor Blaine and her vicious niece in their places. He'd keep his peace about his plan because Beryl didn't want Ruth to be worrying about Devon St. James and those two biddies as well as keeping a smile pinned to her face during the several days it was going to take to get her mother and sister wed. Beryl whispered and continued, "We'll have to see how things go." That was all Ruth's slumbering body needed to know while Beryl figured out his strategy.

❦

ST. LOUIS – 1967

"Well, she's always wanting to steal the family's thunder. Started with the Carter mess," Eleanor Blaine said. Ruth shook her head. *The lady never learned, or was it some kind of bloodlust?*

So the biddy was bold enough to say things in eyeshot of his wife? Beryl turned his gaze on Eleanor Blaine. The lady must think he was a much milder mannered man who didn't mind people talking about his beloved wife.

"I don't think so," Beryl replied with a wide smile that didn't reach his eyes. He knew this woman was trying to hurt Ruth and he saw red. This woman wouldn't bother his wife in public anymore. "As I was saying to my dear friend, Emmitt Pearson, just the other day...," Beryl began. All eyes turned toward him and away from the Blaine woman. Everyone knew Judge Pearson was one of the first black judges on the appeals court. Just the thought of this newly introduced man having eloped with Ruth Yuell, and now telling them he stood in the company as a friend to such an important person, certainly was a more interesting development than listening to Eleanor's rehash. "As my lovely Ruth tells me, and the court documents Judge Pearson unearthed seem to corroborate, Ruth was one innocent defending an innocent pregnant woman. Wasn't her name Stella Carter?"

Beryl didn't look at Ruth but the rest of the group of these gossiping crows nodded their assent. He could almost feel the heat from his wife's flaming cheeks. "It's so sad to see how these things can get so twisted and why *some people* would want to keep things twisted is such a *sin*," Beryl's head shook sadly as he heard the gasps. "So glad to think how a few short years ago we couldn't get any justice at all and now we're able to get redress in the courts." Beryl shook his head again. "Emmitt's going to revisit the case in the next session to show everyone about the past injustices. The judge says it was a brave and wonderful thing for Ruth to stand up to such brutality. Ed Carter's going to say the same thing." He smiled and raised Ruth's hand to his lips. "Judge Pearson wants to tell Ruth himself next week. Such heroes and heroines will *finally* get their due."

Intakes of breath all around, including one from his Ruth, was just the reaction Beryl wanted. He raised Ruth's cold hand to his lips again. Beryl had to get this just right, so this piece of gossip might be put to rest once and for all. "Now, now, Ruthie," he said with a slow smile as he raised her knuckles a second time to his lips. "You've never wanted to raise a fuss about anything brave you've done. But facts are facts," Beryl continued. There were so many gaping mouths; these people all looked like a crowd of open-mouthed, dry-land fish, waiting to be thrown back in the water. They weren't going to feast on his wife anymore if Beryl had anything to do with it. "Judge Pearson thinks you should get a commendation." He gave these people an exaggerated wink. "You've got a real hometown heroine here." He gave Ruth another loving look and then led her stiff body away toward her family. "Yes, sir. The judge will see to it."

A million thoughts whirled in her head and she said in a voice only Beryl could hear, "Did you really talk to Judge Pearson about this?"

Beryl tried to give his best impression of innocence. "Of course, darling. Isn't that what you would do for me if the situation were reversed?" He hoped the myriad of emotions cascading in her eyes would subside as her mind considered the logic and the love behind his question. Beryl was rewarded with a smile of wry mischief as his wife's thoughts cleared and she could see how he was championing her cause against Eleanor Blaine's attack.

"I see," was all Ruth said with humor beginning to dance in her eyes.

Thank God! Beryl cast his eyes heavenward in thanks; not able to give a sigh of relief of his own. Ruth was now with him in this. The masquerade had to continue in this public space in order for long-misconstrued and misinterpreted facts about his wife to get straightened out at long last.

Their pleasant moment fled as Ruth saw Devon and Meggie walk over the living room threshold. Ruth's walk slowed.

"It's time," Beryl whispered as he dipped his head to kiss Ruth's temple, letting go of his wife's hand. "Best to get this over with, too, while you go to check on your mother."

Ruth knew she could trust her husband but old habits were hard to shake.

Beryl watched his wife's stiff steps toward the stairs. At least she was still moving.

❦

Devon thought he remained undetected as he saw Ruth going up the stairs. He dreaded the confrontation with her but it had to come, as would his long overdue apology. First love, he remembered. His high-minded talk in person and in letters, all washed away with his jealousy of Jace Prue, his family's coddling, and his leaving town. Even if it had been well-meaning, Devon knew what was truly right and he should have been stronger. He regretted all those decisions.

In hindsight, he should have been a more mature man in handling his feelings, dealing with the interference from his family, and the neighborhood gossip. They were trying to protect him from heartache, Devon knew, but that didn't make it right. Everyone had been so wrong.

Devon mentally listed the transgressions. They'd all been ham-handed during the scandal and left the Yuells to fend for themselves, especially Ruth. Devon hadn't even given Ruth a chance to explain herself! There was nothing much more to say except he'd acted like a jealous fool when he was courting Ruth and needed to state his sincere regret. He'd met his Meggie but stepped on Ruth's heart in the process. Devon sincerely hoped the years-ago-errors were mended with time.

The vestiges of guilt were somewhat assuaged by the surprisingly troubling, and yet welcome, news that Ruth had wed. Troublesome because he hadn't been able to check with his contacts in Chicago to find out about this Beryl Sikes fellow and identify if Ruth was still doing well with Sikes and in her professional nursing career. If he were honest with himself, he suffered more than a twinge when thinking about his first love, now truly gone, from his life.

He and Meggie were happy and he hoped Ruth was, too.

His musings were interrupted by the approach of a large burly, bald-shaven man whose eyes never wavered from his as Devon met his stare. All Devon could think was that the man was fighting mad. There was no time to consider anything else.

"I'm Beryl Sikes," Beryl said in a clipped introduction as he smilingly gestured toward the door. "I'd like to speak to you on the porch." Under his breath, he whispered like a ventriloquist. "You better smile too or we'll raise a scene."

Devon quickly recovered as he pondered this information and gave out a short laugh. He hoped this gesture would comply with the man's request as he headed for the door. Devon didn't want to create a scene either.

◎◎

Beryl looked at Devon straight in the eye, extended his arm for a handshake, and introduced himself in full view of the living room picture window. "I'm Beryl Sikes. Ruth's husband." Everyone was watching their every move because there were few things more juicy to observe than an old love meeting a new one.

Devon continued the polite repartee while extending his arm and shaking Beryl's hand in what he hoped would be construed as a most cordial first meeting.

Beryl turned a bit so the assembled crowd could get their eyeful. "We're going to have to stay out here a few moments and chat, both smiling and gesturing at each other, like a couple of civilized fools. But I need to speak to you in private about a matter concerning a family member of yours in the next few hours. You can approach me at any time you might think is appropriate. You know this crowd better than I do."

Devon's eyes clouded when he heard Beryl refer to a "family member" but he was thoroughly schooled in public manners and hid his surprise in another laugh. He thought the man wanted to talk about Ruth.

Beryl kept his part up by laughing as well. "How is your baseball team been doing this year?" Beryl masked the real intent of his conversation, signaling he wouldn't broach any more questions concerning the matter until the crowd thinned after the ceremony and Devon was sure they could talk in private.

Meggie would be at his side in a few minutes, Devon knew. Sikes was right. There wouldn't be any time to talk until later. Devon would be busy as a groomsman and both his wife and Ruth would be walking the aisle as attendants before Mrs. Yuell became the new Mrs. Means and Thelma was wed.

"Don't ask Ruth about any of this," Beryl said before turning to the door. He felt like a jackass with all this polite talk and false smiles. "I don't want her day clouded by this." Beryl turned away with a smile and left as quickly as he came.

♋♋

Beryl did his best to watch out for Ruth and stay by Sylvie's side as well. Since Sylvie was going to relocate to Chicago with them in a few days, he wanted her to be as comfortable as possible with him so he could be a second anchor with the new places, sights, and sounds she was going to have to face.

Sylvie tapped his arm. "Cake?" Sylvie held a generous slice of the vanilla crème wedding cake. Lady Dee and Dr. Means had cut into their multi-tiered vanilla cake and Thelma and her new husband had cut into a chocolate-swirled pound cake with yellow butter cream.

"This one is fine," Beryl replied with a smile. "Do you have one?"

"I serve first. Then I'll eat both!" Sylvie said with great enthusiasm.

Beryl smiled widely, enjoying his new sister-in-law's energy and willingness to help. He knew Ralph and she would get along very well in their new living and working settings.

A tap on the shoulder interrupted them. "Sylvie? Can I get a piece of the pound cake?" Devon asked.

"Yes," Sylvie replied. Beryl felt grateful for the love everyone lavished on his new sister-in-law, Sylvie. The Yuells undoubtedly had spent many hours assisting Sylvie in her vocabulary and pronunciation over the years.

"Let's go out to the porch. I've got two cigars," Devon said, hoping the smell would keep away the women and the men without smokes, giving them some peace. Both men abandoned their cake plates on the porch railing as they lit the fat brown cigars. "What is it you wanted to say?"

"I'll make this quicker than I might considering we're in too public a place to be safe for long. It can't be helped," Beryl said, sounding conciliatory. "When Jace Prue died that night, Sylvie came to Ruth's room to tell her your sister Alice was in Prue's room." Anybody looking closely at the two men might have thought Devon St. James had been hit in the back because his neck reared up and his posture became rigid like a soldier at attention.

"What did you say?" Devon spat between clenched teeth, leaning on the porch post, away from the windows, so no one could see his cold eyes and stiff expression.

"Ruth and Leroy saved your sister. Jace started getting drunk-mean and brought out a gun," Beryl replied. The worst was yet to come, he knew, and there was no way to soften it. "You got to stay steady on this, but it was Alice who shot Prue and Ruth took the blame."

Devon wanted to reach for this stranger's throat or at least to ball up his fists and hit this square-jawed menace. It took every ounce of his breeding to resist the impulse. No one slandered his family and got away with it! "If I weren't a gentleman I'd hit you right here," he growled, blowing smoke to hide his expression.

"If it's not the truth, I'll let you," Beryl replied. "Think you might need to call you sister in Detroit and get this whole thing laid to rest." He walked a step closer to St. James. "Ruth didn't want the scandal landing on your family, but it needs to be put to rest for her sake. She's carried this, along with Leroy, for too long. That's going to stop now."

Devon was going to protest but his lawyerly side surfaced. He needed time to get things straight again and clear his family name. *His sister Alice killed Jace Prue?* What a horrible, unfounded accusation! This Beryl Sikes, or whoever his name was, couldn't be right about this thing or anything concerning his family. Alice certainly would have confided such a horrible experience. *Who had Ruth married and brought into her family and their community?*

◐◑

Four hours later Devon St. James was reeling from the news. He kneaded the worn leather on his father's favorite chair in his parents' home. Alice had kept the shooting a secret all these years! Not wanting the scandal or shame on her family...and allowing Ruth Yuell to take on the blame. Alone. Alice had been young, so afraid and so ashamed. Ruth had told her to stay quiet and Alice blindly followed Ruth's orders.

Devon's face scalded with shame. With the specter of her cousin and her cousin's baby's death when Ruth was a teen, Ruth had been tarred a second time. Devon felt responsible for his family's rejection and his own complicit absence. More hot blood flowed to his face.

Ruth willingly sacrificed herself for her friends. *Had Ruth thought his love would sustain her?* She'd been sadly and sorely mistaken. Devon now knew he not only had been a jealous fool, easily swayed by his family; he had been a weak and unworthy friend and boyfriend to a brave young woman. Ruth deserved more then, and certainly deserved more now.

Not much could be done now. What Ruth *deserved* as her heroic due, and what her crusading husband *wanted*, was to allow Ruth to lay her almost-solitary burden down and have the truth come out to the St. James family. Ruth had rescued them long enough.

Alice couldn't come down to St. Louis. But Devon could apologize to Ruth and Leroy, for himself and his family...and he would, to Ruth, Lady Dee, and her children—if Ruth would let them.

CHAPTER NINETEEN

"It felt so good to be able to get that blot off my record, so to speak. I'm amazed!" Ruth whispered as Beryl enfolded her in his arms as they lay in her childhood double bed. Lady Dee had supplied a new mattress. "I was feeling so unsure about things for awhile."

"I felt even better when Eleanor and her sourpuss niece got a dressing down by Dr. Means when the truth came out about Alice," Beryl replied. "I'll never forget him saying the both of them could scat back north and never speak to him again, if he *ever, ever* heard they were causing any more trouble for his new wife or the other Yuells...and everyone gained his permission to come to his door if they heard either Eleanor or Calli laying down any more mischief!" Beryl pushed a few stray strands of his wife's hair from her face. "I was relieved when he said he'd been much too lenient in the past and those two gossips, even they were his blood kin, weren't going to ruin his and your mother's newfound happiness."

Ruth laughed at that, her shoulders shaking the bed covers. "Could have used his fervor years ago...but late is better than never, I guess."

"Perhaps, but this isn't your home anymore, fair lady," Beryl whispered. "We're going to make our home in Chicago and we're taking Sylvie with us." He kissed Ruth's temple and gave her a mischievous grin. "Besides, I've got other things in mind for this new mattress tonight."

EMERGENCY ROOM AT 6:45 P.M.
CHICAGO – 1967

"I think we've got enough for a fairly complete history." Norma smiled, thankful both she and Ruth had gotten through this tumultuous story. Norma only wished she had some better light and a more comfortable writing space besides this small, curtained emergency room cubicle. Sitting on a low visitor's chair and scrawling as fast as she could from her lap was making her back and neck hurt again. She was about to ask Ruth to give her a break to stretch her stiff muscles and get some coffee. "Now will you rest?"

Norma would have said more but Beryl burst through the door, interrupting her. "Where's Ruth?"

Pete followed in his wake. "He just about broke all our necks getting back here from the airport."

"I'm fine. I'm fine!" Ruth replied. Ruth's assurances didn't ease her husband's thunderous looks as he inspected her right arm, and then her left. "I just got pushed over a barricade, bumping my head and shoulder and am here for observation. Really, Beryl," she insisted as she shook his arm, gaining eye contact as she moved her neck to keep his gaze. "Just evaluating the motor skills tests and some blood work before I get released. I'll be fine!" Ruth emphasized the last three words and repeated, "I'll be fine!"

Beryl kept the thunderous look, but seemed to slow his inspection of Ruth's face, neck, and shoulders as he looked deeply into his wife's eyes and considered her assurances.

"I see you've got visitors," the neurology resident in charge of Ruth's care observed as he entered the room and reached for his penlight. He needed to check her pupils one last time. "They'll be one more doctor coming to call and then you'll be released for a day or two of home rest because you're doing so well."

"Can it be soon, doctor?" Ruth asked plaintively. Telling her part of the family history had passed the hours since Norma arrived but now she was anxious to get home. "All my work and doctors are south of here."

"Dr. Gill will be here in a few minutes and you'll be discharged in an hour," the lanky resident replied. "Only about enough time for a cup of coffee!" He looked at Beryl. "You look like you could use one."

👁️👁️

True to the resident's word, Dr. Gill came striding into the cubicle. Only Ruth and Beryl remained.

Norma had to meet her husband and work on compiling her day of note taking. Ruth certainly had an interesting life! Pete had to go relieve his mother from her longer-than-anticipated temporary duty with the shelter students due to Ruth's hospitalization.

Dr. Gill hoped his news would be welcome to Mr. and Mrs. Sikes. After introducing himself, Dr. Gill looked at both his temporarily-hospitalized patient and her husband. "This might be a bit of a surprise, but in the preliminary exam that the intern ordered, we get some extra bloodwork." There was no use making small talk. "Seems like you, Mrs. Sikes, are about two months pregnant and will be expecting a baby in late spring."

Dr. Gill was greeted with intakes of breath and open-mouthed stares for a few split seconds before Beryl grabbed Ruth and hugged her neck. "A baby."

"A baby?" Ruth questioned. She wanted to feel her abdomen to welcome their child, who she hadn't even known was there. But first, as the wonderful reality blossomed in their minds, she and Beryl opened their arms to hug each other joyously.

❦

"Twins. Scott Beryl Sikes at 4:17 a.m. and Allie Endicott Sikes at 4:20 a.m. on April 17, 1968. I thought everything went OK," the attending nurse wrote on the chalkboard as the other nurse wrote in her own patient's chart.

"I've checked with the parents for the correct spellings for the birth certificates," the taller nurse said, eyeing her paperwork. "But I think I'll take some juice and graham crackers in there, just in case. Her husband seemed to know what she was talking about, so I didn't ask, but she might need some extra sugar and fluids because what she was saying made no sense to me." The nurse kept writing as she continued, "The mother, Mrs. Ruth Sikes, said something strange about the twins being born between the stars and bluebird skies."

Made in the USA
Charleston, SC
27 April 2012